THE FATE SWITCH

BY
JEANETTE DYSON

copywrite

copywrite

First published in the United Kingdom by Jeanette Dyson in 2020

Copyright © 2020 by Jeanette Dyson

The moral right of the author has been asserted.

A CIP catalogue record for this book is available from the British Library.

ISBN 978-1-9163878-1-2

Typeset by Tim Collier.

www.cwrite.co.uk/books

Acknowledgements

To Scott, Gabrielle and Olivia,
for your love and support.

To Mum and Dad for pretty much everything.

To Ron Phillips for turning me into a writer
and giving me belief.
To Anne, Betty, Geoff and Judith, for the support,
advice and cups of tea, and to Tim for
turning my manuscript into a book.

The Fate Switch is dedicated to the memory of
Syd Boothroyd, who gave so much of his time to the
sport of diving and gave me a lifelong love of the sport.
Quite simply, thank you.

Apologies to the diving community
For the sake of the story, I've played fast and loose with
training processes, and the timings and organisation of national
diving competitions. I've also created my own selection process
for the GB squad. For this I'm sorry. Hopefully, you'll forgive me
and understand it was purely plot driven. Hopefully, I've made up
for it with the descriptions of the feelings and experiences
of diving, which come straight from my memory, and heart.

Chapter One

Angelina's vision cleared surprisingly quickly. But as the fuzziness drained away and the world around her came into sharp focus, she gasped.

There was a man staring at her. His face, underneath his flat peaked cap, frozen in terror.

The train's conductor.

And he'd seen her.

She couldn't help but stare back.

Where had *he* come from?

She watched as the man backed away from her, slowly, as if any sudden movement would cause her to pounce.

The train lurched to the left, flinging the conductor off balance. Angelina made a grab for him but he recoiled from her touch and she missed. She gasped as the man fell and landed in the lap of a plump, old woman.

Where had *she* come from?

Angelina glanced round, terrified that the train carriage held more surprises, but thankfully all the other seats were empty.

"Get off!" screamed the woman.

Angelina's gaze swung back. The woman was now belting the conductor with a hefty-looking book.

"Get off!"

"Sorry, sorry," said the conductor. He'd raised his arms and was trying to block the blows. "But that girl. Did you see? Her over there. Did you see? - Ow!"

"Help! Get him off me! Help!"

The woman's book connected with the conductor again, this time knocking his cap flying.

She doesn't look as if she needs any help, thought Angelina. That man's going to get hurt and it's all my fault. I bet the Assessors are loving this– what if they leak it to UVue? I'll be finished.

Not knowing what to do, she turned away, staring out of the grimy window at the trees and bushes racing past. If only he hadn't fallen on the old woman, she thought. I might have got away with it then. After all, it would be my word against his, and there's no way anyone would believe his story.

"Sorry, Missus." Angelina heard the conductor say, his voice high-pitched, almost hysterical. "I didn't mean to. I fell, after she- she- she- *appeared*."

Hearing his words, dread rose from Angelina's heart and coiled around her neck, squeezing the breath from her newly-formed body. Cautiously, she turned her head, peering through the long black hair that fell across her face, shielding her from the chaos she'd caused.

The conductor had regained his footing and untangled himself from the old woman. Now, out of her reach, he was bending forward holding on to the seat for support, the computerised ticket machine swung from its leather strap around his neck. His ill-fitting uniform was crumpled and skewed on his thin, angular frame and without the cap, his straw-coloured hair stuck out in uneven tufts.

Angelina could see the terror in his eyes as he stared at her.

"What are you talking about, you silly man?" said the woman, holding the book like a club, ready to strike.

"That girl. Her. Her there." He jabbed a bony finger in Angelina's direction. "She just appeared. Right in front of me."

Why did he have to say that? Angelina wanted to run but didn't dare move.

"What girl?" The woman shifted her weight so that she could see over her shoulder to where he was pointing. "That girl, there? What do you mean, appeared? You're talking nonsense. You attacked me. I'm calling the police."

She pulled a mobile phone from her handbag.

Police?

The last thing Angelina wanted was more attention. She had to do something. She could hear the beeps as the woman pressed the numbers on the phone.

"It was an accident," Angelina stammered, finally finding her voice.

The woman looked up, her chubby finger hovering over the screen.

"I was getting something out of my bag and then I sat up." Angelina warmed to her story. "I think I made him jump."

The conductor had stayed silent, but Angelina could feel his eyes still fixed upon her, as if he expected her to disappear again at any moment. Suddenly he blurted:

"No, no, no. She didn't. She appeared. Materialised. Yes, that's it. *Materialised.*" He nodded vigorously, seeming pleased that he'd found the right explanation. "One minute there was no one there. Then– then she started *appearing.*" He became animated, his hands carving the outline of an invisible head and body. "All fuzzy she was for a start, like you could see right through her. Then she got more and more solid. It was quick, but that's what happened."

Great! Angelina thought. He saw it all.

She glanced at the old woman, who was staring at the conductor as though he'd lost his mind.

Angelina said: "Do you think he hit his head when he fell?" She wrinkled her brow and tried to look concerned.

"Or perhaps he's completely mad," said the old woman. "I'm calling the police."

This time the word 'police' seemed to get through to the conductor, who looked at the old lady in alarm.

"Police? No… I'm just…"

"In shock?" Angelina finished for him. "Do you need to lie down?"

He whipped round to face her.

"Lie down? Yeah. I need to lie down."

And he rushed from the carriage.

As the compartment door slid shut behind him Angelina bent to retrieve his cap, which lay half under the seat where it had fallen. Wonderful, she thought as she turned the cap round in her hands. The Assessors will have seen everything, it'll all be in the Arrival Report, and even worse, it'll probably be number one on UVue for the next millennium. I'll be expelled before I even start this assignment.

"I'd leave that on the seat. No doubt he'll come back for it later." The old woman's voice broke into Angelina's thoughts.

"Hopefully much later," she added. Tucking her phone back into her handbag she leaned towards Angelina. "Are you okay, love? He didn't upset you, did he?"

"No. I'm fine." Angelina tried to smile, thinking that the conductor was the least of her worries.

"Anyway, love. Where are you going to? You look young to be travelling by yourself."

Angelina wanted to think, not talk. But she couldn't afford any more slip-ups, so recited the story she'd rehearsed.

"I'm older than I look. I was fourteen last month and I'm staying with my Aunt in Little Ingworth. Her house isn't far from the station."

"Little Ingworth? That's where I live. Isn't that a coincidence?"

Just my luck, Angelina thought.

The old woman continued. "I'm Rose, by the way. Rose Garden." She chuckled. "I couldn't help falling for the charms of Henry Garden. Married 53 years next March. And you are?"

"Angelina Crossland." It was the first time she'd spoken her new surname aloud and it sounded strange.

"Well, pleased to meet you, Angelina Crossland. Now, who did you say your Aunt was?"

"Dorothy Devin. She's known as Dee."

Rose pursed her lips. "Hmm. Dee Devin. Can't say the name rings a bell. Where does she live?"

"Hermit Hill Lane."

"Ah, well, that's the other side of the village from me. And Little Ingworth is bigger than you think these days, especially now they've built the new houses up by the park. Well, Angelina Crossland, this is our stop coming up. You wouldn't like to help an old woman from the train, would you?"

Thankfully there was no sign of the conductor as she helped Rose down on to the deserted platform. The oily train fumes mingled with the sickly-sweet scent of wet, rotting grass cuttings, and as soon as the door hissed back into place, the train pulled away. Angelina watched it gathering speed, whipping the leaves of the overhanging trees as it disappeared down the track, as if it couldn't wait to leave her and Little Ingworth behind.

Can't say I blame it, she thought, looking around at the decaying station. Weeds grew through cracks in the platform and someone had painted over part of the sign so that the station name now read 'Little …worth'.

Just about says it all, she thought. And I get to call this home!

Still, it might not be home for long, she reflected. Once word got out about this mess, her apprenticeship would be over before it had begun.

The station seemed strangely silent now the train had gone. Only the buzz of insects disturbed the peace as Angelina headed towards a sagging bench at the station's entrance, weighed down by her backpack on one arm and Rose on the other.

"Thanks, love." Rose lowered her bulk to the wooden seat, which creaked worryingly under her weight. She gave a sigh and pulled a hanky from the pocket of her floral sundress to mop her brow. "You know, this must be the hottest day we've had this August. No good for me at my age.

Looking at her, Angelina realised that Rose might expect help all the way back to wherever she lived.

"You're not walking home, are you?" Angelina asked.

"Oh, no, no. I usually get the bus, but with it being Sunday, my daughter's picking me up. She has one of those daft sports cars, two seats, and no roof as soon as the sun shows its face – no good to anyone and it messes up your hair something shocking." Rose patted her tight grey curls. "So, I'm afraid I can't even offer you a lift."

That's fine by me, thought Angelina.

"You're not far away anyway," Rose continued. "Take the snicket and you'll be at Hermit Hill Lane in no time."

She gestured across the road towards a tree-lined path, where a couple of drinks cans loitered and a crisp packet fluttered in a vain attempt to break free from the tacky clutches of a discarded blob of chewing gum.

"It brings you out by the church. Take the road on your right and Hermit Hill Lane is up the hill on the left."

Angelina looked to where Rose pointed. "Thanks. Well, goodbye then."

"Let's say TTFN. Isn't that what you young ones say? You never know, we might meet again, Angelina Crossland."

Knowing my luck, we probably will, thought Angelina. When she was half-way along the path, she risked a glance back towards the station and saw that a man was now sitting next to Rose. They obviously knew each other, so at least Rose would be occupied until her daughter arrived.

Angelina was in no rush to reach Hermit Hill Lane. As she dawdled down the alley, she tried to work out what had gone wrong. There'd been no sign of anyone when she'd run the Prelim Checks. She'd checked the train's location and speed. She'd scanned for human life forms and chosen a carriage that registered 'clear'. She'd even remembered to disable the CCTV. Only then, when she was sure there was nobody in the carriage, had she begun the Physicalisation process.

Could Rose and the conductor have arrived in the time it took for me to Transformate? Angelina thought. Possibly, but Rose had looked so settled.

Turning a corner, Angelina found herself on Hermit Hill Lane. She stopped to adjust the strap on her backpack, which was starting to dig into her shoulder. Resting against the blackened, dry-stone wall, she gazed up the hill and, beyond a small field, saw a row of cottages set back from the road.

So, this was where Dee lived.

Angelina hitched her backpack on to her shoulder and set off up the hill. With every step she wondered how she was going to explain this disaster to the Great Dee Devin.

Chapter Two

As Angelina trudged up Hermit Hill Lane the drone of an electric motor grew louder, reaching a crescendo at the second cottage where a man, his bald head pink and beaded with perspiration, was mowing the lawn. He looked up as Angelina approached, and waved.

"Hello," he called above the noise of the mower.

Angelina smiled but hurried past before he could say anything else. She'd had enough of talking to strangers for one day.

Breathing heavily, she stopped at the driveway to number four, the last cottage in the row. She peeled her backpack from her sweat-soaked T-shirt, pulled out a water bottle and took a long drink.

Hermit Hill Lane certainly lives up to its name, she thought, as she looked around. *Not much life here.*

Beyond the gate to Dee's home, the pavement disappeared into a shallow ditch full of dandelions, wild grass and nettles, which accompanied the road as it wound its way up the hillside, flanked by fields where black and white cows grazed. The fresh smell of cut grass mingled with a pungent earthy odour that Angelina assumed was the cows.

She studied Dee's cottage. Unlike the tidy neighbouring homes, the garden crawled with brambles, and dandelions and buttercups had colonised the ankle-high grass.

Even the house knows I'm doomed, she thought, taking in the sagging windowsills that gave the impression the cottage was sneering at her. *Perhaps it won't be so bad if I am sent straight home.*

She picked up her backpack and headed down the driveway. Ahead squatted a detached, stone-built garage. It was huge and, unlike the ancient cottage, looked clean and new, the woodwork recently varnished.

Reaching the cottage, Angelina felt her stomach twist into a knot.

I might as well get this over with, she thought.

Taking a deep breath, she rapped on the door, straining to hear over the noise of the neighbour's lawn mower for any sound from within.

Nothing.

She knocked again.

Still no reply.

By the fourth attempt, Angelina's knuckles were sore and she gave up.

Oh, great, she thought. Could this assignment get any worse?

Dropping her backpack on the ground, she sank down on the doorstep. Tiny ants streamed in and out of a crack in the driveway a few feet from where Angelina was sitting. Watching them was strangely soothing until her thoughts returned to what might happen once Dee read the Arrival Report.

Being caught in the act of her first Physicalisation broke almost every rule. The conductor would probably have to be sorted out and they might even have to re-tune Rose's memory.

Angelina groaned. No wonder Dee wasn't answering. She would be the one called out to deal with this mess. Right now she was probably redefining the mind of the conductor. And when she'd finished there –

Angelina slumped back against the door. It didn't bear thinking about. She'd probably be spending the next millennium as a filing clerk in the FFU Tax Returns Department.

At that moment the buzz of the mower came to an abrupt halt. The sudden silence made her realise how loud the lawn mower had been. Now she could hear birds singing and the breeze ruffling the leaves in the trees and –

Music!

Someone was playing music close by. Very close by. In fact, it was coming from the garage.

Scrambling to her feet, she followed the path at the side of the garage. It led to a door next to a large window with blackened glass. Music was playing inside.

Standing on tiptoe, Angelina tried peering through the window but the glass was so dark that even with her hands cupped around her face to block out the sun she couldn't see what was inside. Frustrated, she gave three sharp knocks on the door.

Almost immediately, the music was turned down. Angelina knocked again.

"Who's there?" The voice was muffled.

"I'm looking for Dee Devin," Angelina shouted.

"Who are you?" The voice was clearer, as if its owner had moved closer.

"I'm Angelina. Are you Dee?

The door cracked open, a shoulder-length mop of bright orange curls filling the gap. Angelina made out a wrinkled face underneath the frothy hair.

"Who are you?" The orange curls bounced as the face looked Angelina up and down.

"This is four, Hermit Hill Lane, isn't it?" Angelina demanded.

"Might be. Depends who's asking."

"I've told you already. I'm Angelina Crossland and if you're Dee Devin, then you should be expecting me."

"No need for the attitude. You're not due until Sunday. Come back then."

The head disappeared and the door slammed shut.

It wasn't the welcome Angelina had expected from the Great Dee Devin. Forgetting about the trouble she was already in, she rapped hard on the door.

The orange curls reappeared.

"I said come back Sunday."

The woman tried to shut the door again, but this time Angelina stuck her foot in the way.

"It is Sunday."

"No, it's not." The woman tried again to close the door.

"Yes, it… Yow!" The woman had banged the kick rail against Angelina's foot. "Ow, that hurt. Ask your neighbour. He was cutting his lawn. He'll still be in."

The pressure on Angelina's throbbing foot eased.

"Pete? Pete was cutting his lawn?"

"How should I know his name? It was some man with no hair."

"Pete," the voice confirmed.

Without warning the woman reappeared, causing Angelina to stagger backwards.

"If Pete was gardening, you're right, it's Sunday." The woman slammed the garage door behind her.

Angelina stared at the tall, thin figure now standing before her.

The woman was dressed in hideous, pink dungarees over a purple T-shirt. With her wild orange curls, making her hair almost as wide as it was long, the overall effect was of a lighted stick of dynamite.

"Don't stand there gawping, girl. Now you're here we might as well get on with it."

"You are Dee, then," Angelina said.

"Of course, I'm Dee. Who else would I be?"

"It's just, I thought you'd be..."

"What? Spit it out girl."

"I... it doesn't matter." How did she say 'more professional' without getting into any more trouble?

Dee didn't react. Instead she locked the garage door and strode towards the cottage. She was agile for someone who looked to be at least seventy.

Bewildered, Angelina hurried along after the strange-looking woman.

If Dee didn't even know what day it was, then she couldn't possibly know about the train. Should I say something? she thought. Or wait until she reads the Arrival Report?

At that moment, Dee stopped abruptly and whipped round, causing Angelina to pull up short to avoid bumping into her.

"Before I forget, the garage is out of bounds. You stay out of there. Understand?" Dee jutted her chin forward, fixing her bright blue eyes on Angelina, like an eagle surveying its dinner.

Before Angelina could answer, Dee set off again. At the cottage door she stopped and pointed to the backpack on the step.

"If that's yours, bring it in."

The door led straight into the kitchen. She followed Dee who squeezed past a hefty wooden dining table, strewn with papers, and through into a hallway.

"Your room is upstairs, first door on the left. Change the posters if you want, they were left by the last apprentice. My room is past the bathroom at the front. Stay out of there unless you have my permission to enter. Right, let's see." Dee checked her watch and disappeared through a door to her right. She reappeared a few seconds later a wad of papers in her hand.

The Arrival Report.

Angelina felt an icy trickle down her spine. She wanted to speak, to defend herself but she couldn't find the words and stood there, staring hopelessly while Dee squinted at the top sheet of paper, a frown deepening the wrinkles on her face.

Dee raised her eyes, glaring over the paper.

"I think I need to read this by myself."

Chapter Three

Angelina sat on the edge of the bed in her new room. She didn't bother to unpack. What was the point? She'd only have to pack up again when Dee had finished with her.

She fiddled with the fastenings on her backpack, opening and closing the clips until she nipped the soft part of her middle finger and yelped. Unfortunately, this reminded her of the conductor on the train and the knot in her stomach tightened.

Sucking on her sore finger, she looked around the room. It was tidy and clean, with lines vacuumed into the grey, shaggy carpet. Posters, yellowed by the sun and curling at the edges, were pinned to the walls. Most were pictures of sports teams.

"Liverpool FC – 1983." Angelina read the caption on the poster near the door. "No wonder this room smells like a museum," she muttered.

Underneath the poster, there was a bookcase crammed with dull-looking, chunky textbooks. She ignored them, turning instead to the laptop sitting on a wooden desk near the window. She was about to switch it on when she noticed the time on the desk clock.

Fifteen minutes had passed.

Surely Dee had read the report by now.

Angelina crept downstairs and eased open the kitchen door. Dee was seated at the table, her head bowed over a printed report. The bony fingers of her left hand were curled around a purple mug from which rose a wisp of white steam. As Angelina watched, every now and again Dee frowned and scribbled something on the paper.

She must know the truth by now, thought Angelina, as the door clicked shut behind her.

Dee started and looked up from the report. "How long have you been there?" she demanded.

"Just now. Not long. Have I failed?" Angelina blurted out.

"Failed?" Dee snorted. "What kind of a question is that? You know, I could do without this right now. If it wasn't for all these ridiculous cutbacks." Dee gestured impatiently to the chair opposite. "Well, you might as well sit down."

Is that a no? thought Angelina as she slipped into the chair Dee had indicated.

Dee shuffled the report back together, straightened the edges by tapping them on the table, and glared over the top of the paper at Angelina.

"Well it wasn't a perfect arrival, was it?"

"I know, but I don't know how it happened, I…"

Dee interrupted. "Well, I do. You forgot the notification call. Ridiculously simple but apparently beyond your capabilities. Which surprises me, as most young people appear to be surgically attached to their phones these days. Unfortunately, for me, it isn't an automatic fail."

Angelina opened her mouth, and closed it again. She stared at Dee.

The notification call. She'd forgotten to phone ahead to say that she'd arrived. But what about Rose and the conductor? Did Dee know about them?

Dee's voice interrupted her thoughts.

"Well, I see you managed to land on the train. I suppose you've got that going for you. One trainee missed the carriage completely. The fool ended up in the ladies' toilets at Sheffield Station, in a cubicle that was already occupied - and they wonder why I won't have anyone arriving at the cottage." Dee shook her head, glaring at Angelina, as if she were to blame. "I tell you, that mess needed cleaning up in more ways than one."

Angelina's thoughts whirled around her head, Dee didn't know about Rose or she'd have mentioned it straight away. That means there couldn't possibly be any video evidence. And it can't be broadcast on UVue. And…

"I can still do the assignment then?"

Dee looked up and frowned. "Well I presume that's why you're here. Otherwise I'm completely wasting my time. Now, where was I?"

Dee shuffled through the pile of papers in front of her and selected a slim, official-looking document. The front cover was a deep, mottled purple, made from thick card, and in the centre Angelina recognised the stamp of the FFU. Dee opened the front page and smoothed her hand down the spine, flattening the cover so that the document remained open.

Looking directly at Angelina, she gave a smile that never quite made it to her eyes.

"I suppose I have to say congratulations. You're now officially a Trainee Guardian Angel."

"You mean, GA," Angelina said automatically.

Dee peered at Angelina over her glasses. "I beg your pardon?"

"GA. No one calls us Guardian Angels anymore. They've rebranded. The new logo is amazing, you must have seen it."

Dee's face turned scarlet, and when she spoke the words left her mouth like bullets. "The Fate Federation of the Universe -"

"You mean the FFU," Angelina interrupted.

"- might like to talk in acronyms, but I do not. If they stopped these stupid marketing exercises, they could stop these cutbacks and we'd have enough Guardian Angels to offer a decent service on Earth. Mark my words, this would never have happened had I still been on the Board. Now, where was I?" She turned her attention back to the file.

Angelina opened her mouth to protest but thought better of it and sank back in her chair. For another twenty minutes they continued with the paperwork, and Angelina could feel her eyes drooping. Finally, Dee turned the document around and slid it across the table.

"Sign here. Use your real name, not your training alias."

Angelina scrawled her name and pushed the form back.

Checking the signature, Dee looked up in surprise.

"You're Angelina Lachesis. Are you related to Morten?"

"My grandfather was called Morten. Why? What's that got to do with anything?" Dee looked at her thoughtfully.

"I knew him well. Before he went missing, of course. I always thought he was a good man."

Angelina flinched as if she'd been slapped.

"You knew him? Do you know what happened?"

Dee shrugged. "Only what it said in the official report."

"But that didn't say any-"

"I know nothing more."

"But if-"

"I said, I know nothing more."

Angelina opened her mouth to protest, but the hardness in Dee's eyes stopped her.

"I... never mind," said Angelina quietly.

Dee looked down, almost as if she were embarrassed, and scribbled a note on the report before speaking again. "That's almost everything done. Well, Angelina you're officially on the Sector Earth, Trainee Guardian Angel Programme. If you pass this practical, you'll still have your final exams to sit before you officially graduate."

Closing the file, she checked her watch and frowned. "Let's make this quick." She plucked a piece of paper from a pile to her left. "Your assignment is a Fate Switch."

"A Fate Switch?" Angelina brightened; the previous tension forgotten. "I get to do a Fate Switch? A real Fate Switch."

"Well it would hardly be a pretend one, would it? Don't get too excited, it's a level-two. You won't be changing the world just yet." Dee glanced back at her notes. "It takes place in February, so you'll have plenty of time to practice."

"February? But that's six months away. You mean I'm stuck here until then?" Angelina asked in dismay.

"I can't say I'm pleased about it either. But don't worry, once you go to school I'm sure the time will pass quickly."

"School?"

"You'll be joining Ingworth High when term starts on Tuesday." Dee stood, swept the files up into her arms and headed for the door, where she stopped, and turned back to Angelina.

"I've scheduled a training Fate Switch for Saturday. Make sure that you're ready."

Chapter Four

At 9am on Tuesday, wearing a grey school skirt, white shirt and oversized black blazer bearing the red emblem of Ingworth High, Angelina was standing next to Dr Arif, Head of the Science Department, and her new form teacher.

"Angelina is new to the area and will be joining us for the next school year. I'd like you all to make her feel very welcome." With his hands in his white lab coat, Dr Arif beamed at his class of twenty-eight fourteen-year olds.

Angelina didn't feel particularly welcome as she cast her eyes cautiously around the room. Most of the pupils were lounging across their desks, using their arms as pillows, while others whispered and giggled together. On the back row, a girl with straightened, bleached blond hair and heavy make-up caught Angelina's eye. She was leaning back, balancing her chair on its two back legs and watching Angelina with a look of amused consideration. She looked like a cat about to stick its paw into the fishbowl.

"Right." Dr Arif turned to her. "You can sit next to Joe on the second row. Joe, can you please make sure that Angelina doesn't get lost today?"

Conscious that all eyes were now on her, Angelina squeezed through the first row of desks towards the spare seat.

Joe shifted his bag to make room for Angelina. His long blond fringe fell across his face, which he swept back with one hand.

"Hi," said Angelina. She hung her bag over the back of the chair and slid into the seat beside him.

"Hi," he replied.

His expression remained serious and the single syllable gave no clue as to whether he was pleased to be sharing his desk or not.

The rest of the morning passed in a blur as Angelina discovered, to her annoyance, that Dee had already chosen the options for her, including the worst subject Angelina could imagine: ICT.

When lunchtime came, Joe showed Angelina to the canteen. He didn't have much to say and, to Angelina's relief, wasn't interested in asking about her background, or anything else for that matter.

"I need to sign on for circuit training. Can you find your way back?" he asked.

"Don't worry, I'll be fine, thanks."

Joe nodded and disappeared into the crowd.

Sitting in the canteen, surrounded by the greasy smell of fried fish and overcooked carrots, she nursed a limp cheese sandwich and a watery, strawberry milkshake.

Out of the corner of her eye she caught sight of a man carrying a mop and bucket, whom she thought she recognised, but as she turned to get a better look at him, her milkshake was sent flying across the table. She looked up to see the hair-and-make-up-girl from her class, flanked by a posse of followers, standing over her.

"Tut, tut, tut. Seems like the new girl's had an accident. You need to be more careful, Angelina." Her group of friends giggled as she stretched out the name.

Angelina picked up the empty glass and started mopping up the spilt milk with a tissue.

"I said, you need to be more careful." The girl grabbed hold of Angelina's hair and pulled.

"Ouch!" The girl dropped the hair as if she'd been burned. Her other hand flew to her own head. Angelina, meanwhile, looked at her and smiled.

"Who pulled my hair?" The girl swung round and glared at her friends.

The three other girls looked at one another. Finally, one of the girls, with short dark hair, died purple to match her eye make-up, spoke. "No one touched you, Serena."

At that moment, a teacher on lunchtime supervision duty appeared.

"Serena Jackson, please don't tell me you're causing trouble already." The woman stood in front of the group with her arms folded, a weary look said that she'd seen this all before.

"No, Miss Milner. Of course not." Serena pasted a syrupy sweet smile on her face. "We're helping the new girl to settle in."

It was obvious that Miss Milner didn't believe her for a second.

"Is that right?" Miss Milner directed the question at Angelina.

Knowing that she could easily handle Serena and her gang, Angelina simply nodded.

"Well," said Miss Milner, still not convinced. "It looks as if you've already helped her settle in." She eyed the puddle of strawberry milk, which despite Angelina's best efforts, had spread across the table. "I suggest you leave now."

"Just going, Miss. Bye, Angelina," Serena called over her shoulder as she led her giggling group away.

After she'd helped Angelina to clean up the mess, Miss Milner said: "Are you sure you don't want to tell me what really happened?"

"Thanks, but don't worry, I'll be okay."

To Angelina's relief the afternoon bell prevented any further conversation and she set off to look for room 3E. Double French was next on the timetable. She found the lesson incredibly dull. Reciting lists of French verbs was pointless for Angelina. Like all GAs, she had the ability immediately to adopt the language of whatever country she happened to find herself in. Not to mention being fluent in the dialects and languages of the thousands of inhabited planets that made up the Solar Union.

Maths, the final lesson for the day, was equally tedious, and she quickly realised that she'd have to be careful not to do too well in class. It could be quite tricky explaining why she knew far more than the entire teaching team put together.

It was after the final bell that she saw Serena again. Angelina was almost at the bus stop when someone bumped into her shoulder, sending her stumbling forward. Just managing to stop herself from falling, she regained her balance and came face to face with Serena.

"What did you say to Miss Milner?" she demanded.

Angelina sighed. "I can't quite remember, word-for-word. Something about 'do you have a cloth to wipe this mess up with?'."

Serena brought her face so close that Angelina could see the rough, pockmarked skin beneath a thick layer of foundation. "Think you're clever, do you? Don't mess with me, Angelina, or you'll know about it."

Angelina wanted to laugh, Serena sounded ridiculous, but she couldn't afford any unwanted attention, so fought to keep her face straight.

Serena continued. "I'm expecting you to buy me lunch tomorrow to make up for spilling my milkshake. And remember, this is what you'll get if you don't."

Angelina felt something hard kick her shin, but there was no pain. Instead, Serena, looking shocked, was limping and rubbing her own leg as she danced in circles.

"Oh, dear. Did you bang into something?" asked Angelina. "You want to be careful." She smiled and stepped on to the bus, which by now had arrived.

She watched through the window as Serena's friends clustered around in concern.

"Are you okay? Was Serena hassling you?"

Joe had followed Angelina on to the bus and swung into the seat next to her.

Angelina looked round and smiled. "Oh, hi. She's trying to, but I don't think it's working."

She pointed to the side of the road, where Serena was nursing her leg. Even from this distance, the purple bruise on her leg was visible.

Joe gave a short laugh of admiration. "You did that to Serena?"

Angelina looked at him. It was the first time that she'd seen him smile. His entire face became animated and made you want to smile along with him. Angelina couldn't help but grin as she said: "She did that to herself, I didn't touch her. I guess she must have hit something when she tried to kick me."

Joe turned his serious face back on. "All the same, I'd stay out of her way, if I were you."

"Believe me, I'll try," murmured Angelina.

The next day, at lunchtime, Serena and her three friends were waiting for Angelina at the entrance to the school canteen.

"Hope you've brought enough money with you, new girl. You owe me," Serena hissed, falling into step with Angelina.

"No, I don't, Serena." Angelina's tone remained pleasant, as she collected a tray and joined the queue.

19

Serena's friends looked shocked that someone had dared to disagree.

Her voice quivering with anger, Serena said: "I don't think you heard me. You owe me and you'd better pay or else."

The queue shuffled forward.

Calmly, Angelina looked Serena straight in the eye. "I heard you fine, but I don't owe you anything. Why don't you leave me alone?"

Serena shot out her fist, punching Angelina in the stomach. But Angelina didn't react. Instead, it was Serena who doubled up in pain clutching her middle. As she staggered backwards, she bumped into two Year 11 girls who were both carrying full dinner trays. The food was sent flying into the air as Serena lost her balance and went crashing to the floor.

Then, silence.

The entire canteen stopped, everyone turning to stare at Serena. She was sitting on the floor, knees pulled up to her chest, nursing her stomach and moaning as globs of yellow custard dripped from her blonde hair.

A cheer broke out, joined by whistles, whooping sounds and laughter from all four corners of the hall.

Miss Milner, on duty again, was first on the scene.

"What is going on?" Her face was fixed in an angry frown as she shouted above the noise.

No one answered.

"Well?"

She stood, hands on hips, looking at each girl in turn, but then seemed to register the cacophony of noise. Turning to face the seating area, she clapped her hands loudly. Immediately the cheering stopped.

"Enough!" she said in a loud, firm voice that left no doubt that she meant business. "Get on with your meal, or you'll all be in detention."

The noise in the canteen returned to a low, but excited buzz, as Miss Milner turned her attention back to the mess in front of her.

"It was her, Miss. She pushed Serena." Serena's purple-haired friend pointed her lilac, painted finger at Angelina.

"Is that true?" Miss Milner looked at Angelina.

"No, it's not."

Everyone turned towards the voice. Joe stepped out of the queue from behind them.

"Carrie's lying. Serena hit Angelina and then fell into those girls. I saw it all, Angelina didn't move."

"Is that what happened?" Miss Milner turned back to the purple-haired Carrie, who looked away and shrugged.

"I see," said Miss Milner. "You and you, follow me." She pointed to Carrie and Serena who, by now, had struggled to her feet trying to brush the more solid food from her uniform with one hand, while her other arm curled protectively across her waist.

To the two Year 11 girls who were looking on with bemused interest, she said: "Go and get another tray. Everyone else" -she glared at the rest of the queue- "get on with your lunch and mind this mess."

As Miss Milner moved off with the two girls, the caretaker and canteen supervisor appeared with a mop, bucket and a 'Wet Floor' sign. Angelina thought that the caretaker looked familiar but before she could get a good look at him, Joe pulled her back into the queue.

"What's going on?" he asked. "She hit you, but she got hurt."

Angelina thought quickly. There was no way that she could tell Joe the truth about what happened. She could imagine the conversation: 'Well, Joe, it's a little thing called Transference – an automatic self-defence mechanism for GAs. If anyone intentionally tries to harm me, they are the ones who will suffer. Hence, Serena punched me in the stomach and she got winded.'

No, she had to come up with a plausible explanation, fast.

"I didn't feel a thing." At least that bit was true. "I wonder if she missed me and hit her hand on the wall instead."

Wide-eyed, she looked anxiously at Joe. He didn't seem convinced, but Angelina knew that, in his world, the truth wasn't possible.

He shook his head in amazement. "It looked like she caught you from where I was standing. Are you sure you're okay?"

"I'm fine, honest. But thanks for sticking up for me."

"I wasn't going to let Carrie put the blame on you."

Angelina smiled. "Most people wouldn't want to get on the wrong side of Serena and her gang. Half the school is terrified of them."

"She's a bully and the rest are a bunch of cowards. It's about time someone stood up to them."

News of what had happened flew around the school. At the end of the day, as Angelina stepped on to the school bus, she could see people looking up from their phones and shooting curious looks at her. Thank goodness phones weren't allowed during school hours, at least her run in with Serena couldn't have been filmed. She dropped hurriedly into one of the seats near the front, trying to ignore the murmurs and looks. She was supposed to be keeping a low profile. If Dee found out about this, it wouldn't go down well.

Chapter Five

Joe Brennan stared through the dining room window. Gazing down across the park and playing fields, he could see Little Ingworth Church in the distance and hear the faint chime of bells as it struck nine o'clock.

"That's it," he murmured, and bent over his maths book, jotting down the formula he'd been trying to remember.

"Joe, can you watch Nell and Evie for me while I put the washing out, please?"

Joe looked up, brushing his fringe out of his eyes. His mother was standing in the doorway, balancing one of the twins on her hip, while the other ran to him, arms open wide, giving Joe no choice but to hoist her up on to his knee.

"Sorry, Mum. I'm training in an hour and I need to finish my homework."

"Training again? But you were at the pool last night. Since when do you train on a Saturday morning?"

"I told you, Mum. The Nationals are in October and we're putting in extra sessions. Evie, don't. That tickles." Joe laughed as his two-year-old sister grabbed at his mouth with her chubby fingers.

"No talk. Joe-Joe play?" she asked.

"Sorry, Evie. Not now."

"I know you said something about extra training, but I didn't know you meant this morning. Your dad has had to work today and he wants to meet us all for lunch."

"I'll be done by twelve. I can't miss training, though. This competition is important."

His mother sighed. "I'll call your dad and see if he can make one o'clock instead. I'll tell him how important it is for you."

Joe looked down at Evie, who was now bouncing up and down on his knee.

"He won't care. After all, it's not like diving is a proper sport." Joe mimicked the scornful tone that his father had used when Joe came home with his first springboard trophy.

There was silence and Joe immediately regretted his words.

"I didn't mean that."

"Yes, you did, Joe."

She put Nell down. "And I can't blame you. Look, give me twenty minutes to sort this washing out and I'll drive you to the pool. You'll be in plenty of time."

Joe's face brightened. "Thanks, Mum."

He turned to the twins. "C'mon you two. Race you to the play-room."

Squealing with delight, blond curls bouncing up and down, Evie and Nell chased after him.

Joe listened to the twins happily babbling away to each other in the back of the car, as his mum drove him to the leisure centre in Ingworth Town. It always amazed him how the girls talked complete nonsense yet seemed to understand exactly what the other one said.

"Joe," said his mother, staring straight ahead at the road. "You know that Dad is proud of you, don't you?"

Joe turned to look at his mother's profile. She looked tired but then again, she always looked tired these days. Much as he loved them, the twins were a real handful and since his mum had recently started working again all she seemed to do was rush around after everyone else. The last thing she needed now was extra worry about him.

"Course I do, Mum." He gave what he hoped was a convincing grin as his mother flicked her eyes towards him before returning them to the road.

"What you said earlier-"

"That wasn't anything, honest. I was worried you were going to make me miss training."

Indicating left, his mother manoeuvred the car into the lay-by in front of the leisure centre. When the car stopped Joe already had his seatbelt unbuckled and was opening the car door. His mother put her hand on his knee.

"You sure that's all it was, Joe?"

"Yes, Mum. I'm sure." He could tell that she still wasn't convinced so he changed the conversation. "This competition is my big chance, especially as it's at our pool. If I promise to keep on top of my homework, will you still let me do extra training, even though I'm back at school?"

"We'll have to see, Joe. Year ten is important."

"Please, Mum. This is important too."

His mother smiled. "Well, I suppose as long as you don't neglect your work, I won't stop you diving."

"Thanks. And thanks for the lift."

Before she started worrying again, he leaned over and gave her a quick peck on the cheek, then clambered out of the car.

"Bye, bye, you two," he called to the twins.

"Bye, bye, Joe-Joe," called the twins in unison and both waved.

His mother laughed as Joe waved back. "I'll pick you up at half past twelve. Be ready," she said.

He kept waving while the car pulled away from the kerb and disappeared into the flow of traffic. Slinging his sports bag over his shoulder, he headed towards the leisure centre entrance.

"Joe! Wait on."

Joe stopped and turned. He grinned when he saw his coach, Nick Tyler, with his father, Steve, striding towards him. "Hi, Nick. Hello, Steve. I didn't think you'd be here yet."

"Getting in a bit of extra driving practice," said Nick. "Did I tell you I passed my theory? Got the real test in a fortnight. Can't wait. Two more weeks and I'll be free. Won't need the old man to run me around anymore."

"Hey, less of the old, thank you very much," said Steve. "You'd better watch what you say. Whose car do you think you'll be borrowing?"

Nick's lucky, Joe thought for the millionth time. I could never see my dad becoming Club Secretary like Steve is. At least, not unless I start playing rugby.

At the end of the morning session, Joe was tired but happier. He was towelling himself down at the side of the pool when Nick came over.

"Keep diving like that and you'll have that forward three-and-a-half nailed when it comes to the Nationals," he said.

"It's getting there," admitted Joe. "It still feels a bit low on entry."

"You need a bit more power out of the board. Wait for the take-off then squeeze into the pike. It's a big dive. Nail it at this competition though and you could be looking at the national squad."

Joe glanced at Nick. "Are you serious?"

"Too right. I wish I'd had half as much talent as you have, Joe."

Joe was still on a high when his mum arrived to pick him up.

"Good session?" she asked, as he opened the door.

"You wouldn't believe it! Nick thinks my forward three-and-a-half will be ready for the Nationals."

His mum laughed. "Glad to hear that all this training is paying off. Now, put your seatbelt on or we'll be late. The traffic was terrible getting here. I think there's been an accident down by the garden centre."

His dad was already waiting for them at the table, when Joe, his mum and the twins arrived at the restaurant.

"How are my girls?" Nell and Evie gave twin squeals of delight when they saw their dad and raced towards his outstretched arms. Gathering them up, he planted a kiss on the tops of both heads, before smiling at his wife and asking: "All right, Joe?"

"Yeah, thanks." Joe sat opposite his father as his mum settled the twins into their highchairs.

"Well, I know what I'm having, I've been waiting that long." His dad pushed the menu towards Joe.

That would be my fault, I guess, thought Joe, opening the menu and ignoring his dad's comment.

When they had chosen and the waiter had collected the order, Joe's dad leaned back in his seat and ran a hand over his bristly fair hair. "I've got a surprise for you all," he began.

Joe's mum was in the middle of taking the salt and pepper away from Nell, but stopped to look at her husband. "What kind of surprise?" she asked.

"No need to look worried, it's a nice surprise." He grinned and looked around at his family. "We had a special offer through at work and I've booked a long weekend break at Centre Parcs."

Joe looked up in delight. "When? Do I get to miss school?"

"I hope not!" said his mum.

His father laughed. "No, such luck, I'm afraid. It's the weekend you break up for half-term. If I take the afternoon off we can go Friday afternoon and come back early evening Monday."

Joe's face dropped.

"Dad, we can't go then."

His father frowned. "What do you mean?"

"It's the weekend of the Nationals." Joe looked at his mum in dismay.

"Is that all?" said his dad. "Well, you'll have to miss it for once. There'll be other competitions. It's not often we all get to go away together, and your mum could do with a break."

"I can't miss it! I've been training for this for months. Dad, it's important."

"Important to you, maybe. A holiday is important to us." His father's tone turned angry.

"Mum…" Joe looked towards his mother.

"David, Joe's been working hard for this competition. Could we go the weekend after, instead?"

"No, we can't. The offer is only for that weekend and I've paid a deposit, which I can't get back. We're going and that's the end of it."

"Well you can go without me. I'm not missing the Nationals."

"Shh, Joe. We're in a restaurant. Keep your voice down." His mum looked around and smiled at the diners on the next table who had turned to stare at the raised voices.

"Diving! That's all he ever thinks about. It's about time he concentrated on something worthwhile."

"Diving is worthwhile. If you were interested, you might find that out."

"Joe! Don't speak to your father like that." His mother's voice was hushed but stern. "We'll talk about this later."

"There's nothing to talk about, as far as I'm concerned," said David. "We're going to Centre Parcs as a family. End of story."

Joe slid down in his seat; head bowed his mouth set in a tight line. He didn't care what they said. There was no way he was missing the Nationals to spend a weekend with his dad.

Chapter Six

A pigeon ventured closer to the table where Angelina was sitting. Flashes of purple and green luminescence brightened its neck feathers as it pecked at the crumbs littering the floor. She scraped back her chair and the pigeon fluttered into the air, it landed a few feet away and returned to its foraging.

She took a sip of fresh orange juice and glanced at her watch: ten-to-ten. Five more minutes to wait; she settled back trying to get comfortable on the café's hard plastic chairs. The sun had somehow managed to squeeze between the high-rise buildings that surrounded the small square and was pleasantly warm on her face.

Dee seemed perfectly happy to wait and reached for her cup of camomile tea.

Should be called *infusion of old wet socks,* thought Angelina, catching a whiff of the smelly drink.

Apart from the pigeons the streets were almost deserted.

"Why is it so quiet?" Angelina asked.

"It's mainly offices around here. Most are closed on Saturday." said Dee.

Angelina looked at her watch again. Four minutes until her first training session was due to start.

"Nervous, are we?" Dee asked.

She was wearing a pair of large, black sunglasses with opaque lenses. It gave Angelina the rather unsettling feeling that she was talking to a giant fly. Although at least she's dressed like a normal person for once, thought Angelina, taking in the grey linen trouser suit that hung off Dee's bony frame.

"No. I'm fine," she said. Hopefully Dee couldn't tell how nervous she was really feeling.

Dee said: "Follow me, watch and listen, and you'll be fine. Once we're in, stay close and don't say a word."

Angelina sipped her drink. This was her first Fate Switch and she knew all the theory, but performing one was a whole different matter.

She remembered the first thing she'd ever been taught about them: *Fate Switches can change the future – some impact the whole of humanity, others affect only the individual concerned.*

This was a level-two Fate Switch. There wasn't much at stake, but Angelina still couldn't stop her hands from shaking. She closed her eyes and thought back through everything she'd learned, the voice of her tutor echoing in her mind.

Fate Switches occur at a junction in time. Think of a train on a railway line. If the Fate Switch happens, the points on the railway change and send the train to a different destination. If the Fate Switch doesn't happen the train continues to its original destination. Your job is to make sure the train of destiny arrives at the right station. That is, the Fate Switch should give the most favourable outcome for that person. Sometimes your job will be to make sure that the Fate Switch happens, and at other times you'll need to stop it from taking place.

But it was her tutor's final lecture that had always stuck in her head.

Some of you, much later in your career, will be faced with a Fate Switch that's level-ten or above. These are known as Significant Fate Switches. Do not take this responsibility lightly. Significant Fate Switches affect the entire world you're inhabiting. Get it wrong and the consequences are catastrophic.

Dee's voice cut into her thoughts.

"It's time. We need to get into position."

Leaving her drink, Angelina hurried along at Dee's side as she walked briskly across the square towards the front entrance of QuickQuote Insurance, the building they'd been watching.

This was it. Her first Fate Switch. No turning back now.

As they walked, Dee ran through the instructions.

"Vicky Philips will walk through those doors in exactly one minute and twenty seconds. Remember what she looks like?"

Too nervous to speak, Angelina nodded, her mind flying back to the previous evening.

She'd been sitting with Dee in front of the computer in the cluttered study, staring at a Umail, the FFUs universal electronic mailing system.

"It's a level-two Fate Switch, we'll be doing. I don't usually have time to bother with anything less than a level-eight these days, but they're useful for training," Dee had said, as Angelina read the message.

To: Dorothy Devin, Earth
From: Notification Department FFU
Sent: 12 July, 15:12
Subject: Training Fate Switch, Level-two

Herewith advance notice of a level-two Fate Switch, Ingworth, Yorkshire, England, Earth.

Date: Saturday 6 September
Time: By 10.32am (local time)
Location: Ingworth, Church Rise
Target: Vicky Philips

Action: On way to 11am appointment in Sheffield to take Church Rise instead of Market Street and pass the Garden Centre.

Background available:
Age: 23
Address: 22 New Street, Ingworth, Yorkshire, England, Earth
Interests: Works as insurance advisor, QuickQuote Insurance; pilates; gardening.

Desired outcome: Fate Switch to take place.

"Is that all they tell you?" Angelina asked.

Dee barked a harsh laugh. "You only get so much information because I asked for it as a training project."

"How do you know what to do?" The textbook exercises she'd completed at college had seemed much easier.

"Research and preparation, my girl! You are expected to do *some* work."

"What does it mean: by 10.32am?"

"There's a twenty-minute window in which every Fate Switch must take place, but if it's not completed by 10.32 then it won't happen," Dee explained.

"Let me get this right; tomorrow we're going to jump into this Vicky person's mind and tell her to take Church Rise?"

"No. We don't *tell* her what to do, we *Influence* by making suggestions."

"What if she makes the wrong decision?"

Dee shrugged. "It happens all the time. They say that for every successful Fate Switch, there are two unsuccessful ones. If we get the important ones, that's all that matters. It's like anything: the more you practice, the better you get. If you want to pass this assignment you need to work hard."

"What do I say to her?"

"You say nothing!" Dee said. "Tomorrow you will follow me, watch and listen. You need far more experience before you take part."

Now, standing in the sun waiting for Vicky Philips to appear, Angelina was glad that she wasn't expected to say anything.

Dee was talking in a low voice. "Vicky has to come this way, her Mini is in the car park across the road. As soon as she's gone past, we make the Mind Jump."

Mind Jump. The words sent a shiver of apprehension through Angelina. It wasn't a jump in the physical sense where you bend your knees and leap into the air. This was different. She knew the theory: concentrate hard on your target, free your mind from any other thought and allow yourself to be sucked into the subject's unconscious. It was more a case of letting go rather than jumping.

But the doubts were welling up, threatening to engulf her. Now that it was happening, she wasn't sure she wanted to do a real Mind Jump.

"Set your watch now."

Angelina looked at her special-issue digital watch. It was eight minutes past ten; thirty seconds before Vicky Philips was due to appear.

By pressing the top left button, she changed the display. The red, LED letters TIM REM, replaced the time. Almost running on automatic, Angelina accepted the 'Time Remaining' mode by pressing the bottom left button; 60:00 flashed on the display.

"Let me look." Dee grasped Angelina's wrist and peered at the watch. "Good." Her voice was terse. "We have one hour, when we get in. Any longer and I don't need to tell you what will happen."

Angelina felt queasy. She knew exactly what would happen. It was something they'd drilled into her during the Fate Switch module; stay in a target mind for longer than sixty minutes and it's goodbye for ever… Vaporisation.

"You'll hear a single beep every fifteen minutes," Dee continued. "If you're still in the mind after three beeps, exit. Immediately. Got that?"

Not trusting herself to speak, Angelina nodded again.

"Start the countdown when I say 'now'. When the seconds get to fifty-seven, we jump. Here she comes!"

Angelina's pulse quickened as she saw a young woman, dressed in a pale blue dress, step through the revolving doors of QuickQuote Insurance. A red handbag was slung over her right shoulder and she carried a black briefcase in her hand. With her short, curvy frame and shoulder length brown hair, Vicky looked exactly like the photo Angelina had seen.

As the woman hurried towards them, tapping along the pavement on red stiletto heels, Angelina's heart hammered in her chest.

"This is it. Get ready." Dee's voice was barely more than a whisper.

In a flash, Vicky had passed them.

"Now!"

Hearing the whispered command as if it were a klaxon, Angelina pressed the button on her watch. The display changed immediately to 59:59.

Panic bubbled to the surface, I can't do this, she thought…

59:58…

I don't know how…

59:57…

It was now or never.

Concentrating hard, Angelina surrendered to the pull of Vicky's mind.

Instantly, she felt a strange tugging sensation as if she were being sucked out of her Earth body. A thick blackness enveloped her, as she hurtled forward into space. Her ears were filled with a strange whooshing sound and she wanted to scream, but she was travelling so fast into nothingness that she couldn't even catch her breath.

Then it stopped. Suddenly.

She stared wide-eyed into the heavy darkness. There was no sound apart from her quick shallow gasps.

Had she made it?

She couldn't see or even feel anything, it was as if she no longer had any control over her limbs.

Don't panic. Don't panic, she repeated.

Inhaling deeply, she managed to steady her breathing. As the initial fear subsided, she became aware of a new sensation. There was a rawness surrounding her that she'd never experienced before. It felt as though the darkness had some kind of substance to it and there was a faint aroma that Angelina couldn't quite place. She sniffed, or at least thought that she did. Strawberries! She could smell strawberries.

Where was she?

Where was Dee?

If she was in Vicky's mind, then surely Dee should be here? But all Angelina could feel was this syrupy blackness and a faint, fruity smell.

The panic started to return.

She had to get out. Now!

Chapter Seven

"Relax. You made it."

Instinctively, Angelina turned towards the voice.

"Dee? Is that you?"

"Of course, it's me. Who else would it be?"

Although Angelina couldn't see anything, she could hear the sarcasm in Dee's voice.

"Where are we?"

"Exactly where we should be. Not a bad effort for your first jump, I suppose."

"You mean we're in Vicky Philip's mind?"

"There's no need to whisper, she can't hear us in here."

"Something's wrong, Dee. I can't see anything or feel anything. Everything's gone numb!" Angelina felt herself struggling to control the panic.

"Calm down." It was an order, not a request.

"We're in Miss Philips' subconscious, the mind's dark storage bin. That's why you can't see anything. We're right in the middle of all the thoughts, ideas and knowledge that even Vicky Philips doesn't know she has."

"Why can't I feel anything?"

Dee gave an impatient sigh. "You've studied this, remember? The basic theory of Fate Switches? Only your Essence enters the mind. It might feel as if you're breathing and moving, talking and listening, but that's just the way your Essence allows you to understand things. Everything in here is controlled by sense and thought, don't forget."

34

The knowledge came flooding back. "My Earth body has gone? What if I can't find it again? How do I get back to being me?" Although she knew it wasn't real, Angelina felt as if she were shaking.

"Relax. Yes, your body has dissolved into millions of atoms that no one can see, but your Essence keeps them close. Now, microscopic bits of our bodies will be swarming round Vicky. Not that she'll know. But remember" -Dee's tone sharpened- "the bonds weaken quickly around living humans because there's conflict between our Essence and their Aura. Any more than an hour and the bonds will be too weak to reform."

"Vaporisation." muttered Angelina.

"Enough." Dee's voice became business-like. "We'll be Vaporised if we don't get a move on. Follow me. We're going through to the conscious mind where Vicky Philips will hear every word we say. Keep quiet and leave the Influencing to me. Do you understand?"

"How can I follow you? I can't even see you."

"Concentrate and you'll sense the way. You need to let go and head down, as if you're going deeper into the mind."

Trying to quell the growing sense of panic, Angelina once again surrendered to the unknown. As she did so, she felt a faint pull, like an undercurrent gently tugging her down into the sludgy darkness. Resisting the urge to fight against it, she allowed herself to be carried along; desperately hoping that she was going the right way.

As she floated down, the current seemed to gain momentum, moving faster and faster, twisting and turning. It was as if she were shooting through a giant flume at a water park, but in complete darkness, not knowing which way the ride would throw you next. To Angelina, it seemed to last forever, though it was only a couple of seconds before the ride ended abruptly. But instead of a waiting pool of water, she was hit by a blast of light.

Growing accustomed to the brightness, Angelina realised that she was looking through the windscreen of a car. The view changed. Disoriented, Angelina found that she was now looking at a red handbag on the passenger seat. A strange hand, decorated with scarlet nails and chunky rings, came into view and rummaged through the bag before pulling out a lipstick.

'Ah, there it is!'

Even more bewildering, an unfamiliar woman's voice seemed to be inside Angelina's own head.

As she watched, another hand came into view and pulled the lid from the lipstick. Angelina finally worked out what was going on.

She was in Vicky Philips' conscious mind, seeing and hearing the things that Vicky saw, heard and thought.

It was strange having no control over where you were looking or what you were doing, but as Angelina gradually became accustomed to her new environment, she knew that she wasn't alone. Somehow, she could sense Dee nearby, yet knowing that Vicky could now hear every word she said aloud, Angelina didn't dare even to whisper Dee's name. She'd just have to sit tight and see what happened.

Vicky had obviously crossed the road and got into the car, while Angelina and Dee had been in Vicky's subconscious. There was the sound of the car engine starting up and the car moved forward. It crawled out of the car park and turned left on to the road.

After a few minutes they stopped at a junction. Angelina could hear the ticking of the car's indicator but felt dizzy as Vicky quickly swept her eyes right, then left and right again, seeking a break in the continuous stream of traffic.

'Come on, come on.'

That was Dee's voice, thought Angelina. Yet strangely, Vicky accepted the thought as her own. This was how Influencing worked. Dee was tricking Vicky into thinking that the voice she could hear in her head, was her own.

'For goodness sake, where has all this traffic come from?' Vicky thought. *'Right, go.'* Vicky pressed her foot hard on the accelerator and Angelina almost screamed as the car shot forward into the traffic. From somewhere to the side, a horn blared. Vicky had misjudged the speed of the car approaching from the right, which had had to slam on its brakes to avoid a collision.

"Oops." Vicky said the word aloud. She gave the driver a quick glance and an apologetic wave, allowing Angelina to catch sight of the angry motorist, who was gesturing wildly and mouthing something at Vicky.

'Same to you too! Shouldn't have been going so fast,' said Dee's voice. Again, Vicky happily agreed.

The journey continued, the occasional thought interrupting the drone of the car's engine.

'Is that house for sale again?' Tearing her eyes from the road, Vicky let them rest for a second on a large, detached house to her left.

'That's twice within a year! Must tell Rachel. Wonder how much they want for it? Still would you want it to be on a busy road like this?' Angelina could hear Vicky's wandering thoughts as clearly as if they were spoken aloud.

'How am I doing for time?' Dee's voice again.

Assuming it was her own thought, Vicky's eyes turned to the dashboard clock. 10:22, Angelina read. Only ten minutes remaining.

Again, Vicky continued the thought that Dee had started. *'Should be there by quarter to, as long as this traffic keeps moving.'*

A sign for the ring road passed the car. What was Dee playing at? thought Angelina. From the maps that Dee had shown her yesterday, she knew that the ring road would take them straight on to Market Street. Yet Vicky was supposed to take Church Rise instead, which would take her past the garden centre.

Another minute passed and still Dee stayed silent. Angelina was starting to get fidgety. What if Dee had forgotten the instructions? Perhaps she should say something after all.

Angelina heard a beep. The first time-warning. Fifteen minutes had passed since they'd made the Mind Jump. That made it 10:24, eight minutes to go.

Another sign; half a mile to the ring road.

She could hear Vicky going over the details of her forthcoming meeting as the junction for the ring road loomed in the distance.

Do something, Dee, she thought. We're nearly there! On cue, Dee's voice broke into Vicky's thoughts.

'Ten twenty-five. It's time for Dear Sarah on Radio Sheffield. You get some real nutcases on that show.'

Obediently following what she thought was her own memory, Vicky fiddled with the controls on the car radio.

"...news just in." The programme had been delayed for the start of a news flash. "A lorry has overturned on the clockwise carriageway of the outer ring road close to the junction with Park Drive. Police are at the scene and long delays are expected. Motorists are advised to avoid the area if at all possible..." the newsreader continued in her sombre tone.

'*Oh no, that's my direction.*' Angelina could hear the frustration in Vicky's thought.

'*But if I take a left here it leads onto Church Rise and I can cut through the town centre.*' Dee's voice made the suggestion.

Considering her options, Vicky's thought argued against the idea. '*But that way is so slow and they've got those speed cameras now. Should I risk the ring road? The accident might not be that bad after all.*'

'*Although if I go down Church Rise, it'll take me past the garden centre and I could see if they've still got that deal on lawnmowers…*' Dee's voice became persuasive.

'*…and if I'm a bit late I can always blame the traffic anyway,*' thought Vicky agreeing, or so she thought, with herself. '*Oh, but I need to be back for half past twelve. Perhaps I should risk the ring road after all.*'

She's not going to do it, thought Angelina. The left turn was almost upon them and Vicky was still dithering over the decision. We're going to miss the turning, she thought, I'll have to do something.

'*The ring road's blocked, I need to turn here.*' Angelina's voice was so forceful that Vicky immediately pulled down on the steering wheel, swinging the car to the left with a squeal of tyres. She received another blast on the horn from the car behind but they made the turn.

Yes, I did it, thought Angelina. Yet, her relief was fleeting. A wave of hostility washed over her and she knew immediately that it came from Dee. What's wrong with her? She should be thanking me, thought Angelina. Any longer and we'd have had no chance of making this Fate Switch.

Four minutes remaining.

Another minute passed. Vicky turned right on to Church Rise and seconds later brought the car to a halt behind a long line of traffic that was waiting for traffic lights to change.

The garden centre was up ahead on the corner of the junction. They just had to get through the lights. Time was running out, but Dee spoke again.

'*Is that sign still there about the mowers?*'

A line of cars was in the way and Angelina could feel Vicky straining to look for the sale sign.

'*Oh, I can't see from here,*' thought Vicky.

'*I'll have to wait until I'm through the lights.*' Dee's suggestion.

Another two minutes passed as they crawled towards the front of the queue.

'I'll get through this time.' Dee spoke confidently, even though there were three cars still in front of Vicky.

Seconds ticked by. Eventually the amber light joined the red, then both disappeared as the glowing green light appeared. There was a short time delay as the first car eased forward through the lights. But the lights changed quickly and amber was showing by the time Vicky's car arrived at the junction.

'Made it. Now, where's that lawnmower sign?' Dee's voice was insistent and Vicky never even considered stopping. Instead she accelerated through the lights.

'Great, the sale's still on,' thought Vicky, craning her neck to read the A-board outside the entrance to the garden centre. *'Even better, 75% off now. Glad I waited a week.'*

There was a screech of tyres.

Vicky's Mini was sent spinning as a car crunched into the passenger side door. Vicky lurched sideways, the seatbelt keeping her body in place but her head, jerking around like a rag doll, hit the side window with a crack.

Everything went black.

Chapter Eight

"Angelina! Angelina!" The voice was hushed but insistent.

Dazed and disoriented, Angelina couldn't seem to get rid of the ringing in her ears and it took a few seconds to register that someone was calling her name.

"Angelina! Come on. Concentrate!"

Everything was in darkness.

"Who... who's that?"

"It's me, Dee. Now listen."

"Where am I?"

"I said, listen! Vicky is unconscious, that's why it's dark. We need to leave. Concentrate and follow me. We're going back into the subconscious and then straight for the exit. No stopping this time. Got that?"

"I... I think so."

"Good. You shouldn't have a problem; the mind opens when they're unconscious. Ready?"

Trying to shake off the dizziness, Angelina surrendered to her senses. This time, she found herself travelling upwards, accelerating through the twists and turns until she felt the viscous, strawberry-scented atmosphere of Vicky's subconscious slow her down. But before she came to a complete stop, she felt another pull, gentle at first as if easing her out of the sludge, then increasing in speed as she seemed to fly higher and higher, faster and faster, spiralling upwards until she burst out into daylight.

The next she knew she was standing next to Dee on the pavement. She could see Vicky's crumpled Mini, which had been flung across the road by the impact. Its passenger door was sunken and scarred. A silver, sporty-looking car, with a battered left wing and smashed headlamp, had come to rest by its side.

As Angelina watched, the man from the sports car rushed towards the Mini, yanking open the driver's door as he yelled into his phone.

"Ambulance. We need an ambulance!" She heard the man shout.

"You've made a mess of this." Dee hissed the words from between clenched teeth, her eyes fixed on the carnage in the road.

Angelina looked at her in surprise. "Me?"

"You had to open your mouth, didn't you? You were given one instruction. That was it. One thing you had to do, but no, you couldn't keep quiet, could you?"

Shaking her head, Dee turned and stalked away.

Angelina ran after her, bubbling with indignation. "I made it happen! If I hadn't said something Vicky would have missed the road altogether."

Dee stopped and spun round to face her. "Thanks to you she did miss the road. There's another left turn before you hit the ring road that joins Church Rise. She'd have joined the queue of traffic closer to the junction. If you'd kept your mouth shut, she'd have reached the junction before that silver car was in sight and there wouldn't be this mess now."

A knot twisted in Angelina's stomach and her mouth dried. What had she done?

"I... I didn't notice that road on the map," she stammered. "Does that mean the Fate Switch didn't happen?" Her voice was barely more than a croak.

"Oh, it happened all right. You heard the bell, didn't you?"

Of course, the ringing in her ears. Angelina knew that a bell sounded every time a Fate Switch happened. She just hadn't made the connection.

"But it was messy." Dee flicked her hand back towards the driver from the silver car who was still tending to Vicky. She was now conscious but holding the right side of her head and looking rather shocked. "That man was supposed to scrape Vicky's car. Bit of damage to the paintwork, but nothing serious. They swap insurance details and move on." Dee shook her head. "It was only supposed to delay Vicky, otherwise she'd have knocked down a dog that runs into the road in about two minutes' time on Market Street. Thanks to you, all that changed. Everything had to speed up and now it's caused a much more serious incident."

"How do you know all this?"

"FutureVision. It shows what could happen if the Fate Switch occurs or what will happen if it doesn't."

"I thought that was banned?"

"It is. Officially."

Angelina waited for an explanation, but Dee just stared at the wrecked cars, her mouth in a tight line.

"But you said that the Fate Switch happened. Surely, everything's okay," said Angelina.

The wrinkles on Dee's forehead bunched together as she frowned at Angelina.

"I said it only shows what could happen and that's if everything goes according to the forecast. This didn't. For one thing, they're spending too much time here and they've caused a traffic jam, delaying all these other people." She swept her arm around in an exaggerated arc to emphasise her point. "There'll certainly be some RIPles from this Fate Switch. You'd better hope that they don't lead to anything serious."

Angelina felt the knot in her stomach tighten again. She knew that RIPles, or Random, Inadvertent Phenomena, were the unknown consequences that happened when something went wrong with a Fate Switch. Years from now it might be possible to trace a major event back to this one mistake.

The wail of an ambulance sounded in the distance and Dee sighed as if defeated.

"More RIPles," she said, shaking her head. "We need to go home."

Back at the cottage on Hermit Hill Lane, Dee stormed straight into her study and slammed the door.

Angelina crept upstairs and hid in her room. She lay on the bed replaying the Mind Jump over and over in her mind. Why hadn't she trusted Dee?

Half an hour passed before she heard Dee calling for her.

She hurried downstairs and eased open the study door. Like Dee, the small study had a wildly disorganised look about it.

Dee was seated at the large desk that ran almost the length of the room and was piled high with documents, books and loose papers.

She was staring at a film clip playing on the computer screen. Without turning to greet Angelina, she said: "Come and look at the RIPles you've caused."

Narrowly avoiding kicking over the waste bin where a banana skin hung over the side looking like a forlorn escapee, Angelina dragged a spare chair across to the computer and perched on the edge of the seat.

Dee clicked play and the film reloaded.

As Angelina watched, the scene of the earlier car crash filled the screen, digits in the bottom right corner gave today's date and a time five minutes after she and Dee had left for home.

A paramedic was helping Vicky into the back of an ambulance. The time skipped forward as the film jumped to a live view of Vicky exiting the hospital. At the door a man, whom Angelina recognised as the driver of the silver car, walked up to Vicky. There was no sound with the film, but Angelina could tell that they were talking and eventually they moved off together, smiling. Another skip. This time the date was two years in the future and the scene on screen showed a churchyard; autumn leaves were strewn like ashes among the head-stones. The film froze.

Were Vicky's injuries worse than they'd thought?

Angelina glanced at Dee. "Is Vicky...?"

"Perhaps. We don't know. There are too many variables after the hospital. It could be a funeral." Dee frowned. "However, it could be a wedding, or even a Christening."

"She might be okay?"

"All we know is this church is important. More Fate Switches must happen before we discover the outcome. For your sake, I hope it's not the first option."

Chapter Nine

Perched on the church wall next to the bus stop, Angelina was busy checking messages on her phone.

"Hi."

She looked up. "Oh. Hi, Joe. Good weekend?"

Joe pulled a face. "Okay," He hoisted himself onto the wall next to Angelina. "How about you?"

"About as good as yours by the sound of it. Did you do the ICT homework? I thought it was hard."

"Yeah, but don't worry, Mr O'Leary never checks. Hey, look who's coming."

Serena was walking towards the wall on which they were sitting, waiting for the school bus to arrive. Halfway across the road she looked up, caught Angelina's eye and changed direction, slouching off towards another group of girls.

Joe laughed. "Looks like you've scared her off."

"I don't know about that but if she stays away, that's fine by me. Come on, the bus is here."

After school on Thursday, Angelina was working at her desk and had almost finished her homework when Dee knocked on the door and strode into the bedroom.

"I've arranged another Fate Switch for this evening," she said. "But if you dare to say one word while we're in there, I'll have you thrown

44

off the programme."

A shiver of excitement and apprehension shot through Angelina.

At last, another chance.

"I'll stay quiet. Promise."

It was a simple Fate Switch. Dee had to persuade a 30-year-old man called Steve to stay home that evening instead of going to the gym. As his favourite film of all time, so Angelina learned during the Influencing stage, was on television that evening, he didn't need much persuading and they were in and out in fifteen minutes.

"It's straightforward when you follow the instructions," Dee said, on the way home.

I wouldn't have said anything to Vicky if you'd briefed me properly, Angelina thought but knew better than to express her views aloud. "What would have happened if he'd gone to the gym?" she asked.

"Nothing serious. He'd have slipped in the shower and broken his ankle. An inconvenience but no long-term consequences."

There was something else about the Fate Switches that was bothering Angelina.

"Dee, when we were in Vicky's subconscious, I could smell strawberries. Yet, with Steve it wasn't like that at all. In his mind I was reminded of the railway station. Is that normal?"

Dee paused, staring thoughtfully at Angelina. "You could smell his mind? That's interesting."

"It is?"

"You have aromawareness. You're lucky. Only ten percent of all Guardian Angels have that ability. You'll find it a useful skill."

"I don't understand."

"Each mind has a dominant odour that reflects the individual's personality. Vicky is a happy, friendly person, hence the pleasant fruity smell. Steve has a passion for cars. His scent was industrial, that's why it reminded you of the train. It reflects his love of machinery."

"How does that help anyone?"

Dee sighed, as if it were obvious. "It's an early warning system. If you ever smell anything bad, like something is rotten or has gone off, then get out of there fast. It means that individual has an infection, giving them a capacity for evil."

"Can they be cured?"

"Sometimes. But there's nothing you can do from inside the mind. The infection is programmed to destroy anything that can prevent evil, including Guardian Angels. It takes about five minutes for the infection to recognise you, then it closes the mind, trapping you inside until you are Vaporised."

Angelina shuddered at the thought. "Is there any way to beat it?"

"Not that I know. There is a theory that if the person falls unconscious, the mind will automatically open, but I don't know if it works in practice. I've never met anyone who's survived an infected mind."

"How do they become infected in the first place?"

"Who knows? With some it's inherited, with others it can be an event that they've experienced, which makes them more susceptible."

"If you don't have this aromawhatever, how do you know when a Mind Jump is safe?"

"Common sense, girl. The Fate Federation automatically screens all Fate Switch subjects before the notification goes out. Anyone who tests positive for the infection is blacklisted. Unless you go jumping into unchecked minds, you'll be absolutely fine."

Despite Dee's confidence, Angelina still felt uneasy and vowed to take a deep breath as soon as she arrived in anyone's mind from now on.

Saturday morning Angelina awoke to discover a note waiting for her on the breakfast table. Apparently, Dee was already up and in the garage, working. As she munched her way through a bowl of slightly stale cornflakes, Angelina started to read through the list of chores Dee had left for her.

"What?" she spluttered through a mouthful of milk and cereal. "Stack dishwasher; put out washing; take package to post office, first class special delivery; do shopping."

Angelina stopped reading after half a page. This was ridiculous. She was here as an apprentice, not free labour.

A knock on the kitchen door interrupted her thoughts.

"Parcel to sign for." A hand-held electronic console and stylus was thrust at Angelina as she opened the door. A huge cardboard box, twice as wide and almost as tall as the uniformed man with the clipboard, stood at the side of the door.

"What's it for?" Angelina scribbled her name on the screen where the man pointed.

"No idea. I just deliver 'em. It's a bit heavy. Where do you want it?"

Angelina was about to say that she had no idea, when Dee appeared. Today, she was dressed in a long, green-and-blue patterned gypsy skirt with a pink-and-white flowered blouse. The combination made Angelina wonder if Dee had dressed in the dark.

"You can take it straight into the garage," Dee said.

"Righto. You lead the way." The man whistled cheerfully as he jacked the box back onto his trolley and followed Dee.

Angelina stood watching.

Before pulling the garage door open, Dee turned back to Angelina. "I left you some jobs to do."

"I know, I want to talk to you about that." Dee looked annoyed by this and waved her hand in a shooing motion.

"Go inside, I'll be with you in a minute."

Anyone would think that she didn't want me to see inside her precious garage, thought Angelina huffily, as she returned to her breakfast.

She was draining the last drops of her orange juice when she heard the delivery van drive off. A couple of minutes later, Dee re-appeared.

"These jobs" -Angelina picked up the list- "you can't expect me to do them all. I'm not a housekeeper, I'm an apprentice!"

Dee remained silent, as if waiting for a toddler to finish a tantrum.

Angelina waved the list in the air. "This will take me all day. Surely I should be studying?"

For effect, Angelina threw the list onto the table and folded her arms.

Dee stared at her. The silence made Angelina uncomfortable and she fidgeted under Dee's steady gaze.

"Have you quite finished?"

Pursing her lips and tilting her head, Angelina shrugged sulkily.

"I'll take that as a yes, shall I?" Dee raised her eyebrows questioningly. "You're right, you're not a housekeeper, but you are living under my roof and while I don't expect you to pay board, I do expect a little help around the house in return. Any objections?"

Dee had a point. Angelina knew that she'd acted like a spoilt brat, but there was no way that she was ready to admit it yet.

"I suppose not," she said. Then, to save face, added: "As long as it doesn't interfere with my studies."

"Those chores will only take a couple of hours. If you spend the rest of the day studying, you'll be one of my most conscientious apprentices ever!" And with that, Dee headed back to the garage.

Dee was right; there was no way Angelina needed to spend the entire day studying. She sat for a few minutes, nursing her bruised pride, but with no-one around to witness the injustice it became pointless, so she collected the breakfast things and loaded the dishwasher.

An hour later, she was on her way to the post office, happy to be out of the house.

As she reached the bottom of the hill, she caught sight of a man in the distance. He was too far away for Angelina to see his face, but his height and build reminded her of her grandfather. She remembered what Dee had said the day she'd arrived and made a mental note to ask Dee what she knew about his disappearance.

The post office doubled as a convenience store and, having posted Dee's parcel, Angelina was browsing through a selection of magazines, when she heard a familiar voice.

"Oh, hello, my dear. Angelina? That's it, isn't it? How are you enjoying Little Ingworth?"

Turning around, Angelina found herself face to face with the woman from the train. What was her name again? Something to do with flowers... Rose, that was it, Rose Garden. Just what I need, thought Angelina. She'd managed to put the disaster on the train out of her mind for the last couple of weeks.

"It seems nice, thanks," said Angelina.

"That's good. Lovely day again, isn't it?"

"Yes, it is. Anyway, nice to meet you again." Angelina turned as if to go but Rose called to her.

"I couldn't ask a favour, could I? This shopping is so heavy for an old woman like me." She nodded to the two bulging bags in her hands. "I don't suppose you'd help me home with them, would you?"

Rose looked hefty enough to carry at least another four bags in each hand, thought Angelina. But before she got the chance to make her excuses, Rose continued.

"It's on your way home, and" -she paused for effect, her eyes twinkling conspiratorially- "I've baked a chocolate cake this morning,

48

which should be ready to eat when we get back."

Without further ado, Rose placed one of her shopping bags in Angelina's hand and hooked her chubby arm through the other.

"This is kind of you, Angelina. I don't know many teenagers that would help out an old lady like me."

You didn't give me much choice, thought Angelina, still a little bemused at how it had all happened.

Rose kept up the chatter all the way back to her house.

"Here we are, Rose Cottage," she announced proudly as she pushed open the gate to a pretty little cottage near the village centre. "Mr Garden gave it that name when we moved in. Almost three years ago now. He bought that rose bush there and even made this wooden plaque on the gate."

Rose beamed and Angelina gazed around the garden. It was alive with every colour of flower imaginable and as they walked down the path, Rose called out their names to Angelina.

"They're dahlias, over there campanula and coreopsis, and this is my favourite, monarda." She pointed to a clump of spiky red flowers. "Gardening is a passion of mine. When we moved here a couple of years ago, the front garden was neglected. Weeds were everywhere, but plants are resilient, don't you think?"

Angelina didn't know much about flowers and was more concerned with trying to avoid the cloud of bees buzzing angrily around the tall, purple plants, close to the path. Yet, she could tell that Rose was proud of her garden and was waiting for some comment.

"It looks lovely."

"Doesn't it just?" Rose beamed with delight as she unlocked the front door. "Come in, come in."

Although the day was warm, the thick stone walls and small windows of the old cottage kept it cool and Angelina shivered slightly as they stepped through the front door into the darkened hallway.

"Have a seat in the sitting room and I'll bring the cake in." Rose took the bag from Angelina and gestured towards a door on the left. "Won't be a minute," she called as she bustled down the hallway.

The room was as dimly lit as the hallway, with the sun struggling to fight its way through the tangle of rose brambles that curtained the windows outside.

As Angelina's eyes adjusted to the gloomy light, the shadows withdrew and she was surprised to see how large the room was. From the outside, Rose cottage had looked minute.

The sitting room was as fussy as Rose. Lace doilies were everywhere; underneath half-dead pot plants, protecting the arms and headrests of battered chairs and balanced on the top of the display cabinet, which held hundreds of ornaments, figurines and crystal glasses. Pink roses patterned the sofa and chairs and the flower theme continued across the carpet, its gaudy hues climbing up the wallpaper and across the curtains.

Stepping carefully around the footstools and side tables, Angelina perched on the edge of the chair by the window to wait for Rose. As she looked around, she noticed a computer tucked away in a corner of the room on a small office table. Multi-coloured shapes chased each other around the screensaver. It looked so out of place in this old-fashioned sitting room that Angelina got up for a closer look.

She was about to reach for the mouse when Rose's voice made her jump.

"Ah, now you'd better not be messing with that."

Angelina swung round to face Rose, who had entered the room carrying a tray laden with chocolate cake and drinks.

"Sorry, it looked interesting." Angelina moved away.

"That's Mr Garden's pride and joy and he doesn't like anyone else touching it, not even me. Not that I'd want to, anyway. I haven't got the faintest idea about how computers work."

"I didn't touch it."

"No harm done, then. Now, tell me what you think of this." Rose beamed as she handed Angelina a generous slice of gooey looking chocolate cake and lowered her bulk onto the sofa.

The cake did look tempting and seemed a worthwhile reward for helping Rose with her shopping. As Angelina bit into the moist sponge it disintegrated in her mouth.

"Mmm, this is *good*." Angelina mumbled the words as she chewed.

Rose tapped the side of her nose with her forefinger. "Secret family recipe." She sighed. "Only, I don't suppose the tradition will continue. My daughter doesn't care much for baking, more's the pity."

"What about Mr Garden? Doesn't he want some?" Angelina asked between mouthfuls, curious to know what kind of man could cope with being married to Rose.

"Oh, he's up at his allotment. He loves his gardening. Spends most of his time there in the summer."

Angelina couldn't say she blamed him. Rose was rather full on, to say the least. As she washed the last of the chocolate cake down with a sip of water, she heard the Grandfather clock in the hall strike eleven.

"Oh no! Is that the time?" Angelina checked her watch.

"Thanks for the cake, Rose, but I have to go."

"That's all right. You run along, love. I wouldn't want to get you into trouble. But come again whenever you want. There's usually a chocolate cake on the go for welcome visitors."

Chapter Ten

Listening to Mrs Wright, the biology teacher, explaining the Darwinian theory of genetics, Angelina stifled a yawn.

Monday morning was the worst part of the week.

She began doodling a caricature of Charles Darwin in the back of her exercise book.

Suddenly, she looked up.

Someone had called her name.

Mrs Wright was still writing on the blackboard, drawing lines connecting upper- and lower-case letter 'B's to show how the gene for brown eyes was passed on from one generation to the next.

The voice called again.

"Angelina, Angelina."

Furtively, she looked behind her, but no one in the room was looking her way. Nor did anyone else appear to have heard the voice.

"Angelina, now."

This time, she felt a strong urge to follow the voice. She knew that she had to get out of the class immediately.

She raised her hand.

"Yes, Angelina," said Mrs Wright.

"Could I go to the toilet, please?"

Looking irritated that the question was not genetics related, the teacher frowned. "We've just had morning break, why didn't you go then? You're not at infant school now."

All heads turned towards Angelina and a tittering of laughter rumbled around the class.

"Sorry, Miss. I… I don't feel very well." For emphasis, Angelina clutched her stomach and gave what she hoped was a pained expression. It must have looked convincing.

"Oh, right. I see. Well, in that case, you'd better go."

With one hand nursing her stomach and the other clamped across her mouth, Angelina rushed from the room.

"Go and see the nurse," Mrs Wright called after her.

Hurrying down the corridor, Angelina turned the corner and headed away from the classroom towards the cloakrooms. Confident that she couldn't be seen, she stopped, listening for the voice.

It came again, this time louder and more insistent. "Angelina, come now."

Come where? Angelina thought, the urgency in the words starting to make her panic. Without knowing why, she closed her eyes and concentrated.

There was a sensation of movement. Wind was blowing through her hair, she could hear the rustling of leaves, birds were singing and the air had turned cool and fragrant. She'd only closed her eyes for a second but, when she opened them again, she was standing by the gate at the edge of the school playing fields.

"Angelina, come. Now!"

The voice was coming from outside the school grounds. Following its command, she hurried through the gate to the pavement. Turning left she jogged along next to the busy main road that ran parallel to the school.

"Angelina, come. Now!"

As she reached the zebra crossing, she slowed and stopped.

This is it. This is where the voice is coming from, she thought. But what now?

Nervously, she looked around, waiting for another command, but the voice had fallen silent.

What do I do now? she thought. Wait?

A minute passed. She tried closing her eyes and concentrating again but this time nothing happened. Yet, she couldn't leave: some instinct was making her stay. On edge, she kept fidgeting, taking a few steps to the left, then to the right, craning her neck to see if she could see anything that might offer a clue as to why she was here.

As she watched, a woman, pushing a pram, approached the crossing and stood by the kerb. She was too busy smiling and making gurgling noises at her baby to take any notice of Angelina.

A red car slowed and stopped to let the woman cross. Angelina felt the urge to follow, and the reason she was here became clear.

As the woman stepped on to the crossing, the baby threw its blue teddy bear from the pram. As the woman bent to retrieve it Angelina caught sight of a black car racing up the road towards them. It was travelling much too fast and even from this distance she could hear loud music pumping from its stereo. She watched as it moved out into the middle of the road, preparing to overtake the red car and she could tell that the driver hadn't seen the crossing. Neither could the driver have seen the woman or the pram as they were hidden by the red car. In horror, Angelina saw that the car wasn't going to stop.

Frantically, Angelina looked at the mother who, by this time, was handing the teddy back to the baby, wiggling it in front of his face to make him laugh. She was so engrossed in this private game that she hadn't seen or heard anything. Pushing the pram with one hand she continued to cross the road, heading straight into the path of the speeding black car.

Chapter Eleven

Joe gazed up at the fluffy white cumulus clouds, then glanced down and added a few more curved lines to the cloud he was sketching in his geography book.

He was quite enjoying this unexpected outdoor geography lesson. In fact, school wasn't that bad at all this year. It certainly beat being at home and having to talk to his dad.

Glancing up at the sky again, he held up his geography book to check the result. Not bad. That one looks a bit like Angelina when she wears her hair in a ponytail. He flushed at the thought and lowered his book. If he was honest, she was another reason he was enjoying school this year.

There was something about her that he couldn't work out. She wasn't like the other girls in his year. She didn't seem bothered about trying to impress people. Neither had she taken any nonsense from Serena, although he still couldn't work out what had happened in the canteen. He'd been right there and could have sworn that Serena had hit Angelina.

He turned the page and started sketching the thin wispy, cirrus clouds, which according to Mr Pickering, lived twenty thousand feet up in the atmosphere. A movement near the gate at the far end of the playing fields caught his eye. A figure was hurrying away from the school.

That looks like Angelina as well, he thought. But it can't be. She's supposed to be in biology.

While he watched, the person passed through the gate and continued towards the road.

If it is her, she'll be in big trouble if she gets caught out there, he thought.

He glanced over to Mr Pickering, who was busy helping another pupil. Confident that no one was watching him, Joe clambered up the banking and behind one of the thick bushes that grew alongside the boundary railings. From there he had a clear view of the pavement and could see that the person had reached the zebra crossing.

It *was* Angelina. He was sure; there was no mistaking that long black hair. She looked agitated, as if she couldn't decide whether to cross. She was about twenty metres from where Joe was standing and he started edging towards her across the top of the banking, taking care to stay hidden from Mr Pickering and the rest of the geography class.

"What are you doing?" he muttered.

A woman with a pram joined Angelina at the crossing and a red car pulled up to let them pass. Angelina started to follow the woman. Joe slowed, realising that there was no way he could get close enough to call out to her before she crossed. Where could she possibly be going at this time of day? He thought.

The sound of an engine made him look to the right. What he saw made him freeze. A black car was on a collision course with Angelina and the woman.

In a split second his brain had processed everything he was seeing. The car was going too fast; the woman was still moving towards it; Angelina was following; and he was too far away to do anything. The car was going to hit them.

"Nooooo!"

Time seemed to slow as he heard Angelina cry out and grab the handle of the pram. He watched as Angelina, the woman and the pram tumbled backwards and the black car streaked past, leaving the pram rocking in its wake.

Adrenalin shot through Joe's body, freeing him from the momentary paralysis. Without stopping to think, he leapt over the railings and sprinted towards the zebra crossing. As he approached, he could see that the mother, pale and trembling, had snatched up her baby and was clutching him to her chest as if to reassure herself that he was still there.

"Thank you, thank you, thank you," he heard her say over and over again to Angelina, before convulsing into sobs.

The man from the red car rushed over to the woman. "Hey, are you okay. That idiot nearly killed you. Here, come and sit down for a while." He guided the mother and her baby away from the road.

Angelina was backing away from the scene when Joe arrived, and he grabbed her shoulder to stop her from bumping into him.

"Angelina!"

She jumped and swung around to face him. Her blue eyes widened with surprise when she saw who it was.

"Joe? What are you doing here?"

"I was about to ask you the same thing. You just saved that woman and her baby."

Looking around, as if to make sure that no one had heard, she grabbed Joe's arm and ushered him back towards the school railings.

"No…, yes, I…, look it was nothing, I stopped her from walking into the road. That was all."

Still breathless, more from fear than from his sprint, Joe looked at Angelina in bewilderment. She looked nervous, as if she'd been caught doing something wrong, instead of someone who'd no doubt just saved the lives of a mother and her baby.

"It didn't look like nothing from where I was standing."

They had reached a break in the railings. Angelina squeezed through, pulling Joe after her and into a clump of bushes. She turned to him.

"Look, Joe. Please can you do me a big favour and don't mention this to anyone."

"Why not? You should get an award or something for what you did."

The shadow of a smile flashed across Angelina's face but quickly disappeared. "Thanks, Joe, but I don't deserve it. I happened to be there, that's all. And if anyone finds out, I'll probably get into big trouble for being out of school."

That reminded Joe. "Why are you out here?" he asked.

Angelina looked back towards the road before answering. The red car was pulling away and the woman and pram were safely across the road.

"I wasn't feeling well in biology and Mrs Wright sent me to the nurse. I thought fresh air and a walk might make me feel better." She turned back to him. "And it did. I feel fine, now."

Joe had the feeling that there was more to Angelina's story but before he could say anything, she interrupted with her own question.

"Anyway, what are you doing here?"

"Me? Geography. We're on a field exercise. Drawing clouds." He held up the clipboard that he was still carrying."

"You mean there's a class out here?" Angelina looked stricken.

"Joe, I can't let them see me. Please, I need your help."

Her panic was so real Joe felt that he had to do something.

"It's okay, they won't. Follow these railings to the top of the playing fields. The bushes will hide you until you reach the school. They never lock the side entrance; you should be able to get in without anyone seeing you."

"Thanks, Joe. I'll see you later," she said, giving him a smile that made his heart lurch.

What is it about her? Joe thought, staring at where she'd disappeared through the bushes.

Joe had circuit training at lunchtime and didn't see Angelina again until after school. His final lesson of the day finished a few minutes late and she was already waiting in the corridor for him.

His face brightened when he saw her, and he ushered her away from the crowd of students spilling out of the classroom.

Making sure that no one could overhear them, he asked: "Did you get back to biology okay? What about Wright? Did she give you any hassle?"

A guilty look came over Angelina's face. "I bumped straight into Dr Arif when I got back to the science block and had to pretend that I was on my way to the nurse's room. They kept me in there until halfway through lunch."

Joe laughed. "Well, it's got to be better than lessons."

"I think even biology would have been more interesting than sitting in that room by myself." Angelina smiled. "Thanks again for earlier."

"I didn't do anything; you saved that woman. When I saw that car coming, I thought you were all goners."

Angelina shook her head, as if to get rid of the image.

"I was in the right place at the right time. Thanks for helping me get back, though."

Without warning, Angelina threw her arms around Joe and gave him a hug.

Flushing, Joe gave her a quick squeeze back and broke free.

"Hey, no worries. Look, we'd better get to the bus or it will go without us, and I've got training tonight."

"Training? I heard you were good at sport. Diving or something isn't it?"

He found Angelina easy to talk to and before he knew it, they were on the bus and he was telling her all about how unreasonable his dad was being over the Nationals.

But another part of him couldn't stop thinking about that hug.

Chapter Twelve

Why had she hugged him? Angelina thought. She hadn't known she was going to hug him. It had just happened. A bit like a sneeze that takes you unaware.

What if he got the wrong idea? She was here to do a job and getting too friendly with the locals was not a good idea. It led to problems. But she liked Joe and spending time with him made living here bearable. As she walked up Hermit Hill Lane, she tried to put Joe out of her mind and turned her thoughts back to the voice she'd heard that morning.

Arriving home, Angelina found the door to the cottage unlocked.

"Dee," she called.

The only reply was the ticking of the hall clock.

She'll be in the garage! Angelina marched into the garden and banged on the garage door.

"Who is it?" Dee's voice came from within.

Angelina rolled her eyes. "It's me. Who else would it be?"

"Is it that time all ready?" Dee's orange topped head poked out of the door.

"I need to speak to you. It's important."

"I'll be out in a minute. I need to finish this."

"Can't I come in? I'll tell you while you work," said Angelina, bobbing her head up and down as she tried to see into the garage beyond Dee. What could Dee possibly do in there all day? She was so precious about her stupid garage.

"No, you can't."

"Why? What do you do in there?" From where she was standing, she'd caught a glimpse of piles of cardboard boxes, all different shapes and sizes. It didn't exactly look interesting.

"Nothing to do with you. I'll be with you in ten minutes." Dee slammed the door shut and there was a click as a key turned in the lock.

Angelina raised her fist and was tempted to hammer on the door, but she knew it wasn't worth it. Dropping her hand to her side, she stormed back to the cottage to wait. She was at the kitchen table, finishing her maths homework when Dee eventually walked in, a quarter of an hour later.

Picking up the kettle and taking it to the sink to fill, Dee called over her shoulder: "What's this *big* event that you're desperate to talk about?"

"As if you care," muttered Angelina without raising her head from her books.

Dee turned off the tap, replaced the kettle and flicked the on-switch, before giving Angelina a cold stare. "If that's your attitude, I'll get back to my work." She started towards the door. "Give me a call when it's boiled please."

"Wait. I'm sorry. Something really strange happened at school today."

Dee paused, her hand on the door handle, and studied Angelina as if deciding whether to accept the apology.

"Please, I need to talk to you."

Pursing her lips, as if to indicate that Angelina wasn't entirely forgiven, Dee pulled out a chair and sat down at the table. "I'm listening."

Still trying to control her anger, Angelina took a deep breath and began. She told Dee all about the voices she'd heard and how, somehow, she'd been transported outside. As she talked, her anger dissolved.

After describing the way she'd pulled the woman and the pram out of danger she stopped. For some reason, she didn't want to mention Joe or his involvement.

"That was it. I managed to get away before any of the teachers saw me." She looked at Dee expectantly.

Dee gave her barking laugh.

"Is that it?" she asked. "I thought you said it was important."

"It seemed a pretty big deal to me." Angelina could feel the annoyance growing again.

"You mean you don't know what it was? Have you never heard of an AutoESC?"

Angelina shook her head.

"You're so fond of acronyms, you surprise me."

Knowing that it would be considered a stupid question even before she opened her mouth, Angelina couldn't resist asking: "What's an AutoESC?"

"Automatic Emergency Saviour Call. I can't believe you've never heard of an AutoESC." Tutting, Dee shook her head. "What do they teach you at that college, these days?"

"Obviously nothing about Autowhatevers," Angelina murmured.

"An AutoESC is an automatic, last minute, response call."

"Which means?"

"It means that if a human is about to be placed in a life-threatening situation, like the woman and baby with the car, then the Integrated Fate Monitoring System, no doubt you'll know it as the IFMS, puts out an automatic message. They've changed the system in the last couple of months. The message used to go out to all Guardians stationed in that country, but with the cutbacks they've narrowed it down to a half-mile radius." Dee tutted again. "It's all about budgets. They're making more and more cutbacks these days."

Dee looked thoughtful. "In fact, it's only since they changed the system that they've used trainees for AutoESCs, I suppose that's why they haven't bothered teaching you about them yet. I'll have to have a word and make sure that they change the curriculum."

"They called me by name. How did they know who I was?"

"Automatic Identity Recognition software. All Guardian Angels, including trainees have their identity logged in the system. The signal radiates out from the point of danger, a bit like GPS, and when it comes across a Guardian Angel, he or she is recognised by the software and the command personalised. It stops any confusion about who the call is for and makes sure that we respond as quickly as possible. That's new too."

"Shouldn't we be able to stop the situation from happening in the first place? I thought that's what the Fate Switch was for?"

"That's the theory but they've slashed our budgets and cut the number of Guardians on Earth. Now, we're contracted only to deal with high priority Fate Switches, which have long-term consequences for human society. Unless, of course, it's for training purposes. Then we take our pick from whatever's out there."

"But that woman and her baby could have been killed. Isn't that a high priority?" Angelina was stunned by what she was hearing.

"It would certainly have been tragic, but the consequences would stay within the immediate circle of family and friends. That's why it didn't warrant a high enough priority Fate Switch. It's life, deal with it. I don't respond to AutoESCs at all, these days. I haven't got the time."

Angelina had a sneaking suspicion that she already knew the answer to her next question. "What would have happened if I hadn't been in range of the AutoESC?"

Dee shrugged. "She might have seen the car in time, otherwise there would have been an accident."

Standing up, Dee returned to the kettle. Reaching for the handle, she stopped and looked at Angelina. "It happens all the time. You can't let it bother you or you'll be no use to anyone. You're only one Guardian Angel; you can only do your best."

Dee gave a humourless laugh. "There are people on Earth who still think that everyone has a Guardian Angel sitting on their shoulder waiting to save them from every inconvenience." She shook her head. "Ridiculous! Can you imagine the cost?"

On Tuesday morning of the following week, Angelina was seated at the kitchen table eating a bowl of dry breakfast cereal. The milk in the fridge was sour. Unfortunately, she'd only discovered this when she'd taken a mouthful of her first bowl of milk-covered cereal – the rest of which was now in the bin.

Dee was seated opposite, sipping camomile tea and browsing through the morning paper. Casually turning the page, she said: "I think you might be ready to do a solo Fate Switch by the weekend."

Angelina almost choked on her cereal.

"What?"

Wiping flecks of cornflakes from her mouth, she stared at the newspaper that Dee was hiding behind.

Lowering the paper, Dee peered at Angelina over her purple glasses. "You've logged fifteen successful practice sessions. If we reach twenty by Sunday, I might let you have a go by yourself."

"Are you serious?" Angelina didn't know whether to be delighted or terrified.

"Your assignment is in February and you need as much practice by yourself as you can get. Mind Jumping and Influencing must be second nature by the time you take your test." Dee had turned on what Angelina had come to call her 'lecturing' voice.

"What will it be? Is it anyone I know?"

"Slow down. I only said you *might* be ready. We'll see how you go this week before I make any firm decisions."

Angelina still had a grin on her face when she reached school. In registration, when Joe dropped his bag on the table and sat down next to her, he commented: "Someone's happy."

"Looking forward to computer class."

"Yeah right. You hate ICT."

"Yes, but at least I get to copy from you and get top marks without doing any work!" She said.

Joe laughed and, for some reason, she wanted to hug him again. Since the day of the AutoESC they'd spent more and more time together. When Joe wasn't at football practice they would sometimes walk home together, and Angelina now sat next to him in ICT. This had proved a smart move as she needed his help with the work. She'd never been interested in computers and it was the one subject she struggled with. The technology had been around on Earth for only a few decades and changed constantly, so her curriculum had dealt only with the basics.

On the way to ICT that morning, Joe was telling Angelina all about the forthcoming football match.

"We're playing Stalyborough High in our first league game of the season. They always win. Last year, they knocked us out of the cup in the semi-finals. They scored with the last kick of the match. It was a nightmare."

"People here think that football is important then?" She didn't dare to admit how little she knew about it. She hadn't seen the point in studying the football module very well, after all it was only a sport.

"I don't know about important, but people care about who wins." He stared at Angelina, who was trying to look interested.

"You don't know much about football, do you?"

"No. Sorry."

"Didn't they have a team at your last school?"

"If they did, I didn't take much notice. Is it anything like diving, then?"

Joe laughed. "If you watch some teams you'd think so."

Mystified, Angelina chuckled at what she assumed was a joke.

Still laughing, Joe said: "You haven't got a clue what I'm talking about, have you?"

Angelina shrugged.

"I can't believe you don't know anything about football." Joe's face lit up. "The game is a week on Saturday. Why don't you come with me? I said I'd watch as I'm not training until the afternoon."

They arrived at the ICT room, which gave Angelina a few seconds to consider the invitation while they settled into their seats.

Surprised, she found herself quite excited by the idea. Why not? she thought. Dee's told me to get involved with school activities.

"I'd like that. Thanks, Joe."

"Great. I'll call for you."

By the weekend, Angelina had performed four more Fate Switches. As daylight was fading fast in the evenings, she was learning to Mind Jump in the dark. Although it didn't make any difference whether it was night or day, Angelina was discovering that colder, darker days posed a practical problem.

People tended to stay indoors more and as a Mind Jump can take place only if the GA has a clear line of sight with the target, finding a window of opportunity could be difficult.

She soon became used to making very quick Mind Jumps while the target hurried from the car to their house or nipped out to empty the kitchen bin.

"This kind of practice will stand you in good stead for the future. It's important to make decisions fast in our kind of work." Dee had lectured after one particularly awkward session.

They'd waited outside the woman's house for an hour on Friday evening before she'd finally opened the door to a neighbour. Dee and

Angelina had had less than five seconds to make the jump before the neighbour had entered the house and the door had closed again.

After that mission had been successfully completed, Dee had said: "You're doing very well, Angelina. Perhaps there's hope for you yet."

Wow, thought Angelina. I suppose that's praise indeed from the Great Dee Devin.

On Saturday morning, Angelina accompanied Dee on her twentieth Fate Switch. Their target was a man in his early forties, who lived in Ingworth Bridge with his wife and two sons.

The day had arrived with a relentless, miserable drizzle. Even by mid-morning, when Angelina and Dee were huddled together under a pink and green polka dot umbrella, daylight had barely penetrated the heavy, grey clouds. They were waiting outside Ingworth Bank on the High Street and Angelina was so cold that she began to lose the feeling in her toes as she watched cars splash by, misty rain dancing dizzily in their headlights.

Her teeth were chattering by the time Dee nudged her.

"Here he is."

Angelina saw a powerfully built, bald man, with his hands stuck deep in his jeans' pockets, stride over to the cash point outside the bank. The collar of his short black jacket was turned up and his shoulders were hunched against the rain.

"Let's go."

On Dee's order, Angelina jumped.

At least it's warmer in here, thought Angelina, but what's that smell? The man's subconscious reminded her of the boys' sports hall at school; it had the same unwashed odour of week-old socks. In a panic, Angelina remembered Dee's warning about infected minds. Although she couldn't see, she could sense that Dee was still near her in the subconscious and knowing that the man would be unable to hear them, she called out.

"Dee, something smells bad."

"Shh! You know the rules."

"It smells rotten. It could be an infection!"

"This is unpleasant, but not rotten. You'll know rotten when you smell it. Now, follow me and no more talking. We've got a job to do."

The man was counting a pile of notes that he'd taken from the cash machine when Angelina arrived in his conscious mind. Dee got to work straight away.

'*Maybe I should put this back,*' she said.

'*But it's a dead cert. Barry's had an insider tip.*' The man thought he was arguing against his own conscience.

'*Denise'll go ballistic.*' Dee, again.

'*But if it wins, I could treat her to that new handbag she wants. She's bound to forgive me then.*'

'*Will, she? She was pretty upset last time. What if she's serious this time?*' Dee argued.

By this time, the man had reached a shop with its windows obliterated by bright posters of sporting events. Angelina caught sight of a close-up of a greyhound running and the front view of a line of horses carrying brightly clad riders, their thundering hooves frozen in mid-gallop.

As the man pushed the door open and entered the shop, Dee said: '*It's not too late, I don't need to do this.*'

'*But the odds are twenty-five to one, that's two-and-a-half grand if Barry's right. I missed out on that one last week and it came in. One last time and that's it.*'

'*Yeah, but Denise said if I ever–*'

'*She'll be fine. I can always talk her round.*'

They were now standing at a narrow, chest-high table that ran around the perimeter of the shop, broken only by the doorway and a line of cash registers along the back wall. Holders, containing slips of paper and small blue pens, were fixed to the table at regular intervals. Several television screens hung from the ceiling, like giant flat baubles and the walls were pasted with newspaper cuttings and posters of tables, which Angelina later discovered were racing schedules. The man whipped a slip of paper and a pen from one of the holders. In uneven, looped writing, he scribbled a name on the paper.

'*Mr Lonelyheart, one hundred pounds at twenty-five to one!*' He thought the words as he wrote them.

'*Mr Lonelyheart, that could be me if Denise finds out I'm betting on the horses again. I should stop and screw this paper up right now.*' To Angelina's surprise, Dee was starting to sound desperate.

'*I know, I know. But this can't fail. Barry's never wrong. This is it; I mean it. Just one last time and I can go out on a winner.*'

'*There's always one last time.*'

'*Yeah, but this time I mean it.*'

'*Isn't that what I said last time?*' Dee continued arguing.

'That was different. If this wins I won't do it again, ever. This is one last time.'

'Okay, that's done.'

Had Angelina heard correctly? 'Okay, that's done' was their code to leave if ever something went wrong or they were unable to make the Fate Switch. Dee couldn't leave now or the mission would fail. If that happened, Dee might not let her go solo tomorrow.

But it was too late. Dee had already exited the conscious mind. Angelina considered staying on and finishing the job but knew that if she didn't follow Dee's orders she'd be in even more trouble. Feeling rather bewildered, Angelina made her exit.

They were back in the rain, standing under the colourful umbrella watching the man as he stepped through the door. He stopped, sheltering in the betting shop doorway to stuff something into his wallet, before pulling up his collar and hurrying down the road away from them.

Dee was silent, watching the man as he disappeared around the corner. Eventually Angelina said: "I didn't hear the bell."

"No."

"The Fate Switch didn't happen?"

"No, we can only do our best. They don't always work out the way we want them to. This one will be recorded as a failure."

"Dee, are you all right?"

Dee had a strange look on her face. It was almost as if she looked sad. But this was Dee; Dee got mad, Dee got sarcastic but, to Angelina's knowledge, Dee didn't get sad.

"I'm fine. Let's go, there's no point standing around out here."

They set off in silence. Dee seemed to be lost in a world of her own.

Knowing that something wasn't right but not understanding what she had witnessed, Angelina tried again.

"I suppose he loses all that money on a horse race, then?"

Dee snorted. "There's more at stake for him than one hundred pounds. Anyway, the horse wins."

Angelina had a feeling that there was more to come.

"He's an addict, Angelina. Take a tip from me, never try to Influence an addict. Whatever you do or say, if the addiction is too strong, you'll never get them to change. We can't do a thing unless they want to change."

"I don't understand."

Angelina glanced across at Dee, who was walking so fast that Angelina had to run to keep up with her. Under the pink umbrella, there was a sickly glow to Dee's face.

"That man?" Dee jutted her chin in the direction from which they'd come. "His name is Danny Chapman. I've known him since he was born. Years ago, on one of my previous stints on Earth, his parents lived next door to me on Hermit Hill Lane."

Dee shook her head. "He was a lovely little lad but got in with a bad lot in his teens and by the time he was eighteen he was hooked on gambling. His mother never got over it. There've been a dozen Fate Switches where I've tried to make him take a different path, but they've all failed."

Dee slowed down, at last. "I thought I had a chance this time. He met Denise a few years ago. They married and have two young boys. At first the gambling stopped but recently he started again. Last week he lost the rent money on a horse and Denise gave him an ultimatum. Today's Fate Switch was to try to stop that bet he's put on."

"If the horse wins, why does it matter?"

"It's not about the winning or the losing. He promised Denise he would stop. He's broken that promise and destroyed any trust that she had in him and I couldn't stop him. You don't need FutureVision to know what happens next. Denise leaves him and takes the kids. Not that you can blame her."

"But it's not that serious, is it? I mean, I thought this was only a level-one Fate Switch."

Dee sighed. "You're right. It affects only him. Even Denise and the kids are better off without him if he can't kick the habit. I thought, this time…" Dee broke off and a look of regret crossed her face. Her tone hardened. "His poor mother has suffered enough."

When they arrived home, Dee disappeared into her study. Angelina was munching on a slice of cheese on toast when Dee stuck her head around the kitchen door.

"I thought I could smell something. Make me one of those, please. I need to finish this report. Two slices with a lick of Marmite on top and a cup of my special tea. Call me when it's ready."

It didn't take long for you to get back to normal, thought Angelina.

While Dee was eating, Angelina broached the subject of her solo Fate Switch.

"This morning was my twentieth Fate Switch and you said I could do one by myself when I'd logged twenty."

"I think you'll find that I said twenty *successful* Fate Switches."

Angelina dropped her head. It was as she'd feared.

Dee picked up her last piece of toast and paused, examining it as if it were a priceless vase. "But it wasn't your fault that I chose Danny. And you followed the orders to the letter."

Angelina looked up as Dee took a bite of her toast, chewing slowly and thoughtfully.

"So," Angelina prompted.

"So, yes, you can go solo tomorrow."

With a scream, Angelina jumped up and raced around the table, flinging her arms around Dee. "Thank you, thank you."

"I could always change my mind," said Dee.

Angelina let go. "Sorry. I got carried away."

"Yes, I can see that. I suggest you go to your room and calm down. I'll send the details through to your computer when I've finished here."

It seemed to take an eternity for Dee to finish her lunch but eventually the computer beeped, announcing the arrival of a Umail.

In her haste, Angelina clicked on the wrong icon twice before she managed to bring the Umail up on screen.

Fwd: Angelina.Crossland
From: D.Devin
From: Notification Department, FFU
Sent: 4 October, 12:53
Subject: Fate Switch, Level-one

Herewith advance notice of a level-one Fate Switch, Ingworth, Yorkshire, England, Earth.

Date: Sunday 5 October
Time: By 11.00am (local time)
Location: Martin Grove, Ingworth
Target: Matt Armitage

Action: To accept invitation from friend and decide against bike ride.

THE FATE SWITCH

Background available:
Age: 15
Address: Whitehaven, Martin Grove, Ingworth, England, Earth.
Interests: Pupil at Ingworth High, football, fitness, gaming.

Desired outcome: Fate Switch to take place.

Angelina had finished reading the information for the second time, when there was a knock at the door and Dee entered.

Come in, why not, thought Angelina, but she was too excited to care.

"You've read the assignment?" Dee pulled up a chair and sat down next to Angelina. "Even you should be able to cope with this one. It's only just arrived but you might know this boy. He's the year above you at school."

"I recognise the name." Angelina knew from classroom gossip that Serena used to be his girlfriend.

"Good. Well, it's straightforward enough and shouldn't take long at all. I can't see that he'll need much influencing to go off with his friends, although it doesn't say where they're going. Any questions?"

Angelina was so excited that she couldn't think of anything to say and shook her head.

"Good." Dee stood. "I'll be in the garage for the rest of the afternoon. I want you to look over the theory of Fate Switches again and we'll go through everything this evening. Then I suggest you get an early night. Tomorrow's a big day for you."

Chapter Thirteen

Despite taking Dee's advice about an early night, Angelina found it almost impossible to sleep. After tossing and turning for what seemed like hours, she finally drifted into oblivion just after midnight. But, like a kid on Christmas morning, she awoke at half past six and was unable to get back to sleep.

She was still buzzing with nervous energy when Dee finally said: "Right, we need to go."

Yesterday's rain had finally stopped, although the menacing clouds remained. To Angelina they looked like a brooding jury gathering to pass judgement on her performance, a feeling which intensified as she and Dee approached their destination.

Matt Armitage lived in a pleasant neighbourhood on the outskirts of Ingworth Town. The detached houses were large and expensive looking, separated by generous groomed gardens.

"That's where your target lives." Dee pointed to one of the larger houses across the road from where they were standing. "He should be appearing in the next five minutes, but you'll have to be ready. He'll only be in your sight line for one minute."

The enormity of what she was about to do finally hit Angelina and any excitement that she'd felt dissolved in a fluttering of nerves.

"I want you to go through the check list and tell me exactly what you're going to do," said Dee.

Taking a deep breath, Angelina began. "I set my watch, then jump." She clutched her left wrist with her right hand to illustrate the action. "When I'm in his subconscious I move straight into the conscious mind. I'll have ten minutes to do the Influencing." She looked at Dee for reassurance.

Dee nodded. "Keep going."

"I listen until I get used to his thought patterns before joining in. I agree with him or continue his line of thought so that he accepts my voice as his own. Then, when he gets the invitation from his friend, I start the Influencing and make sure that he says yes." She looked at Dee. "What if I don't know when to begin the Influencing?"

"Don't panic. Listen to his thoughts and you'll be fine. After all, you knew when to butt in when I was trying to Influence Vicky Philips."

Angelina's cheeks coloured at the memory and she turned her gaze back to the house.

"What do you do next?" Dee asked.

"When I hear the bell, the Fate Switch has taken place and I move immediately back to the subconscious and exit."

"Good. And emergency procedures?"

"If I can't Influence him to accept the invitation and I hear a single beep from the watch, I must exit anyway."

Dee looked stern. "Make sure that you do. You'll still have forty-five minutes remaining, but I want you in and out within quarter of an hour. This is your first time and it's only a level-one Fate Switch, with nothing significant at stake. If your watch beeps before the bell rings, leave immediately, even if you think that you're almost there. Understand?"

"I said I will." The nerves were growing, making Angelina tense.

"Don't take that attitude. I mean it, Angelina. You'll receive higher marks for missing the Fate Switch but following instructions than you will for breaking the rules to get the job done."

Chastised, Angelina nodded.

"Good." Dee glanced at her own watch. "He should be out in about ninety seconds. I'll leave you to it."

"What? You're going? I thought you'd be here, waiting for me!"

"I can't be there when you do your assignment, so we might as well start things as we mean to go on. Besides, I've got work to do at home. I'll see you back at the cottage when you're finished."

Dee must have seen the look of panic on Angelina's face, as she added: "You'll be fine. You've mastered Mind Jumping and if you don't manage the Influencing this time, don't worry. What's important today is that you do this by yourself."

"I don't think I can." Angelina's voice was a whisper.

"Stop being ridiculous and I'll see you back at the cottage." Without a backward glance, Dee walked away, leaving Angelina standing on the pavement, staring at her receding back.

As she watched Dee go, Angelina caught sight of a movement out of the corner of her eye but when she turned to look there was no one there. Strange, she thought, then jumped as a loose carrier bag skittered across the path in front of her. She almost laughed out loud with relief. Stop being so jittery, she told herself.

A sound from across the street focussed her attention. Matt Armitage had appeared from the side door and was heading towards the garage.

Sixty seconds, she thought. I've only sixty seconds before he disappears from view.

If she was going to do this, she had to move now or she'd miss her chance. But there was no way that she would reach him if she jumped now, she was too far away. She had to move closer.

Flicking her head from side to side to check for traffic, she darted across the road. By the time that she judged herself close enough to make her move, Matt had reached the garage and was using both arms to lever up the heavy door.

Time was running out. Within seconds he would be inside the garage and out of her sight line. Her nerves forgotten, Angelina kept her eyes fixed on Matt as she set her watch, concentrated and jumped. In an instant she felt the familiar sucking sensation as she was pulled into his mind. Seconds later the movement slowed and there was nothing but the silent, sludgy blackness of Matt's subconscious. Without stopping to think, she felt for the vortex that would take her through to the conscious mind.

As she whirled along again, moving faster and faster, she felt euphoric. She'd made it. Her first solo Mind Jump. Now that it was happening, her nerves had evaporated and the excitement had returned.

Light splashed over her as she landed in Matt's conscious mind. He was inside the garage now and she could see him searching among a line of tools, which were hung neatly along one wall.

'That'll do!.' Matt's thoughts came as clearly as her own.

He selected a spanner from the rack. Picking his way past a lawn mower and a pile of boxes he made for a purple mountain bike, encrusted with mud, which was leaning against the back wall of the garage.

'One twist should do it.' Angelina heard him think. He placed the jaws of the spanner around the nut on the handlebars and gave a firm twist.

"Got it," he said aloud.

Returning the spanner to the rack, he wheeled the bike outside, looking up at the sky as he came out into the open.

'I hope this weather holds up. I want to get up Yarn Bank and back today.' Matt's internal voice was becoming familiar to Angelina.

Right, my cue, she thought. *'It doesn't look promising.'*

'Those clouds are looking a bit black.'

That was Matt, thought Angelina. He accepted my words, it's working.

"Matt." A shout from the street caused Matt to turn around.

'Carl, what's he doing here?' Matt thought. Aloud he said: "Hey, Carl, what's up?"

Carl sauntered up the drive. "I'm meeting Dom at the pool. Want to come?"

"Since when did you start swimming?"

Through Matt's eyes, Angelina saw Carl grin. "Since Dom found out that Elle Wilson, Megan Gallagher and Faye Bradshaw are going to be there."

"Megan Gallagher?"

"Yep. Dom was talking to Ella yesterday. They're on some health kick and going for a swim today. Thought we'd join them." Carl's grin grew wider.

'Megan's gorgeous,' thought Matt.

"Are you up for it?" Carl asked.

"I'm supposed to be training this morning. My football coach set me this schedule."

'But it does look like rain.' Angelina started placing doubts in Matt's mind.

'That's true,' thought Matt.

Carl shook his head. "You can't be serious? It looks like it's going to chuck it down. You must be mad."

'Megan's gorgeous.' Angelina emphasised Matt's earlier thought, even though she couldn't recall what Megan looked like. *'And it does look like rain,'* she repeated for good measure.

"Come on," said Carl.

"I *should* do this bike ride," said Matt.

Angelina put on a persuasive tone. *'Then again, swimming is good exercise too.'*

'Better even. It works arms and legs.' Matt's mind latched on to Angelina's argument.

'I could always do the bike ride later if the weather clears up.' Angelina finished for him.

"Come on, mate. I'm meeting Dom in ten minutes." Carl checked his watch.

'Why not?' Angelina suggested before Matt had the chance to think of another excuse.

"Yeah, okay then," said Matt.

He stashed his bike back inside the garage and, as he ran towards the house, Angelina heard the faint ring of a bell.

The Fate Switch! She'd completed her first Fate Switch. All by herself. And in time!

'Yes!' Angelina couldn't stop herself from shouting out.

"Megan Gallagher. Yes!" Matt muttered, as he bounded up the stairs towards his bedroom.

Matt had heard her exclamation but luckily, it appeared that he was still accepting her voice as his own thoughts.

Oops, I'd better get out of here before I say anything else, she thought.

Concentrating, she felt for the pull that would take her back into Matt's subconscious and was soon whirling back into the gluey darkness.

The momentum slowed as she reached the subconscious and, with Matt no longer able to hear her, she let out a whoop of delight.

"I've done it, I've done it I've done it!"

She shouted into the empty blackness. "Now let's get out of here and see what Dee has to say about this brilliant effort."

Relaxing, she felt for the exit, waiting for the familiar sensation of rising up and out into the atmosphere.

But nothing happened.

Angelina berated herself. "Come on, you're too wound up. Calm down and concentrate," she said aloud.

She collected her thoughts, breathed deeply and focussed on feeling for the exit.

Nothing. She couldn't sense anything.

She tried again.

It wasn't working.

What am I doing wrong? she thought. I can't be focussing properly. Okay, loosen up and relax.

She counted to ten slowly, concentrating on relaxing a little more each time she felt the sensation of breathing out.

"And go." She tried again.

Still nothing.

Again and again she tried but something was wrong. She couldn't feel the exit. Panic started to seep through as she tried over and over again to sense the way out. It was no use: the exit wasn't there. Matt's mind was closed. She was trapped.

Realisation opened the floodgates of panic.

She had to get out. Her breath seemed to be coming in short sharp gasps and it felt as if she couldn't breathe. Frantically, she searched through Matt's mind for a way out, but it felt as if she was clawing her way through a pool of mud, floundering and sinking in the viscous milieu.

"Help!" She tried to cry out, but her voice was a muffled whisper. She was suffocating, drowning in the sludge.

A high-pitched sound pierced through her panic.

It was the first beep from the watch alarm, signalling that fifteen minutes had passed since she'd entered Matt's mind.

The noise was like a slap in the face and it shocked Angelina out of her panic.

Calm down, I need to calm down, she thought and forced herself to relax. Remember, I'm not really breathing in here so I can't be suffocating. Like Dee said, it's the way my Essence makes sense of things.

"Come on, Angelina, you need to calm down, you need to stay in control," she said in a stern voice. It worked, the panic subsided and her head started to clear.

She continued speaking aloud, the sound reassuring in the black void. "Think! The first alarm has just gone off, so I've got almost forty-five minutes before…." She stopped. "No. No. I'm not going there. I need to focus. I need to find out why Matt's mind is closed."

Thinking back to her studies, Angelina tried to remember all the circumstances that might cause a mind to close. To her knowledge, there were only two possibilities that could apply in this situation. One gave her a chance, the other didn't bear thinking about.

"An argument! That's it, he's started an argument." If Matt was arguing, she knew that his mind would close to all other suggestions and ideas, which would also prevent her from leaving.

"That has to be it. He's having an argument with his parents about going swimming."

She almost laughed with relief. It would only be a temporary closure. As soon as the argument finished or Matt allowed himself to listen to another viewpoint, he would open his mind again and Angelina could escape.

"Let's see if we can Influence him to speed this up. Otherwise Dee will start marking me down." Encouraged, Angelina headed back into Matt's conscious to see what was happening.

It took a second for her to adjust to the daylight that she could see through Matt's eyes. But when she saw where he was, her heart dropped.

Matt was already on the bus, joking around with Carl. He was talking, listening and thinking, with what should have been a completely open mind. In fact, it was so busy with conversation in Matt's mind that Angelina couldn't think properly and slipped back into his subconscious.

Only one possibility remained.

She felt numb. It was as if she'd gone beyond panic and could no longer feel anything. With a perfectly rational mind, she accepted the facts that she could no longer hide from. There was only one reason for the exit to remain closed.

His mind was infected.

"But I didn't smell anything. Nothing at all." She called out in frustration.

Dee had said she would recognise an infection immediately by its foul, rotten odour. Yet, Matt's mind didn't smell of anything.

That was when it hit her.

Dee had also told her that every mind has its own scent, so she should be able to smell something. It hadn't dawned on her until now, but Matt's odourless mind should have been a warning that something was wrong.

"How could I have been so stupid?"

She fell silent, going over and over her actions, pointlessly working out the things she should have done differently. Finally, she gave up; wishful thinking wasn't going to change a thing.

"Well, I'll probably go down in history as the GA who performed her first and last Fate Switch at the same time." She laughed aloud, a strange hysterical sound with no humour.

"What now? I've got about forty minutes. Do I sit here and wait to be Vaporised?"

Strangely, she felt calm. It was almost as if by saying the words aloud and accepting her fate, it no longer held any fear for her. If anything, she felt revitalised by the revelation.

I wonder if this is how Grandad felt, she thought. Before she could give this any further contemplation, an article she'd once read came to mind. It was about a technique known as 'Tuning In', which GAs could use during a Mind Jump to access the thoughts and ideas that were stored in the deepest parts of the subconscious.

From what she could remember, the technique was like meditating. You relaxed your senses to such an extent that you became as one with the mind of the individual.

"I've nothing else to do. I might as well try to find what it is that's finally destroyed me."

With an almost cavalier attitude, she let go, relaxing deeper and deeper. To her Essence it felt as if she was falling into a bed of marshmallow, the sludge oozing around and over her, warm and comforting. She entered a dreamlike state, giving her the sensation that she was about to drift off to sleep.

Then the whispers came.

Instead of falling asleep, Angelina became wide awake. More awake than she'd ever felt in her entire life. It was as if she'd fallen through a thick, spongy cloud and emerged in a huge, cavernous room. Here her thoughts were crisp and clear, and she felt hyper-alert. Although she knew that it was still pitch black, her senses were so in tune with her surroundings that it gave her the impression that she could see.

In this infinite, resonant space she could see Matt's store of knowledge stacked next to a bank of images and visions which only surface at night in his dreams. Ideas fluttered around like caged birds; darker ones like crows, pleasant ones in the fragile form of hummingbirds and, with the precise aim of an eagle, Matt's focussed determination soared past her. All the while, whispers of long forgotten thoughts echoed around her.

Almost in awe, she scanned the dark expanse of his deepest mind. The scene was continually flowing, as if the walls and ceiling were melting and reforming around her. In the centre of the vast space a sphere of light glowed brightly. Unlike the rest of the shifting scene, the light was completely still. To Angelina's mind it looked like a burning glass ball. Yet, she knew that this orb was Matt's spirit, his soul. It was held in place by a strong magnetic column – his life force. If this was disturbed, then the orb would disintegrate and Matt's life would be gone, and Angelina with it.

Careful to stay away from the orb, she searched Matt's deep subconscious. As she reached a heavily shadowed corner, she shivered. Here the darkness was more intense, almost physical. As she looked closely, she saw fetid thoughts squirming and writhing like maggots, giving off a vile, rancid odour that could not be missed. Angelina had never sensed anything like it before, but she knew what it was: pure evil.

With her heightened sense of knowledge, Angelina knew for sure that it had been placed there deliberately. It certainly hadn't grown from Matt's mind, nor had it been here very long, otherwise it would have damaged the thoughts and ideas around it. No, this was new.

The clarity with which she could think in here was amazing. Thoughts and answers were tumbling over one another so quickly that she was almost struggling to keep up. It was all becoming obvious.

This was no accident. She'd been trapped on purpose. Someone had infected Matt's mind to destroy her. They'd used something - she didn't know what - to neutralise any odours meaning that she wouldn't know what was happening until it was too late. This was part of a bigger plan; she was sure of it.

"But who would want to get rid of me? And why? I'm only a trainee. Dee only gave me the assignment yesterday, who else could have known that I was going to be here?" Angelina voiced her questions.

Dee! The mention of her name brought another memory rushing back to Angelina. It was something Dee had said about escaping from infected minds.

Perhaps I've a chance after all, Angelina thought. At that moment, the alarm sounded its second beep. It gave her such a jolt that it broke her concentration and she lost her connection with the inner recesses of Matt's subconscious.

Back in the thick darkness, the speed of Angelina's thoughts slowed to their normal pace, but she held fast to the last memory that she'd had.

Half an hour gone and half an hour left, I've got to move fast, she thought.

Chapter Fourteen

The noise was deafening when Angelina returned to Matt's conscious mind. Screams, shouts and laughter did battle with the occasional blast from a shrill whistle; the sounds bouncing off the high, white tiled walls. She was struck by the sanitised smell of chlorine that chased away the repulsive odour of the infection.

Finally making sense of what she was hearing and seeing, she realised that Matt and Carl had already changed into swim-shorts and were now strutting along the poolside.

As Matt glanced down into the pool, Angelina saw that it was a soup of bodies so thick that it was difficult to tell which limbs belonged to which swimmer. But through the chaos, Angelina saw that Matt and Carl were heading towards Dom, whom she recognised from school. He was sitting on the edge of the pool, legs dangling in the water and acknowledged Matt and Carl with a wave.

'Who's Dom waving at?' Angelina put the question in Matt's mind. As planned, his automatic reaction was to look behind him, giving Angelina the opportunity to check out her surroundings.

She could see that they were walking away from the changing rooms. To the right, the viewing balcony ran the length of the pool. Ahead, beyond the main pool was a smaller, square pool with deep-blue water. Metal barriers separated it from the main pool and a strange arrangement of platforms and aqua-green boards were located along one side.

On the far side of this smaller pool Angelina caught sight of a familiar figure and almost gasped out loud.

It was Joe.

That must be the diving pool, she thought. I should have known that Joe would be here: he trains every Sunday morning. Seeing Joe's familiar face boosted Angelina's determination.

Matt and Carl joined Dom on the side of the pool.

"Are they here yet?" Carl asked.

Angelina could see him scanning the pool for the girls.

"I haven't seen them, but I've only just arrived," said Dom.

'Why don't I get my training done before they get here,' Angelina suggested to Matt's mind.

'Then it's done and I can be back with the boys when Megan turns up.' Matt continued the thought.

To his friends he said: "I'm going to do a quick twenty lengths, want to join me?"

"That sounds way too much like hard work," said Carl.

"Yeah, I'll pass, thanks," said Dom.

"Please yourselves. Call me when the girls arrive."

Matt pulled something down and over his eyes, which turned the world a bright yellow colour. Then he dropped into the water.

Angelina had never experienced swimming and almost screamed as Matt's head became submerged. The noise from above was blotted out and replaced by a faint, high-pitched buzzing noise. Whatever Matt had covered his eyes with allowed him to see underwater, giving her a clear view of the yellow-tinged thrashing legs and squirming bodies of other swimmers as he navigated his way around them.

Angelina jumped as a swarm of bubbles passed in front of Matt's eyes, accompanied by a strange gurgling noise. Then she realised that it was just Matt, blowing air bubbles from his mouth. Seconds later, she jumped again as Matt broke through the surface to breathe, the commotion from the pool taking her by surprise. Angelina felt disorientated by the whole experience and Matt was on his third length before she became acclimatised to the rhythmic, up and down motion of Matt's swimming.

She'd suggested the swim to give her time to think. In the clarity of Matt's deep subconscious, she'd remembered Dee telling her that infected minds automatically open if the person falls unconscious. It was only a theory, but if there was a chance it might work she had to try. If she could somehow knock Matt out, there might be a chance that she could survive this disaster after all.

It was a long shot, but it was better than hanging around waiting to be Vaporised. The problem was, how could she make Matt fall unconscious in a way that wouldn't cause him permanent damage, especially now that he was in the swimming pool?

She would have to be very careful. It couldn't happen in the water, it was too dangerous for Matt. Also, where could she materialise? She would be fully clothed, which would be incredibly conspicuous in the middle of a swimming pool.

Considering her options, Angelina felt her heart drop. The viewing balcony was out; it was too high for her to reach from here. The pool side was too busy, she'd be seen immediately and if her aim was out and she landed in the water, she'd be in even more trouble.

It was hopeless.

Angelina felt like crying. For a brief moment she'd thought there was a chance she might escape. But there was no way out; it was impossible.

What will Dee do when I don't return? She thought. How long will she wait before realising something is wrong and sending out an alert? What will Dee tell the school? Will anyone care if I don't turn up in the morning? Joe might. He's a good friend and always seems pleased to see me-

Joe!

An idea flashed into Angelina's thoughts. It would rely on Joe, but she knew that she could trust him, and it might just work.

As Matt ploughed up and down the pool, Angelina formulated her plan. It wasn't perfect and would be a huge risk, but she had to give it a go. Matt was now halfway through his fourteenth length and she knew that the third alarm would be sounding soon. Once that went off, she would have only five minutes before her energy would start slowly sapping away.

Wasting no more time she launched into the first part of her plan.

'I've had enough of this. What are those two up to? If they're talking to Megan…,' she said.

'I'll have a quick break and see,' Matt finished. He stopped at the end of the pool, pulled the yellow things from his eyes and looked around for Carl and Dom. He spotted them in the deep end, taking it in turns to dive underwater. Angelina saw three girls sitting on the side, chatting with each other and the boys.

'I knew it. Megan's here and they didn't call me,' thought Matt.

Angelina saw her chance. *'If they think that will impress the girls, I'll show them.'*

'I can swim better than those two idiots.' Matt kept the thought running as he swam over to Dom and Carl.

'I bet I can dive better too, that would impress Megan.' Angelina held her breath after she delivered this suggestion. She had no idea whether Matt could dive or not, yet she had to persuade him to have a go or her plan didn't stand a chance.

'Yeah, I'll show them.'

To her relief, Matt wasn't concentrating on what she was making him think. He was too busy staring at the pretty brown-haired girl in the middle of the group, whom, Angelina assumed, must be Megan.

'I'll challenge them to a dive.' She kept Matt's mind filled with her ideas.

"Hey." At Matt's shout, Carl, Dom and the girls looked over.

"Hi, Matt. Didn't know you were here," said the girl to Megan's left. She had long cornrows tied in a ponytail that had yet to get wet.

"Oh, hi, Elle. Hey, Megan, Faye, you're here too?"

Despite her predicament, Angelina almost laughed out loud. Matt's attempt at playing it cool by pretending he hadn't seen the girls was pathetic.

"Trying to get fit," said Elle. She lifted a slender arm and pouted at Matt, while pretending to flex her biceps.

'Megan's not taking much notice. I need to get her attention. If I could get the others to go diving that would impress her.' Angelina knew that she was starting to sound desperate.

"I was coming to see if you losers dared to go on the diving boards."

"Us losers! I'd like to see you up there."

'I've been on loads of times.' Angelina was hoping to plant a false memory in case Matt had never dived from the boards before.

"Want to bet?" said Matt.

"You're not serious. You wouldn't dare," said Dom.

The three girls were looking very interested in the exchange between the three boys.

The girl Angelina guessed was Megan, spoke: "That must be soooo scary. Look, isn't that the kid from Year 10 up there now? He's called Joe, isn't he?" She gasped. "Did you see that?"

Everyone turned towards the diving boards, but Joe had already disappeared beneath the water.

Angelina stepped in. *'If Megan's impressed with that, wait until she sees me.'*

"I can do that. Anyone else coming?" With a kick of his legs, Matt swam to the side.

"Go, Matt!" said Elle.

"If you can do it, I can." Dom was taking up the challenge.

Angelina heard a loud beep. Fifteen minutes left, she thought. This must work.

'I've got to beat them,' said Angelina to Matt. *'Come on.'*

Matt hoisted himself out of the pool.

'Dom's just behind, I can't let him get there first.' Angelina's voice was urgent in Matt's mind. *'Run!'*

Matt set off towards the diving pool. Through his eyes, Angelina could see Joe up ahead. He was standing with his back to Matt, listening to his coach's instructions.

I must time this right, thought Angelina.

'Dom's catching, faster,' she said, encouraging Matt.

As Matt tried to put on a spurt of speed, he lost his footing on the wet tiles. As Matt fell backwards, the last thing Angelina saw was condensation running down the glazed roof of the swimming pool. Without waiting for him to land, she rushed into his subconscious, arriving in time to feel the jolt of his head hitting the floor.

Had it worked?

She couldn't tell yet.

Forcing herself to remain calm, she concentrated.

Nothing was happening.

Panic threatened to force its way through but she held her nerve.

Focussing her thoughts on Joe and imagining his face in front of her, she let go.

There was a faint tug. Was it up or down? She couldn't tell yet.

The feeling became stronger.

It was up! His mind was opening, it was working!

She wasn't out of trouble yet. As she travelled upwards she forced herself to control the elation and keep her thoughts focussed on Joe.

At last, she broke free from Matt's mind and saw the briefest flash of daylight before darkness fell again.

Hurtling down into another mind, she hoped that her aim had been good enough. If she'd timed it right and kept her concentration, then she should have jumped straight from Matt's mind and into Joe's.

The movement stopped. Angelina steadied herself and then breathed in. She burst out laughing. Banana smoothie! She could smell banana smoothie! Joe's favourite drink, full of vitamins and carbs, he always said. This had to be Joe's mind, she was sure of it.

There was no time to celebrate – the clock was still ticking. Switching minds wasn't the same as exiting, time could only recharge fully while she remained out of a host mind for at least an hour. She was still on the same clock.

Angelina reckoned that she had only twelve minutes remaining. That meant she had to be out within seven minutes or else she wouldn't have enough strength left to exit.

She moved immediately into the conscious mind and heard the comforting sound of Joe's voice. It was definitely his mind! Now, she had to work on getting Joe back into the changing rooms.

A voice interrupted her thoughts.

"He'll be fine. It's just a bump. It'll teach him not to run around like an idiot on this wet floor."

It belonged to a man dressed in shorts and a T-shirt, who was walking towards Joe.

Angelina saw that the man was referring to Matt, who was lying on the floor, with a lifeguard kneeling next to him. Matt was now awake and attempting to sit up but the lifeguard, who was gesturing to a colleague for help, made him lie down again.

Thank goodness Matt's okay, thought Angelina.

"Do you want me to do another three-and-a-half, Nick?" Joe asked.

Nick? This is Joe's coach I'm looking at, thought Angelina.

"Yes. Hold on that fraction longer until you're at the top of the dive before you pull into the pike."

To Angelina it was like listening to someone speaking in code, but it must have made sense to Joe as he nodded and leapt up the ladder to the first platform. For some reason that Angelina couldn't quite fathom, he started wiping his legs and body with a small square piece of blue cloth that he kept wringing out over the side of the railings surrounding the platform. Angelina wasn't all that keen on heights and each time Joe looked over the edge, she felt dizzy.

Within seconds he was back on the diving board, talking himself through the dive.

'Wait on the hurdle, fast swing through, push into the board, ride with it and then pike.' As he thought the words, Angelina could feel Joe performing a dry run of the arm and leg movements, which finished with him pulling his right leg up in front of his face.

He was concentrating too hard for Angelina to risk interrupting him now. I'll catch him after this dive, when he's in the water, she thought.

Taking a deep breath, Joe started walking along the springboard. As he walked out over the water, the drop looked much greater to Angelina as she could now see straight to the bottom of the pool. The board flexed under Joe's weight, bending down towards the water and terrifying her even more. If only she could close her eyes, but in the conscious mind, she could only see through Joe's eyes and had no direct control over where he looked.

Pushing off his right foot, Joe lifted his left knee and, simultaneously, raised both arms above his head. After hanging in mid-air for a split second, Angelina found herself looking down at Joe's toes as he connected with the end of the board, high above the surface of the water.

The sight was too much for her. She screamed.

Joe's knees buckled and he overbalanced, falling forward towards the water.

Chapter Fifteen

What was that? thought Joe.

Someone had screamed in his ear as he was about to take off. Thankfully, his years of diving training allowed him to recover almost immediately and he stretched out, lining up for a perfect headfirst entry.

For a second, the muffled buzz of water filled Joe's ears as he shot through the water. Bending at the waist, he performed an underwater somersault and pushed off from the bottom of the pool. He kept his eyes open as he rose upwards but without goggles all he could see was a blurry image of the swimming pool ceiling. Seconds later the sights and sounds of the pool came back into focus as his head broke the surface.

"What was that?"

The frustrated shout came from Nick, who was standing with his hands on his hips at the side of the pool.

"Didn't you hear that scream? As I took off?" Treading water, Joe shook his head to clear the water. "It sounded to be right inside my ear." He swam back to the side and, placing both hands on the side hauled himself out of the pool with one fluid movement.

"I didn't hear anything. Probably kids messing about in the pool."

"It sounded to be closer than that." Joe looked around, but there was nothing obvious.

That's strange, he thought. I guess it must have come from the main pool, after all.

"You're hearing things, Joe," said Nick. "Now, get back up there and do the dive. Remember, don't sit back on your hurdle step, stay tall."

Joe was about to climb the ladder when he stopped. I could do with the loo, he thought.

"Nick, I'll be back in a minute. Just nipping to the loo."

Nick rolled his eyes. "Okay."

As he hurried back to the changing rooms, Joe realised that he didn't need the toilet. What am I doing? he thought. Oh, I know. I need to get my towel.

Stepping into the changing rooms and through the shower area he stopped, confused. What was it I needed to do? He asked himself. His face brightened again. Go to one of the cubicles, that's it.

Without challenging the logic of his thinking, he set off towards the changing area.

This one here, he thought as he reached the first cubicle and entered. Now, I need to lock the door.

As he slid the bolt on, his mind went blank. He stood for a second, staring at the cubicle door, his hand still covering the bolt as he tried to gather his thoughts.

Why have I locked myself in a changing room cubicle? He thought. I'm going mad.

"Joe."

Joe nearly jumped out of his skin.

Spinning around what he saw shocked him even more, he stumbled backwards into the cubicle door.

Angelina was sitting on the seat looking up at him.

"Joe, it's me." Her voice was barely a whisper and she looked incredibly pale.

"What the.... How did you get here?" He reached out to touch her, wanting to check whether she was real. He stopped before he made contact, almost fearful that his hand would go straight through this strange apparition.

She gave a weak smile. "It's okay, Joe, I really am here." She tried to stand up and move towards him, but her legs gave way and Joe leapt forward to catch her before she fell.

He helped her back to the bench.

"Thanks," she said. "I'm feeling a bit weak but it will pass."

Joe felt as if he was in the middle of a mixed-up dream. "Angelina, where did you come from? I mean, what do you think you're doing? You're in the men's changing rooms. And how come you're in the cubicle that I happened to walk into? I don't understand what's going on."

Angelina dropped her head and sighed.

In frustration, Joe raised his voice. "Tell me what's going on, Angelina."

"Shhh." She lifted her head and looked anxiously at Joe. "Please, keep your voice down, Joe. I don't want anyone to know that I'm here."

"Why are you here?"

"I haven't time to tell you now. I need to get out of here and you need to get back to your training or they'll start to wonder where you are."

"How do you know that I'm ...?" Joe began, but Angelina held up her hand to stop his question.

"Not now, Joe, there's no time. Can you meet me in the café when you've finished?"

Joe nodded. "Yeah, I don't have anything to get back for."

"Okay, I'll wait for you there. I need another few minutes before I can move. If you close the door behind you, I'll make sure that there's no one around when I leave."

"Are you sure you'll be all right by yourself? You don't look well." It hit Joe how ill she looked. "Shall I get a First Aider?"

"No, please. Whatever you do, Joe, don't say anything to anyone about this. I promise I'll be fine in a minute. I'll meet you upstairs when you've finished."

With a last concerned look, Joe opened the door and slipped out. He waited until he heard the bolt slide back into place before returning to the pool.

"You took your time," said Nick. "Anything wrong?"

"I had a quick shower to warm up."

Nick looked at his watch. "I tell you what. Forget your three-and-a-half and move on to your back twister. I've got a driving lesson in twenty minutes."

The rest of the training session passed in a blur, with Joe unable to concentrate on anything other than Angelina. He tried to come up with a sensible, rational reason as to how and why she'd appeared in the men's changing room, but it was impossible. He was so pre-occupied that he kept missing his dives and in the end Nick finished the training session early.

"What's up, Joe?" asked Nick. "You were diving well earlier on. But after that kid knocked himself out on the poolside, you went to pieces."

"Yeah, don't know what happened. Sorry, Nick," Joe mumbled and headed off to the changing rooms.

As he showered and dressed, Joe began to doubt that Angelina had ever been in the changing room and that maybe he'd had some weird hallucination. But when he entered the cafeteria ten minutes later, there she was, sitting at the table nearest the door. She was nursing a drink and smiled when she saw him.

Dropping his bag onto the floor, he slid into the seat opposite her.

"Do you want a lemonade," she asked, gesturing to her drink.

Joe ignored the question. "What's going on, Angelina? I've had the worst training session ever, thanks to you. Why were you hiding in the changing rooms? You scared me stupid."

"I'm sorry, Joe, but there was nothing else I could do. You've got to believe me."

"Believe what, Angelina? What's going on?"

Joe knew that he was sounding angry but wasn't sure why. True, he was annoyed that his training had been disturbed but that wasn't why he was upset with Angelina. No, it was more a feeling of betrayal.

He liked Angelina. A lot. In fact, ever since she'd hugged him in the corridor after school the other week, he'd been kicking himself for just standing there. The next day he'd almost asked her out, but while he was trying to work out what to say, she'd started talking and the moment had passed.

It was precisely because he liked her that he was angry. Something was going on. Yet, she obviously didn't trust him enough to tell him what it was and that hurt.

As he stared across the table at her, his anger faded away. She was still very pale, and her eyes didn't have their usual sparkle. She dropped her head, as if she didn't even have the strength to hold his gaze. She looked completely done in.

"Please. Tell me what's wrong. I might be able to help." Joe's voice was much softer when he spoke, but Angelina kept her head down, her dark straight hair shielding her face from view.

"You know I won't say anything," he said.

Still, she didn't respond. He reached out and touched her arm. "Come on, I thought we were friends."

Angelina lifted her head slightly and tried to smile, which caused the tears that had welled up in her eyes to escape and roll down her cheeks. She dropped her head again as she tried to stem the flow of tears with her hands.

Joe felt completely lost. Was she crying because he'd been angry with her? No, he didn't think so. There was something much bigger going on here. Something that was no doubt linked to her appearance in the changing rooms. He just had no idea what it could be.

"Hey, don't cry. Look, maybe if you tell me, I can help."

This seemed to make things worse, her shoulders shook as she sobbed silently.

Feeling helpless, Joe sat and watched her weep. He grabbed a handful of unused napkins from the next table and passed them across to Angelina.

She looked up, her eyes red and streaming. "Thanks, Joe. I mean it, thank you for everything you've done and I'm sorry I've dragged you into it all this."

What was she thanking him for?

Bewildered, Joe waited for Angelina to explain.

After wiping her eyes and delicately blowing her nose, Angelina seemed to pull herself together.

"Sorry, I didn't mean to break down like that," she said. "It's been a tough morning."

"Don't worry and stop saying sorry."

"Sorry." She gave a half laugh. "I mean, okay."

"Are you going to tell me what all this is about and why you were hiding in the men's changing room?" Joe tried to make the question sound light-hearted, but Angelina's face darkened again and she shook her head.

"You're better off not knowing."

"What do you mean? I need to know what's going on, Angelina. I'm worried about you."

She sighed. "You won't believe me even if I tell you."

"Try me."

Angelina cocked her head slightly to one side and stared at him. Her penetrating gaze made him feel as if she was making a life or death decision and he wanted to look away, but she held him with her eyes.

"Okay, I'll tell you everything. Not here. We need to go outside. Somewhere quiet, where we can be sure no one else is around."

"There's a park near my house. There's plenty of space there."

"Remember, Joe. You were the one who wanted to know everything. Don't say that I didn't warn you."

Joe nodded, but her words sent a shiver of apprehension through him.

Chapter Sixteen

They caught the train back to Little Ingworth, barely speaking a word to each other during the journey.

Angelina was lost in thought. There had been only five minutes and thirty seconds remaining on her watch when she'd finally exited Joe's mind and now, almost an hour and a half later, she was still completely exhausted.

While waiting in the café for Joe, the enormity of what she'd been through had hit her like delayed shock. She'd almost been Vaporised. Extinguished forever. When Joe had started being nice to her it had all become too much and, to her dismay, she'd been unable to stop the tears. The thought that someone had tried to get rid of her had made her feel very alone, very far from home and with no idea who to trust anymore.

Except Joe.

But now she was wondering what to say to him. She no longer cared about breaking the GA code. Nothing could be worse than what she'd been through today, and she could do with someone to talk to right now.

What was worrying her was how he would react. He wouldn't believe her. He couldn't believe her, she knew that. What she was about to tell him was impossible from his experience of the world. But somehow, she had to make him believe. Otherwise she'd lose Joe as well. And she didn't think she could cope with that.

"This is our stop." Joe stood up and grabbed his sports bag from the luggage rack before helping Angelina to her feet. She was still incredibly weak and glad of the assistance.

From the railway station, Joe led Angelina along the same short cut that she'd used when she'd first arrived in Little Ingworth, six weeks ago. This time, however, they turned right, and she followed Joe past the church and across the field to the park.

He steered Angelina up the hill towards the playground, which was deserted, probably because of the weather. The day was still grey, and a chill breeze was rustling the golden leaves that still clung to the branches of trees surrounding the park. It must have rained while they were in the swimming pool, as the swings were wet and a puddle had formed at the entrance to the play area, where excited feet had dented the ground over the years. Joe stopped at one of the two metal benches. Taking a towel from his bag he wiped away the raindrops that stood like tears on the red-painted slats.

"We should be okay here," he said.

Angelina perched on the edge of the bench hugging herself, partly to keep the cold out and partly for comfort.

The park sloped gently upwards towards the new housing estate at the top of the hill. On the side nearest to the play area, a dry-stone wall separated the park from the road, where an occasional car splashed by. She looked around, checking for passers-by but there was no one and, from where they were sitting, no one could come within fifty metres of them without being seen.

Joe sat down next to her, twisting his body to face her. "Well? What's the big secret?" he asked.

Angelina looked down at the glistening brown bark that littered the play area. Where did she begin?

Joe waited and she was glad that he didn't try to push her as she struggled to find the right words. Taking a deep breath, she turned to face him.

"Before I start, everything I'm about to tell you is true. You won't believe me, but it is. I need you to remember that."

Joe looked bemused. "Of course, I'll believe you."

She gave him a sad smile. "No. You won't, Joe."

"Whatever it is, I'm sure it can't be that bad." He fidgeted on the seat, a concerned look on his face.

"It's not that." She paused.

"Well, what is it then. I'm thinking all sorts of things here. You've got to tell me; I can't stand this much longer."

She nodded. "You deserve that much." She took another deep breath. "I'm not like you, Joe."

He gave a snort of laughter. "Well, I know you don't know much about sport, but we seem to get on okay."

"I don't mean in that way. What I mean is that I'm not human." There, she'd said it. She peered anxiously at Joe waiting to see how he would react.

"Yeah, right. What are you then? An alien?" He looked unsure and half-laughed as if waiting for the punch line to come.

This wasn't working. She'd made a huge mistake trying to tell Joe, but she'd gone too far to back down now.

"No, not an alien. Well, not in the way you mean. I'm a GA, what you call a Guardian Angel. Well, a trainee, at least."

There was silence. Even the breeze seemed to hold its breath as Angelina delivered her incredible news and waited for Joe's reaction.

"What are you talking about?"

"It's true. I am a Guardian Angel. I'm here on Earth to complete my practical exam so that I can qualify. Dee's not my Aunt, she's my mentor. Today, I was taking part in my first solo Fate Switch but Matt Armitage's mind was infected and I got locked in. I managed to make him fall and escaped into your mind. That was why I ended up in the changing rooms with you. Another five minutes and I'd have been Vaporised. I know it's hard to believe."

Angelina knew that her torrent of words wasn't making any sense at all to Joe, but she also knew that if she didn't get everything out now, she might not have another chance.

While she was speaking, Joe's face changed from a stunned look of incredulity to… Angelina couldn't tell what; but it soon became apparent.

"If you don't want to tell me, that's fine. But at least come up with something believable." In one angry motion, Joe stood, snatched up his bag and stalked away.

Watching him leave, she whispered: "I knew you wouldn't believe me, Joe."

For the second time in the space of an hour, she felt the tears welling up. Dropping her head, she pressed the palms of her hands to her eyes, in a futile attempt to stem the flow.

"Can you prove it?"

The voice made her jump and she looked up to see Joe standing over her.

He spoke again: "Can you prove what you've said?"

Hastily wiping the tears away with the back of her hand she nodded. "If you'll let me."

"How?"

"There are a few things I can show you. But why did you come back?"

Joe dropped back on to the seat. "I don't know. It was what you said about knowing that I wouldn't believe you. And I've always thought that there was something different about you."

"Yeah, well..."

Joe continued: "I suppose the real reason is that I couldn't come up with a better explanation as to why you were in that stupid cubicle."

He pushed his blonde fringe away from his eyes with both hands, rubbing his forehead as if massaging a headache. "I still don't understand all this, though."

"It's not something a human should ever have to understand. I shouldn't have told you and if anyone finds out I did, I honestly don't know what will happen. It's just..." Angelina paused, struggling to stay in control of her emotions, "....I didn't know what else to do. You're the only person that I know I can trust now."

"You said that you could prove you're an angel."

"Guardian Angel. I'm not dead." Angelina smiled adding: "Thanks to you."

"You mean there's a difference? Geez, this is complicated."

"Angel is the name you give to the spirit of a dead person. I'm a Guardian Angel. We exist in our own right. We live, we work, and we can die. We just come from another dimension where the rules are a bit different."

Shaking his head, Joe said: "This is unreal."

"I know it's hard to take in." Angelina was terrified that Joe might leave again. "Let me prove it to you."

She checked her watch. Almost two hours had passed since she'd exited. Usually, the time she could spend in a mind would be fully recharged by now, but as she'd been so exhausted by the previous Mind Jump, the watch still showed only forty-two minutes. That should be plenty of time though, she thought.

"Can you see that car over there?" Angelina pointed to something behind Joe, and he turned his head away from her.

"What, car?" He turned back. And stared at the empty space where Angelina had been sitting. "Angelina?"

'I'm here, Joe.' Angelina said from within Joe's mind.

"Where?" Joe asked aloud. "You sound strange." He stood, turning in circles, trying to catch sight of Angelina.

'In your mind.'

"What!" He swung around. "I can't see you."

Through his eyes, she could see Joe scanning the playground.

'That's because I'm here in your head.'

"Stop messing about, Angelina. Where are you?"

'You wanted proof Joe; this is it.'

"Seriously, where are you?" Joe's voice had taken on a panicky edge.

'Like I said, you're hearing my voice from inside your mind. Think about something that I couldn't possibly know. Don't say it aloud, think it.'

The way his eyes were flitting about, she could tell that he wasn't listening.

'Is she behind the wall?' Joe's thoughts were loud and clear to Angelina.

'Joe, I'm not behind the wall.'

"I didn't say anything!" Joe said aloud.

'I know, but you thought it and I'm in your mind listening to everything you think and say. I can also see out of your eyes and know that you're now looking straight at the crisp wrapper that's trapped against the wall.'

As if caught in the act of staring at someone, Joe immediately shifted his eyes away, scanning the park for signs of Angelina.

'Will you stop doing that, you're making me dizzy.' Still run down from her earlier experience, Angelina was finding it hard to concentrate in Joe's head. *'Do you believe me yet?'*

"I... I don't know. How can you be in my head?" Joe was still speaking aloud.

'I'll explain in a minute.'

'I'm going mad.' Joe thought.

'No, you're not mad, Joe. Although this is probably why we're strictly forbidden to tell humans, as it would send them mad.'

"You heard that?"

'If you concentrate, I can prove it to you. Imagine something weird. Picture it in

your head but don't say anything, just think it. Can you do that?'

"Yeah, I suppose."

'Shh, don't say anything aloud. Think about the picture in your head.'

Angelina smiled as she heard Joe's thought. A second later she was standing behind Joe. "Hey."

Joe whirled around, looking totally bewildered.

"Where did you come from?"

"Sit down and I'll tell you everything."

"You said you were in my mind. Did you mean that?"

She nodded. "I wanted to prove to you that I'm telling the truth. I asked you to think of something weird, something that I couldn't possibly guess. You didn't say what it was, did you?"

"No, I do know that much."

"The only way that I could possibly know what you were thinking is if I was in your mind, listening to your thoughts, right?"

"I guess so."

"Well, it was certainly weird. You imagined a Tyrannosaurus Rex eating baked beans while roller skating around our classroom."

Joe stared at her.

"How did you do that?"

"Like I said, I was in your mind. I could hear all your thoughts."

"But that's impossible. How could you ..." Joe's voice trailed off.

It wasn't working. She'd shocked him too much by disappearing into his mind. She needed another way; something that would be easier for him to take in. Her face lit up as an idea came to her.

"Joe, do you remember how Serena got hurt when she punched me?"

Frowning, Joe nodded. "I was sure she'd hit you."

"Nip me." Angelina pulled up her sleeve and held out her arm.

"What? Don't be silly." Joe looked taken aback at the strange request.

"Seriously, nip me."

He hesitated.

"Go on, Joe. Nip me. Please."

With a shrug, Joe pinched Angelina's arm.

"Ouch," he cried out, clutching his arm. "I've been stung."

Angelina giggled. "Sorry, I should have warned you to be gentle. It wasn't a sting. It was the pain you tried to make me feel.

It's called Transference. It keeps us safe from harm on Earth. If anyone intentionally tries to hurt a GA – that's what they call Guardian Angels these days – then they're the ones who feel the pain."

"What if I bumped into you? Would I be the one to get hurt?"

Angelina shook her head. "No, then we'd both feel the pain. It's only if you try to hurt me on purpose."

"You're telling me that when Serena punched you, she winded herself?"

"Exactly."

Joe grinned. "No wonder she ended up on the floor."

He frowned again, looking intently at Angelina. "You *are* telling the truth, aren't you?"

She smiled with relief. "Yes, Joe. I promise you everything I've said is the truth."

"I still don't understand how you ended up in the changing room. And what was all that about Matt Armitage being infected?"

"That's all a bit more complicated. It's all to do with why I'm here on Earth. Today was supposed to be a straightforward training session but it went horribly wrong."

For the next ten minutes Joe stayed silent while Angelina told him all about her Fate Switch assignment; how she'd learned to Mind Jump and Influence people, persuading them to make the decision that would prove most beneficial to them.

As she talked, his eyes widened in amazement at her explanations. When Angelina reached the part about how she'd jumped from Matt's mind into his and then screamed when he was about to dive, Joe interrupted.

"I knew I hadn't imagined that scream." He looked puzzled.

"Thinking about it, I didn't want to go to the toilet either. Was that you as well?"

"There wasn't much time left and I had to get you away from the poolside so that I could get out of your mind without anyone seeing me. In the end I had about thirty seconds left.

"If I hadn't gone along with your suggestion, what would have happened?"

Angelina bowed her head as if the weight of the thought was unbearable. Then, sitting up straight, she looked Joe in the eye and said: "I'd have been Vaporised or, in other words, killed."

Joe looked horrified. "My mind would have killed you?"

"No. I'd have run out of energy, a bit like a SCUBA diver running out of air. It's not the sea's fault if that happens and it wouldn't have been your fault if something had happened to me. Thanks to you it didn't. You saved my life, Joe." She smiled.

"But it was close, what if I hadn't…"

He seemed to know that the sentence would be too painful to finish and changed the subject instead.

"You said that you're here as a trainee, aren't you a bit young? I mean you're only the same age as me?"

"It's all relative. Different dimension, different rules." She shrugged. "Besides, I won't be fully qualified for another few years, I'm still only training."

"Does that mean you're not my age?" Joe looked unsure.

"In Earth years I'm fourteen, the same age as you." She placed her hand on Joe's arm. "I know it's tough to get your head round this."

"You're not kidding. I mean, how many of you are there? Are you telling me that there are millions of Guardian Angels walking around on Earth and we've no idea about them?"

"Not millions. In fact, it's probably only a few thousand these days. Dee blames it on budget cuts and lack of funding. Some people never come across a GA their entire lives."

"Yet I manage to become best friends with one."

"That doesn't have to change. I'm around for another few months." Angelina looked hopeful.

"How can it not change! What you've told me changes everything I've ever known. According to you, I'm the only person in the world who knows that another dimension exists and that there are Angels running around on Earth changing our minds without us knowing it."

"We can't change your mind. It's always your decision. We help you to make the decision that will be best for you."

Joe leapt off the bench, throwing his arms in the air as his voice became louder. "It doesn't matter what you do, it's the fact that you do anything at all; that you even exist. What else is there out there?" He held up his hand. "No, wait. Don't tell me. I've found out enough for one day."

"Please. Calm down." Angelina looked anxiously around. A figure, accompanied by a small dog, had appeared at the other side of the park.

"Someone's coming, Joe. Listen to me, we need to be careful. You can't tell anyone about this. You have to promise me you won't say a word."

"Who would I tell? Who would believe this?"

He sank back on to the park bench.

"I'm sorry, Angelina. I don't usually go off on one like that, but this is big. It's huge. It changes everything I know about this world. It's a lot to take in."

"Nothing has changed, Joe. All you know is that there's a force out there looking out for the best interests of people on Earth. It should be quite comforting."

Seeing that Joe wasn't convinced, Angelina continued: "It was unfair of me to put this on you, but I had no one else to turn to."

Sighing, Joe took Angelina's hand. "I'm forgetting what you've been through." He gave a wry smile. "I guess I'll have to get used to having an Angel, GA, or whatever you are, for a best friend."

For the first time since becoming locked in Matt's mind, Angelina felt happy again.

Joe's face grew serious. "You said that Matt's mind had been infected on purpose. Do you have any idea who would do that? What about Dee? You said she was the only one who knew where you would be."

"I know." Angelina bit her bottom lip. "But I can't believe it's Dee. She's not very easy to live with and I get the feeling that she's not keen on having me around, but she's the Great Dee Devin, one of the most respected GA's in the Universe. At least, she was until a few years ago. She resigned from the Board of the FFU and holed up here in Little Ingworth, but still..." Angelina shook her head. "No, I can't see it being Dee. It doesn't make sense. What would she have to gain? Besides, there are much easier ways to get rid of me if she wanted to."

While waiting for Joe in the café, Angelina had considered the possibility of Dee's involvement. It would make sense. After all, like Joe had said, she'd chosen the assignment.

But Angelina didn't believe it was Dee. While looking at the swirling infection in Matt's deep subconscious, when her reasoning was fast and clear, she'd fleetingly sensed something familiar, like perfume that lingers in a room after the person wearing it has gone.

Only this hadn't been a smell, more an awareness. But before she'd identified the elusive sensation the timer had beeped and she'd lost the connection. All she could remember now was that it hadn't felt like Dee.

When she tried to explain this to Joe, he remained doubtful.

"You know best, but I wouldn't trust anyone. Whoever did this will probably try again when they find out that they've failed."

"Oh, no." But Angelina wasn't responding to Joe's warning, she'd recognised the dog walker who was now trudging up the slope towards them, calling out her name.

"Angelina. Yoo-hoo. Angelina."

"Who's that?" Joe asked, keeping his voice low so that the approaching figure wouldn't hear.

"*That* is Rose Garden." Joe pulled a face.

"Seriously, that's her name. I met her on the train. She's a bit over the top but I think she's just a bit lonely." Angelina raised her voice. "Hi, Rose. I didn't know you had a dog?"

Dressed in a thick black coat and matching woolly hat, Rose looked even wider than ever. Arriving at the playground, she leaned on the fence designed to keep dogs out, panting hard at the effort of carrying her bulk up the small hill. A fluffy West Highland Terrier, nose to the ground and tail wagging, scurried around. He finally fixed on a scent trail, followed it to a nearby tree and lifted his leg to mark his territory before setting off in search of another trail. Rose watched him for a couple of seconds while she caught her breath.

"Dog, me? No, no, it's not my dog. Mr Garden is allergic to animal hair. He starts sneezing as soon as old Sweep here puts his nose through the front door. Sweep's my neighbour's dog. I walk him every now and again. Keeps me fit." She patted her generous stomach. "We couldn't get out earlier because of the rain. And who's this?" Rose beamed expectantly at Joe.

"This is Joe. He's a friend from school."

"Hi," said Joe.

"Pleased to meet you, Joe. I'm Rose, Rose Garden." She held out a gloved hand for him to shake. "What are you two doing out here? I'd have thought it's a bit cold to be hanging around the park."

"We're on our way home. We stopped to talk about a school project we're working on," said Angelina.

"School project, eh?" Rose gave a knowing smile that made Angelina blush and Joe look away. "So that's what you call it these days. Don't worry, your secret's safe with me, I was young once." She chuckled. "Well, if you're ever stuck for a warm place to hide out and work on your *school project*, you can always pop in and see me. You never know, there might be chocolate cake on the go as well."

Without waiting for an answer, Rose checked her watch. "Well, I must be off. Pop around soon, Angelina and it's been very nice meeting you, Joe."

With a final beam, Rose turned away and gave a whistle.

"Swee-eep, Swee-eep."

The white-coated Westie came bounding over, his jaws open in anticipation of the doggy treat that Rose was holding out. The dog sat patiently while Rose clipped on the lead and then reared up on his hind legs, deftly catching the biscuit that Rose tossed into the air.

"Bye, bye," she called, waving as she marched towards the road, Sweep prancing along at her side.

Angelina and Joe watched her until she disappeared before catching each other's eye and dissolving into laughter.

"I can't believe she said that!" Angelina said in mock horror.

"She doesn't look as if she was ever young," said Joe.

"I tell you what though, her chocolate cake is good. I'll have to take you there sometime." Angelina looked at her watch. "It's almost half past one. I'd better get back. Dee's probably out looking for me by now."

"Do you want me to come with you? I mean, what if it is Dee who's behind all this?"

"Thanks, Joe, but it's better if you don't. She might work out I've told you everything."

Joe still looked worried. "Well, I'll walk with you to Hermit Hill Lane."

Angelina shook her head. "If she's out looking for me, she might see you. It's not worth the risk. I'll be careful, I promise. I'll see you at school tomorrow."

Still not happy, Joe made her promise to ring him if anything went wrong. Angelina was secretly pleased when she saw him watching her until she left the park and turned the corner out of sight.

Her strength was starting to return and the walk home gave her time to think. Joe had taken things pretty well, considering she'd turned his view of the world upside down. But how would Dee take the news that her trainee had almost been Vaporised?

As she opened the gate to 4 Hermit Hill Lane, she couldn't believe what she was seeing. Dee wasn't out looking for her after all, she was in the garage working. In the gloomy afternoon, light was escaping from the frosted window at the top of the garage door and music was playing within.

Outraged, Angelina stormed down the driveway and banged on the side door.

"One minute." Dee's voice called.

Furious, Angelina banged again.

The door flew open.

"Didn't you hear me? I said I'd be a minute." Dee looked annoyed. "What do you want anyway? Is it lunchtime already?"

Astounded by Dee's obvious lack of concern, Angelina was momentarily lost for words. Recovering quickly, she asked: "Lunch? It's quarter to two. Do you have any idea where I've been?"

Responding to the aggressive tone, Dee folded her arms and glared at Angelina. Using a voice that would freeze molten lava, she said: "I'm assuming that you've been doing exactly as I instructed you to do in the note I left. By now, your report from this morning's Fate Switch should be waiting for me along with my lunch and I told you not to disturb me until that was the case. Are you trying to tell me you've been elsewhere?"

Angelina matched Dee's icy tone. "I didn't get your note, Dee, because I was busy trying to escape from Matt Armitage's infected mind. While you were working" -Angelina flung her arm dismissively in Dee's direction- "I was five minutes and thirty seconds away from being Vaporised. It's taken me until now to regain enough energy to make it home." This was a slight exaggeration but Angelina was past caring. "There's me thinking you might actually care enough to be out looking for me. But no. You're hiding away in here working."

As Angelina ranted on the colour drained from Dee's face, her shoulders sagged and her arms fell loosely to the side. It was like a stopper had been pulled from an inflatable ball.

"Matt's mind was infected?" Dee whispered.

"It hadn't been there long, but it was enough to trap me inside. Whoever put it there disguised the smell so that I wouldn't know."

Pulling the garage door shut behind her, Dee ushered Angelina up the path and into the kitchen.

"This can't be right. I checked that Fate Switch myself. It was all fine."

By the strain in Dee's voice, Angelina knew that she was trying to convince herself rather than Angelina.

On the kitchen table was the note that Dee had mentioned; the words 'Do Not Disturb Me' were scribbled in large black letters at the top of the page. Dee busied herself by filling the kettle.

"Go sit down. Are you hungry? I'll bring you lunch. You need to get your strength back."

Mollified by Dee's concern, Angelina did as she was told. Flopping onto the sofa she discovered that the exhaustion had returned. She lay back on the soft cushions and within seconds was asleep.

She awoke an hour later to discover a plate of ham and cheese sandwiches next to a cold cup of tea and a biscuit, sitting on the coffee table. Rubbing the sleep from her eyes, Angelina found that she was starving and polished off the sandwiches and cookie without leaving the sofa. As she was boiling the kettle to warm her tea, Dee reappeared.

"Are you feeling any better?" Her concerned frown added even more wrinkles to her lined face.

"Much. Thanks for the sandwiches."

"Tell me exactly what happened."

Angelina's tea was almost cold again by the time she'd finished telling Dee her story.

"I can't understand what went wrong. To prevent any mistakes, black-listed names are kept on a different database system altogether. I've checked the file again and Matt was definitely on the list that had been checked and approved." Dee seemed genuinely troubled.

"I'll show you."

She led the way into her study, fiddled with the computer and pulled up the list of Fate Switches that had come through the previous day. Matt Armitage's name was highlighted, and Angelina could clearly see a tick in the 'Safe' column, next to his listing.

"All I know is that I was trapped in his mind and when I explored his deep subconscious there was an evil infected mass."

"You said it was fresh, that it hadn't been there for long?"

"That's how it felt, although I can't explain how I knew. Everything seemed so obvious at the time. It was like my thoughts were working at a hundred miles an hour."

Dee nodded. "The deep subconscious is the purest part of the mind. That's why it was easy to think. There are no lies polluting the atmosphere. Even humans can't lie to their deep subconscious. They can bury the truth in there, but you'd be surprised, it always has a way of surfacing."

Dee tilted her head to one side as she studied Angelina. "I'm surprised you managed to get in there. I know senior Guardians who have never mastered the deep subconscious. You did well."

Despite the words, Angelina didn't get the feeling that Dee was praising her.

"I didn't have anything to lose. I thought I might as well give it a go."

"You were lucky. Very lucky. Matt must have become infected very recently, probably a day or so before you did your Mind Jump. That's the only theory that makes any sense. And it's probably what saved you. The infection hadn't developed sufficiently to keep his mind closed while he was unconscious. But a few more days and you'd have had no chance."

Angelina shook her head. "No. It had been placed there deliberately. It was meant for me. Someone or something wanted to get rid of me."

Dee gave Angelina a look that was almost sympathetic.

"You've been through a terrible experience, but that doesn't make sense. How could anyone have purposely placed an infection in Matt's mind? That Fate Switch came through as I was scrolling through the potential targets for you. No one could possibly have known which one I would choose.

"Besides, I sent the acceptance in on Saturday and the Fate Switch Department closes at the weekend. Even they won't know my choice until tomorrow. Say that someone had been working on Saturday, it takes over twenty-four hours for an infection to become strong enough to close a mind. There wasn't time for this to be a deliberate attempt to hurt you."

"I know what I saw. It had been placed there on purpose to trap me."

Dee sighed. "The problem with the deep subconscious is that your mind can work too well in there. It goes into overdrive and comes up with solutions to problems that don't exist. I think that's what happened here."

"I was so sure." Angelina's conviction started to waver.

"Why would anyone want to hurt you? You're a trainee performing a few easy Fate Switches. Why go to the kind of trouble that you're suggesting to get rid of you? It was a billion to one accident; you've been terribly unlucky."

Angelina dropped her gaze and stayed silent. She'd been sure it was deliberate, but what Dee was saying made more sense. It was as if she'd awoken half-way through a dream where everything had seemed clear and true and yet when she'd tried to remember things in the cold light of day, it was all a jumbled mess of half thoughts and staccato events.

She shook her head again.

"I was certain."

"For what it's worth, you did extremely well. Not many seasoned Guardian Angels would have had the presence of mind or the ability to get themselves out of that one. You've a fine career in front of you, Angelina. Please don't let this terribly unlucky incident get the better of you."

In bed that night, Angelina went over and over everything that had happened that day. Despite Dee's reassurance, she couldn't help thinking that there was more to it; that someone, or something was stalking her, waiting for the next opportunity to pounce.

Chapter Seventeen

The rest of Sunday passed in a blur. Joe tried to come to terms with everything Angelina had told him but it threw up more questions than answers, and he found it all too much to think about.

He was also desperately worried about Angelina. Despite her reassurances, he wasn't convinced that she would be safe. If everything she'd told him was true – and although it had sounded incredible, it had made sense of the inexplicable events he'd witnessed over the last few weeks – then she was probably still in danger.

He'd never met Dee, but as she'd been the one to give Angelina the assignment, logic suggested that she was to blame for Angelina's near-death experience. Then again, Joe wasn't sure that he could rely on logical, rational thought anymore.

When Monday morning finally arrived, he was at the bus stop, outside the church, by eight o'clock; although the school bus wasn't due for another half hour and Angelina never arrived before twenty-past. He wished he had her phone number and could message her or even call. The waiting was agonising.

Gradually more Ingworth High pupils drifted up, forming small clusters, most had their heads bowed over their phones. Joe stayed apart from the crowd, distracted by thoughts of Angelina. He did hear mention of Matt Armitage's name, however, and allowed himself a small smile. Lucky for Matt phones aren't allowed on the poolside or his slip would probably have gone viral.

Twenty-past eight came and went and Joe grew more and more agitated and by twenty-five past he was almost beside himself with worry. Angelina was never early, but neither was she ever late. He heard an engine in the distance and the yellow school bus came into view, grumbling up the hill.

It was no good. He couldn't leave for school without knowing that Angelina was safe. He set off in the direction of Hermit Hill Lane.

As he reached the corner, he saw Angelina's familiar figure hurrying along the road. She waved and relief flooded through him.

He almost set off running to meet her but stopped and waited until she joined him.

"I thought something had happened to you," he said.

"Sorry I'm late. I've got a good reason." She was breathless from rushing. "I'll tell you on the bus."

"You're okay though?"

Angelina laughed. "I'm fine. Come on, the bus is here."

The school bus had pulled up outside the church. With a hiss of escaping gas, the doors concertinaed back and the scrum of waiting kids surged forward. It was pointless joining the rush, so Joe and Angelina hung back. She shook her head.

"How come they're in such a rush to get on the bus when most of them claim to hate school? I don't get you humans."

Her words hit Joe like a bolt of lightning, as he realised how privileged he was to know Angelina's real identity. Yesterday the knowledge had felt like a heavy burden, but with that one sentence the load had vanished, and now all he felt was excitement. He had a direct link to another dimension, one that no one else had a clue even existed.

"What are you grinning at?" Angelina asked.

"It doesn't matter. Come on."

As they were almost last on the bus, all the double seats had been taken and they were forced to sit apart. Joe had to wait until morning break for Angelina to explain.

Strong winds overnight had blown away the weekend's rain, leaving a blustery, bright day. To make sure that they couldn't be overheard, they made their way to the edge of the school grounds and perched on the wall that marked the perimeter.

"What did Dee say." Joe asked.

"I think she was genuinely shocked when I told her. She'd checked everything again, couldn't find a problem so put it down to an unlucky accident. Her theory is that Matt's mind became infected quite recently, probably after the checks were done and the Fate Switch notice was issued. It is possible."

"You don't sound convinced."

The wind whipped Angelina's hair across her face and, with a sigh, she tucked it back behind her ear.

"I don't know. It felt like a deliberate attempt to trap me but what Dee said makes more sense. Perhaps I was just in the wrong mind at the wrong time."

"What about the lack of smell? You said everyone has a smell; surely that must have been covered up on purpose?"

"Dee put that down to the early stage of the infection, saying it hadn't started to smell."

"Do you believe her?"

Looking straight ahead, Angelina shrugged. "Why not? She knows more than I do. Let's face it, it's far more likely to be an accident than a plot to kill me off. Why would they bother? I'm not that important."

A stray football, helped by the wind, bounced against the wall nearby. Joe leapt down and kicked it back to where it had come from.

Hoisting himself back on to the wall, he said: "I'd still be on your guard, if I were you, in case there is more to it. You never know, Dee might be trying to cover up her involvement."

Angelina nudged him with her shoulder. "You're even more of a conspiracy theorist than I am."

"Just be careful. There's no point in taking any silly risks."

"I'm not. I've spoken to Dee about it and she's agreed to let me choose my own training missions from now on. She's even going to register them with the FFU after I've completed them, rather than before. That way no one can sabotage any mind that I'm about to enter. Dee thinks I'm being paranoid, but at least she's willing to go along with it."

"Well, I don't think you're paranoid and anyway, after yesterday who could blame you? Talking of yesterday, what will happen to Matt? I can't say he's ever been particularly nice, but will he become more evil?"

"Not now. Dee's notified the Infections Department at the FFU. They use a private company that specialises in neutralising infections. They'll send a team in to get rid of it and after that he should be back to normal. The infection hasn't been established long enough to do any long-term damage."

Angelina jumped off the wall and turned towards Joe, her mood turning playful.

"I haven't told you why I was late this morning yet, have I?"

"No, go on then?"

She wrinkled her nose. "On second thoughts, maybe it's better you don't know. Anyway, it's too late. Break's nearly over."

With an exaggerated look at her watch, she turned away and, with bouncing steps, headed back to the school building. Scrambling down from the wall, Joe raced after her.

"Angelina, wait. You've got to tell me."

After all the stress of the previous twenty-four hours, Angelina's good mood was infectious and Joe couldn't help laughing.

"Hmm," she pretended to consider the request. "No, I think this news is too much for a mere mortal to take."

He fell into step beside her. "Now, you're driving me mad!"

She turned towards him, tilting her chin and giving him a Cheshire-cat grin.

"Shall I tell you?"

Joe groaned. "After what you told me yesterday, I'll probably regret this, but go on."

"You will want to hear this. It's good news for you. At least it could be."

"Good news? For me? About what?" Joe was intrigued.

"You know that I said Dee is letting me choose my own practice missions?"

Joe nodded.

"She's given me access to the list of forthcoming Fate Switches. Only low-level ones, but still. I was looking through them this morning because Dee wants me to do another solo Fate Switch this week to make sure I don't lose my confidence. Guess what I came across?"

Angelina continued without waiting for an answer.

"A level-one Fate Switch for David Brennan of Little Ingworth."

"Dad?" Joe was aghast. He hadn't known what to expect, but it certainly hadn't been this.

"Well, I don't know many more David Brennan's in Little Ingworth, especially one with a son called Joe."

"It mentions me?" Joe was stunned.

Angelina must have realised that Joe was finding it hard to take in, as she calmed down and her voice became serious.

"That's why I was late this morning. I checked it twice and it's definitely your dad. It's about your diving competition, Joe. About whether he lets you go. It's only low-level so there are no major consequences whether you do the competition or not, which also means that it's not the kind of thing that GA's Influence these days. There aren't enough of us. But if I want to, I can use it as a training session."

It took a few seconds for the news to sink in. The Nationals were less than two weeks away and his dad was still insisting that Joe would have to miss the competition for the family holiday.

"Let me get this right," said Joe. "You're saying that you can tell Dad to let me dive?"

"It's not quite as simple as that, but the FFU is on your side. Their preferred outcome is that you are allowed to dive. I have to persuade your dad that it's the best decision to make, for him and for you."

Joe could feel his excitement growing. "You can do that, though, can't you?"

"I can try, but I've only done one solo Fate Switch and remember how that turned out."

"You still made the Fate Switch happen, though."

"I'll do my best but there are no guarantees. You need to understand there's a chance it won't work."

"I know, but if it does… When does it happen?"

"On Thursday at eleven minutes to six in the evening."

"That's about the time Dad usually gets home."

It was strange to think that Angelina already knew what was going to happen on Thursday.

"To give it the best chance of working, we need to plan this carefully. I need to know things like where you can stay if you don't go with them."

"That's easy. Nick's family are old friends of my parents, I used to stay over when I was young and my parents were away. Nick's mum has already said I can stay with them for the weekend."

A thought crossed Joe's mind and fear made his insides lurch.

"If this FFU knows all about what's going on in my life before I do, does that mean that it will discover that I know about you and what you are and everything?"

They'd almost reached the school and Angelina stopped.

"No, it doesn't work like that. The FFU only monitors native human and animal activity on Earth. GAs are off the radar. If your fate changes because of our conversations they'll think it's happened while I've been doing my research. The only way they'll know about us for certain is if we're overheard or if one of us says something."

Angelina stopped and looked puzzled, as if she'd thought of something.

"What's wrong?" Joe asked.

"Talking of being watched, you know the school caretaker?"

"Yeah, Mr Laker? What about him?"

"Do you know much about him?"

Joe shrugged. "Only that he's probably been around since the school was built. Why?"

"Oh, nothing. I thought he looked familiar and with everything that's happened recently, it made me wonder… but if he's been around for a while then it can't be anything."

"You don't need to worry about Mr Laker. My gran knew him when she was at school. He was the year below her and when I first started at Ingworth High, she told me how all the girls used to, in her words, 'fancy him'. That was more information than I needed to know!"

Still worried about their previous conversation, Joe asked: "Are you sure they won't find out that I know about you and these Fate Switch things?"

"They don't even monitor low-level Fate Switches these days. There are millions of them happening all the time, so it's all automated. It's only Fate Switches at level-ten and above that are ever monitored closely. If we're careful, we should be okay."

The bell rang, bringing an abrupt end to morning break and their conversation. In double Spanish Joe found it difficult to concentrate. He was desperate to dive at the National Championships, but his dad could be stubborn. Angelina will struggle to persuade Dad to change his mind, he thought.

By lunchtime the rain had returned. With everyone inside, there was nowhere for Joe and Angelina to talk in private. They settled for sitting on one of the tables at the back of the classroom, their feet resting on chairs.

"Why don't we go back to the park after school?" Angelina asked.

"Good idea. We might see Rose Garden again and can let her know how our *school project* is going on!"

They both burst out laughing.

"Looks like the lovers are sharing a private joke." Serena and her gang had sidled up to them.

Joe gave her a bored stare. "Go away, Serena."

"That's my desk you're sitting on."

She gave the chair a vicious tug, pulling it out from under Angelina's feet.

"You can have your desk back, Serena. We were leaving."

Angelina slid down from the table and Joe followed.

"That's right, Joe, run after your little girlfriend." Serena smirked and her gaggle of admirers tittered in support.

Angelina stopped and swung around to face Serena. Smiling, she said: "You want to try being nice to people for a change, Serena. Ever heard of Karma? What goes around, comes around? It's where you get what you deserve. You might want to think about that."

Serena's features twisted into an ugly glare and she stepped closer to Angelina. Despite being much smaller than Serena, Angelina refused to be intimidated and stood her ground.

"Is that a threat?" Serena asked.

"Call it friendly advice." Angelina's tone remained calm. "You've got your desk back, enjoy it."

As they walked away, Joe could feel Serena's eyes boring into their backs. When they were out of the classroom, Angelina turned to him and groaned.

"Why did I say that? I'm not supposed to threaten people."

"You didn't. Like you said, it was advice. How can that be threatening?"

"Thanks, but I don't think the FFU would agree if they found out."

She linked his arm and they continued along the corridor. When they reached the P.E department, Joe stopped at the noticeboard.

"Hey, are you still up for watching the football on Saturday?" he asked.

"Definitely, I've already cleared it with Dee. She's happy I'm trying to blend in. And probably wants me out of the way so she can work."

"The team has been picked." Joe pointed to a list on an A4 piece of paper that was pinned to the board.

Before they had chance to study the team, footsteps sounded along the corridor. As he glanced around, he heard Angelina stifle a gasp. The unmistakable figure of Matt Armitage was walking towards them. He shot her a concerned look, but she gave a quick nod, indicating that she could cope.

"Hey, Matt. How's your head? I saw that fall yesterday. Looked nasty."

"S'okay now, but I didn't fall." Matt looked annoyed at the suggestion. "Carl tripped me."

Joe didn't dare catch Angelina's eye as he knew he wouldn't be able to keep a straight face.

"It looked as if you slipped from where I was."

Ignoring Joe's comment, Matt swore under his breath. He peered at the noticeboard.

"Is that Saturday's team list?" Matt swore again. "No way! You must be joking! They'll laugh us off the field!"

Mystified, Joe checked out the team sheet and saw what had caused Matt's fury.

He gave an astonished laugh. "Whoa. Nina Kaur. He's picked Nina. Good on him!"

"He can't do that. There must be a rule against it." Matt stalked off in the direction of the P.E. staff room.

"Who's Nina Kaur? Why is he so upset?" Angelina asked.

"Nina, joined the school this year. And Matt's so upset because she's a girl."

"I don't see the problem."

"There isn't one, but it will be the first time at our school that a girl has made the first team. She deserves it though, she's an amazing footballer. I'm surprised she hasn't been picked up by one of the professional clubs. Someone told me that her mum and dad want her to go to university, so maybe that's why," Joe explained. "I think she's a much better footballer than Matt. I bet that's why he doesn't want her on the team."

It was still raining when the school bus dropped Joe and Angelina off at the church. Sheltering by the church wall, under the overhanging branches of a giant yew, they waited for the other passengers to disperse.

"What do we do now? We'll get soaked at the park." Joe looked up at the sky, but there was no sign of a break in the clouds, which looked even darker in the creeping dusk.

"We'll have to go through it all tomorrow." Jiggling from foot to foot to keep warm, Angelina pulled the hood of her coat further down over her brow.

"I can't, I've got athletics at lunchtime and football training after school."

"Well we can't stay here or you'll end up with pneumonia and won't be able to dive anyway."

"Have I caught you two loitering again!" said a friendly voice from behind them.

Joe and Angelina swung around to see Rose Garden watching them with a smile on her face. A piece of clear plastic that tied underneath her chin, protected her white hair from the rain and she wore a long beige Mac. She was carrying two bulging, canvass shopping bags.

"Let me guess. You're looking for somewhere to carry on your school project."

Joe couldn't believe it, but Rose winked when she said the last two words. Before he could deny anything, Angelina spoke up.

"Yeah, you've caught us, Rose. We were going to the park, but it's chucking it down." Angelina held her hand out, palm up, as if to catch the rain as proof.

"Well, don't you two worry. I know somewhere that's perfectly dry and there's hot chocolate to warm you both up. If you wouldn't mind carrying these bags for an old woman, you'd be more than welcome at Rose Cottage."

Joe was about to decline but he felt Angelina's sharp elbow in his side and he kept quiet.

"Thanks, Rose. Here, Joe, you take one bag, I'll take the other."

Making sure that Rose couldn't see, Joe threw Angelina a questioning look, but with a grin, she shrugged and mouthed: "Why not?" Then turned to follow Rose.

Giving a sigh, Joe joined her. Although, once seated at Rose's kitchen table with a steaming cup of hot chocolate and a slice of homemade carrot cake in front of him, he was glad they'd taken up the offer.

"Now," said Rose. "I'd like to make a deal with you two."

She'd settled her bulk on the kitchen chair at the end of the table and was warming her hands around a cup of tea.

"The park isn't the most welcoming of places now that it's coming colder and darker. So, if you two don't mind running the odd errand for me, I'm quite happy for you to meet here when you want to. I know what it's like when you're young and in love."

Joe gave Angelina a wide-eyed look of embarrassment, then dropped his eyes to hide the smirk. He knew that Angelina was having a similar reaction.

"Ah, you may laugh. But it doesn't seem that long ago since I was in your shoes. Mark my words, you'll feel the same when you get to my age." Her eyes twinkled as she became lost in a long-ago memory. "Ah, you should have seen me and Mr Garden when we first got together. Couldn't keep away from each other, you know. I'll tell you, he was quite the romantic in his day."

That was one image that Joe couldn't cope with thinking about and he broke in.

"That's kind of you, Rose. But we can't do that. I mean, won't Mr Garden mind?"

"Don't talk nonsense, of course you can. I'll be glad of the company. Don't you worry about Mr Garden. He doesn't usually get home until after six each evening. He spends a lot of time at his club, now that it's too dark for the allotment. As long as you don't touch any of his things, he won't mind."

"If you're sure, we'd love to, Rose. Thanks," said Angelina.

"That's settled then." Rose put her hands on the table and heaved herself into a standing position. "I'll leave you to it. I'll be in the sitting room if you need me for anything."

Picking up her tea, she bustled out of the kitchen, closing the door behind her. After making sure that she wasn't going to return, Joe leant over the table towards Angelina and, in a low voice, asked: "What did you say that for?"

"Why not? When you think about it, it's perfect," Angelina whispered back. "Rose already thinks we're going out together and she's right about the weather. We can't meet in the park forever. Another couple of weeks and we'll be leaving school in the dark."

"I suppose." Joe still wasn't convinced. "It's just, we don't know anything about Rose, and it seems a bit unfair to hideout here."

"Joe, we'll be doing her a favour. She's lonely. You heard what she said about Mr Garden. He's never here. From what she's said about her daughter, I don't think she visits much either. Come on, Joe, she'll love having us around. We can help out by fetching her shopping and things."

It sounded convincing and Joe couldn't think of any more reasons to say no.

"Okay, I suppose it won't do any harm."

"Great." Angelina brightened. "Now, we need to talk about Thursday."

Continuing in a low voice, she outlined her plan to Joe. Over the next two days he was to arrange for Nick to call his dad, inviting Joe to stay at Nick's parents' house over the weekend.

"Don't worry if he turns Nick down. At this stage we need to put the idea in his mind. I also need you to get your mum to have a word with your dad about the same thing."

"That shouldn't be a problem, she's on my side about this."

"Good, that will help. Now, when does your dad get home?"

"On Thursdays I usually get back from football practice by five and Dad gets home between half-five and quarter to six. Then I'm out again at a quarter to seven for diving. I've been thinking, would it help if you came to tea that day?"

"Probably not." Angelina grinned. "It might look a bit suspicious if I disappear from the dinner table. We'll save it for another time. Also, I'll have to go straight back home and report to Dee, afterwards. I could email you with some kind of code to let you know what happens."

"How about if you put 'computer project okay for next week', if it works or 'computer project cancelled' if it doesn't."

Angelina giggled. "Earth's a lot more interesting than I ever thought it would be."

They stayed for another half an hour, spending the last ten minutes talking to Rose in the sitting room. Joe decided that Angelina was right; Rose was just lonely. When they finally left, Rose accepted their offer to do her shopping the following week.

By Thursday, Nick had called Joe's dad with a formal invitation for Joe to stay with the Tyler family on the weekend of the Nationals. As expected, his dad had politely declined. Joe had also badgered his mum to make his dad change his mind, all to no avail. By Thursday evening, Joe was beginning to worry that nothing Angelina said would make the slightest bit of difference.

Joe was so on edge when he returned from football practice on Thursday evening that after his dinner, he hid in his room. Although he was desperate to know what was going on, he didn't dare risk being in the same room as his dad in case he gave anything away or distracted Angelina.

To keep his mind occupied he decided to search for a new speaker he'd been saving up for. Eventually, he found one that he wanted and placed the order. He looked at the clock. It was half past six. How did it get so late? Angelina should have finished the Fate Switch ages ago. Had something gone wrong? If it had worked, surely his dad would have told him by now, and Angelina would have sent a message. He checked his emails, but there was nothing from Angelina.

His heart sank. It hasn't worked and she doesn't know how to tell me, he thought. For a few minutes he stared at his computer screen, willing a good news message to appear.

Nothing.

He felt sorry for Angelina. She would have tried her best and would be as disappointed as he was that it hadn't worked. He had to let her know that he didn't blame her and typed out a quick email.

'Don't worry if the computer project is cancelled. I know it's not your fault. Joe x'

He didn't see his dad before he left for training, but when his mum didn't mention anything on the drive to the pool, it confirmed his fears. The tiny glimmer of hope he'd had that somehow Angelina had managed to change his dad's mind, vanished. He'd have to accept that he would miss the competition.

To forget about his bitter disappointment, Joe worked harder than ever in training and Nick was pleased with his performance.

"You're diving so well. Any chance your dad might change his mind about next week?" Nick asked, when the session was over.

Joe shook his head. "Can't see it, Nick." Joe was horrified to find himself close to tears and couldn't go on.

Seeing how upset Joe was, Nick said: "Don't worry, you'll have another chance in March. You'll blow the competition out of the water by then."

To Joe, March was a long time away.

Nick's dad dropped Joe at home. He'd not dared to look at his emails in the car in case he broke down again. He ran straight upstairs to his bedroom before checking his phone. Four new messages were waiting.

He scanned the information. The first was confirmation of his recent purchase, the second, a newsletter from a computer components site to which he subscribed. Angelina's name appeared on the third email down. The message had been sent at 7.15pm.

Knowing what to expect, he tapped on the message.

He read it twice, unable to believe what it said.

'Computer project absolutely fine for next week. See you tomorrow xx'

Just then, he heard his dad calling him.

Chapter Eighteen

With everything that had gone wrong since she'd arrived on Earth, Angelina had feared the worst when she'd first entered David Brennan's mind. Immediately, she'd checked for infections but had been relieved to discover that David's mind held a comforting aroma; one that had reminded her of home and had made her feel safe; it smelt like family.

In fact, the entire training mission went incredibly smoothly. Joe's dad had turned out to be a pushover. It had taken Angelina only a few, well-chosen thoughts to change David's mind and the Fate Switch bell had sounded. She'd pointed out how miserable Joe would be and how it would probably spoil the holiday for everyone else; how it would give David a chance to spend time with the twins; and was it fair to force poor Joe to take part in the toddler activities that would interest Evie and Nell? He was so good with the twins, didn't he deserve a break?

During her conversation with David Brennan's mind, Angelina had also discovered why he didn't encourage Joe in his diving. That was something she would have to keep to herself for now; it was an issue that Joe and his father must work out together.

The last thought Angelina had heard from David, before she'd exited his mind was: "I'll tell him tonight, when he gets home from training."

Knowing how happy Joe would be, she'd rushed back to Hermit Hill Lane to email him with the good news. Unfortunately, Dee had caught her as soon as she'd walked through the door, wanting a full report on the training mission and all the necessary paperwork completed. The hallway clock had struck seven before they'd finished and Angelina had finally escaped to her room.

Joe's message was waiting for her and she almost laughed out loud with delight as she'd sent her response.

That'll cheer him up, she thought.

On Friday morning Angelina was up and out so early that she arrived at the bus stop before Joe. It wasn't long before he appeared though, and when he saw her, he gave a whoop and came bounding over, flinging his arms around her waist, lifting her off her feet and swinging her round and round.

"You did it!"

He was almost shouting, and Angelina couldn't stop laughing. Finally, he put her down.

"I couldn't believe it when I got your email. Dad didn't tell me until after diving. By then I thought everything had gone horribly wrong."

"Huh. Glad to hear you've so much faith in my abilities!"

Joe grinned. "I should have known you'd do it." He glanced around but it was only just after eight and there was no one else in sight. "You're the best GA I've ever met." He tilted his head and pretended to look thoughtful. "I have to say, you're also the only GA I've ever met, but definitely the best. No doubt about it!"

Angelina gave him a friendly punch on the arm. "Thanks. I'll take whatever compliment I can get from you. Although" -she stretched the word out- "on Saturday, I might not be the only GA you've ever met."

"What do you mean?" Joe frowned in confusion.

"Dee wants to meet you."

"What?" Joe stepped back.

"I know, I know. I couldn't put her off. Sorry." Angelina could understand Joe's reluctance.

"I didn't think that you'd told her about me."

"I had to. She was talking about me doing another training assign-ment on Saturday morning, so I had to tell her about the school football match."

"Did you have to mention me? Isn't she going to be suspicious when you go off to some football match with the son of your last assignment?"

Angelina could hear the panic edging into Joe's voice. "That was exactly why I had to tell her. If I hadn't, she'd have known that some-thing was wrong."

By this time a few more early risers were heading towards the bus stop. To keep their conversation private, Angelina pulled Joe away from the front of the queue and back against the wall.

"What you need to understand is that it won't even cross Dee's mind that I've told you who I really am. No GA in their right mind would ever take a human into their confidence. Dee knows that I chose your dad's Fate Switch on purpose. After what happened with Matt and because I know you, I said that I thought it would be the best way to get my confidence back. I told her that I knew all about your diving and so I'd probably find it easier to Influence your dad."

Joe still looked doubtful, so Angelina pressed on.

"I'm allowed to make friends with humans. In fact, it's encouraged. It makes it easier for us to do our jobs and, let's face it, it would be a bit strange if I joined your school and never spoke to anyone."

"I suppose so."

"I'm here for another few months and the chances are your name will come up at some point. I have an interim report to submit before Christmas, which includes who I spend time with, what I've learned about your culture and about a million and one other things. I can't possibly leave your name out of that. If Dee remembers that I did a Fate Switch for a David Brennan, whose son, Joe, is a diver and attends Ingworth High, she'll wonder why I didn't mention it earlier. That would look far more suspicious and she'd wonder what I was hiding." Angelina finally ran out of breath. She gazed up at Joe, begging him to understand.

"You're saying the more open we are about our friendship; the less likely Dee is to suspect that I know everything?" He still didn't sound convinced.

"Pretty much."

"What if I say something to give it all away?"

Angelina smiled reassuringly. "You won't. You haven't said anything to anyone at school or home, have you?"

"I suppose not." Joe conceded. "Why does she want to meet me?"

"I think after Matt she feels as if she should be keeping an eye out for me a bit more. You won't have to spend much time with her. If you call for me on Saturday morning, she can say hello to you and then we'll be off. Simple."

Joe groaned. "Angelina, nothing is simple around you."

On Saturday morning, Angelina awoke to a cloudless morning and the first frost of autumn. Fingers of sun had begun to creep around the edge of the curtains as, still snuggled up in bed, she heard the kitchen door slam: the signal that Dee was on her way out to the garage. Angelina raised her head to glance at her bedside clock. Sure enough, it was eight o'clock. It didn't matter what day it was, at the same time, every morning, Dee was always up and on her way to the garage to do whatever it was that she did in there.

Although Angelina had no idea exactly what it was that kept Dee so busy in the garage. She assumed that it was important research and planning for the FFU. After all, Dee was the senior GA coordinator on Earth. It also explained why so many parcels were continually coming and going. They were obviously packs of correspondence from GAs stationed in various countries around the world. Dee acted so secretive about her work in the garage that it couldn't possibly be anything but highly classified FFU projects.

It was so cold in the cottage – Dee had yet to turn on the central heating even though it was the middle of October – that it was another twenty minutes before Angelina dragged herself from her warm, cosy bed. Even after she'd showered and dressed, she was still shivering as she stood in the kitchen waiting for the toaster to pop up. To keep warm, she took her toast and juice into the sitting room. The fire wasn't lit, but Dee kept an electric heater in there and Angelina turned it on, huddling up close. The smell of burning dust soon filled the room and her toes were almost smouldering from the scorching air blown out by the small heater.

She was still relaxing in the sitting room, watching Saturday morning television, when there was a knock on the door.

She grinned as she opened the door to Joe.

He looked nervous and whispered: "Is she here?"

"No, don't worry. She's in the garage working. We'll call in when we're ready to go."

Looking relieved Joe stepped over the threshold and followed Angelina towards the hallway cupboard. As she scrambled around for her boots, she heard Joe call out. He was standing at the doorway to the study.

"Is that Dee's computer?"

"Yes, why? What's wrong with it?" Angelina was busy pulling on her fur-lined boots.

"That's one of the most powerful computers you can get. They're brand new, cost an absolute fortune and do everything." Joe's eyes gleamed in admiration. "I'd love to have a go on that."

"There you go. You've something to talk to Dee about, after all. Although I'm not sure she knows much about computers either and personally, I can't think of anything more boring," said Angelina. "Come on, stop drooling on the carpet and let's get this over with."

Locking the kitchen door behind them, Angelina led the way down the path towards the garage. She rapped on the door and stood back waiting, giving Joe an encouraging smile as she did so.

There was no answer. Neither could she hear the radio, which Dee always turned on when she was working.

Puzzled, Angelina knocked again. "Dee? Hello? We're about to go?"

"Perhaps she's changed her mind about meeting me," said Joe, hopefully.

"She mentioned you again last night. I wonder where she's gone?" As she spoke, Angelina pulled down the handle and pushed against the door with her shoulder, to confirm that the garage was locked.

When the door yielded, swinging smoothly inwards, it caught her by surprise and she half-stumbled into the garage.

The light was off and, although the garden was bathed in the bright morning sun, barely any daylight penetrated the window's blackened glass. The square of yellow light from the open door had fallen onto a pile of boxes, which for a split-second, was all that Angelina could see.

Joe, who had followed her into the garage, flicked a switch that he found by the door and the entire room exploded into life under the harsh glare of fluorescent lighting.

"Whoa," said Joe. "What the…? What does Dee do in here?"

Ignoring Joe's question, Angelina gazed around, her mouth hanging half-open in dumb astonishment. She stepped forward, her eyes moving slowly, trance-like, around the room as she tried to make sense of what she was looking at.

From inside the garage looked enormous, the effect helped by the white-painted, breezeblock walls, which reflected the bright, artificial light. It wasn't the size of the room that amazed her, it was what it contained.

Whenever she'd thought of Dee in the garage, Angelina had always had a picture in her mind of Dee working away at a desk, surrounded by filing cabinets and bookcases, with rows and rows of lever arch files and textbooks: in effect, an extension of her indoor study. Never had she imagined the scene that she was now staring at.

"What is all this," she whispered, talking more to herself than Joe.

It was true that there were shelves, bookcases and cabinets, but they didn't contain textbooks and files. Instead, it was an Aladdin's Cave of goods. Toasters, radios and hairdryers waited on the shelves along with stacks of boxes and books; jewellery sparkled from open boxes, while large cardboard packs with outline diagrams of TVs were stacked against one wall. Instead of the usual oil and petrol fumes that most garages reeked of, Angelina's senses were assaulted by a potpourri of sweetly floral perfumes combined with the decidedly chemical flavouring of new electronic equipment.

To the left, was a large worktable, laden with packaging materials and a gigantic roll of bubble wrap, while against the far wall a swathe of white material hung from the ceiling, providing a backdrop to an eerie-looking, headless, tailor's dummy.

"What is she, some kind of burglar?"

"I… I don't know," said Angelina. "I don't understand this. I mean, this isn't GA work. It can't be."

"It looks like she's got some kind of warehouse here. Does she store things for a living?"

Angelina shook her head. "No, we're not allowed to work for personal gain. We can do voluntary work, but we can't take employment away from humans. The FFU provides an allowance that covers all living expenses. We don't need money."

"She could be a fence."

"A what?" "A fence. You know, someone who handles stolen goods for thieves."

Angelina looked bewildered. "Whatever it is she's doing in here, it's not official business. No wonder she's been so keen to keep me out."

A sound from outside made Angelina start. In horror, she looked at Joe.

"That's the gate. It must be Dee. Quick, turn off the light, she can't know that we've been in here."

Scrambling back towards the door, Joe flicked the lights off and taking care not to make a sound, Angelina gently pulled the door closed behind them.

It was definitely Dee. Angelina could tell by the short fast footsteps tapping down the driveway; it was the way Dee walked when she was in a hurry.

Angelina only had a couple of seconds to decide what to do. Although the side door to the garage couldn't be seen from the driveway, Dee would be turning the corner onto the garden path any second now and would immediately spot them. Even if Dee went into the cottage first (assuming that she had her key with her, which Angelina doubted) she would see them through the kitchen window.

They had to hide.

Desperately Angelina scanned the small, overgrown garden for inspiration, then an idea came to her.

"Follow my lead," she whispered to Joe.

Balling her hand into a fist, she knocked loudly on the garage door and called out: "Dee, it's me. Are you in there?"

Hearing Dee's footsteps speed up, she knocked again.

"Dee, are you there?" For effect, she placed her ear to the door, knowing that Dee would see her. "We've got to..."

"I'm here."

Dee sounded annoyed as she hurried towards them. She pushed past Angelina, placing her back protectively against the garage door.

Acting surprised, Angelina stepped back. "Oh, I thought you were inside."

"I had to go to the post office. What do you want?"

"We're off to the football match, like I told you. You said it was okay."

Dee's face creased into even more wrinkles. "Hmm, yes, I remember. It's today, is it?" She fixed her stare on Joe. "And ...?"

"This is Joe, my friend from school that I told you about. The one you wanted to meet." Angelina looked at Joe as she introduced him.

His eyes were wide and he gave a nervous smile.

Dee treated him to her impression of a hawk contemplating a wounded sparrow, jutting her head forward and narrowing her eyes.

"Hi. Nice to meet you." Joe gave a tentative smile and held his hand up in a half wave.

Angelina wasn't sure what was scaring him most – Dee almost catching them in the garage or how she looked. Having become used to Dee's weird and wonderful outfits, Angelina had forgotten to warn Joe how eccentrically Dee sometimes dressed. Today her ensemble included a purple anorak open to reveal a lime green jumper hanging over a pair of dark blue denim jeans; maroon baseball boots added the finishing touch.

"So, Joe. Where do you live?"

"Err, the new estate up by the park."

"Where's this football match?"

"It's at the school playing fields."

"What time will you be back?"

"I'm training this afternoon, so we won't be late." Joe was looking rather shell-shocked by Dee's quick-fire interrogation.

Trying to save Joe, Angelina interrupted: "Dee, we've got to go or we'll miss the match. We only came to say goodbye."

Angelina made a point of looking at her watch. Backing away and dragging poor Joe behind her, she said: "I've locked the cottage door. Have you got your key?"

Dee patted her purple pockets and finding them empty, turned to the garage. Angelina could have kicked herself for asking the question. It was obvious from the frown on Dee's face that she'd remembered where her keys were and that the garage door was unlocked.

"I'll be back by lunch. See you then." Holding her breath, Angelina turned and started walking away but Dee's sharp voice stopped her.

"Have you two been in the garage?" The accusation rang heavy in Dee's voice.

Angelina froze. Half-turning, she looked over her shoulder, pretending that she hadn't understood the significance of the question. "I thought you always kept it locked when you weren't there?"

Her innocence must have been convincing, as Dee looked unsure; almost flustered.

"Yes. Yes. Yes, I do." She patted her pockets again, looking around on the ground as if checking to make sure her keys hadn't fallen out. Taking advantage of Dee's confusion, Angelina gave a wave and backed away towards the driveway.

"Bye."

"Nice to meet you. Bye." Joe followed Angelina's lead and before

Dee had chance to say anything else, they turned the corner and were gone.

Half-expecting Dee to call them back, Angelina and Joe sped up the drive. Pete, from next door was in his garden and called out a cheery hello to Angelina and Joe as they ran past. Not wanting to stop, Angelina simply waved back at him.

It wasn't until they reached the bottom of Hermit Hill Lane, and were sure that Dee had not followed them, that they slowed down enough to talk.

"That was close. I thought she was bound to see that you were lying," said Joe.

Nowhere near as fit as Joe, Angelina was still trying to catch her breath.

"I wasn't lying," she managed to say between gasps. "All I said was that I thought she kept the garage locked."

Joe grinned in admiration. "Yeah, you did. That's clever."

Angelina finally got her breathing under control. "Thanks. I thought Dee might pick up on it though. If I'd told her an outright lie she'd have known immediately. You can't hide a lie from a GA."

Joe's face clouded over and he grabbed Angelina's arm. "What if she does that Mind Jumping thing and finds out what we know. She could do that, couldn't she?"

"Not to me. I'd know straight away. And she can only jump into your mind if she has a direct sight line and I kept my eye on her until you were around the corner."

Joe seemed to accept Angelina's reassurance, but he still looked worried when he spoke. "She's been lying to you, though. About the garage."

"Thinking about it, she's never lied she always refused to tell me what was in there. I thought it was top secret, but I'm certain that what we've just seen has nothing to do with the FFU."

They continued in silence for a few minutes, Angelina trying and failing to come up with an explanation that made sense. As she'd looked around Dee's garage a knot of uncertainty had formed in her stomach, and the more she thought about what she'd seen, the tighter it coiled.

Before she'd arrived on Earth, the boundaries between right and wrong had been perfectly clear. To her, the thought of breaking GA laws was unimaginable. The laws had to be kept. GAs provided moral guidance for a planet's inhabitants. If GAs started breaking the laws, how could they possibly help their targets?

Yet, over the past few weeks, those boundaries between right and wrong had become blurred for Angelina. She'd broken the most important law of all by telling Joe who she really was. Angelina might have been trying to stay alive, while Dee was probably doing something illegal or worse, but did that matter? Were Angelina's reasons for breaking FFU law any more justifiable? She didn't know.

Joe interrupted her thoughts, voicing something that she'd not allowed herself to consider.

"You need to be careful, Angelina. Whatever Dee is doing in that garage, it might have something to do with you getting trapped in Matt's mind. It looks more and more likely that she was the one trying to get rid of you."

He was right and Angelina knew it.

"I have to find out what she's up to."

"No!"

Surprised by Joe's reaction, she looked up at him.

"I need to know what's going on."

Joe was shaking his head, frowning with worry. "Please, Angelina, promise me that you won't go looking in that garage again, or do anything to make Dee think you've already been in there. Please, promise me."

"I need to find out. Like you said, she could be the one trying to get rid of me."

"She'll probably try even harder if she finds out that you know about her secret life. Then you'll be a threat she'll have to deal with. You said there are easier ways for her to get rid of you than Vaporisation."

"I can't let her get away with this."

"You don't have to. Wait until you've finished your assignment. When you're back in your world, you can tell the FFU police or whoever needs to know. For now, you have to keep yourself safe."

"How do I do that without help?"

Joe had obviously given the question some thought already. "You've got the upper hand now. You know all about Dee, but she doesn't know that you know."

"I'm not sure I know anything," said Angelina.

"You know that you need to be careful, which is the most important thing. Dee won't be able to surprise you with any more tricks like Matt's infected mind. If you're not a direct threat, she probably won't dare to try anything else. That's why you can't go digging any more. You can't risk making her suspicious."

Angelina looked troubled. "I can't do nothing." Then she brightened. "I could send a Umail to the FFU and let them know what's going on."

Joe didn't share her optimism. "You can't risk it. From what you've said about the FFU, it's busy and understaffed. What if the Umail gets lost or it takes a couple of months for someone to get around to doing something about it. Don't forget that Dee gave you that computer. How do you know she hasn't installed some kind of Guardian Angel Spyware and is reading all your messages?"

"I hadn't thought of that." Angelina's brow once again furrowed with worry. Joe recognised how scared she was.

"For what it's worth, if you let Dee get on with whatever she's doing, I think you'll be fine. You've been okay so far."

"Apart from almost being Vaporised."

"You know to be careful now. That won't happen again. As far as Dee is concerned, nothing has changed. She doesn't know you've been in the garage. Keep quiet about that and you'll be fine. Remember you've got me to help you too."

Angelina smiled. "Okay, okay. I promise to be careful. I promise not to go snooping. And I promise to try not to worry. There. How's that?"

Joe linked her arm. "Fantastic. Right, let's get to this game."

As usual, what Joe had said made perfect sense. She had to see this assignment through and then there would be the chance to bring Dee to justice; she must be patient.

For now, she put Dee and the garage out of her mind and tried her best to make sense of Joe's GA guide to football. At least, that was what he called it. To Angelina it sounded complete nonsense, but she tried to nod and shake her head at what she judged to be the right times.

It was almost eleven by the time they arrived at the school playing fields and the sun had chased the frost into the shadows, leaving the grass under their feet wet and soft.

"It'll be like a mud bath by the time they've finished," said Joe.

Nina's place in the team had caused a real stir around school and a crowd had gathered to watch the match with Stalyborough High. The two teams of supporters had already staked out their territory. Along the edge of the field closest to them, Angelina recognised quite a few people from school.

"Come on, they're about to start."

Grabbing Angelina's hand and pulling her with him, Joe hurried towards the football field. They found a space along the touchline, almost level with some white lines on the field that Joe said was the penalty box. The players were already on the field, the red and black clad Ingworth High players dotted around the half where Angelina and Joe were standing. It looked a curious arrangement to Angelina but she could see that the players were placed in some sort of formation.

She recognised the tall, powerfully built figure of Matt, shaking his arms and legs as he waited by the edge of the centre circle. He was listening to Mr Stephens, the boys' PE teacher and football coach, who was shouting instructions from the side-line.

"Matt's the captain, although it looks as if Stalyborough won the toss."

He pointed towards two players from the opposition, who were standing in the centre of the pitch, a ball at their feet.

"Toss? I thought they had to kick the ball, not throw it?"

Amused, Joe looked at her. "I should write these down! They don't toss the ball: they toss a coin. The team who calls heads or tails correctly, wins the toss and will usually decide to take the kick-off. That leaves the other team to choose which way to play first."

"I see, I think. Is he the goolie?" Trying to remember what Joe had told her, Angelina directed Joe's attention to the Ingworth High goalkeeper who was clapping his gloved hands and shouting words of encouragement to his teammates.

Joe gave a snort of laughter. "I think you mean, *goalie.*"

At that moment, the only adult on the pitch, a man dressed in black shirt and shorts (the referee, according to Joe), checked his watch and blew a whistle. The two teams ran towards each other amid cheers of encouragement from the crowd. To Angelina, it looked like complete chaos but Joe assured her that there was some order to their movements.

The ball ricocheted between players and, although Angelina had no idea what was going on, she soon became caught up in the excitement, shouting and cheering along with Joe and the rest of the crowd.

At one point, when the noise from the supporters had died down for a moment, she asked: "Which one's Nina?"

"She's over there on the left wing."

Joe pointed to the far side of the field and Angelina saw a small but wiry figure with straight, black hair, pulled into a tight ponytail running towards the ball. She was being chased by a much taller boy from Stalyborough High.

Nina reached the ball first and with a flick of her feet, wrong-footed her opponent and accelerated effortlessly away, the ball at her feet. She didn't slow, even as she dribbled the ball down the wing, keeping perfect control before delivering a cross into the centre as Matt came running in. Unfortunately, Matt's timing was wrong and the ball went sailing straight past him and straight to the Stalyborough defender.

A collective groan went up from the Ingworth supporters, immediately followed by cheering, acknowledging the good play.

"Did you see that?" Joe was clapping hard. "I told you she's good."

Even with her limited knowledge of football, Angelina had been able to appreciate Nina's skill. Over the sound of their applause, she noticed Matt's reaction.

"Why is Matt shouting at her?"

"Because he's an idiot. He messed up and now he's trying to blame Nina's cross." Cupping his hands around his mouth, Joe yelled: "Great cross, Nina."

The home supporters agreed, and the clapping and cheering started all over again. Angelina noticed Matt, glaring in Joe's direction but the match had already moved on, the ball now in the Ingworth half. A shot from a Stalyborough player glanced off the crossbar and bounced out of play behind the goal, bringing equally frustrated cries from the away supporters.

Joe's hands flew to his head at the near miss and he turned to Angelina.

"That was close. We were nearly one goal down, then."

For the next half hour, the ball seemed to bounce from one end of the field to the other as each team tried and failed to take the lead.

Just before half time, Matt collected the ball inside the Ingworth half. A defender soon caught up with him but across the other side of the field, Nina was free and the supporters were calling and gesticulating for Matt to pass. He ignored their shouts. Keeping possession, Matt was forced out wide by the defender and Angelina could see that he was running out of room. Finally, he made what looked like a desperate attempt at a shot on goal, but he was so close to the corner flag when he kicked the ball that it bounced harmlessly across the mouth of the goal and in easy reach of the Stalyborough goalkeeper. Yet the keeper fluffed his attempt to clear the ball, managing only to knock it towards the edge of the penalty area. Fortunately for Stalyborough, it went straight to one of their players.

Then, without warning, a streak of black and red plucked the ball away from the feet of the defender. It was Nina. The green and white shirted player was left standing as Nina rolled around him and from twenty yards out, kicked the ball towards the goal. Still stranded from his earlier mistake, the goalkeeper could only watch as the ball flew into the top corner of the goal.

The Ingworth crowd went wild, jumping around, cheering and yelling. On the field, the home team, with the notable exception of Matt Armitage, ran over to Nina, high-fiving her.

"What a time to score, just before half time. Did you see that goal?"

Joe was jumping up and down with excitement and didn't need an answer, so Angelina nodded and clapped enthusiastically as he continued cheering.

Stalyborough had barely had time to kick off again before the referee blew his whistle again

"Half time," said Joe. "Well, what do you think? It's not a bad game, is it?"

"It's more fun than I expected. Matt didn't seem happy about Nina scoring, though."

Joe shrugged. "That's his worst nightmare: someone else taking the spotlight."

The second half started slowly with few shots on goal. For the first ten minutes, Nina barely touched the ball. Two of the biggest Stalyborough players on the pitch were flanking her, using their strength, rather than skill, to keep her out of the game.

"They know she's a threat," said Joe. "Their coach is trying to keep her out of the game."

The new tactics worked, and it wasn't long before one of the Stalyborough attackers dribbled into the Ingworth penalty area. His shot flew over the Ingworth goalkeeper, whose last-ditch attempt to dive on the ball failed, and hit the back of the net.

The groan from the Ingworth High crowd almost matched the cheer that went up from the Stalyborough supporters. The score was one all with only twenty minutes left to play.

By now, Angelina was as carried away as Joe was with the tension and excitement. Time was ticking by quickly, yet it was stalemate out on the pitch. Matt managed a weak kick on goal that was easily collected by the opposition's keeper. At the other end, a Stalyborough shot narrowly went wide of the post, causing gasps of relief from the Ingworth crowd and gasps of despair from the travelling supporters.

Joe checked his watch. "Only five minutes left," he said.

A minute later, the ball rebounded from a failed Stalyborough attack and bounced up the field to where Nina was tussling with her markers. She dodged as one of them tried to grab her and they tackled each other, giving her time to break free and collect the ball. Cutting inside, she made a run down the centre, the ball at her feet. With only the goalkeeper to beat, the Ingworth High crowd were going wild.

"Nina won't miss from there. She can't."

Joe's voice was confident, but Angelina hardly dared to look. As Nina edged closer to the goal she slowed, picking her spot she drew back her left foot to shoot.

"No!"

The shout went up almost in unison from the Ingworth supporters.

Nina lay sprawled on the ground, clutching her shin with both hands, her face in agony. One of the Stalyborough defenders had made a desperate lunge, chopping her feet from under her as she prepared to shoot.

The referee ran up blowing his whistle. He pointed to the penalty spot with one hand and with the other, brandished a red card in front of the offending Stalyborough player.

Mr Stephens ran on the field to tend to Nina. The referee, meanwhile, was having a stern word with the Stalyborough defender. After a dressing down, the player slouched off the pitch in the direction of the opposition's stony-faced teacher, his head bowed in disgrace or anger, Angelina wasn't sure which.

With the help of Mr Stephens, Nina made it to her feet. Gingerly she took a few tentative steps, limping around while flexing and stretching her lower limb. Eventually her gait became stronger as the initial sting of the tackle eased.

"What happens now?" asked Angelina.

"It's a penalty!" Joe was hopping about with excitement. "That means one of our players has the chance to kick at goal from the penalty spot, with only the keeper to beat."

"Who takes the kick?"

"I don't know. It's usually Matt, but it looks like Mr Stephens has given the ball to Nina. This could be interesting."

An angry looking Matt was saying something to Mr Stephens, but the teacher obviously didn't agree and pointed Nina towards the penalty spot. As Mr Stephens turned his back and jogged off the field, Matt said something to Nina. Angelina was too far away to hear what was said, she saw Nina's eyes widen and she shook her head. The next moment, she handed the ball to Matt and ran to take up a position at the edge of the white box.

Joe cursed under his breath. "Matt's scared her off. He's a selfish…" Joe didn't bother to finish his sentence.

Mr Stephens was shouting from the side-line and the rest of the team and the referee, looked unsure as to what to do. Matt, meanwhile, had placed the ball on the penalty spot and was pacing slowly and deliberately away from the ball. He looked at the referee and nodded that he was ready.

Still wary, the referee cast his eyes towards Mr Stephens, who was standing at the edge of the field, hands on hips, his mouth in a tight line and an angry frown causing his bushy eyebrows to become one thick slash across his brow. A sharp jerk of the teacher's head instructed the referee to continue.

Matt's blatant disobedience had caused a hushed murmur to rumble around the field, but with a shrill blast from the whistle, the crowd fell silent in anticipation.

Angelina couldn't work out whether she wanted Matt to score or not. Although she wanted Ingworth High to win, part of her was hoping he would miss, to punish him for whatever he'd said to Nina. The ball shot hard and true from Matt's foot straight towards the centre of the goal. Had the keeper stayed upright, the ball would have hit him in the chest, but he dived to his right and the ball hit the back of the net behind where he'd been standing a split second earlier.

From the muted applause, the rest of the Ingworth High supporters felt like Angelina. Even the players on the field didn't show their usual enthusiasm for the goal, although Matt jumped up and punched the air in a victory salute.

For the final five minutes of the game, the atmosphere remained subdued. Stalyborough battled hard but without luck or success and at the final whistle, Matt's goal was the only difference between the two sides.

As they made their way home after the match, Joe said: "That was such a good game until Matt ruined it. I can't believe Nina gave in to him like that."

"It's her first game," said Angelina. "From what you've said, she'll have to be ten times better than anyone else on the pitch as it is, and Matt's the captain. If she'd missed, Matt would have used it as an excuse to get her knocked off the team."

"Well, I hope Mr Stephens gives Matt detention for a month."

"What for?" Angelina looked amused. "For scoring the winning goal? I can't see that happening. Matt might not be very sporting but he got the job done."

"It still doesn't excuse what he did." Joe said.

When they reached Little Ingworth, Joe accompanied Angelina back to the cottage on Hermit Hill Lane. They stopped at the gate.

"Are you going to be all right?" he asked.

"I think so."

There was no sign of Dee, but the street was quiet and Angelina could hear the faint tinny sounds of the radio coming from the garage.

She'd been so caught up with the excitement of the football match that she'd managed to forget about her problems with Dee. Now that she'd returned to the cottage they came flooding back.

Joe must have been thinking along the same lines.

"Promise me you won't do anything to make Dee suspicious." He looked down at her, his face serious.

She gave a brief smile of reassurance. "I promise. What you said made sense. Don't worry, I won't do anything silly. You'd better go or you'll be late for training."

"Cal if you need me."

Angelina could tell that Joe was reluctant to leave her, but she gave him a push.

"Go on. You've a competition to train for."

She watched him until he reached the bottom of the hill where he turned and waved before vanishing around the corner. Despite her reassurances to Joe, Angelina wasn't looking forward to seeing Dee again. Resisting the temptation to go straight to her room, Angelina headed for the garage and banged on the side door. This time, Dee called out, although she didn't rush to open the door.

"I'm back. I'll be inside if you need me," Angelina shouted through the closed door.

Without waiting for a reply, she started up the path, then heard the garage door open.

"We need to talk."

Angelina's heart almost stopped as she turned to see Dee locking the garage door.

Dee must know about her and Joe being in the garage. Frantically, Angelina tried to remember if she'd touched or moved anything inside that would have given her away but nothing came to mind.

Trying to keep her voice steady, she asked: "What about?"

"I'll tell you when we're inside."

Feeling like a condemned man walking to the gallows, Angelina followed Dee into the cottage.

"In here."

Dee walked through the hall and into the study. As Angelina closed the study door behind her, Dee turned.

Angelina's heart started hammering away in her chest. Oh no, she thought. This is it.

Dee, her right arm extended in front of her, bore down on Angelina, reaching forward, towards the young girl's neck.

She's going to strangle me! Her thoughts and heart were racing and involuntarily, she squeezed her eyes shut, flinching away from Dee's grasp.

"What's wrong with you?"

Opening her eyes, Angelina saw Dee standing there, clutching a sheet of paper. Heart still hammering, realisation dawned on Angelina. Dee hadn't been trying to strangle her; she'd been reaching towards the printer that was on top of the cupboard behind Angelina's left shoulder.

"Err, nothing. I think I've got something in my eye. It might be a fly." She rubbed her eye and blinked a few times. "I think it's gone, now."

"Good, because I need you to concentrate on this." Dee sank into the office chair and motioned for Angelina to take a seat.

Puzzled, yet relieved that she was still alive, Angelina complied.

"I received a Umail this morning from the FFU."

Angelina leaned forward slightly, listening intently. She couldn't tell from the brusque tone that Dee was using, whether this was a good thing or a bad thing. She waited for Dee to continue.

"It's the full details of your official assignment: who the target is, when and where it all happens." She pushed the piece of paper she was holding into Angelina's hands. "Read it carefully and we'll go through it later."

Holding the paper as carefully as a mother holds a new-born, Angelina sat looking at it, as if it might vanish before her eyes. This was what she'd been waiting for: information about her assignment. So, this was what Dee had wanted to talk to her about.

"I've forwarded the original Umail through to your computer." Her eyes glinted behind her purple-framed glasses. "It certainly looks interesting."

Rising from her chair, Dee added: "Right, I've some work to finish."

When Dee had gone, Angelina carried the piece of paper to her room, settled on her bed and started reading the assignment that she must complete before she could escape this uncertain world.

Chapter Nineteen

When Joe arrived at school on Monday everyone was talking about the football match, and, to Matt's obvious annoyance, Nina's outstanding performance.

Joe was too preoccupied with thoughts of Angelina to take much notice. She'd texted him saying she had something important to tell him, but they barely had any time alone during the day. It wasn't until after school when they reached Rose's house that they had a chance to talk.

On the way, they'd called at the village store to collect Rose's grocery order. Once again, Rose had welcomed them with cake and hot chocolate before retiring discreetly to the sitting room.

Finally alone, and certain that Rose had closed the door behind her, Joe turned to Angelina.

"Go on, then. What's been up with you all day?"

Angelina could barely contain herself as she reached into her bag and brought out a folded piece of white paper. She held it out to him.

"What's this?" Mystified, Joe reached for the paper.

"Open it," she whispered.

Slowly and deliberately he unfolded the paper, smoothing out the creases as he laid it on the oak table. He read the first line and looked enquiringly at Angelina.

Biting her lip, she nodded at his unspoken question.

"It's my official assignment. This is what I've been waiting for! Can you believe it? It's finally come through. Go on, read it," she urged.

Joe's eyes skimmed over the printout.

THE FATE SWITCH

To: Dorothy Devin, Earth
From: Notification Department FFU
Sent: 18 October, 10:53
Subject: Angelina Crossland, TGA A 3A

Trainee Test: Assignment DD01402/98443
Level-one Fate Switch, Ingworth, Yorkshire, England, Earth.

Date: Saturday 14 February
Time: By 14.10 (local time)
Location: Main hall, Ingworth High School
Target: Serena Jackson

Action: For Serena to invite Nathan Bird to school Valentine's Ball and for him to accept.

Background available:
Age: 14
Address: 17 George Street, Little Ingworth
Interests: Art, fashion and music.

Desired outcome: Fate Switch to take place.

When he came to the end, he read it again to make sure that he hadn't been mistaken. Eventually he lifted his head and stared at Angelina.

"*Serena*? It involves Serena?"

"Shh. Keep your voice down." Angelina glanced at the door that led to Rose's sitting room.

Joe followed her eyes but the door was still closed.

"Sorry. I didn't mean to say it so loud. I can't believe that you have to jump into Serena's mind. If any mind is infected it has to be hers."

Angelina shook her head. "She's mean, not evil."

She leaned forward, her long black hair trailing on the table, her face alive.

"At last, I'm getting somewhere. I know exactly what I've got to do and once it's over I can get out of this world and make sure that the FFU do something about Dee. It feels more real somehow, doesn't it?"

To avoid answering the question, Joe looked down at the paper again. Angelina was right; it did seem very real. Yet, he wasn't sure that he wanted it to be real. 'Being real' meant that Angelina would be leaving, returning home to whatever dimension she had come from, not just another town or even another country where they could perhaps message and even see each other every now and again during the holidays. No. Where she was going, she'd be gone for good and Joe didn't think he was ready for that.

Of course, he knew that she couldn't stay here forever. He'd known when she'd first told him who and what she was that she would eventually leave again. They'd also talked about her Assignment and about her going home when it was over; about her being safe again. He did want her to be safe. But seeing the date and time of the event that would bring their friendship to an end made everything a little bit too real. He didn't want to lose her so soon.

He knew that he couldn't say any of this. Instead, Joe looked her in the eye and smiled.

"It's great news. What do you have to do? It doesn't say much."

"They never do. There's even more work to do on this as it's an exam. We're supposed to treat this level-one Fate Switch as if it's a high priority Fate Switch, a level-ten or above."

"How can you pretend it's more important than it is?"

"It's not about pretending it's important; it's about the preparation you have to do before the Fate Switch can take place."

"Now you've lost me."

She looked to the ceiling as if seeking inspiration on the best explanation. "I've told you that the consequences of low-level Fate Switches are pretty limited and only affect that person and maybe their immediate family, right?"

Joe nodded.

"For my training so far, I've just gone in and had a go at influencing. Sometimes it works, sometimes it doesn't."

"You've told me that before."

"Well, with a high-level Fate Switch, it's different. As lots of people can be affected if the wrong decision is made, you have to do more preparation. You must make sure that you've set everything up so that the Fate Switch has the best chance of happening - or not happening - depending on the FFU's advice. Some Fate Switches take years of planning, with lots of different people involved. That's why they send the information through so early. It's a bit like a game of chess. You have to plan your final, winning move, right from the start."

"I'm not very good at chess."

Angelina laughed. "I'm being serious. My official assignment will be set up so that I have to put together a strategy that involves lots of little moves that will eventually, and hopefully" -Angelina crossed her middle and index fingers on both hands and held them up in a gesture of luck- "get me to the point where the Fate Switch has the best chance of taking place. They're testing that I'm capable of thinking strategically and putting it all into action."

Angelina continued, excitedly telling him how, over the next few months, she would Influence Serena and Nathan to make a series of decisions so that on Saturday the fourteenth of February, at around five to two, they'll both be in the same place and Serena will ask Nathan to go to the Valentine's Ball with her.

"At that point, I'll be in Serena's mind, influencing her to ask the question." Angelina finished.

Joe looked incredulous. "Do you know who Nathan Bird is?"

A shadow of a frown crossed Angelina's face. "I think so. He's in Mr Frazer's registration class, isn't he? Tall; black hair?"

"That's him. Do you know what Serena's pet name for Nathan Bird is?" He gave a slightly hysterical snort of laughter.

"No," said Angelina, doubt clouding her face.

"Nathan Nerd!"

"She doesn't like him?"

"Like him? Serena wouldn't be seen dead with Nathan. You'll never get her to ask him to the Valentine's Ball."

"She has to. I have to make it happen. She must ask him, or the Fate Switch doesn't happen and I fail the assignment. That can't happen. I have to pass." She looked anxiously at Joe.

Unable to offer any reassurance, Joe said: "That assignment is next to impossible. I mean, Nathan and Serena... they're just... well, it's like they're..."

Joe was struggling to find the right explanation. He pushed his blond fringe away from his brow and tried again.

"You know how we come from different dimensions? Well, the dimensions that Nathan and Serena come from are even further apart.

Serena is vicious, bullies people and hates school. Nathan is quiet, works hard, always gets As and plays the classical guitar. See what I mean: worlds apart."

To illustrate his point, he held his arms out to the side, palms up, as if cupping two imaginary worlds.

While Joe had been speaking the colour had gradually drained from Angelina's face. He saw her fear but couldn't offer false comfort.

Covering her hand with his, he spoke gently. "Serena and Nathan, it's just not going to happen, Angelina."

"Yes, it is."

With one sharp movement, she drew her hand out from under Joe's grasp and snatched the printout from his other hand. Joe could see that she was trembling as she folded the paper precisely along its previous creases. Startled by her reaction, he tried to take her hand again but she pushed her chair back and moved out of his reach, grabbing her bag and stuffing the paper inside.

"I didn't mean to upset you. I just thought you ought to know."

She stopped what she was doing and stared at him. Joe had never seen such a determined look in anyone's eyes before.

"I know you didn't mean to, but you don't get it, do you?" She looked accusingly at him. "I don't have a choice. I must find a way to make this Fate Switch happen. If I don't, I'll be stuck here for another six months or however long it takes for a retake to come through and if Dee's got anything to do with it, I probably won't last that long. Either that or I give up any hope I had of graduating and I won't do that. When Grandad died, I swore that I'd become a GA, just like him."

Her tirade stopped, as if she'd run out of things to say or had said too much.

Joe sat back in his chair. Although the words had been spoken in little more than a whisper, the force of emotion behind them had landed like a blow to his stomach, taking the breath right out of him.

For a moment, neither of them spoke. It was as if the outpouring had congealed into a physical entity that now stood like a barrier between them.

Joe broke the silence.

"I'm sorry. You're right, I didn't get it. I guess we'll just have to find a way to make this work."

It was as if Joe had cast hot water on to ice. Angelina's face melted into a smile and the tension evaporated.

"You mean you'll help me?" she asked.

"Of course, I'll help you. What did you think I was going to do?" Joe turned serious again. "It won't be easy. It's going to take a lot to get Nathan and Serena to agree to a date."

"Well, we've got together and we really are from different worlds. At least they're both human."

Joe's heart leapt at Angelina's words. Did she think of them as a couple? He didn't get the opportunity to question her about the comment before she continued speaking and the chance had gone.

"Although I suppose it's doubtful whether Serena is human!"

The door to the sitting room opened, dousing any further conversation.

"Ahh, hard at work on your school project, I see."

Rose gave an enormous wink as she squeezed past the kitchen table and flicked the switch on the kettle. "Can I get anyone another cup of hot chocolate?"

"Not for me thanks, Rose," said Joe. "I'll have to be going soon. I'm putting some extra training in this week."

"Ah, yes. Didn't you say you were a diver? How did you get into that? It's quite an unusual sport."

"I guess it is a bit different. Nick, my coach, is a few years older than me, and when I was young, his family and mine used to go on holiday together. I guess Nick was my hero. He was a diver so I wanted to be one too." Joe shrugged. "It went from there. I started training at the club, then a couple of years ago, Nick started university. He gave up diving, passed his coaching qualifications and took over as my coach."

"Joe's amazing, Rose. It's the Nationals this weekend and if he wins, he could be selected to dive for Great Britain."

Blushing, Joe tried to play down Angelina's boast. "There's no guarantee of being picked for an international competition. If I do well, I might get selected for the squad, but that's all at this stage."

"That's all? That sounds rather exciting, if you ask me, my dear." Rose looked suitably impressed. "And what are these 'nationals'?"

She joined them at the kitchen table, nursing her mug of tea.

"Oh, it's just a big diving competition, where divers from all over the country compete. They're every few months on springboard and

147

highboard but you have to qualify to enter."

"Sounds intriguing. I've never seen real, live diving before. I've watched it on television and it always looks so difficult. I mean how do you do all those twisty and turny things in the air and land without a splash. It must be terrifying."

"It is," said Angelina.

Joe knew that she was remembering about the time she'd jumped into his mind just as he was about to take off for his dive. He shot her a warning look; it would be rather difficult to explain to Rose how Angelina knew that diving was scary.

Angelina recognised her mistake and quickly continued, trying to explain her words.

"I've seen him dive and it looks pretty terrifying to me."

"Are you watching him in the competition?" Rose asked.

"Of course. His mum and dad can't go, so someone needs to cheer for him."

"Well, parents can't be everywhere, but it'll be nice if you're there, Angelina. Mr Garden is away at a convention this weekend so I'm going shopping with my daughter on Saturday afternoon. I'll keep my fingers crossed for you, Joe."

"Thanks, Rose."

The sound of the phone ringing in the sitting room interrupted the conversation.

"Won't be a minute." Rose pushed herself up from the chair and bustled out of the kitchen.

"Stop being so modest about the competition. You know how good you are," said Angelina.

Joe shook his head. "It doesn't matter how good you are if you lose it up here." He tapped the side of his head with his forefinger. "My first ever competition, I remember being so nervous that my knees wouldn't stop shaking when I was standing backwards on the end of the board. It was like an earthquake had struck the board. I almost fell off on my inward dive."

Joe tilted his head to one side and looked at Angelina.

"You know, it's not that different to the stuff that you're doing. It's like a little voice inside your head that tells you what might go wrong." He narrowed his eye. "It couldn't actually *be* one of your lot, could it?"

Angelina gave a sly grin. "Might be."

Joe's eyes opened wide. "Seriously?"

"Of course not. As if we've got the time." She laughed. "People are full of doubts, especially about themselves. Although once we find out what your doubts are, it makes it much easier to Influence you, so I suppose sometimes it might be us."

Joe didn't get the chance to reply as the door to the hallway opened and Rose returned. He had his back to Rose but noticed Angelina's expression change as she glanced up at the old woman.

"Are you okay?" she asked.

Rose fended off Angelina's question with a wave of her arm. "Oh, I'm fine. It's nothing."

"Are you sure? Was it bad news?" Angelina wasn't going to let it go.

"Oh, not really." Rose tried to smile. "I'm being silly. That was my daughter calling."

"Is she okay?" Joe asked.

"Yes, yes, she's fine. It really is nothing." Rose gave a sigh. "She's cancelled our shopping trip on Saturday. Apparently, she and her husband have been invited to some celebration in London. One of her friends is having a surprise birthday party." She shook her head. "Oh, I shouldn't let it bother me. It's just… oh, I don't know. I was so looking forward to seeing her. She's not been around for a few weeks." Rose forced a smile. "Ignore me, I'm just a silly old woman. Now, where were we? You were talking about your diving, Joe."

Since he'd first met her, Joe had always thought of Rose as being invincible. Looking at her now, all he could see was a desperately sad old woman making excuses for her selfish daughter. She reminded him of his own grandma, whom he'd always hated to see upset about anything. He looked towards Angelina for help.

She must have known what he was thinking as she gave him a small nod and stretched her arm across the table towards Rose.

"Rose, I know it's not the same as seeing your daughter, but would you like to come with me to watch Joe dive on Saturday?"

Rose patted her hand. "That's very kind of you, Angelina, but you young ones don't want some old woman hanging around."

Joe backed Angelina up. "Seriously, Rose, we'd love you to come. Like Angelina said, my parents can't make it and I'd ordered two tickets. Angelina's taking one, but there's still one spare."

Rose gave them both a smile. "You're good kids and the fact that you've asked me has made me feel better, but I couldn't possibly accept."

"Rose, please come. You'd be company for me. I don't know any of Joe's diving friends."

"Well…."

Joe could see Rose's resolve starting to waver.

"Please, Rose. We want you to come."

"We wouldn't ask if we didn't mean it," Angelina added.

Faced with this two-pronged attack, Rose crumbled. She looked from one to the other and laughed.

"If you insist, then thank you, I'd be honoured."

"Great! The competition starts at two. I'll call for you at one and we can get the bus into town?" Angelina said.

"As you're being so good to a poor old woman like me, why don't you come by an hour earlier and I'll treat you to lunch on the way? I know this lovely little café that does delicious crusty rolls." Rose beamed.

Later, as Joe walked home with Angelina, he asked: "You didn't mind inviting Rose on Saturday, did you?"

Angelina looked up, as if surprised by the question. "Of course not. She's been good to us and she was so upset about her daughter. Why? You don't mind her coming do you?"

"Me? No. It'll be like having my own supporters for a change, instead of having to borrow Nick's family to cheer for me."

"Carry on like this and you'll have your own fan club!"

"Yeah, lucky me. And it'll be the only fan club in the world made up of Guardian Angels and little old ladies."

Laughing, Angelina linked her arm through his for the walk home. It felt good.

The rest of Joe's week was taken up by school, training and organising his weekend at Nick's house. He couldn't even find time to join Angelina at Rose's house on Wednesday evening.

His parents were planning to leave for Centre Parcs mid-morning on Friday. His dad suggested the change, saying that as Joe was no longer going with them it was silly to wait until after school and they might as well make the most of their weekend away. Joe didn't mind and it was arranged that Friday evening he would go straight to Nick's house from school.

On Thursday night, his dad drove him to the pool for training as Joe was laden with luggage. He had an overnight bag and extra training gear that Nick would be taking home that evening, to save Joe from having to lug it to school the following day.

When they reached the leisure centre, Joe was about to open the car door when his dad stopped him.

"All the best for Saturday, Joe. We might not be there, but we'll be thinking about you. Call and let us know how you go on. Remember, if you do your best, it doesn't matter where you come."

It was the closest his dad had ever come to supporting him in his diving and Joe wasn't sure how to react. Part of him was pleased and grateful for the attention, but a bigger part resented what his dad had said. Joe could tell that it was his mum that had put his dad up to this; the words just didn't ring true, somehow. It also annoyed him that his dad was making out that there was no way they could be at the competition. Had he ever taken the slightest bit of interest in Joe's diving, he would have known which weekend the Nationals were being held and could have booked the holiday for a different week.

It had been his dad's final sentence that had angered Joe most. What did he mean, 'it doesn't matter where you come'? Of course, it mattered. It was the only thing that had mattered since he'd started diving. Obviously, his dad just didn't get it at all.

Not wanting to start another argument, Joe quashed his feelings. Trying to smile, he said: "Thanks, Dad."

It must have satisfied his dad, who was looking equally uncomfortable about this attempt at a father-son talk, as he nodded and smiled.

"Good lad," he said.

Joe stood and watched until his dad had driven off, a swirl of emotions running through his mind. By not thinking about it, Joe had become very good at ignoring what his dad thought about diving. Yet, his father's clumsy attempt to make Joe feel better had made things far worse. It was as if the words had unlocked a part of his mind, allowing hidden feelings to come rushing back to taunt him. Miserably, he recognised how much he longed for his father's approval.

Shocked to feel the hot prickle of tears in his eyes, Joe pulled himself together. I will not let him ruin this for me, he muttered. With a deep breath he held back the tears and dismissed the thoughts, refusing to give them a voice.

He was so well practiced that within seconds he had regained control of his emotions. Hoisting two of the bags on his shoulder and, carrying the third in his hand, he jogged towards the leisure centre entrance.

At seven-thirty on Saturday morning, Joe's phone alarm beeped. Immediately he was wide awake, the nervous excitement of his forthcoming competition crushing any lingering lethargy. Throwing back the thick, feather quilt, he swung his legs out of bed and sank his toes into the soft cream carpet of Nick's parent's spare room.

Like the rest of the Tyler house, the guest room was warm and welcoming. He pulled back the heavy, plum coloured curtains before starting his morning stretches. Joe could do the splits and sit quite comfortably in the pike position - his legs outstretched in front of him and his body bent double, chest resting on his legs.

By the time he'd finished, had showered and dressed in his club tracksuit, he could hear movement downstairs. As he reached the hallway the smell of toast caused his stomach to give a loud growl and he could hear Nick's mum humming along to the radio.

As Joe entered the kitchen, Jill Tyler was stirring something in a pan over the hot plate. She looked up and smiled.

"Morning, Joe. Help yourself to juice and cereal. You know where the glasses are, don't you?"

"Morning, Jill," he said, opening the cupboard and taking out a tumbler. "Smells good. No wonder Nick stayed at home when he went to university."

She chuckled. "He finishes this year but I doubt I'll get him to move out. This, by the way, is my speciality: ham and cheese omelette. Whenever I made it for Nick before a competition he always did well. I'm not superstitious or anything, but I didn't think it would do any harm. Besides, you need a good breakfast. If you're diving at two, I'm guessing that you're not going to want much for lunch."

"Thanks. That would be great."

"Hey, talk about favouritism. There'd better be enough for me, Mum. Morning, Joe. Ready for today, then?"

Hearing Nick's voice, Joe turned and grinned. "Course I am."

Jill swatted at Nick's hand as he stole a slice from the pile of buttered toast waiting on a plate.

"After one of my omelettes he'll be well and truly ready. You'll have to wait for yours, Joe was up first."

"Like I said, favouritism." Still munching his toast, Nick joined Joe at the breakfast table.

"Let's talk about today," he began.

"Oh, Nick. Let the poor boy eat his breakfast first." Jill placed a plate of steaming omelette in front of Joe.

"It's fine, I want to talk about it. This is great, Jill. Thanks."

"Right, as I was saying before we were so rudely interrupted." Nick pretended to give his mother a disapproving look.

"I'd be careful, if I were you." Jill wagged her wooden spoon at Nick. "You'll be getting your own breakfast, at this rate."

Nick blew his mother a kiss and turned back to Joe.

"We'll get down to the pool for half past nine. It's training until eleven but I don't want you tiring. A quick run through is all you need. You know the dives. This morning is just about fine tuning. Remember what I said about that forward three-and-a-half of yours."

For the next half hour, over omelette, tea and toast, the conversation stayed with diving and preparing for the competition. As they talked, Joe could feel the excitement growing. This was what it was all about. Ever since the day he'd first stepped on to a diving board he'd been hooked. It had been the exhilaration when he'd landed safely in the water, and the accompanying adrenaline rush that had done the damage and kept him addicted ever since. To Joe, there was nothing in the world like the euphoria of performing a new dive for the first time – the harder the dives became, the bigger the fear and the greater the rush.

It was also the drive for perfection that kept Joe dedicated to his sport. Each time he stepped onto the board, his elusive endeavour was for the next dive to be better than the last; a desire to achieve that sweet feeling of connecting with the springboard at just the right moment, knowing that the angle of take-off was true and feeling his body disappear vertically into the water through the hole made by his hands.

Competitions were an opportunity to show off his mastery of the sport. Joe loved the challenge of competing. Given only one attempt at each dive, there was no room for error and in competition it was often the mental battle that decided the medals.

The morning training session went well and, at twenty minutes to two, Joe was on the pool side, feeling comfortable and relaxed as he went through a gentle stretching routine to keep his muscles loose. He was facing the spectator balcony, knowing that Angelina would be arriving any moment with Rose in tow. When she finally appeared, his heart leapt and he realised how much he'd been looking forward to seeing her.

Everything was coming together so well. This was the biggest competition of his life so far and Angelina was here to support him. It couldn't be better.

Standing up he waved and saw Angelina smile and return the greeting.

"Whoa, so that's who you've been waiting for. You've done all right there, Joe."

Blushing, Joe whipped round at the sound of Nick's voice behind him.

"What?"

"I've seen you. You've been staring at the balcony or the last fifteen minutes. Are you going to introduce me to your girlfriend?" Nick nudged Joe.

"She's not my girlfriend!"

"Really? Why not? She's come to watch you, so she must be keen. Go say hello and then I want your mind on the competition. Afterwards, you can ask her out before she gets fed up with waiting."

"Nick, it's not like that."

"Well, if you've any sense it should be." Nick gave him a friendly push.

If only you knew the truth, thought Joe as he bounded up the steps to the balcony. It was always hot and humid on the spectator gallery and Rose, who was leaning against the safety barrier, was fanning herself with the competition programme. Angelina was beside her, peering down at the poolside.

"Looking for me?" he asked as he approached.

Angelina whipped her head round at the sound of his voice, giving him a delighted smile that made his heart somersault.

"Hello, Joe," said Rose.

"How was lunch?" he asked.

"Great. You'd like that place. They do all sorts of health foods and smoothies."

"It's all right for some. All I've had is a toasted teacake and banana."

"It's lucky I've brought you a slice of my chocolate cake for afterwards then, isn't it?" Rose reached into her old-lady-sized handbag and brought out a foil-wrapped package that looked extremely generous for one slice of cake.

"It's also by way of an apology. My daughter's trip was cancelled, so I hope you don't mind but she's picking me up in ten minutes to go on that shopping trip we'd planned. I wanted to wish you luck, dear."

"Thanks, Rose. And don't worry, I'm glad your daughter could make it after all."

"What happens now?" Angelina asked.

"I'll finish warming up, then we'll have time for a last-minute bounce on the boards before the competition starts."

"When do you dive?"

"It'll be in the programme. I think I'm up fourth."

Rose was studying the sheet of paper in her hand. "Yes, you're fourth on the list." She lowered her voice. "Go on, then. Who's your biggest rival?"

Joe laughed at Rose's conspiratorial tone. "There are a couple of new names but out of the divers I know Seth Palmer is the only one I've never beaten. He's a year older than me and was selected for the GB Development Squad last month."

"Well, never mind that. I'm sure you'll win this time. I'll have to leave you now but good luck, Joe."

"Thanks, Rose. Enjoy your afternoon."

"Thanks for lunch. I'll let you know how he goes on," said Angelina.

She gave Rose a hug before taking her seat. Joe sat next to her.

"I bet Rose was pleased about the shopping trip," he said.

"She got a call while we were at lunch. You should have seen her face. She really misses her daughter but she'd never say."

Angelina nudged Joe. "I think someone wants you."

Turning to face the pool, Joe saw Nick beckoning to him. Joe raised his hand in acknowledgement.

"It's Nick. I've got to go."

"Best of luck. Dive well," said Angelina.

"Thanks." He stood, then turned back to Angelina and smiled. "I'm glad you're here. It makes a difference."

Back on the poolside, Joe became focussed on the competition. While he stretched, away from the other competitors, Nick gave him a final pep talk.

"I've been watching the others train and there's no one you can't beat. Seth's still good but you've improved beyond recognition these last few months. I saw him watching you this morning and you've got him worried. He knows he'll have to raise his game to beat you today. He's diving sixth, so you've got the advantage over him. You can set the standard that he'll have to follow. You can do this, Joe. Just go out there. Dive like you did in training earlier and this competition is yours."

Ten minutes later, the boards were cleared and the competitor's names announced in dive order.

The pool was calm and, without the underwater pumps agitating the surface, would have looked like glass. For the divers, the pumps were vital, helping them to see the surface and judge their entry.

Joe was standing with Nick in one corner of the pool, going through the motions of his first dive, feeling confident and relaxed. He knew his greatest battle was with himself. It was up to him whether or not he dived well. Once he was on that board he was on his own.

The seven judges – three on one side, four on the other – climbed on to the high chairs that were positioned level with the diving boards.

As the first diver and dive was announced, Joe kept his back towards the pool. Nick didn't allow him to watch other divers during a competition.

"If they do a poor dive, it puts doubt in your mind as to what can go wrong. If they do well, you start thinking that they're better than you. But if you don't watch, there's nothing to worry about," Nick had explained when he'd first started coaching Joe. It was good advice.

After the second diver had completed his first-round dive, Joe made his way to the bottom of the steps leading to the diving platform. As etiquette dictated, he waited until the diver before him had entered the water before leaping up to the platform. Feeling the reassuring prickle of the aquamarine non-slip surface below his feet, Joe used his right foot to adjust the fulcrum wheel into his preferred position and stood waiting, three metres above the surface of the water, for the previous diver's scores to be read out.

"Joe Brennan, forward one-and-a-half somersaults in the piked position."

The announcement was accompanied by a short sharp blast from the referee's whistle, signalling that Joe could start his dive.

Taking a deep breath, Joe pushed his shoulders back and, after a mental run through of his dive, commenced his hurdle step – the walk and jump that would take him to the end of the board.

It was a relatively easy dive to start with and Joe felt good as he soared into the air and completed the dive above the level of the board, leaving him plenty of time to stretch for the entry. As he hit the water, he pulled his arms apart and piked again, rolling over to create a vacuum that would suck any splash down with him and create the perfect 'ripped' entry.

His head broke the surface of the water to the sound of cheering and clapping. "...eight and a half, eight, eight." He caught the announcer reading out the last three judge's marks. With strong over-arm strokes he swam back to the pool side and lifted himself out of the water. A huge grin on his face, he headed straight for Nick who was still whistling and clapping.

"Fantastic dive, Joe. You nailed that one," said Nick.

Joe's good form continued for his next four dives, but he could tell from listening to the judges' scores that Seth was diving equally well. By the time the final round arrived, Joe and Seth were way ahead of the field, with Joe leading by ten points. In the final round, he was performing his new dive; forward three-and-a-half somersaults in the piked position. It was the same as Seth's final dive.

"All you need to do is keep your head with this one. Strong on the board, wait for the take off and pull into that pike." Nick demonstrated the actions that Joe knew so well.

Nodding, Joe set off to take up his position for the final dive. Standing on the board, waiting for the referee's whistle, Joe knew that this was the biggest dive of his career so far.

"You can do this," he muttered.

The whistle blew. He ran through the dive in his mind, breathed in and slowly exhaled. Keeping his head up and eyes on the end of the board, he started walking. One, two, three, wait for the board...

...Joe's mind went blank.

Chapter Twenty

Angelina was surprised to find how nervous she was for Joe. Every time he stepped on the board, she felt a potent mixture of pride and fear that set her heart racing. Part of her wanted to turn away but a stronger desire, to see how Joe performed, kept her eyes fixed on the pool.

Yet, time after time, as he landed in the water with barely a splash, she felt a thrill of relief and happiness that was so strong she virtually jumped out of her seat each time Joe dived, clapping so hard that her hands hurt.

He was doing well. The final round of dives was announced.

When it was Joe's turn to dive, Angelina's hands were clammy and her top was sticking to her back, as much from nervous tension as from the chlorine-drenched heat of the spectator gallery. Her heart thudded louder and louder, seemingly in time with Joe's steps, as he climbed the steps to the platform.

"Come on, Joe, you can do this," she muttered.

The dive was announced and the referee blew his whistle. The pool fell silent in anticipation. Joe was seconds away from a perfect competition and Angelina found herself holding her breath, as if afraid that the slightest disturbance would knock him off balance. But Joe looked completely in control as he moved smoothly along the board.

"That's it, Joe. Another good dive." Angelina's words were little more than an exhalation.

She watched him lift his arms and knee, in a move he called the hurdle step.

"You can do it," she murmured.

He landed, two-footed on the end of the board but instead of flying into the air, his knees buckled under him and his feet seemed to stick to the board, killing the spring and leaving him balancing on the edge.

Angelina heard a collective gasp from the watching spectators and divers and, in surprise, found that she'd joined in, her hands instinctively covering her mouth.

It seemed as if everyone had frozen except for Joe. He raised his hands to his head, as if in total disbelief. Even from the balcony, Angelina could see the look of dismay on his face as he turned and stalked back to his starting point. Head tilted back, as if the reason for his mistake lay in the condensation-soaked windows bordering the high ceiling, Joe continued until he reached the back of the board. He stopped abruptly and turned to face the water, breathing deeply as he composed himself.

Everyone else remained frozen, the only sound coming from the background hum of swimming pool pumps.

What happens now? Angelina's unspoken question was answered as Joe set off again, moving smoothly down the board. She hardly dared to look as Joe completed his hurdle step. For a split second she thought he was going to stop again but this time he exploded from the diving board, quickly folding in two and spinning so fast that his body was a blur. Just in time, he straightened out to enter the water headfirst.

In relief, Angelina jumped to her feet with a cheer.

"You did it. Fantastic, Joe," she breathed.

The announcer's voice interrupted her celebrations.

"Two points will be deducted from each judge for a restart. Six reads four, five-and-a-half reads three-and-a-half, six reads..."

"Oh, no!"

In dismay, Angelina sank back into her seat, realising that the rest of the applause for Joe was muted. By this time Joe had surfaced, but instead of swimming back with his head held high, as in previous rounds, he'd submerged again and swum to the side under the water.

His body language expressed his despair as he climbed out of the pool. Head hung low he collected the little piece of cloth he used to dry himself with and almost ran back to the corner where Nick was waiting. Taking a towel from his bag, he leant his back against the tiled wall and slid to the floor. Resting his elbows against his bent knees, he buried his face in the towel.

159

Angelina saw Nick squat down and put an arm around Joe's shoulder. She could see Nick's mouth moving and whatever he said made Joe raise his head and nod. Nick pointed to the pool and Angelina saw that Seth was about to do his last dive. Like Joe, he was performing a forward three-and-a-half somersaults piked. Unlike Joe, Seth did the dive first time.

"That wasn't as good," Angelina murmured, sensing a glimmer of hope that things might work out for Joe after all.

The judges entered their scores into the electronic consoles. Seth had scored half a point less from each judge than Joe, but without the deduction, he'd scored much higher on the dive in total. Knowing that there was the degree of difficulty to consider, Angelina wasn't sure if Joe had gained enough points to win. That was, until she caught sight of Joe's face.

He was marching over to Seth, who had just climbed out of the pool and was studying the scores. Joe shook Seth's hand and smiled at something Seth said to him. Even with the smile, there was no hiding the look of disappointment on Joe's face. The announcer confirmed the result, Seth had beaten Joe by less than two points.

Angelina watched Joe graciously accept congratulations from the other divers and coaches. But she could tell it was forced.

Joe managed to maintain his act through the medals ceremony but quickly disappeared into the changing rooms afterwards. Angelina returned to the café to wait for him.

She'd finished her drink and was beginning to think she'd missed him when he finally appeared. He slumped into the seat opposite her.

She knew not to congratulate him, even though he'd come second in the entire country for his age group, which was a pretty big deal.

Instead, she asked: "Are you okay?"

"Not really." He slumped back in the chair and looked at the ceiling, his face a blank mask. "I blew it. Plain and simple."

"What happened?"

Joe shrugged as if he didn't have a care in the world. But then he seemed to come back to life. Sitting up he leaned forward and the mask fell from his face revealing the agonising torture he was feeling inside.

"I don't know. I just don't know. I was feeling so good and then as I landed on the board…" his hands mimed the motion, "… my mind went blank! Totally blank."

He looked almost bewildered and so lost that Angelina didn't know what to say.

"It was like I'd never done the dive before. I just didn't know what to do or where to go. There was nothing up here." He was speaking quietly, in a monotone and he tapped the side of his head with his finger for emphasis. "That's never happened to me in competition before. Ever. I blew it. The best chance I've had, and I stuffed it up, big time."

"You don't know that, Joe. You came second, which I know seems like a disaster, now, but even with that dive you only just missed out on first place. The selectors will have to take that into account."

Joe snorted and looked away. "You're right," he said.

His even tone belied the look of bitterness on his face.

"What do mean?" she asked, although she already knew that she wouldn't like the answer.

"I mean that they have taken it into consideration. They've already spoken to Nick about me." He gave a short, ugly burst of laughter.

"And?"

"And do you know what's funny? It turns out that if I'd come second to Seth, I'd be in the squad."

"You did come second, I don't understand."

"It was the restart." He dropped his head and stared at a stain on the plastic table, absentmindedly rubbing it with his finger as he continued talking. "Because I had the restart, they don't think I'm quite ready for the pressure of being in the national squad. Forget that I nearly beat Seth anyway. They think I'm too young and don't want to put more pressure on me at this stage of my diving career. They want to look at me in another few months and see how I do then." He spoke as if reading from a script and Angelina knew that he was repeating the words that the officials had used.

"That's not fair. Oh, I'm sorry Joe."

"They're wrong. It wasn't the pressure. I don't know what made me stop, but I know it wasn't the pressure. I tried explaining that to Nick, but he doesn't seem to mind. He was pleased with how I dived. He agrees with the selectors and says I've plenty of time." He shook his head. "And I can just imagine what my dad will say. 'Good lad, silver medal, well done, Joe'." He mimicked his dad's voice.

"Go easy on him." Angelina was remembering the thoughts she'd heard while in David Brennan's mind. "You can't blame him if he congratulates you on coming second."

Joe had slouched back into his seat, the fight leaving him. "Yeah, whatever."

"Come on, Joe. I know it's disappointing but when you think about it, it's not that bad. They're seriously considering you for the national squad. That's got to be a good thing, hasn't it? Today, you almost won the competition. In a few months' time you can prove to them how big a mistake they've made not picking you today. What's a few months, anyway? It might seem like forever now, but just think how quickly it will pass. You'll be in the British squad before you know it."

Joe stared at her, the mask back on his face. "The next Nationals are at the beginning of March, Angelina. Think about it. That's three weeks after you leave here for good. I'm not sure I want time to go all that fast."

Chapter Twenty-one

Despite Angelina's best efforts to cheer him up, Joe remained down for most of the week. Unbeknown to him, she'd even risked her career with an off-the-record Mind Jump into his dad's head, where she'd persuaded David Brennan that sympathising with Joe, rather than congratulating him, was the best course of action. Although her plan worked, it did little to raise Joe from the depths of despair.

Finally, on Friday morning, the old Joe returned. The clocks had gone back at the weekend and, for the time being at least, the mornings were lighter, despite the blanket of low cloud that seemed to wash all colour from the world. It was still mild, and fallen leaves were crowding together in the gutters, giving the air a damp, autumnal fragrance that Angelina found surprisingly comforting.

Joe was sitting on the wall behind the bus stop and waved as she rounded the corner. He gave her a huge grin as she jumped up on the wall next to him.

"You look happier."

"I've been a nightmare, haven't I? Sorry." Joe flicked his fringe out of his face.

"Yep. So, what's changed?"

"Training was terrible and Nick had a go at me last night."

"That made you smile?"

"He said that I can't change what's done and if I carry on like this, I'm likely to mess up again."

"Good, I'm glad someone's made you see sense. You were the best diver there. You know that."

Joe nodded. "I hate to admit it, but you were right. It's not that long to wait until my next chance. Anyway, how's the assignment going?"

Angelina held up her hand. "Wait, just repeat that bit about me being right, again."

"No chance!"

Grinning, Joe tried to shove her off the wall.

Laughing Angelina resisted and they started tussling. Grabbing Joe's waist and pushing her shoulder into his chest, she somehow managed to unbalance him. Rather than fall, Joe jumped from the wall, keeping hold of Angelina's wrist and pulling her down with him. Still giggling, Angelina found herself falling towards the pavement. Then she felt the world tilt as Joe grabbed her and lifted her back to her feet. Shrieking with laughter, she finally regained her balance and found herself wrapped in his arms. As she looked up, all she could see were his concerned blue eyes, staring down at her. The laughter stopped, dried by an incredible warmth that shot through her. She became conscious of the strength of his arms as he held her and she knew by the intense look on Joe's face that he was experiencing it too.

"Are you okay?" He spoke in barely a whisper but emotion weighted the words.

She nodded, unable to tear her eyes away from his intense stare.

"Kissing at the bus stop now, are we?"

Starting at the shout, Angelina broke out of the embrace.

Serena.

"Don't let me interrupt you." The girl sauntered up to them, chewing gum, a sly smirk on her heavily made-up face. She stopped a couple of paces from them, obviously still wary of getting close to Angelina.

"Serena, I'm glad I've seen you." Smiling, Angelina stepped towards her.

Taken aback by the friendly greeting, Serena curled the corner of her lip in distaste, looking as if she'd just had a whiff of something rotten. "What?"

"I saw the pictures you've been doing in art class and I wanted to tell you, I think they're amazing. You're talented."

As anticipated, Angelina's enthusiastic friendliness caught Serena off guard. She'd obviously expected a confrontation and wasn't prepared for Angelina's praise.

For a moment, Serena was stunned into silence, without the reaction she'd wanted from Angelina, she was lost. The encouraging words had completely thrown her off balance and she didn't know how to respond.

"You don't know what you're talking about. Stay out of my business!"

"I'm serious, Serena. Those pictures are good."

The internal turmoil that Serena was enduring was almost visible and Angelina knew that she'd found the Achilles heel she needed. Watching Serena battle with the mixed feelings caused by being praised for something she actually cared about, made Angelina want to laugh. She maintained her look of genuine interest, until eventually Serena swore at her and stalked off to abuse a group of younger girls, who were waiting by the wall. Angelina turned to Joe with a triumphant grin, the earlier embrace totally eclipsed from her mind.

"What was all that about?" asked Joe.

"That was the first step towards completing my assignment."

"You're going to make friends with her?" Joe's voice was incredulous.

"No, don't worry. I don't intend to go that far. I just need something that will let me connect with her."

"Connect? With her?"

Angelina nodded. "If I'm going to persuade her to do anything, I need to know what drives her."

"I didn't know she was an artist." Joe was watching Serena over Angelina's shoulder.

Turning to follow Joe's gaze, Angelina admitted: "Neither did I until yesterday. I was in Mrs McCauley's art room and one of Serena's pictures had been placed in the middle of a big display. I couldn't believe it; she's got talent."

"I thought the only thing she had a talent for was ruining people's lives."

As they watched, she shoulder-barged one of the smaller girls in the group that she'd been bothering, before slouching away to join her own friends.

"It made me wonder if art was something that she cares about. From that reaction, I'd say it is."

At that moment, a low rumble and grating of gears announced the arrival of the school bus. Standing near the front of the queue, Angelina and Joe found themselves caught up in the daily surge, as the school children jostled forward.

"One at a time." Came the automated response from the bus driver as the doors hissed open.

Crushed once again against Joe, Angelina felt a jolt as the memory of his arms holding her close came rushing back. The thought caused her heart to race and brought a flush of heat to her cheeks. Thankfully, Joe was too tall to see her blushing but the feeling shocked her.

What was she thinking?

This was not supposed to happen. Joe was human. She'd already broken one unbreakable rule by telling him who she was. Now, what was she playing at? Joe is a good friend, a very good friend. For his sake, as well as hers, that is all he is. All he can ever be.

But no matter how much she wanted it to, the memory of that warm fuzzy feeling, when Joe had held her close, refused to disappear.

Chapter Twenty-two

To Angelina's relief, Joe didn't bring up their encounter at the bus stop. After a few days, she'd almost managed to believe that it hadn't really been such a big deal anyway. He'd stopped her from falling, end of story. Anything else was just her overactive imagination.

Only now she couldn't stop her imagination.

It was as if that silly play-fight had smashed open a phial of captured emotions that now refused to be contained. Instead, like fireflies, they'd flutter around inside her heart or pretend to hide until Joe appeared, when they'd soar from her stomach to light up her face.

At night, they'd creep into her mind playing the 'what if' game. Encouraging her to imagine what might be possible if she was human or he wasn't.

She knew that they had to be controlled. If Dee started to suspect anything at all, that would be it. She'd be sent home; banned from any future human contact. No second chance. Ever.

It was only the thought that she'd never even have the chance to say goodbye to Joe that gave her the strength to keep the futile fireflies hidden.

She continued with what was now an act, giving Joe no reason to believe that she thought of him as anything other than her best friend.

Thankfully, Dee had been distracted over the past few days, spending even more time in the garage and hadn't seemed to notice Angelina's turmoil.

It was almost a week before Angelina had the chance to tell Dee about Serena's love of art, but Dee had simply dismissed her with a wave.

"Good. That should keep you busy. I need to get back to work."

The next morning was Friday again and, as usual, Angelina had caught the school bus with Joe. She was telling him about Dee's reaction as they entered the school and was so busy chatting that she knocked into a broom that had been propped up against the wall at the side of the door. She tried without success, to catch it before it fell.

"Sorry about that. Are you okay?" It was the caretaker.

"It just made me jump." Angelina picked up the broom and handed it to him.

"Thanks," he said and, whistling, headed off towards the hall.

Angelina watched him go. "You know, Mr Laker still looks familiar, but I can't think where I've seen him before."

"Mr Laker?" Joe looked surprised. "That's not Mr Laker. I think he must be an assistant or something. Anyway, what are you going to do about Dee, then?"

Angelina sighed. "What can I do? I'll just have to get on with trying to pass this assignment. I'm going to follow Serena home from school tonight and find out what's going on in her head."

Joe frowned.

"I don't think you should do that without Dee knowing. If anyone's mind is filled with evil, it has to be Serena's."

"I didn't think you trusted Dee."

"I trust Serena even less. What if I come with you, just in case?"

Angelina looked amused.

"No offence, but what do you think you could do?"

Joe shrugged. "I don't know. Hit her over the head if you don't appear within half an hour. Give you somewhere safe to jump. Whatever I have to."

He turned to look her in the eye, his face serious. "You know I'd do anything for you."

The meaning was clear and set the fireflies fluttering around Angelina's heart again, but she worked hard to keep the mask in place. To her relief, the bell for morning registration sounded, giving her a few seconds to regain control and consider her reply.

"I promise not to take any risks, anyway you've got training tonight," she said.

"Not until six. I could come with you straight after school."

Angelina shook her head. "Don't you think she might notice if we're both hanging around? That could make it more dangerous for me."

They'd reached the classroom by this time and there were too many people around to continue the conversation.

As they took their seats, Joe whispered: "Okay, go but call me as soon as you're safe."

Angelina saw the concern in his eyes. "I promise."

Later that day, as the school bus pulled up next to Little Ingworth Church, Joe held Angelina back, blocking her way while everyone pushed past down the aisle. Angelina saw Serena force her way down the steps and watched through the window as she linked arms with Carrie and flounced off into the churchyard.

"Let me go. I'm going to lose her." Angelina's voice was low but urgent.

Joe refused to be moved. "You'll catch her."

When the bus was almost empty, he stepped into the aisle and finally allowed Angelina to leave her seat. As she jumped on to the pavement, Joe caught her arm.

Angelina tried to pull away. " I have to go."

Ignoring her, Joe held her tight. "It's almost four o'clock. If I don't hear from you by five, I'm calling Dee."

His eyes were fierce, and Angelina could tell that it wasn't an idle threat.

"You can't. You don't know what might happen."

"I don't care. If you don't call, then it means that you're in trouble and whether Dee's involved or not, it's worth the risk to stop you being disintegrated or Vaporised or whatever you call it."

"Okay, okay. I'll call you by five. Promise. Just don't ring Dee, whatever happens, please."

"Then make sure you call me first."

With that, he stalked off, leaving her standing at the bus stop, staring after him. For a second she just stood there, fuming at Joe for threatening to go to Dee. Didn't he know how dangerous that could be for him and for her? Whether Dee was involved in all this trouble or not, letting on that Joe knew her true identity would cause so much trouble for both of them.

With a sigh of frustration, she turned and hurried into the churchyard, where she'd last seen Serena and Carrie heading. Following the uneven paving towards the church, she scanned the overgrown grave-yard for any sign of the two girls. The path led towards the steps for the main entrance of the church and then branched off to the left and right, presumably encircling the old stone building. Taking the right-hand path, which looked well used, Angelina continued along beside the main body of the church.

Still there was no sign of Serena or Carrie. As Angelina neared the corner, she was beginning to think that she'd lost them and would have to give up. Then she heard voices.

Slowing down, she moved more cautiously, edging towards the corner of the church. She recognised Serena and Carrie's voices but couldn't make out what they were saying or how far away they were. Moving as close to the corner as she dared, Angelina stopped and waited, her back to the wall, trying to decide what to do next. The girls were close, but she had no way of knowing exactly where they were. If she risked a look, there was a chance she'd be spotted, but she had to do something. Without a clear line of sight, she wouldn't be able to make the Mind Jump.

Angelina looked at her watch. Five past four. If she left it any longer, there was a chance she'd miss Joe's deadline.

Why had she agreed to that stupid promise? she thought.

There was nothing else for it. Taking a deep breath to steady herself, she stepped away from the wall and strolled casually around the corner.

Serena and Carrie were facing her, a few metres away, sheltering in a corner where the building jutted out to form a porch for the back entrance to the vestry.

A look of startled fear crossed the girls' faces and Carrie instinctively hid her hand behind her back. Realising who it was, Serena recovered quickly and stared defiantly at Angelina, holding a lit cigarette close to her lips, as if waiting to be challenged.

Carrie swore in relief and brought her cigarette out from behind her back.

"What do you think you're doing?" Serena stepped towards Angelina.

Acting as if she was surprised to see them, Angelina stopped.

"I could ask you two the same thing." She looked at the burning cigarettes and snorted. "I didn't think that even you two would be stupid enough to start that pathetic habit. Then again…"

Serena looked as if she was about to say something, but Carrie beat her to it.

Throwing the glowing stick on the ground and grinding it into the gravel with her boot, she said: "You won't say anything, will you."

"Don't be stupid. She wouldn't dare say anything, if she knows what's good for her." Serena took another threatening step forward.

Standing her ground, Angelina shook her head.

"Don't worry, Carrie. I won't need to say anything. You'll give yourself away."

Fearfully Carrie looked around, as if expecting to see someone else approaching.

"What do you mean?"

"Ignore her. She's only winding you up." Serena breathed in another lungful of smoke and blew a stream of acrid grey soot towards Angelina.

"What I mean, Carrie, is that you stink of smoke and before you know it, you'll be addicted."

Carrie turned her head to her shoulder, furtively sniffing her jacket to check if Angelina was telling the truth.

"Get out of here and leave us alone." Serena raised her voice and started walking towards Angelina.

"Don't worry, I'm going." As Angelina continued past them, through the corner of her eye, she could see Serena glaring.

Carrie said: "I'm going, Serena. I don't think this is a good idea."

"You're not going to let her scare you off?" Serena's attention was back on Carrie and both girls were looking the other way.

With a quick look to make sure there was no one else around, Angelina focused on Serena and jumped. A fiery smell assaulted her senses as she arrived in the darkness of Serena's subconscious.

That figures, after what I've just caught them doing, thought Angelina.

A second later she was looking at the world through Serena's eyes. She was watching Carrie, who was glancing around nervously.

"Where's she gone now?" Carrie asked.

"I don't know. Who cares? As long as she has gone."

Angelina could sense that Serena was becoming frustrated with Carrie.

"You don't think she'll tell anyone, do you?"

"I don't care if she does. Who's she going to tell? The teachers?"

Serena laughed, acting for all the world as if she didn't care. Inside her mind, Angelina could feel Serena's anxiety and realised that deep down, she was as nervous as Carrie.

"I don't know but I'm going home." Carrie pushed away from the wall but then stopped and sniffed the arm of her coat. "Do you think she was right about stinking of smoke?"

"Who cares? Let's just go. I'm getting cold anyway."

Although she'd only intended to listen and watch on this first Mind Jump, Angelina couldn't resist having a bit of fun with Serena.

'When you think about it, smoking's pretty boring really.' Angelina had no idea how Serena would react to this thought, imagining that she'd automatically rebel against it, yet what she heard in Serena's mind, surprised her.

'And it tastes horrible'

'And gives you wrinkles.' Angelina reinforced the idea. *'I'm going to tell Carrie I'm fed up with it.'*

"I've had enough of smoking. I don't think I'll bother any more. Anyway, it's more mature to give up."

Carrie looked at Serena in surprise. "You said it was cool?"

'It's even cooler to give up.' Angelina quickly put the thought in Serena's head.

"That was before I knew it was so boring." Serena yawned to emphasise her point.

By this time, they were back at the bus stop.

"I'm off," said Carrie. "See you tomorrow."

"If I decide to bother with school. Not sure if I will, yet."

Serena gave a lazy wave as Carrie, still looking nervous from the earlier encounter, hurried across the road and headed into the village. Hitching her school bag higher on her shoulder, Serena dug her hands in her coat pockets and set off in the opposite direction.

Even though the evening was becoming colder as the light began to fade, Serena dawdled along the road, seemingly in no rush to get home. Ten minutes later she reached a large house. It was set back from the road and protected by high metal gates. A silver sports car was parked on the driveway. At the sight of it, Angelina felt Serena's anger grow.

'Great, devil woman's back,' thought Serena. Angelina was surprised at

the venom and frustration in Serena's thoughts.

Pushing through the gate, Serena's footsteps crunched on the gravel drive and she kicked the wheel of the car as she walked past. She paused before opening the front door, as if preparing for battle. Once inside, she dumped her bag in the hallway and started up the stairs, her feet making almost no sound on the thick carpet. She was halfway up when a voice stopped her.

"Serena?" It sounded like a woman but as Serena didn't turn around, Angelina couldn't see who it was.

"What now?"

"I thought I'd heard you come in. I've had a call from school."

"And?" Serena still didn't turn around.

"They said you've been skipping classes again."

"They're lying." Serena's voice gave the impression that she was bored, but inside her mind, Angelina could sense the resentment growing.

"Is everything all right, Serena?" The voice was anxious.

"I thought you were dealing with things much better since the last time."

Rolling her eyes and giving a sigh, Serena turned slowly to face the voice and Angelina caught her first glimpse of a pregnant, blonde-haired woman. She looked to be in her thirties and had a concerned frown on her face.

"The head wants to meet with your dad and me."

"What!" The fury in Serena's voice made Angelina jump. "What do you mean, you and Dad?"

"We're just trying to do what's best for you."

"You've no right to be there. You're not my mother." Serena spat the last four words out.

The woman flinched as if the words had been stones, her right hand moving protectively to rest on her bump.

"I'm not trying to be, Serena, but your mother..." The woman stopped abruptly, obviously deciding against saying anything more.

"What, Laura? My mother what?" Serena was shouting by now. "My mother lost everything, that's what. You took Dad and the house away from her and now you're trying to take her place."

"Serena..." The woman, Laura, sounded hurt.

"I hate you!" The words hissed from between Serena's lips as she turned and flew up the stairs, racing across the landing, slamming the bedroom door behind her and throwing herself on the bed.

Angelina felt stunned. She knew Serena was angry at something but what had that woman done to deserve that kind of reaction. From the little Angelina had witnessed, Laura had seemed to care for Serena.

It dawned on Angelina that the scent in Serena's mind had nothing to do with cigarettes. It was from the fiery thoughts; Serena was literally smouldering with anger.

There were no clues from Serena's thoughts, as to why she was so angry. Her mind was still going over the argument and she was obviously worried about her father being summoned to the school. Serena was now lying on her back across her bed and Angelina found herself staring at the bedroom ceiling. Daylight was failing but from Serena's peripheral vision Angelina could tell that the cream walls were almost obliterated by posters of film and music stars. Then, before she could take in anymore, Serena sat up.

'I wish Dad had never married that woman. All she cares about is his money! I hate her!'

Serena fired off the thoughts one by one and Angelina could feel her passion. For a moment, Angelina was afraid that Serena would return downstairs to continue the fight but instead she reached under the bed and pulled out a sketch book and pencil.

Switching on the bedside lamp, she flicked through pages of drawings, until she came to a clean sheet where she started scribbling furiously. For the second time in as many minutes, Angelina was taken aback. Serena's drawings were amazing, but it was the subject of the drawings that Angelina found so intriguing; nearly every page featured the same woman in some guise or another. Although much older than Serena, the woman's features were so similar that it could only have been her mother.

Angelina stayed inside Serena's head, listening to her thoughts. It was only when two beeps sounded, her warning that half an hour had passed, that Angelina realised she had to make a move.

'Was that a car door?' she said in Serena's mind.

'Did I hear something?' Serena questioned the thought that Angelina had planted.

'Maybe it was Dad. If I get to him before Laura, maybe he won't be so cross about school.' Angelina's suggestion was enough to get Serena moving.

Stuffing the sketch pad under her bed she ran quietly down the stairs and carefully twisted the latch to open the front door, peering out into the gloomy evening. It was enough time for Angelina to exit Serena's mind and disappear into the shadows out of sight.

From her hiding place, Angelina could see Serena frown as she looked round one last time before pulling the door closed. Angelina waited a couple of minutes in the darkening driveway before moving.

Unfortunately, the security light turned out to be rather sensitive and she had to make a dash for the street to avoid being caught in its glare. Slipping through the gate she forced herself to slow down and stroll casually along the pavement as if she was supposed to be there. Thankfully, the road was deserted.

Once she was safely out of sight of Serena's house, Angelina checked her watch. It was a quarter to five; fifteen minutes left until Joe's deadline. Pulling out her phone she swiped the screen to bring up Joe's number. The screen lit up for a second, the battery empty icon flashed and the phone died.

"No!" Angelina continued staring at the phone, willing it to light up again, but the screen remained blank. With a groan, she realised she'd forgotten to put it on charge the night before.

She couldn't even ask a stranger to borrow their phone, as she'd never bothered to memorise Joe's number. She had less than fifteen minutes to get home before Joe called Dee, yet she was ten minutes from the church and it was almost another ten-minute walk to Hermit Hill Lane from there.

At least Joe didn't have Dee's mobile number, not that she ever switched it on anyway, so he'd have to call on the house phone. With a bit of luck Dee would be in the garage out of earshot. Just in case, she started running.

It was two minutes to five when she reached the foot of Hermit Hill Lane and by now Angelina was completely out of breath. Gasping for air, she half-walked, half-jogged up the hill.

At one minute past five she pushed open the gate of number four and heard the faint sound of a phone ringing. Sprinting down the driveway, she reached the kitchen door as the ringing stopped.

Chapter Twenty-three

Pushing the door open, Angelina could hear Dee's voice coming from the sitting room. Without hesitating, she rushed into the room.

"Is that for me? I'm expecting a call."

Dee swung round.

"One minute," she said to the person on the other end of the telephone. Covering the mouthpiece with the palm of her hand, she held the phone out to Angelina.

"It would appear that it is."

Dee sounded annoyed and fear shot through Angelina.

Keeping her tone casual as she accepted the phone, she said: "It's probably Joe about the homework."

Dee gave her a funny look. He must have already said something, thought Angelina. But then again, Dee always gave her a funny look. The phone felt like one of the weights from the school gym as she lifted it to her ear.

"Hello." She was convinced that Dee would hear the waver in her voice.

"Angelina, is that you?"

"Yes." She breathed the word with relief. "Rose, how are you?" How come old people never called you on your mobile?

"I hope you don't mind me calling, my dear. It's just that I wondered if you'd be so kind as to collect a loaf of bread with the shopping on Monday? Wholemeal if you don't mind. I forgot to put one on the list and I'm almost out."

"No problem, Rose. I'll make a note straight away. Is there anything else you need?"

"No, no, love. That's it, thanks. It's ever so good of you. I was telling your Aunt how good you've been to me. She should be very proud of you."

Wonderful, thought Angelina, I'm sure Dee's incredibly proud to hear how well I'm mixing with more humans than I need to.

"Thanks, Rose. See you Monday."

"Who is Rose?" Dee stood with her hands on her hips, glaring.

Angelina smiled with relief. Dee might be angry about Rose, but it could all have been so much worse.

"Rose is a lonely old lady who we've been helping by doing her shopping."

"We?" Dee jumped on the word as Angelina realised too late, her mistake.

"Yes, Joe and I." There was nothing else for it but to come clean.

"Joe? Isn't he the one from school who took you to the football? A diver or something?"

"Yes, he's a friend." Angelina tried to brush off the comments, acting as if Dee should already know all this.

"Friend? What do you mean, friend?" Dee folded her arms and narrowed her eyes. "While we're on the matter where have you been tonight?"

Angelina couldn't believe what she was hearing, and her own frustrations came pouring out.

"Tonight, I've been doing exactly what I should be doing, research for my assignment. Serena Jackson? I did tell you about it, not that you ever bother to listen. In fact, I'm not even sure why you're called my mentor. You're not exactly doing much mentoring these days." Angelina gestured wildly in the general direction of the kitchen door. "All you ever do is hide away in that stupid garage. I've been left to do all this alone.

"And Joe. If you want to know who Joe is." Angelina was unable to stop now that she'd started. "Joe is a friend. He's proving to be the perfect cover for me at school. I might not be getting much help from you on my real assignment, but at least Joe's helping me with my computer project at school, so the teachers don't flag me up as a special needs case and start looking into my background. So, if you don't mind, I'm going to catch up with Joe now."

Dee had stayed silent throughout Angelina's tirade and she

remained still, her arms folded, waiting. As Angelina's anger subsided and she became acutely conscious of the silence, broken only by the background hum of the central heating system, the horror of how much trouble she'd landed herself in came sharply into focus.

Dropping her head, she mumbled. "I'm sorry, I shouldn't have said all that."

"No, you shouldn't. But don't worry, your appalling attitude has been noted and will form part of my final report." Dee's matter of fact tone hardened as she continued. "For your reference, as a mentor, I'm here to guide you and offer advice when necessary. What I am not here to do is hold your hand every minute of the day. You are not the only responsibility I have, and you are certainly not the most important one."

Angelina kept her eyes on the floor, not daring to look at Dee.

"Now, I don't suppose helping an old woman with her shopping is a problem, but in future, keep me informed of anyone you regularly see out of school who is not connected with your assignment."

Contrite, Angelina nodded as Dee continued.

"If this Joe is helping then fine, but be careful. While you're on Earth, you're susceptible to human feelings. Make sure they're kept under control. Do I make myself clear?"

"Yes," said Angelina, finally daring to raise her head.

Checking her watch, Dee said: "Dinner will be ready in ten minutes. You can set the table and tonight I want a full, written report on your research from earlier this evening."

Giving Angelina no chance to respond, Dee stalked out of the room. That is so unfair, Angelina thought. Dee's never bothered about reports before. I bet she's doing it on purpose to get back at me. I bet she'll only chuck it in the bin.

The ringing phone interrupted her sulky thoughts.

Joe! She still hadn't called him. Grabbing the receiver, she glanced at the clock, it was almost ten past five, he'd be worried sick by now.

"Hello?"

"Angelina, is that you?"

"Oh, hi, Joe. How's things?" She tried to keep her tone light in case Dee was still listening.

"How's things? How do you think? What happened? Why didn't you ring? Is everything okay? I couldn't get through on your mobile, then the home phone was engaged. I was about to come looking for you."

"Oh, yeah, I'm fine, thanks." It wasn't easy pretending to have a normal conversation when Joe sounded so panic stricken. "Sorry I didn't call earlier, my battery died on me. Drives me mad, that thing." She gave a false laugh.

"What's wrong with you? Don't you know how worried I've been?"

"I know, the homework is a nightmare tonight."

"What? Oh, is Dee there with you?"

At last, thought Angelina. He's finally calmed down enough to work it out.

"I think so, but I'm not sure about that bit of the project. Can you explain it?"

"I guess that means you can't talk properly."

"Yeah, that's it. I see what you mean now." Angelina sounded enthusiastic.

"Well, you listen and I'll ask the questions. Did everything go all right with Serena?"

"Yes, I don't have a problem with that bit."

"Did you find out what you needed to?"

"I might need to work on that section some more."

She heard Joe sigh over the phone.

"This is ridiculous," he said. "At least you're okay. Please, don't ever do that to me again. Next time make sure your phone is charged."

"And I think I'm okay with that part, now you've explained it."

"We can't talk like this. Look, what are you doing tomorrow? The football team is playing in the second round of the cup. I was thinking of going to watch, if want to come with me?"

His voice turned shy, as if he'd realised halfway through the sentence that he was asking her on a date and that she might say no. Had he been able to see the delighted grin that spread across Angelina's face, he wouldn't have been worried.

"The football again? Yes, why not." Angelina successfully kept the excitement out of her voice.

"Great." The relief in his voice was clear. "I'm training in the morning, so I'll call for you about one."

"Okay. See you then, Joe."

It was almost ten o'clock before Angelina finished her report. As predicted, Dee barely glanced at it, but as she'd been given permission to go to the football match with Joe, Angelina didn't even care.

It had just stopped raining when Joe turned up the next day.

Dee had been busy on the computer in the study all morning and didn't bother to respond when Angelina called goodbye. By the time they reached the school playing fields the wind had blown in more rain and Angelina could feel the cold seeping through her thick winter coat. She glanced at the dark seething clouds lurching across the exposed field and hunched her shoulders to keep the wind from blowing the rain down her neck.

"Can't they play indoors?" she asked.

Joe laughed. "If only. Get used to it, this is typical football weather."

By half time Angelina could barely feel her feet and was sure that the rain was seeping into her boots. The only consolation was that the Ingworth High team was four goals to nil up against Millbank High School, thanks to two goals from Mat, one from Nina and an amazing long range shot from Sam, a defender from Year Eleven.

Ten minutes into the second half, two more goals had been added to Ingworth High's total and Angelina couldn't stop shivering.

"You're frozen." Joe put his arm around her shoulders, pulling her into him.

The move seemed the most natural thing in the world and Angelina didn't think to resist. It wasn't the heart-stopping feeling she'd experienced at the bus stop. This was different, more natural, it felt right. Relaxing into his shoulder, she enjoyed the warm feeling it gave her.

Joe looked down at her, a contented look in his eyes.

"Come on," he said. "Let's go. There's no way Millbank are coming back from six goals down."

His arm still around her shoulder, Angelina allowed Joe to guide her away from the football field. They were now walking into the stinging rain and Joe was doing his best to shield her with his body as they battled against the weather, which gave Angelina an excuse to stay close to him. But her head had caught up with her emotions and she was thinking about what might happen next. She wasn't sure how she should react if he tried to kiss her. She should move away from him now to prevent the situation from even arising, but she was shocked to discover that a strong part of her wanted it to happen and so she did nothing.

The rain was coming down harder than ever by the time they reached the road.

Shouting to be heard over the wind, Joe said: "Come on, the leisure centre is near here. We can warm up in the café."

At least there'll be too many people around for him to make a move, she thought, relieved but disappointed.

"Here you go," said Joe as he placed two tall mugs on the table, frothy cream slopping over the sides.

"This looks good," Angelina wrapped her frozen hands around the mug.

She'd chosen a corner table where no one could overhear their conversation. As the warm, sweet drink gradually thawed her from the inside out, Angelina told him the full story of the previous evening at Serena's house.

"She only arrived in the area a few years ago. I think her dad owns a design company. They do adverts or something for big companies," said Joe.

"When she first started at our school, she used to threaten the other kids that her dad was rich and would have them arrested if they ever told on her. I know it scared some of them."

"Do you know anything about her mum? She hates this Laura, who must be her stepmum; she was wearing a wedding ring. I think whatever's causing Serena's attitude has to do with her mum. That sketch book was full of pictures. I'm sure they were of her mother."

"I've never heard her mention her mum, not that I've ever taken much notice of Serena." He looked at his watch. "Oh no, we've been here for over an hour already. We're going to have to go, I'm babysitting the twins this evening."

Angelina groaned. "Just when I was starting to feel my feet again."

On the bus back to Little Ingworth, Joe rested his arm around Angelina's shoulder as they chatted easily about Serena and the football match. For the twenty-minute journey home, Angelina couldn't think of anywhere in the universe that she'd rather be.

Joe had to dash as soon as they stepped off the bus and Angelina walked slowly home in the rain allowing herself the luxury of thinking about the afternoon. About Joe's arm around her. About how right it had all felt. Even though she knew that it was all wrong.

She was hanging up her dripping coat and still thinking about Joe when Dee marched into the kitchen, glasses perched on top of her red curls and a calf-length green cardigan flapping behind her.

"I thought it was you. I have to go away tomorrow."

"Pardon?" Angelina turned to look at Dee, confused by the unexpected announcement.

"An emergency in the Middle East." Dee walked over to the sink and started drying plates that had been left to drain, something that she never usually bothered with.

"Bit of a situation that needs sorting out and they need my help."

"What kind of a situation? How long will you be away?" Angelina was balancing on one foot, while tugging her wet boot from the other.

Dee busied herself putting the plates away. "It's classified, but all being well I should be back by Wednesday. You'll have to miss a couple of days of school."

Angelina had swapped legs, but as Dee's last comment registered, she looked up and lost her balance, falling against the kitchen wall.

"What do you mean? Why do I have to miss school? I can't miss school, we're in the middle of a project."

Dee whipped her head up, peering suspiciously at Angelina. "I thought you hated school. Are you sure you're handling this Jim situation properly, or is there something I should know?"

Horrified, Angelina felt a flush creep up her face. She pushed away from the wall and bent down, to pull off the remaining boot, hoping that Dee hadn't noticed.

"He's called Joe and I'm handling it fine. I told you, he's a useful friend. That's nothing to do with this."

The blushing under control, Angelina lined up her boots by the door and turned back to Dee.

"I've got to do a computer presentation with Joe tomorrow and he'll be marked down if I'm not there. Besides, I'm finally getting somewhere with Serena and I was planning to follow up on all that stuff I found out about her. It'll go to waste if I have to come with you."

"You're not coming with me. I told you it's classified."

Angelina opened her mouth to speak, stopped, frowned and started again. "What's the problem then? I can stay here."

"You can't stay by yourself." Dee had picked up the dishcloth and was now vigorously cleaning the worktop surfaces, which Angelina had never seen her do before.

"Why not?"

"Because you're a fourteen-year-old girl and too young to be home alone overnight in this country. All it takes is for someone to call social services and they'll have you taken into care, which would cause all kinds of problems."

"That wouldn't happen." Angelina didn't sound convinced. It was a small village and she'd discovered that gossip was rife.

"Wrong, it could happen. I'm going to arrange for you to stay with one of our operatives in London while I'm away. It won't be a problem and you may as well do some sightseeing while you're there."

I don't want to do any sightseeing, thought Angelina. She might have a soft spot for Little Ingworth but had no desire to explore the rest of this world. Her face brightened as she thought of a way out.

"What if I stayed with Rose? You know, the woman you spoke to on the phone yesterday. I'm sure she'd enjoy the company and I wouldn't need to bother her much. I'd only have to be there to sleep. I could keep an eye on things around here too."

Frowning, Dee paused her scrubbing. Seizing upon the hesitation, Angelina tried to strengthen her argument.

"We could ask her. It would save you bothering another GA. Like you say, they're overstretched and I'll probably be in their way. If you haven't even arranged it yet, what does it matter?"

Dee looked up. "I don't even know who this Rose person is."

"She's an old woman who's retired to Little Ingworth. Her daughter avoids visiting and her husband is never around. Rose is lonely and I'll probably be welcome company for a few days."

"It would make things easier…"

"If you're leaving tomorrow don't you have enough to do without sorting out a babysitter for me?"

"…but I haven't even met her. I can't let you stay with someone I've never met. It's not good practice."

"Who's going to know, Dee? I'm not going to tell anyone, and Rose certainly won't. It might not be the done thing but there's nothing in the rule book to say you can't stay with humans, is there?"

"No, but…"

Angelina could see that Dee was wavering. "I'll be staying with a friendly old woman for a few days. Where's the harm in that?"

Dee sighed. "Well, I should be back by Tuesday evening, so I suppose you could be trusted not to do anything stupid for a couple of nights. I am expecting a delivery on Monday, it would be better if there was someone here to take in for me."

"I could do that. I'll come straight home after school and do that before going to Rose's house."

Frowning Dee said: "All right. Because it's an emergency and because I have very little time to sort anything else out, I'll let you stay with Rose. If it's okay with her. Any hesitation and you're going to London. And I want to speak with her."

Grinning, Angelina nodded. "No problem, but I'm sure she'll say yes. Shall I call her now?"

Five minutes later and it was all arranged. Rose had sounded delighted at Angelina's request and even Dee appeared happy - or as happy as she ever appeared - with the final arrangements.

Angelina could hardly wait until the next day. Almost three full days without Dee, she thought. Wait until Joe hears this.

Chapter Twenty-four

"What time is this parcel arriving?" Joe asked Angelina as they trudged up Hermit Hill Lane after school on Monday.

The weekend's rain had finally stopped but the clouds and wind had remained, and in the failing light shadows of bare branches brushed the road in front of them.

"I'm hoping it's already there, although delivery can be any time before six."

"I've got to leave at quarter to five. I hope it's arrived by then."

"Joe, I'll be fine." Angelina's laugh materialised as little puffs of cloud in the cold November air.

"I know, but it's almost dark now and it'll be pitch black out here by six."

"And nothing can happen to me, remember?"

He knew that what she said was true, but he couldn't help feeling protective towards her.

"Yeah, well. You never know who or what's about."

Not for the first time, Joe felt a confusing mix of emotions. He knew that he'd fallen head over heels in love with Angelina. That wasn't in doubt. But he was clueless as to what he could or should do about it. Once again he replayed the scene after the football match in his mind, remembering how amazing it had felt when he'd pulled her close and she'd stayed there, happy to let him hold her as they'd hurried through the rain like any normal couple. Yet, they were anything but, and he hadn't dared to take things further for fear of losing the precious little contact with her that he had.

As they turned into Dee's driveway, Angelina had obviously picked up on how worried he was.

"The package is probably already here and we can go straight back together," she said.

"You're probably right." Joe tried to brush off his earlier worries.

With its darkened windows, the cottage looked as if it were gently sleeping, but then Joe caught sight of the oversized garage. In the shadowy half-light, its doors appeared like the bared teeth of a giant monster lying in wait. He shivered involuntarily and quickly put the image out of his mind.

"It will be round the back out of sight, if they've already been."

Angelina left him at the cottage door while she checked on the agreed hiding place.

"Doesn't look as if they've been yet. We might as well wait inside."

"It's colder in here than it was outside," said Joe, as Angelina unlocked the door and led him into the kitchen.

"Dee must have turned the heating off. At least we know she's gone. Let's hope this delivery arrives before we freeze. Shall I put the TV on?"

Joe shook his head as an idea came to him. "If Dee really isn't here, there is something I wouldn't mind doing."

Angelina frowned, looking wary. "What?" she asked.

Joe grinned. "Could you show me your computer? I want to see this Versalnet that you were talking about."

"Versalnet? What do you want to see that for?" She seemed surprised at the request.

"Are you kidding? You're talking about a universal internet and email system and I could be the first human to see it. That's unreal."

"It's not that interesting, you know. It's just the same as your email."

"Believe me, it'll be interesting."

Angelina shrugged. "Whatever."

He followed her upstairs and stood staring at the outdated posters on her wall as she booted up the laptop. Suddenly, he became very aware that he was in Angelina's bedroom and they were all alone.

"What's with the posters?" He asked the question more to fill the silence than to find out why she had Madonna as a pin-up.

Busy tapping away on the computer keys, Angelina didn't even look up as she answered. "They were here when I arrived. I haven't got anything to replace them with so I thought they might as well stay. There you go."

Joe watched as the screen dissolved before his eyes and reappeared with the thick white 'V' slowly rotating in its purple sphere. Intrigued, he sank into the chair she offered him.

"Woah. How does it work?"

"How do you think? You use the mouse, double click on the 'V' and it opens – like your internet. I thought you knew something about computers?"

"Ha, ha," he said, following her instructions. "It needs a password."

Leaning over his shoulder, Angelina typed in her password and the screen automatically loaded up her Umail account.

"Wow, this is amazing." Although it was laid out like a standard email inbox, the senders' domain names were unlike anything he'd ever seen.

Wide-eyed, he looked up at Angelina. "Would it be okay to look through some of these? Could I check out the code?"

Angelina shrugged. "Look at what you like, as long as you don't make any changes or send any Umails."

"Don't worry, I won't leave a trace. Promise."

"If you're doing that, I might as well start my homework. I've a ton of biology to do."

Joe scrolled through Angelina's emails, examining the operating system. Although there were some structural similarities, the code was very different from any he'd seen before. For twenty minutes, he was oblivious to anything other than the figures and symbols on screen. Then something caught his attention.

That can't be right, he thought.

Frowning he checked it again, and then three more times, each time coming to the same conclusion. If he was right…

He turned to where Angelina, still in her coat, was sprawled on the bed drawing a diagram of the human digestive system.

"You need to see this."

She looked up. "See what?"

Joe didn't need to say anything; the look on his face was enough to make her move.

"What's wrong?" Angelina pulled up a chair and sat beside him.

"This isn't right." He turned back to the Umail inbox on screen. "I was looking at your assignment message, the one that Dee forwarded through to you from the FFU."

He highlighted the Umail he was talking about and Angelina nodded. Opening it, he continued: "It gives all the details of your assignment, including the status level, which it says here is a level-two." He turned to Angelina again to make sure she was still following his explanation.

"Yeah, so what?"

"I looked through the history, to see where it had originated and saw this." Scrolling down the page, he came to the anomaly that had caught his eye. "Can you see? It looks like something's been deleted."

Angelina bent forward, concentrating on the screen. "There's a bit of space and a few extra straight lines, but that's all I can see."

"That's what caught my eye. It's different, but there didn't seem to be any reason for it to be different, so I played around a bit to see if I could find out what was going on. Now, from what I can see, your Umail system has a kind of in-built history file that records any changes made in the messages. It's a sophisticated system, but that's where I found this." Joe clicked on the history button and waited for Angelina's reaction.

"I don't understand."

"Your assignment has been changed." Joe's voice was almost a whisper as he pointed at the words on the screen. "This has been deleted" -he moved his finger down to the next line- "and this has been added."

He watched Angelina as she registered the meaning of the words on screen.

She shook her head. "That can't be right."

"I've checked it four times and the only thing that makes sense is that the Umail you received about your assignment has been changed."

The colour had drained from Angelina's face and her voice shook when she spoke. "You mean that I've been given a level-eleven Fate Switch for my assignment?"

"All I know is that according to the history, this Umail was changed from a level-eleven to a level-two." Joe pointed to the words on screen. "And it's been changed from 'High Priority' to 'Trainee Assignment'. Your assignment number has been added as well, probably to make it look real. I checked it against the first Umail you received to make sure; it's definitely your number."

"What's this bit about formatting?" She pointed to a line underneath the section that Joe had indicated.

"I'm not sure, but whoever did this probably had to make the typeface match the rest of the message. The only thing that makes sense is that someone has changed this deliberately to set you up."

"But why? You need to be really experienced to even attempt such a difficult Fate Switch." Angelina was still staring at the screen in disbelief.

"I think someone wants you to fail your assignment."

Angelina whipped around to face Joe. "Fail? Why? Who would care so much if I passed or failed? I'm only a trainee. I'm not important. Who would go to so much trouble?"

Joe bit his bottom lip, deliberating whether to tell Angelina what he feared most. To avoid Angelina's stare, he turned back to the screen.

"The changes were made after the email left the FFU but before it came to your machine. According to the history, there's only one person who's received the message in between..."

"Dee." Angelina finished the sentence for him.

"No one else has had access. It must have been Dee."

"I don't understand. If I fail this assignment, she's stuck with me until another one comes through. It could be months. If she's doing this to me, why does she want to have me around for even longer?"

Joe had had the same thought when he'd first seen the changes.

"I think it's all linked to the garage. Whatever she's doing in there, it's against your rules. You've said as much yourself. I think that she's worried you'll say something about it when you go back. But if you fail your assignment, you'll lose all credibility, everyone will assume that you're trying to get back at Dee. Either that or she wants to stop you from saying anything until she's finished whatever she's doing around here."

"Or both! I lose credibility and she has chance to finish up, so there's no evidence anyway."

At that moment, Angelina looked very small and vulnerable, as if the weight of this new knowledge had caused her to shrink into herself. Seeing her like this, Joe didn't want to tell her his greatest fear, but knew that he had to. She needed to know so that she could be prepared.

"There could be another reason."

"Like what." She shrugged as if she hadn't a care in the world. "You might as well tell me; it can't get any worse."

Yes, it can, thought Joe. "I'm scared that Dee's buying time, so that she has more time to get rid of you."

"Get rid of me? I don't understand."

"The accident with Matt," Joe explained. "Maybe it wasn't an accident after all."

"That's ridiculous." Angelina shook her head.

"Is it?"

"Of course, it is." But she sounded less convinced.

"I hope you're right." Joe bit his bottom lip. "Be careful, that's all I'm saying."

A banging on the door downstairs caused them both to jump. Looking at Angelina, Joe's first thought was that Dee had returned early, but Angelina had realised what was going on.

"It's the delivery. I'll see to it, while you close this down. Don't leave any trace that we've looked at it. I don't want Dee, or whoever has done this, to know that we're on to them."

Chapter Twenty-five

Too stunned to speak, Angelina barely said a word as Joe accompanied her back to Rose Cottage.

At the gate, Joe caught her arm as she turned to go.

"I'll help you get through this, I promise," he said. "Be careful when Dee's around. Don't let her suspect that you know anything."

Unable even to form a smile, she nodded. She knew that Joe would only stay longer and worry more if she didn't agree, and she couldn't take that tonight. Not even from him. She needed some time alone to think things through.

Arriving at Rose Cottage, the door opened almost as soon as Angelina rapped on the oak frame and Rose's round silhouette appeared, black against the warm light from the hallway.

"Come in, come in. I've told you already, there's no need to knock. Not when you're staying here."

"It's habit, I guess."

Angelina tried to act normal but even the cosy cottage couldn't thaw the cold numbness she felt inside. Rose bustled back down the hallway towards the kitchen.

"Dinner's on. It's just you and me again tonight. Mr Garden called to say he wouldn't be back from the club until after eight," she called over her shoulder.

Surprise, surprise, thought Angelina. The previous evening, it had been ten o'clock, before Mr Garden had returned from his club. Angelina had already been in bed, reading, when she'd heard the door open and the sound of voices downstairs. In the morning, he still hadn't surfaced by the time Angelina had had to leave for school, so she had yet to meet Rose's absent husband.

This evening she had more things to worry about and was quite relieved that she wouldn't have to make small talk with a stranger.

"Can I help?"

Angelina had followed Rose into the kitchen and was watching as she struggled onto one knee, awkwardly bending her bulky body low enough to reach into the oven.

"You can set the table, if you would, dear." Rose was panting as she heaved herself into a standing position once again, balancing a steaming pie in her oven-gloved hands. "Hope you're hungry. I've some roast potatoes to go with this."

"Sounds great."

Angelina tried to sound enthusiastic even though her stomach was in knots and the last thing she felt like doing was eating. As usual, Rose gave her a huge helping.

"You could do with a few good meals inside you, my girl. You're nothing but skin and bone."

Having managed to swallow a few mouthfuls of food, she pushed the rest around her plate.

"Are you okay, dear?" Rose had obviously noticed that something was wrong. "You've not had an argument with that boyfriend of yours, have you?"

"Joe's not my boyfriend, Rose."

"So you keep telling me."

"Joe's fine."

For a split second, she considered telling Rose everything. Explaining how Dee was supposed to be there to help her, but instead she'd betrayed her, had set her up to fail or was planning something even worse. But she knew she couldn't. It was bad enough Joe knowing. Instead she said: "I'm a bit worried about school. I've so much homework tonight and we've an important test in biology tomorrow."

Rose frowned. "They put too much pressure on youngsters these days. All this worry about exams, it's not good for you."

"It's not too bad. I just don't like failing anything." At least that bit was true.

After she'd helped Rose clear away the meal, Angelina excused herself, saying that she had to study. "I'll probably go straight to bed afterwards, if that's okay."

"That's fine, love. Don't stay up too late studying or you'll be neither use nor ornament to anyone tomorrow."

Not quite sure what Rose meant, Angelina nodded and disappeared to her room. Rose Cottage had two bedrooms and Angelina was sleeping in the smaller box room that overlooked the back garden.

She sank down on the thick flowery eiderdown that covered the single bed, leaned over to the bedside cabinet and reached under the pink tasselled lampshade to switch on the brass table lamp. Falling back on to the bed, she lay there, curled in a foetal position while the words from the computer screen swam through her mind.

Dee was a legend in the FFU. Could she really be behind everything that had happened? She'd written almost every text on Fate Switches that existed. She'd been the first female GA to join the Inner Union of the FFU. She'd almost been elected President; that was when they'd started calling her the Great Dee Devin.

Angelina's vision blurred with tears. The day of the election was the day her grandfather had disappeared. They'd just announced that Dee had lost to Ven Goodfort, when she'd been told the news.

Tears rolled down her cheeks, soaking into the white pillowcase as Angelina cried silently. Finally, her sobs subsided and she sat up, rubbing the tears from her eyes and face.

"Whatever's going on, I will not fail this assignment," she whispered.

She pulled her schoolbooks from her bag in case Rose came up to offer her supper, as she had the night before, and started jotting notes in the back of her biology exercise book.

The incident with Matt could have been an accident, she reasoned. Dee had certainly acted with what appeared to be genuine concern at the time. But the stuff in the garage and the altered Umail – that didn't add up.

What could Dee be up to? And why? Could this be some twisted form of revenge against the FFU because she'd lost the election? Was Dee so bitter, even after all these years?

"Evidence. I need to find something that will make sense of all this," muttered Angelina.

The most likely place to find anything useful would be the garage, but that was locked and Dee had taken all the keys with her, Angelina had already checked. There might be evidence somewhere else; a place she could get into: Dee's bedroom. Dee had insisted that Angelina should stay out of the front bedroom. Perhaps there was a good reason. It was a long shot, she knew, but it was worth a try.

Just deciding to do something made Angelina feel better and she even joined Rose for supper at half past eight. Mr Garden was still out, and Angelina felt incredibly sorry for Rose, who made yet more excuses for his behaviour. It was after ten and Angelina was dozing in bed when the sound of the front door opening disturbed her. A man's low, muffled voice could be heard through the floorboards.

He doesn't deserve you, Rose, thought Angelina as she drifted off to sleep.

The alarm woke Angelina at six in the morning. She was hoping to slip out of the house without anyone knowing, but she found Rose drinking tea in the kitchen.

"You're up early, my dear."

"I've left a textbook at home and I'll be in real trouble if I don't have it for school."

"Well, you've time for a spot of breakfast before you dash off."

It was easier to accept than stand arguing with Rose, so it was almost seven o'clock before Angelina managed to escape. Dee was due home today, but Angelina had no idea what time she might arrive. With it being an official mission, Dee had travelled by Instantaneous Translocation: the method of moving instantly from one place to another that Angelina had used to arrive on Earth. It meant that there would be no warning as to when Dee might reappear in her cottage. For all Angelina knew, Dee might already be back.

Thankfully, everything looked exactly as it had the evening before; the package was still on the kitchen table where she'd left it, and the cottage was still icy.

To make sure, Angelina went from room to room, calling Dee's name. Finally satisfied that she was alone, she crept up the stairs, half-expecting Dee to appear. Her heart beat faster as she approached Dee's bedroom door. Carefully, she wrapped her hand around the cold metal handle and eased it down. For a second, she wondered if the door would be locked, but it opened easily, creaking as it swung away from her.

It was the first time that Angelina had even glimpsed inside Dee's room and she couldn't help but feel that the African-style décor matched Dee's colourful dress sense. The room smelled faintly of cinnamon, probably from the fat, church candles that stood on the two bedside tables either side of the large double bed, which dominated the room. Covering the bed, a beautifully embroidered throw, in rich browns and dark reds, blended in with the glowing colours of a large oil painting featuring an African savannah scene that hung behind the bed and fascinated Angelina.

Remembering the task in hand, she tore her eyes from the picture and glanced around the room. Apart from the candles, the bedside table held nothing but a lamp and an open book, which was resting face down, its spine bent and the pages splayed to indicate Dee's place.

That's a strange choice of book, she thought reading the title, *'Cultivating Profit'*.

She turned her attention to the built-in wardrobes at the other side of the bed. She gave a start as the floorboards creaked under the thick, purple carpet when she skirted the bottom of the bed. Opening the first wardrobe yielded nothing but a rack of blouses, skirts, trousers and dresses, their garish, mismatched colours fighting for attention. They reminded her too much of Dee and with a shudder, she quickly shut them away again. The second wardrobe door refused to budge when she tugged on the handle. She tried again, pulling harder, but then noticed a small keyhole peering at her with its single black eye.

Locked and Dee probably has the key with her. I'm wasting my time. What did I think I'd find? A letter confessing everything? A printout of the original Umail? I don't even know what I'm looking for.

Stop it! Think positively. That's what Joe would say.

She scanned the room again. The only place she hadn't looked was Dee's dressing table, which gawped at her from beneath the window. Its spindly white legs looked barely strong enough to hold the mirror, pots and potions resting on its top. Two slim drawers were fixed into the front of the dressing table, each with a central keyhole that watched her with an unblinking stare.

"It's worth a try," she muttered, striding with renewed purpose across the creaking floor.

Both drawers were locked.

Frustrated, she dropped on to the dressing table stool, gazing blankly, at her reflection in the mirror. Without keys there wasn't much more that she could do here. She was about to give up and leave when something in the mirror caught her eye. A shallow, hand-painted clay dish on the tabletop held a jumble of small objects: earrings mixed with nail scissors, brooches and a small, dull, bronze-coloured key.

Carefully she picked up the key, half expecting it to disappear. About four centimetres long, it had an old-fashioned circular loop at the end and looked the right size to fit the wardrobe.

Although Angelina knew that Dee was hardly likely to lock something important away and then leave the key out for anyone to find, she couldn't help hoping that she might find something that would give her a clue as to what was going on. Avoiding the creaking floorboard, she crossed quickly over to the wardrobe.

It was no good. The key didn't even fit, let alone open the wardrobe. It was too small and rattled around in the lock.

It must fit one of the dressing table drawers, she thought. But if Dee hadn't bothered to hide the key, it was unlikely that there would be anything important in them.

With nothing else to do, Angelina tried the key anyway. At least it fits, she thought as it slipped easily into the keyhole of the right-hand drawer.

She eased the key in an anticlockwise direction. It didn't move. She tried the left-hand drawer with the same result. Increasing the pressure, she tried forcing the key to turn. It had to be for one of the drawers! In a fit of frustration, she jiggled the key, trying to loosen the lock. It was then that she felt something yield. Twisting the key again she realised that she'd been turning the key the wrong way. With a twist of her wrist in a clockwise direction, the lock clicked open. Slowly, as if frightened of disturbing something, she eased the drawer open. There was no need to worry. Like Dee's study the drawer was a mess and filled with jewellery, pens, clips and other bits of junk, but nothing important.

Locking the drawer, Angelina tried the key in the second lock, this time turning it clockwise. Like its twin, the right-hand drawer clicked open on the first attempt but this one held bundles of papers. Letters! This looks more promising. Leafing through the papers she came across a credit card-sized driving licence that featured a black and white picture of a startled-looking Dee, who seemed to be staring straight at Angelina. With a shiver, she replaced the licence.

The remaining letters appeared to be bills that, surprisingly, Dee had organised in date order. Six months of electricity bills were followed by six months of gas statements and the yearly council tax notice. She ought to go paperless, Angelina thought. Flicking through the documents, she came across a bank statement stuck to the back of last month's telephone bill, which she carefully peeled away.

Before studying the bank statement, Angelina flicked through the remaining letters but there was nothing of interest, just more utility bills. She returned to the bank statement and gasped.

She double-checked the account name: Dee Devin, 4 Hermit Hill Lane. It was Dee's all right. But the balance; the account held three-hundred-and-thirty-nine thousand pounds.

Angelina stared at the piece of paper in her hand, until the black printed figures began to dance around the page, almost as if they were mocking her. There was no way that Dee could legitimately have that amount of money. Living expenses were covered by the FFU, but that was all, there was no way that Dee could save up that amount of money.

This was nothing to do with revenge, she thought in disgust. It's greed. For the second time in as many days, Angelina felt numb. There could be no doubt now. Whatever it was that Dee was up to, it was all about money.

Chapter Twenty-six

When Angelina told Joe about the bank statement, she had never seen him so angry, especially with her.

They were seated across from each other in the school canteen. Having been there a while, they had the table to themselves. Joe had finished his meal and was sipping on a banana smoothie, while Angelina played about with a baked potato that she'd barely touched.

When she admitted to going back to Hermit Hill Lane alone, Joe almost knocked his drink over.

"Why did you do something so stupid? Dee could have arrived home at any time. If she'd caught you, who knows what she'd have done."

Riled by Joe's reaction and because she didn't want to admit that he had a point, she snapped back.

"I need to know what's going on. Hiding out at Rose's won't get me anywhere."

"Why didn't you tell me what you were doing? I could have come with you. I could have helped."

Joe had immediately calmed down, but everything became too much for Angelina and she wasn't ready to back down.

"How could you have helped?" she challenged. "If I'm so stupid, it would have been even more stupid for you to come along."

She caught her breath, knowing that she was about to cry, but for some reason she didn't want Joe to see her. Pushing her food away, she scraped back her chair and fled from the canteen and out into the school grounds.

As the cold, bright air hit her face, her mind cleared. Fear dried the tears before they reached her eyes as she saw, with acute clarity, the real danger.

Joe.

What if he had been with her this morning and Dee had caught them? Dee was incredibly powerful. Angelina used to think that it was always used for good. Now she didn't know what Dee was capable of. By trying to save herself, Angelina realised that she was putting Joe in danger. She slowed and came to a halt by the edge of the playing fields realising what she had to do. Frantically she searched her mind for alternatives, but there were none that would keep Joe safe. He had to stay out of her life. Otherwise… she stared across the fields barely daring to admit the truth to herself… otherwise Dee could kill him.

"Angelina, wait!"

She turned to see that Joe had caught up with her.

"I'm sorry, I shouldn't have said all that. I was worried. I've been thinking," he continued in a rush. "What if we send a Umail when Dee's not around? I could delete all the evidence, so she'd only know about it if she checked the history and I bet she doesn't do that every day. I'm sure there'd be enough time for them to send help."

As Angelina stared at the determined expression in Joe's eager eyes, she knew that he'd never let her face things alone. He cared more about her than he did about himself. There was only one thing that would make him stay away. She had to make him stop loving her. For Joe's sake, she had to end their friendship. Now.

The weight of this realisation turned her heart to stone. She had to be totally emotionless or Joe wouldn't believe her. It took all her will power to look him in the eye and speak in a normal voice.

"What do you mean, 'we'? There is no 'we'. This is about me. You shouldn't even know who I am. You're not part of this."

"What?"

Joe looked stunned, as if she'd slapped him across the face, and Angelina almost caved in immediately. But the knowledge that this was the only way to keep him safe, kept her going.

"You heard. It's nothing to do with you." She twisted her face into a sneering smile as if she'd just made some connection in her mind. "That's it, isn't it? You think it's all about you, don't you? You're as bad as the rest of them, living in this little bubble of a world and thinking that you're all the centre of the universe. You humans think you're all so superior to any other living thing and yet you haven't got a clue. Any of you. You're nothing in the grand scheme of things." She spread her arms to emphasise her point.

"Look you're upset. I'm not surprised, but we can get through this. I promise, I won't let you down."

The concern in his eyes almost crippled her and for the first time she truly understood why the GA golden rule was never to get personally involved with the locals. It could only end in pain.

Knowing that she couldn't keep the charade going much longer, she had to finish it now. There was no going back. She had to hurt him so much that he'd leave her alone for ever.

"Joe, what do you think is going on here? I mean between you and me." She spoke to him as if he were a child, a condescending smile on her face. "You've been useful a few times. I mean, you did help me out with Matt, and you've taught me about school and everyone here, which was helpful. But what did you think would happen? That we'd be girlfriend and boyfriend, save the world and live happily ever after?"

She gave a harsh laugh, trying desperately to ignore the bewildered look on Joe's face as she twisted the knife. She continued in a chillingly pleasant tone. "You've liked playing GA Joe, haven't you? Well, all good things come to an end. I'll admit, it was fun while it lasted, but let's face it, we both know it was only for show."

"Why are you doing this? Has Dee got to you?"

Angelina rolled her eyes and sighed. "No one has got to me, Joe. I'm saying what we both know. It has to end sometime, so why not now? And, to be honest, your knight in shining armour routine is getting a bit boring." She shrugged. "Sorry, it's how I feel. How about we shake on it and leave as friends?"

She held out her hand. Joe looked down at her outstretched arm in disbelief. He raised his head and his blue eyes burned into Angelina's as she fought to keep her mask in place. His voice was taut with anger when he spoke.

"You're not Angelina." He turned and stalked back towards the school.

"I take it that's a no? See you around, Joe." She called after him. The final twist of the knife.

Keeping the fake smile on her face, she watched him go. Part of her desperately wanted him to turn around and come back so she could tell him that she didn't mean a word of what she'd said. But the stronger part of her loved him too much. He might be hurting, but at least he was safe.

She flinched as he slammed the school door shut behind him, the force so great that the sound carried easily across the school yard. Only when she was sure that he was out of sight, did she let her mask slip and allow the silent tears to roll down her face.

"I'm sorry, Joe," she whispered.

Luckily, she had no lessons with Joe that afternoon and was already settled on the school bus when he boarded. He caught her eye and for one wonderful moment, she thought that he was going to join her. Knowing that if he did she wouldn't have the strength to keep up the pretence, she tutted in contempt and turned her head to stare out of the window.

From the corner of her eye, she saw him purse his lips, shake his head and swing into the seat behind the driver. What Joe couldn't see were the deep gouges that her nails were making in her palms in an effort to stop the tears.

As soon as the bus turned on the road by the church in Little Ingworth, Joe was out of his seat, clinging to the pole while he waited for the doors to fold open. Knowing that it was easier to let him go, Angelina stayed in her seat until the bus was almost empty. By the time she was standing on the pavement, Joe was already out of sight.

She stood for a moment, not knowing what to do or where to go. The thought of heading home to face Dee was too much to bear.

This is it, she thought. Now, I am all alone.

Shivering as the wind picked up and blew loose leaves around her ankles, she hitched her school bag on to her shoulder and set off towards Rose Cottage to collect her things.

Dark clouds had brought dusk even earlier tonight and it was starting to rain as Angelina arrived at the cottage. The door was ajar, but Angelina's knock went unanswered. Cautiously pushing the door wider, she peered into the gloomy hallway.

"Hello? Rose?" Angelina called out. But the words fell dead into empty air. She tried again. "Rose, are you there?"

For some reason, the silence in the cottage didn't feel right. At the end of the hall, a sharp L-shaped crack of light glowed yellow around the door leading into the kitchen. But if Rose was in the kitchen, why didn't she answer. Like a moth drawn to the light, Angelina edged cautiously down the hallway.

"Rose?" Her voice wavered as she twisted the handle and eased the kitchen door open. The room was tidy but empty.

"Rose?"

Starting to panic, Angelina ventured back down the hallway and into the sitting room, only to find it too was deserted. The curtains hadn't been drawn and the faint glow from the streetlights, cast sickly grey shadows around the room. Racing upstairs, calling for Rose as she went, she flung open the door to Rose's bedroom, knowing even before she did, that Rose wasn't there. The cottage was empty.

Unsure of what to do or where to go, Angelina found herself clinging to the banister. Something was wrong. Why was the door open? What if Dee had already got to Rose?

A noise from outside made Angelina freeze. Someone was coming down the path. Before she could move, the front door creaked open again. Carefully she retreated towards the nearest bedroom hoping to find somewhere to hide, but on her second step, the floorboard creaked. Whoever was downstairs had obviously heard as the footsteps stopped and the hallway lit up as the light was switched on.

"Who's there?"

Weak with fear, Angelina almost collapsed when she heard the sharp voice. Thankfully, she managed to stop herself from falling to the floor.

"Rose, it's me. I was so worried. Where were you?" she called running to the top of the stairs.

"Angelina?"

The startled look on Rose's face turned to concern as Angelina stumbled down the stairs towards her.

"You gave me a bit of a fright. Whatever's the matter, dear?" Rose dropped her gloves onto the hallway table as Angelina dived into her arms.

"The door was open, but you weren't here. I didn't know where you were. I was worried that…" Her voice trailed off. She didn't know why she'd been so worried.

Rose gave her a reassuring squeeze. "Oh, you silly thing."

"I didn't know where you were." Angelina repeated.

Rose held her at arm's length, so she could look into her eyes. "It's lovely of you to care so much, my dear. But I was only next door. Lizzie, my neighbour, called to say she'd be working late and could I let Sweep out to lift his leg."

"Sweep? Who's Sweep?" Then Angelina remembered about the little West Island terrier that Rose sometimes looked after. "Oh, the dog!"

"Yes, Sweep. Now, what's all this about? You don't become hysterical because an old woman disappears for a few minutes." She smiled gently at Angelina. "Is it Joe?"

Angelina hadn't realised how shaken she had been by everything that had happened that day, but at the mention of Joe's name a fresh swell of tears rushed to her eyes. Miserably she nodded.

"Thought so, I can spot a heart breaking from a mile away." Rose pulled Angelina back towards her, and the young girl yielded to the comforting warmth of the old woman's embrace.

"Is it definitely over?"

Squashed into Rose's shoulder, Angelina nodded again. It was easier to let Rose think that it was a romance gone wrong, at least that way she wouldn't ask too many questions and it wasn't that far from the truth.

Giving her a final squeeze, Rose released Angelina and handed her a tissue.

"Dry your eyes, dear and I'll put the kettle on."

Allowing Rose to take control, Angelina followed her into the kitchen. Blowing her nose, Angelina collapsed into one of the chairs at the table.

Pull yourself together, you're being pathetic, she thought. Get the assignment over and done with and you're out of this stupid world for good. Joe had to end at some point, she reminded herself.

Leaning across the table, Rose handed Angelina a mug of tea before squeezing into the chair opposite.

"Do you want to talk about it?"

Angelina shrugged. "There's not much to tell. It wasn't going anywhere. He's diving most nights. I said some things I probably shouldn't have done. We argued. He stormed off."

"Perhaps you need to talk to one another. Don't let pride stop you from making things right with him." Rose sipped her tea.

Warming her hands on the mug, Angelina stared at the brown, steaming liquid, avoiding Rose's stare. "No, it's gone beyond that, Rose. It's over."

Rose must have seen that it was pointless trying to change Angelina's mind.

"Well, I've a dozen sayings that are supposed to make you feel better, starting with, you're only young and there are plenty more fish in the sea. But I'm not too old to remember that just now, nothing will help. However, I am old enough to know that time's a great healer and you will feel better eventually."

Angelina raised her eyes and managed a smile. "Thanks, Rose. And thanks for having me this weekend. I'd better finish this and get back home. I guess Aunt Dee will be back by now."

"No problem, my dear." Reaching across the table, she patted Angelina's hand. "Anytime you want to talk, you know where I am."

Looking down at Rose's gnarled hand that still covered hers, Angelina reflected that perhaps she still had one friend left in this place.

Chapter Twenty-seven

As Angelina hurried home in the dark up Hermit Hill Lane, hauling both her school bag and overnight holdall with her, she noticed a light shining from the front bedroom of number four. She halted abruptly at the sight, her heart hammering. The glow was coming from Dee's bedroom. In a panic, Angelina searched her memory; had she left it on after being in Dee's room earlier that day?

Flicking quickly through the events of that morning in her mind, Angelina finally calmed down. She remembered that dawn had already broken by the time she'd arrived at the cottage and there'd been no need to switch the light on while she'd searched.

Stop being so jumpy, it's just Dee, Angelina thought. I must calm down or she's going to get suspicious.

Dreading coming face to face with her mentor, Angelina slipped quietly into the kitchen, thankful that the heating was on and the house was once again warm. A stew was simmering away on the hotplate, filling the kitchen with a rich aroma of onion gravy that made Angelina remember how hungry she was.

Strange, she thought, it's not like Dee to do the cooking. Dee chose that moment to breeze into the kitchen, wearing one of the brightly patterned African robes that Angelina had noticed hanging in the wardrobe. For once, the rusty colours of the flowing garment complemented Dee's wild, red hair.

"Ah, you're back. Right on time for dinner, that's good. How did you get on staying with Iris?"

"You mean Rose." Angelina watched Dee carefully, looking for any sign that she'd been on the computer and was aware that Angelina had discovered the altered Umail.

Dee waved a hand dismissively. "That's it, Rose. Knew it was a flower. Did you have fun?" Dee stared at her with what appeared to be a genuine smile.

Worried that Dee might be toying with her, Angelina answered cautiously. "It was fine, thanks. By the way that package arrived yesterday. I left it on the kitchen table."

"Yes, I got that. Thank you." Dee moved to the oven and lifted the stew pan lid, releasing a puff of steam that rose and hovered over the pan before evaporating. Her back to Angelina, Dee stirred the stew with a wooden spoon. "It's a good job you were here. With this weather it would have blown away by now."

She sounds like she means it, thought Angelina. This isn't like Dee. She's never this talkative and she certainly doesn't cook; she opened tins and warmed meals, but she didn't cook. It was almost as if she was… happy.

"How did your trip go?" Angelina asked.

Dee stopped stirring and turned to face Angelina, a beam deepening the lines on her face. "Very well. Extremely well, in fact. Couldn't have gone better."

Dee turned her attention back to the stew.

"Is the situation in the Middle East sorted?" Angelina held her breath as she waited for Dee's response.

"Middle East?"

Dee frowned as she stirred the bubbling mixture, appearing distracted or perhaps, thought Angelina, confused.

But Dee continued quickly. "Oh, that, yes. Middle East, yes. The Middle East is fine. Like I said, it all went very well."

Dee's gushing response confirmed Angelina's suspicion. Dee wasn't telling the truth. At least she wasn't telling the entire truth. Whatever she'd been up to while she'd been away had had nothing to do with sorting out a crisis in the Middle East. In fact, Angelina was willing to bet that whatever Dee had been doing wasn't official business at all. More likely, it had something to do with the money stashed away in her personal bank account.

Excusing herself, Angelina headed upstairs and was unpacking her bag when another thought dawned on her. No wonder Dee had given in so easily when Angelina had suggested staying with Rose. Leaving Angelina with a GA operative in London would have caused complications. Dee would have had to give a reason to her colleague, which might have led to some awkward questions. With Angelina staying at Rose Cottage, Dee was free to do whatever she wanted.

The only thing that cheered Angelina up was that Dee didn't appear to know that she'd discovered the truth about the Fate Switch, or the bank statement. At least I'm safe for the time being, she thought.

Over the next few weeks, Angelina tried to adjust to life without Joe. A couple of times on the day following their argument, he'd approached her, obviously with the intention of making up. Each time she'd cut him dead, pouring scorn on his attempts at friendship. Eventually he'd stopped trying. In morning registration class, Angelina had moved so that she was no longer sitting next to Joe and in ICT, the only other class that they had together, Joe had taken the initiative, sitting at the other side of the class before Angelina had even arrived in the room.

Rumours about their broken relationship were rife. Angelina knew they were saying that Joe had caught her with a boy from another school. She suspected that the story had been invented by Serena's vicious tongue.

To avoid thinking about Joe, Angelina threw herself into her Fate Switch assignment, which had the added benefit of keeping her out of the house and away from Dee. Not that Dee was ever around anyway. She was spending almost all her time in the garage and the number of packages being delivered to and taken from the house was increasing daily. It was as if Dee was no longer bothering to hide what she was doing.

The beginning of December marked the halfway point of Angelina's assignment. Twenty-five per cent of her marks rested on her interim report, which she spent a week preparing and presented it to Dee one evening over dinner.

Barely glancing at it, Dee said. "Leave it on the table. I can't look at it now. I have some work to finish first."

The next evening, it was still on the table. Dee obviously hadn't even bothered to read it.

Angelina felt a surge of anger. I've been written off, she thought in disbelief. Dee knows a trainee can't perform a level-eleven Fate Switch, so she's not even going to waste her time marking this, she thought.

"If Dee thinks I'm finished, it's going to be the biggest mistake she's ever made. I'm going to make this Fate Switch happen, no matter what." The words came out in a fierce whisper.

Angelina spent almost every spare moment researching Serena Jackson and Nathan Bird; the boy who Serena had to ask to the Valentine's Ball. Joe had been half-right. Nathan was quiet, serious and did well at school, but Angelina soon discovered another side to Nathan, when she followed him home one night.

He lived with his mum and younger sister in a small end terrace on the outskirts of Ingworth. His mum worked as a receptionist for one of the large accountancy firms in the town and his sister Tamzin, or Taz as Nathan seemed to call her, was in her first year at Ingworth High. As their mother worked full-time, Nathan walked Tamzin home each evening.

Nathan was the type of boy you'd pass on the street without noticing. He was average height with short dark hair framing a pleasant but still boyish face, which always looked very serious. Tamzin was a younger, female version of her brother, only with much longer hair and her features were always incredibly animated. She was a confident, bubbly girl, who seemed to talk non-stop as she walked home with Nathan.

The first time Angelina jumped into his mind, it was a complete waste of time and she learned nothing more than she already knew. It was a Tuesday evening and Nathan and Tamzin spent the entire time doing their homework.

The next day, when Nathan and Tamzin arrived home, they didn't stay. Instead they dumped their school bags in the hall and left the house.

"Ben shouldn't be long. We'll set up," said Nathan as he locked the door again.

"Can we work on that new one again?" Tamzin asked.

"Yeah, you like that, don't you?"

Intrigued, Angelina watched through Nathan's eyes as the brother and sister made their way along the side of the house towards a shabby looking garage at the end of the garden. Nathan unlocked the side door, releasing a musty smell and stepped into the darkness, Tamzin following close behind.

She shivered. "It's going to be cold tonight, I'm glad I kept my gloves on."

"I'll put the heater on. It'll soon warm up."

Nathan flicked a switch and the garage filled with light, making Angelina almost gasp in amazement. The walls were covered with old carpet and in the centre of the small space stood a drum kit. It was flanked by two microphone stands and a couple of large, black speakers. Nathan headed towards a steel cabinet at one end of the garage, from which hung a large padlock. Selecting the right key from his pocket, Nathan unhooked the padlock and opened the door. Reaching inside the cabinet, he pulled out a set of drumsticks, handing them to Tamzin, before pulling out two electric guitars.

Joe had told Angelina that Nathan played the classical guitar, but he hadn't mentioned the electric guitar or that Nathan played in a band. This was obviously something that nobody at school knew about. Perhaps he was afraid of being ridiculed because his little sister was involved, or perhaps he didn't think it was anything to do with anyone else.

There wasn't a lot of room in the garage and Tamzin picked her way past the microphones and sat down behind the drums. Angelina could hear her tuning the various drums as Nathan concentrated on plugging in and testing the sound levels for the guitars. He was tuning the large guitar when the door opened, and another boy walked in. He looked about the same age as Nathan, but Angelina didn't recognise him from school.

Nathan looked up and held out one of the guitars. "Hey, Ben, you've missed the hard work again."

Ben grinned. "You could have warmed it up in here, I'll never get my fingers to work. Hi, Taz."

"Ben, before we start, Nath has something to show you." Excitedly, Tamzin jumped off the stool and skipped deftly around the equipment towards the cabinet. Rummaging inside, she pulled out a thin cardboard file and handed it to Ben, the phrase 'bursting with pride' came to Angelina's mind: the young girl could barely contain herself.

"Don't, Taz, it's not finished yet," Nathan protested.

"But it looks great. Have a look, Ben." She bounced up and down on tiptoe as Ben opened the file and slid out a piece of paper.

"What do you think? It's fantastic isn't it?" Tamzin couldn't wait for an answer.

Ben studied the paper, then turned his gaze on Nathan. "This is good, Nath."

Ben held up the paper and finally Angelina could see what all the excitement was about. An image, drawn in pencil, of a horse rearing up on its hind legs, as if it were leaping through a diamond-shaped hole, dominated the page. The words 'DIAMOND BLACK', were written in curly, fluid letters along the top left-hand side of the diamond. "It's not finished. I need to add colour, for a start," said Nathan.

"It's good, isn't it?" Tamzin asked Ben again. Without waiting for an answer, she squealed and jumped up and down. "Our first album cover, I can't believe it."

Nathan laughed. "Calm down, Taz. We haven't even recorded a song yet, never mind got a record deal."

"We will one day and that's what the album cover will look like." She jabbed her finger towards the picture, jutted out her chin and stalked back to her drum kit. "Come on, let's start."

Hidden in Nathan's mind, Angelina was as excited as Taz. This was what she'd been looking for: something to link Nathan to Serena.

Art.

Wait until I tell Joe about this. The thought popped into her head before she could stop it. She missed him. And it hurt.

Pushing thoughts of Joe away, she concentrated on leaving Nathan's mind.

'What was that noise outside,' Angelina said inside his head.

'Did I really hear something?' Nathan challenged the thought.

'I'd better check,' Angelina continued.

Nathan walked obediently to the door.

"Where are you going?" Ben asked.

"I heard something outside. Just seeing what it is," Nathan said.

"I didn't hear anything." Ben turned to Tamzin.

She shrugged. "He did this yesterday, kept thinking he was hearing things. I think he's going mad." Tamzin gave a quick drum roll and bashed the cymbal to finish.

Nathan ignored them and opened the door, giving Angelina the chance to leave his mind without being seen.

"No, nothing there." She heard Nathan say as he closed the door.

Crouching in the shadows, Angelina waited until Diamond Black started playing. Their music was muffled, the carpet on the walls doing a reasonable job of sound-proofing the garage, but they sounded good and Taz was amazing on the drums.

As she crept away from the garage, she thought about what she'd learned: Nathan played in a rock band and loved art; Serena loved music and had a talent for art.

In one sense, they're not quite so far apart as Joe thinks, but in another, they might as well live on different planets. How will I ever get those two together?

Chapter Twenty-eight

Serena was in her room. Her music was so loud that Angelina, hidden in the mind of Dan Jackson who was downstairs in the kitchen, could hear and feel the rhythmic thump of bass in the background.

Ten minutes earlier, she'd been hiding in the shadows of the garden, waiting for Serena's dad to arrive home from work. He'd parked his car in the garage, which, like the front gates, had opened and closed automatically, almost catching Angelina out. She'd seen the garage door slowly descending and had had to move quickly into a position where she could see Dan in the car. He'd only just opened the car door, giving Angelina the clear sightline she needed before the garage door had swung shut.

As was her habit now, she stopped to sense the scent of Dan's mind before moving towards his conscious mind. She didn't plan on getting trapped in any more infected minds.

Dan had used the internal door that led directly from the garage into the kitchen. As soon as he'd entered the house, he'd been hit by Serena's pulsing music.

Now, as he dropped his briefcase on the floor and hung up his coat, Angelina could sense his frustration and his thoughts came clearly to her: *'Not again. I've told her about that music.'*

Laura waddled up to him and planted a kiss on his cheek.

Angelina didn't think she'd seen anyone looking so pregnant yet from what she'd learned from Serena, the baby wasn't due until the New Year, which meant that Laura still had at least another four weeks to go.

"Don't say anything about her music. We need to talk," Laura said.

Dan let out a sigh. "She's not in trouble at school again, is she?"

"No, it's not that."

"What then, the police?" Dan sounded resigned to bad news.

Laura shook her head.

Angelina sensed Dan's anxiety levels rising, as he placed his hand on Laura's bump.

"You're okay, aren't you? The baby?"

Laura smiled at his concern. "The baby's fine and I'm fine, apart from being the size of a whale."

Dan relaxed. "Well, what's wrong then?"

"Let me sit down first."

Moving to the island in the middle of the kitchen, Laura hoisted herself onto one of the white, swivel-topped bar stools. Dan perched on the stool next to his wife. Unlike Laura, who was so small that she could barely reach the footrest, Dan was so tall that he left one foot on the floor. Angelina could tell that he was anxious to know Laura's news.

"Tell me what's wrong."

Laura bit her lip nervously. "She's back. She called at the house this afternoon, wanting to see Serena."

Immediately, Angelina could feel anger bubbling away inside Dan.

"I didn't think she was due out yet."

"Apparently she got out last week."

Who is 'she'? Angelina wanted to blurt out, but all she could do was remain silent and hope that things would become clearer.

"Was Serena here? Did she see her?"

"No, she hadn't arrived home from school." Laura looked away from Dan. "That's if she's been to school. I think she's been playing truant again."

"Not again. Great, and with Cathy back on the scene it's only going to get worse."

"Cathy didn't seem quite as bad. Perhaps it's worked this time."

Angelina shivered, as Dan's mind became as cold as his words.

"That woman will never change. She had me fooled for too many years. Don't let her get to you, Laura. In fact, I think it's time we told Serena the truth."

"Dan, you can't do that!"

"Why not? She thinks we're to blame for everything and her behaviour is getting worse. We can't let her go on like this. We've got the baby to think about, Serena's acted like a spoilt child for long enough. And it'll serve Cathy right if Serena knows the truth."

"No, Dan, that's not fair. Cathy's her mum. You'd destroy Serena if you told her the truth." Laura placed a hand on her swollen stomach.

Dan's attitude thawed and Angelina felt a rush of warmth as he looked at his wife.

"After the way Serena's treated you and the things she's said, I can't believe you're still trying to protect her. She doesn't deserve you. I don't think I deserve you."

Laura shifted her weight, looking uncomfortable on the hard seat. "Yes, you do. I'm no saint, I just know what she's going through, and to her I deserve everything I get." She gave a bitter half laugh. "I always swore I'd never be the other woman. I didn't want to put anyone through what I went through."

Dan got up and encircled Laura in his arms. "You're not the other woman. You never have been, so don't forget that."

"I am as far as Serena's concerned." Laura stayed rigid, refusing to yield to Dan's embrace.

"This is nothing like your mum and dad. Cathy is a manipulative alcoholic who would have wrecked Serena's life if I hadn't got out when I did. You played no part in that." Dan held Laura at arm's length. "I happened to get lucky when I met you. When Serena finally wakes up to what's going on, she'll know how lucky she is too."

He pulled Laura to him again and this time she didn't resist.

Her head resting against Dan's arm, she said: "Maybe the rehab's worked this time. Cathy did seem better."

Dan gave a sigh, raising his eyes to the spot-lit ceiling. "I wouldn't bet on it. I've spent so much money on clinics for that woman I could have bought one by now. She'll only be cured when she wants to get better. Did she say when she was going to come back?"

"She wants to take Serena out for lunch on Saturday. We'll have to let her."

Dan sighed again. "I don't suppose we can stop her. Let's hope the benefits of rehab last until then." Dan looked around. "Did you hear someone at the door?"

It was a ploy that seemed to work every time and, as Dan investigated, Angelina made her escape. It was cold outside, no doubt there would be a frost overnight. As she made her way home, she replayed

Dan and Laura's conversation in her head. She knew one thing for certain; she had to find out more about Serena's mother.

On Saturday morning, Angelina was once again hiding in the bushes near Serena's house when a silver sports car roared into the driveway. A woman, wearing high heeled boots, black trousers and a cream fur coat, that might have been real for all Angelina knew – climbed out. Swinging a black diamante studded bag onto her shoulder, she sashayed across the pebbled driveway. Her neatly bobbed, ash-blonde hair swaying in time with her steps. As she turned to lock the car door with the remote control, Angelina caught a glance of her heavily made-up face. This was obviously Cathy, but whilst her features were scarily similar to Serena's, the thick foundation couldn't fill the deep lines around her eyes and mouth. The woman looked at least ten years older than Dan, but from what Angelina had learned, Cathy was a year younger than her ex-husband. Her addiction was obviously ravaging her body.

She rang the bell but didn't wait for an answer before rapping sharply on the door.

The door flew open and Serena stood in the doorway. It was the first time that Angelina had seen Serena looking genuinely happy.

"Mum!" She squealed and threw herself into Cathy's arms.

"Hello, sweetie. How's life been in Castle Drudge. I hope you've managed to survive."

Serena pulled away and curled her lip up at one corner. "Horrible. They're getting worse, Mum."

"Well, come on then. Let's get out of here."

Slamming the door behind her, Serena linked her mother's arm.

Wanting as much time as possible, Angelina waited until the last minute to make the Mind Jump. As Cathy was about to pull the car door shut, Angelina made the jump into her subconscious. She wanted to see what was going on in this woman's head. Taking a deep breath to check for infections, Angelina almost gagged on the smell of stale tobacco and alcohol; Cathy's mind wasn't infected, but it was certainly derelict.

Once in the conscious mind, Angelina watched as Cathy concentrated on her driving. Somehow the woman managed to agree and disagree with Serena in all the right places, but Angelina could tell that she wasn't really listening or caring about what her daughter had to say.

Cathy drove Serena to a café in Ingworth, which (Angelina noted) didn't serve alcohol. They settled in a booth at the back of the room, Serena with a club sandwich, chunky chips and fruit juice, Cathy with a green salad and espresso.

They talked about music and Serena's friends as they ate. Cathy barely touched her salad. Instead her mind kept drifting to thoughts of a bottle of vodka stashed in the linen cupboard in her flat.

Eventually, Serena asked: "Mum, when can I come and live with you?"

"As soon as I beat those fancy lawyers that your dad keeps paying to keep you away from me."

"I hate him. Why can't he just let me go." Serena pouted.

"It's a power struggle, darling. Keeping us apart is his way of getting back at me for leaving him."

"Well, he can't do that forever. As soon as I'm eighteen I'm coming to live with you."

Cathy smiled, but Angelina could tell that she wasn't happy with the idea.

"They could have let me go on that cruise with you. I can't believe they didn't let me go. I'd have learned more than I do at that stupid school."

"That's what I thought too, darling, but you know what they're like. Laura's probably jealous because she can't even walk in her state, let alone go on a cruise." Cathy pulled a face. "I can't imagine how anyone gets so huge because they're pregnant. I certainly didn't look like that with you."

Cathy smoothed a bony hand across her own emaciated belly.

For a second, Angelina thought she saw a flicker of distaste in Serena's eyes, but Cathy quickly softened her words with a grin.

"Tell me about the cruise. Did you get back on Monday? What was the Caribbean like? Was it amazing?" Serena changed the subject.

"Oh, it was fabulous. You'd have loved it and they'd have loved you. It could have done with some younger people."

For a second Angelina was confused by what Cathy was saying, but as the woman's real thoughts flitted through her mind, Angelina

pieced the truth together. To explain her long absence in the reha-
bilitation clinic, Cathy had invented an eight-week cruise around the
Caribbean. She'd also pretended to invite Serena along, knowing full
well that there was no way that Dan and Laura could agree and so
they would look bad in Serena's eyes. What's more, Cathy knew that
Dan wouldn't tell Serena where her mother was really going.

As Angelina heard more and more of Cathy's poisonous lies, she
began to understand why Serena acted the way that she did, and for
the first time felt a hint of sympathy.

After half an hour, Cathy looked at her watch.

"Time to go if we want to catch the film."

*'At least I don't have to talk to her anymore and then I can take her straight
home. I deserve a drink after today. Just one won't harm.'* Cathy's unspoken
thought, as they left for the cinema, shocked Angelina. Thankfully, it
was time for her to make her exit.

Hidden in the alley by the café, she watched Serena and her mother
as they headed back towards the car.

"Thanks, Cathy," she whispered. "You've given me a chance with
this assignment."

There were only two weeks left until school broke up for the
Christmas holidays.

Being careful not to let Dee know what she was doing, Angelina
became the nagging voice of doubt in the back of Serena's mind. She
planted questions and thoughts that gradually opened Serena's eyes
to the cracks in Cathy's stories. Eventually the confusion and doubt
started creeping into Serena's own thoughts.

As Angelina visited the minds of Cathy, Dan and Laura, little by
little she laid the foundations of her plan.

Chapter Twenty-nine

At lunchtime on the last day of term, Angelina was in the corridor reading the latest football report on the notice board. The team had beaten Ashfield High in the quarter final stage of the cup and Nina had scored twice.

I wouldn't have minded seeing that game. She thought back to the football matches she'd watched alone over the past few weeks, and the sense of loneliness returned. Watching the school team play helped her remember how good it had felt when she was still with Joe. Especially the time in the rain when he'd held her close.

A noise made her start and she turned to find herself looking straight into Joe's expressionless face. She couldn't move or speak as all the emotions she'd tried hard to keep locked up broke free from her heart and flooded into her head. Joe spoke first.

"You may as well have this."

He held out a small box-shaped gift wrapped in silver foil paper and tied with a purple, organza bow – jewellery store packaging.

It was the closest she'd been to Joe since the argument and she didn't trust herself to speak.

"Take it." He sounded impatient as he thrust the gift towards her.

She couldn't tear her gaze away from his face. He was trying to act as if he didn't care but she could see the hurt lurking behind his eyes.

"What is it?" she asked.

"Your Christmas present. I bought it ages ago. I can't give it to anyone else and the shop won't take it back, so you may as well have it." The words came across flat and emotionless.

Taking the gift, Angelina began: "Joe, I ..." She stopped knowing that she couldn't say all the things that she wanted to say. In the end, she said: "Thanks, that's kind. Sorry, I didn't get you anything."

"Doesn't matter. I didn't buy it for that. Happy Christmas." Joe's gruff voice sounded anything but happy. He turned and left Angelina standing in the corridor. She watched him walk away. He didn't turn around.

In the week leading up to Christmas, Dee was working later and later into the night in the garage. During the day it wasn't unusual for three or four vans to appear outside the house, collecting and delivering various parcels. Although she was curious to know what was going on, Angelina resisted the temptation to question Dee or do anything that might make Dee suspicious. It was too risky.

Also, while she was locked away in the garage, Dee had no idea what Angelina was up to. In fact, Angelina rarely saw Dee apart from mealtimes. Sometimes, if she remembered, Dee would ask about the assignment and Angelina would offer a brief update, careful to play down how well things were going.

When she wanted company, Angelina escaped to see Rose, whose cottage had been transformed into a fairy grotto on the first day of December. It was a cheerful place and helped Angelina to forget about Joe, Serena and Dee for a little while.

Three days before Christmas, Angelina was helping Rose with her baking. I'm actually having fun, she thought as she curled pastry lids over the tops of open mince pies.

"You're doing a lovely job, my dear. I can't believe this is the first time you've ever baked mince pies." Rose, dressed in a flowery apron her sleeves rolled up to her elbows, had her hands in another bowl and was busy rubbing flour, sugar and butter together for an apple crumble.

Angelina found herself smiling back at Rose. "I've never eaten one either."

"What?" Rose feigned horror. "We'll have to do something about that. In fact, I've been meaning to ask" -she rested her flour-covered wrists on the edge of the bowl- "are you and your aunt doing anything on Christmas Day? If not, you're both welcome here. We won't be seeing my daughter and her husband; they're staying with his parents." Rose's face dropped for a second. "That leaves me and Mr Garden, and it will be ever so quiet. It would be lovely to have company."

It was a tempting offer. She planned to visit Serena's house on Christmas morning to put the next phase of her plan in place, but apart from that she was free.

"I have some people to visit in the morning, but I should be back by lunchtime and we haven't got any other plans that I know of."

Angelina thought about the bare cottage on Hermit Hill Lane. Dee had allowed a small artificial Christmas tree that Angelina had found at the back of one of the wardrobes to be decorated but there had certainly been no mention of a Christmas Day meal.

"I'll ask Aunt Dee and let you know. Thanks, Rose."

"Good. Oh, I do hope you can both come."

When she returned home, Angelina wasn't surprised when Dee declined the invitation. "I need to catch up on some paperwork, but you go if you want. I'll get through things much quicker if there are no distractions," said Dee.

I'm just a distraction now, am I? Angelina thought.

By Christmas Eve, Angelina was feeling more and more nervous about her plans for Christmas Day morning. She spent a restless night and woke before it was light. Realising it was pointless trying to get back to sleep, she switched on the bedside lamp and reached for the gift from Joe that she'd hidden under her bed.

Slowly, she pulled on one end of the organza bow and the filmy purple ribbon unfolded, slipping away from the silver paper. A small tab of clear tape held the gift wrap in place and, as Angelina edged her fingernail under the folded corners, the paper sprung free. An emerald green jeweller's gift box was half hidden in the folds of silver paper. Lifting the box gently away from the wrapping, she eased open the lid.

Attached to a silver chain and resting on a small, plump, green cushion, was a silver angel. Angelina lifted the necklace from the box, allowing the inch-high charm to pirouette freely as she gazed at the delicate design. The intricate wings were spread wide, and the half-smile that played on the lips gave Angelina the impression that she too was hiding a secret. Delicate hands were clasped in front of the figure, while moulded silver legs were held in the passé position: one leg straight, the other bent so that the toe touched the knee. It was beautiful.

Under the cushion, Angelina found a small, gift card that matched the silver gift wrap. Her fingers felt thick and clumsy as she opened the card.

She's not quite as stunning as my real angel! Love you, Joe xx

Angelina read the message twice before tears blurred her vision. She presumed that Joe had written the tag when he'd bought the gift, which had been before the argument. He must have forgotten the message he'd left inside.

She fastened the chain around her neck, knowing that she'd have to keep it hidden from Dee. Once dressed, she slipped the angel beneath her jumper, hiding it from view. Knowing it was there was enough to make her feel slightly less alone.

By eleven o'clock on Christmas morning, Angelina was crouching behind a clump of conifers in the Jackson's garden. She knew that Serena, having opened her presents, was now back in her bedroom listening to the music that was blaring from her new speakers: a Christmas present from her dad and Laura.

Dan had left on the hour-long round trip to collect his parents and mother-in-law, and Angelina knew that Laura was in the kitchen preparing Christmas dinner.

It was cold and damp outside and the earthy smell of rotting wet leaves surrounded Angelina in her hiding place. So much for deep and crisp and even, she thought, shifting position to stop her leg from going dead. She glanced at her watch.

"Come on, come on. You should be here by now," she whispered.

Angelina was beginning to think that it had all gone wrong when she heard the growl of a motor and a car turned into the road. She stiffened, but the car accelerated as it drove past the Jackson's house.

"Where are you?"

Straightening her legs, which were aching from crouching in the same position for so long, Angelina rose into a half-standing position, stamping her feet silently on the soft ground to bring back the circulation. She was still upright when another car turned the corner and Angelina almost slipped into the mud as she threw herself down behind the nearest bush.

This time the car pulled up outside the house. Her vision partly obscured by the feathery branches, Angelina could see the front end of a white taxicab. She heard a car door open, then slam shut before the taxi, its back wheels spinning, sped off.

From her hiding place, all Angelina could see was a pair of high heeled black boots crunching unsteadily across the gravel driveway. Hardly daring to breathe for fear of making a noise, Angelina eased her weight slowly to the left to give her a better view. She smiled in relief as she saw Cathy press the bell and knock on the front door.

Cathy raised her hand to knock again, when the door swung open and Angelina glimpsed Laura standing in the doorway holding a tea-towel.

Angelina couldn't hear what Cathy said, but whatever it was, it made Laura drop her head and step back, allowing the older woman to enter the house.

"Yes!" Angelina hissed the word excitedly.

With a quick check to make sure that there was no one around, Angelina dashed from her hiding place and down the path at the side of the house. The Jackson's back garden was large, private and backed on to a wood, so there was no chance of Angelina being seen by the neighbours. Collecting a handful of tiny pebbles that decorated the water feature, she flung them at a window on the first floor, pressing her back against the wall of the house as she heard them clatter against the glass.

No response.

She tried again. This time the window opened and as soon as Angelina saw a head poke out, she jumped.

'I'm sure I heard something.' Serena was still peering out of the window when Angelina arrived in her conscious mind.

'It must have been birds.' Angelina's suggestion was readily accepted by Serena's mind and she pulled the window closed.

Serena had turned her music down and was about to press the

volume button on the remote control when Angelina's next suggestion stopped her.

'What was that?' Angelina asked.

Serena tilted her head, listening. *'No, it wasn't anything.'*

'There! That noise.'

There was nothing to hear, the house was so well insulated, but Angelina's convincing tone made Serena believe that she had actually heard something.

'I'm sure it was voices. Who's she talking to.' Angelina reinforced her suggestion.

Out of curiosity, Serena crossed her bedroom and opened the door. Now she could hear for herself the faint sound of people speaking.

'Someone's in the kitchen. Who's here and why hasn't Laura told me?' Angelina asked.

As anticipated, Serena crept down the stairs to find out. The door to the kitchen was closed and it wasn't until Serena was outside the door that she recognised the voice.

'Mum!' she thought, a smile breaking out on her face.

'Why is she here? And why didn't she come up to see me?' Angelina added the doubt.

Serena brushed off the thought and pulled down the door handle. The latch clicked and the door opened a crack.

'Wait!' Angelina's order stopped Serena before she could open the door further. *'What are they saying?'*

Now that the door was ajar, everything the two women were saying inside the kitchen could be heard clearly by Serena. Registering the argumentative tone of one of the voices, she followed Angelina's advice, leaning close to the door to listen, instead of pushing it open.

"Are you going to give me my money then?" It was Cathy.

"I've told you, Cathy, there's no cash in the house. I haven't been out lately and Dan's taken his wallet with him. He won't be more than an hour. Why don't you spend some time with Serena? I'm sure she'd love to show you her Christmas things. I know she was disappointed when she couldn't see you today. It'll be a lovely surprise for her." Laura was trying hard to keep Cathy calm.

Angelina could sense Serena's confusion; Laura was encouraging her mother to see her.

"I'm not bothered about seeing that spoilt brat. I bet you've both bought her far too much for Christmas."

Angelina felt a surge of almost physical pain shoot through Serena as her mother's venomous words hit home. For a second, Angelina was frightened that Serena would collapse as she staggered back from the force of the words.

"Don't speak like that about Serena. She adores you, and what if she hears you? She's only upstairs…" Laura's voice faltered. "She can be a lovely kid, she's just got a lot to deal with."

"Lovely kid? Who are you fooling? Dan tells me what the teachers say about her. She's only allowed to stay at that school because Dan keeps handing them huge donations."

This wasn't going the way that Angelina had planned. She'd wanted Serena to see what her mother was really like, but even Angelina hadn't realised that Cathy could be this nasty. She needed to get Serena out of here.

'I can't listen to this any longer. I'm going back to my room.' Angelina suggested.

But Serena didn't move. She was beyond listening to reason. Her mind couldn't process anything other than the words that were coming from the kitchen.

Laura was speaking again, her voice unsteady with shock and anger. "Don't you dare…"

Laura stopped, and Angelina wondered if she'd broken down in tears, but then she spoke again.

"You've been drinking! I can smell it on your breath. I thought you might have changed this time. You've been out of rehab less than a month and you're drunk again."

Cathy swore. "Don't you judge me."

Serena and Angelina both jumped as something crashed to the ground. It sounded like one of the bar stools had been knocked over.

"Think I wouldn't do anything because you're pregnant with another of Dan's brats?" Cathy's voice was loud and taunting.

"Leave her alone."

With Angelina powerless to stop her, Serena had pushed open the kitchen door and was now staring at her mother. The two women whipped their eyes to the door and froze. Laura had her back against the breakfast bar and Cathy was looming over her.

"I said, leave her alone." Serena stepped towards her mother.

Cathy drew back from Laura and pasted a smile on her face. She turned and started walking unsteadily towards Serena, her arms open.

"Hello, darling. Happy Christmas."

She stumbled over the fallen bar stool but managed somehow to keep upright.

"You are drunk!" Serena spat the words at her mother.

"It's Christmas. Everyone has a drink at Christmas." Cathy dismissed the accusation with a wave.

"I heard everything you said."

Angelina could feel the emotions tumbling around Serena's mind.

"That? Oh, don't take any notice of that silly argument." Cathy tilted her head and looked amused. "You don't think I meant any of it, do you?"

"No." Serena shook her head, keeping eye contact with her mother. "I don't think anything. I know you meant it. Get out of our house."

Serena was almost shaking with rage as she raised her arm and pointed towards the door.

"Darling, you don't mean this." Cathy pouted, as if her feelings were hurt and reached forward to hug Serena, but the young girl stepped back out of reach.

"I said get out. Get out. Get out!"

Serena's voice was trembling as much as her body and Cathy, even through the haze of alcohol, saw that she'd gone too far.

"Don't worry, I'm going. You're as bad as they are."

Serena stepped back as her mother snatched up her handbag and stumbled past. She watched while Cathy slammed the door shut behind her, before turning back to Laura who was still at the breakfast bar, one hand clinging to the work surface the other clutching her stomach.

"Did she hurt you?"

Laura shook her head, trying to catch her breath. "I'm okay, I think it's just a twinge. I'll be fine."

Angelina, still hiding in Serena's mind, could tell that the girl was still too shocked to know what to do.

'She needs to sit down.' Angelina took control.

"Come and sit down," said Serena. She helped Laura over to one of the dining room chairs.

'Perhaps she needs some water,' said Angelina.

"Do you want a drink? Some water?" Serena asked.

"Yes, please," Laura gasped.

Serena returned within seconds, almost spilling the water in her hurry to get back. Having taken a long gulp, Laura smiled at Serena.

"I think it's easing. Thank you."

'Is the baby coming?' Angelina asked, although she didn't know what Serena could do if the answer was yes.

"It's not time, is it?" Serena pulled a chair up as she gestured towards Laura's bump.

"Don't worry. It's settled down again." Laura gazed at Serena. "Are you okay?"

Serena dropped her head, looking at the floor, and Angelina could feel the memories of her mother's conversation tumbling through her mind.

"I... I don't know." Serena sounded lost.

"How much did you hear?" Laura's voice was gentle.

"Everything after she demanded money." Serena raised her eyes again. "That was all she came for, wasn't it? She was drunk." She looked accusingly at Laura. "You said she'd been in rehab, but you told me she'd been on a cruise."

Laura sighed. "I'm sorry we lied to you. Your mother didn't want you to know she has a drink problem and I didn't want you to think badly of her. I made your dad go along with it."

"Why would you do that?"

"I know what you're going through. I've never told you, but my dad went off with another woman when I was fifteen, a year older than you. She used to say some horrible things about my mother and eventually the woman stopped my dad from having any contact with us. He had another family and died before we made up."

"I didn't know that," said Serena.

"I met your dad after he'd separated from your mum, but I still didn't want you to go through what I went through. I know you probably won't believe me or your dad, but we've tried to encourage your mum to spend more time with you."

Serena sank back in her chair, her eyes wandering around the kitchen, but Angelina could tell she wasn't focussing on anything. "She always told me it was you and Dad who wouldn't let her see me. I don't understand."

"Don't think badly of your mum, Serena. She's an alcoholic, which means she'll do anything to justify having a drink and to avoid taking responsibility for her actions. What she said today, try to remember she doesn't really mean it. It's all part of the illness."

"You're still defending her?"

"She's your mum, I don't want you to lose her, like I lost my dad."

The front door banged open and Dan rushed in, his face full of panic.

"What's going on, I saw Cathy outside. Has she been here?" He stopped, obviously surprised that Serena and Laura were sitting next to each other. "Are you okay?"

Angelina wasn't sure who he was talking to, but Serena answered first.

"I heard Mum saying things. Laura's told me everything. I'm sorry, Dad. I thought it was you." Serena burst into tears and ran into her father's arms.

Two older women, accompanied by an older man, followed Dan through the front door. Serena's grandparents, Angelina thought. Seeing her exit clear, she left Serena's mind.

Outside, Angelina saw that the taxi had returned to collect Cathy who had flopped into the back seat.

That wasn't quite what I planned, Angelina thought. But at least it worked. She checked her watch. Just in time for Christmas dinner.

Chapter Thirty

The door to Rose Cottage flew open almost as soon as Angelina had finished knocking, the warm smell of cooked turkey curling around her.

"Oh, thank goodness you're here, dear." Rose looked unusually flustered as she opened the door.

"Why? What's wrong?"

"Oh, it's Mr Garden."

Rose's face crinkled into a frown as she stepped back to allow Angelina into the hallway. For a second, Angelina thought that she was going to burst into tears.

"Is he all right?"

"Yes, he's fine. But his friend…" Rose plucked a tissue from the pocket of her dress and held it to her mouth as if to stem the flow of emotion. "Oh dear, I'm not making much sense, am I?"

Taking Rose by the arm, Angelina steered her into the sitting room and settled her into a chair. Perching on the edge of the sofa, Angelina squeezed Rose's hand.

"Tell me what's happened."

Rose stifled a sob. "It's terrible. We had a call this morning. Bob Woods – that's Mr Garden's good friend from the allotment – they think he's had a heart attack. His wife called to tell us. She's in a terrible state. Mr Garden's gone to the hospital to help out." Rose gave a sob. "On Christmas Day, of all days. Oh, it's so awful. Poor Mr Woods. Poor Mrs Woods."

Rose was obviously distressed, and Angelina felt like a burden.

"Why don't you go to the hospital to be with them? I'll walk you down there and you can come back with Mr Garden. Come on, let's get your coat." Angelina stood but Rose shook her head.

"He's in intensive care. They only let family in. They've made an exception for Mr Garden because Mrs Woods is by herself."

"Why don't you call the hospital to see how he is? It's better than sitting here worrying. I'll make you a cup of tea while you phone."

"Yes, yes, dear. That's a good idea, I'll do that."

Rose had obviously kept occupied by cooking Christmas dinner and the smell in the kitchen made Angelina's stomach rumble. She couldn't help hoping that Rose was still in the mood for eating after all the upset.

The tea was brewing when Rose bustled into the kitchen, a relieved beam on her face.

"That was such a good idea of yours, Angelina. They let me speak with Mr Garden and apparently things are looking promising. Mr Woods still needs more tests, but they don't think it's as bad as they first feared. He's stable and conscious now, which is a good sign, they say."

"That's a relief for you. Is Mr Garden coming home then?" Angelina was thinking hungrily of her Christmas dinner.

Rose shook her head again. "I told him to stay there. Mrs Woods needs all the support she can get. He'll bring her back with him later, she can stay here tonight. Until then, he's told us to get stuck into the food but to save some for him and Mrs Woods. So, we'd better do as we're told. Forget that cup of tea, I'm having a sherry!"

Rose had surpassed herself with the meal and Angelina could barely move when she'd finished her last spoonful of Christmas pudding.

It was late afternoon and the light was fading when Angelina left Rose Cottage. Still feeling full, she walked the long way home, which skirted the edge of the park. As she approached the lower perimeter, movement in the children's playground at the top of the hill caught her eye. Her heart jumped as she recognised Joe's familiar outline. His back was to her as he pushed his twin sisters on the swings, racing backwards and forwards to keep each one swinging in turn. The toddlers' happy screams carried easily on the frosty breeze that whipped long black strands of hair across Angelina's face, and stirred the fallen leaves that remained scattered over the damp grass.

229

For a few minutes, she watched as Joe entertained his sisters, pretending to let the swing hit him before skipping out of the way at the last minute. She couldn't help but smile at the twins' laughter. She felt for the angel necklace hanging around her neck.

"Happy Christmas, Joe," she whispered before turning and hurrying home.

Although she still wore the same heavy makeup, Serena was almost unrecognisable when she returned to school after the Christmas holidays. Instead of the arrogant, bored attitude, she seemed quiet and uncertain.

The teachers had obviously been told something of what had happened in the Jackson household over Christmas, as Dr Arif was especially gentle with Serena during registration.

It's almost as if she's been broken, thought Angelina with a twinge of guilt. But she consoled herself with the knowledge that if the next part of her plan worked, Serena would be happier than she'd been for a long time.

It was during assembly, at the start of the second week of the spring term, that the announcement Angelina had been expecting was made.

Mrs Page, the head teacher was reeling off the school notices, when she came to one that made the entire school sit up and listen.

"As I'm sure you're all well aware, the highlight of this half term is our famous Valentine's Ball."

A cheer rang out around the hall, followed by a cacophony of voices as the pupils chattered excitedly among themselves. Mrs Page held up her hand, waiting for quiet.

"All right, all right." she said. "Now, in previous years this has always been a great success, so you've a lot to live up to if you're going to throw the best Valentine's Ball yet. Do you think you're up for it?"

Mrs Page drew back, holding her hands up in mock defence, as the roar confirmed the school's assent.

"Glad to hear it. Now remember, it's your Valentine's Ball and it's up to you to make it a success. We'll be putting together a committee and we'll need student representation. Mr Stewart will also require help from all you budding artists to decorate the scenery and prepare the hall. We're hoping to have live music and singing on the night, so get yourselves involved."

After school, Angelina made her first jump into Serena's mind since Christmas Day. Arriving in Serena's subconscious, Angelina knew immediately that something was different. It was the scent: the aroma of burning had gone. In its place all Angelina could detect was the smell of ash.

Her fire has burned out, thought Angelina, concerned by the change within Serena. There's nothing to replace it with yet. I'll have to help change that.

In Serena's conscious mind, Angelina was in for another shock. Serena's thoughts were faint and unsure. She was polite and friendly enough to Laura, but quickly excused herself and hid in her room, where she lay on the bed staring at the ceiling, her music on low.

Angelina knew that she had to do something to bring her round.

'Where's my sketch book?' Angelina asked.

Serena's eyes moved lazily towards her chest of drawers, where the pad was balanced on a pile of novels.

'I could draw some ideas for the Valentine Ball.' Angelina suggested.

'What's the point,' Serena dismissed the thought.

'I bet they've never had anything like my designs.' Angelina tried again.

This time, Serena showed a glimmer of interest.

'They've always had boring artwork. They wouldn't know what had hit them if I designed it.'

'I'll jot down a few ideas.' Assuming this was her own thought, Serena obediently got up and collected her pad.

From her vantage point, Angelina watched in amazement as Serena drew a dramatic, stylised heart that almost appeared to pulse on the page. After adding banners, her own distinctive lettering and a horned cherub, the effect was amazing.

'That's even better than I thought. Perhaps I should show Mr Stewart,' Angelina suggested.

'What's the point?' Serena disagreed with, what she thought was herself.

Angelina tried a different tack. *'Although I suppose he might let me use if for my next project. That would save me some work.'*

'But what if it's not really that good?' Since her confidence had been shattered, Serena was proving harder to convince.

'I could see what Laura thinks.' Angelina held her breath, not knowing

how the suggestion would be taken, but to her surprise, Serena didn't question it and headed downstairs.

Serena's relationship with Laura had apparently improved enormously in the three weeks since Christmas Day. Laura was in the lounge, lying on the sofa looking incredibly uncomfortable. When she saw Serena, she struggled into a sitting position and smiled.

"Are you ready for something to eat?" Laura asked.

"I'm fine. You rest. I..," Serena stopped and looked down at the sketch pad in her hands, unsure of herself again.

'I might as well ask. It doesn't matter what she thinks.' Angelina urged Serena on.

Serena held out her sketch pad. *"It's probably silly, but I wondered if you thought this was any good. They're looking for designs for the Valentine's Ball and I thought...."* Trailing off, she thrust the book towards Laura.

For what seemed like forever, Laura studied the pictures. Eventually, she asked. "Did you do these?"

"Yeah, they're not that good. Don't worry about it."

Serena made a move to take back the sketch pad, but Laura moved it out of reach.

"Unlike your dad, I don't know much about art but I can tell when something is amazing." Laura looked up at Serena, a look of genuine surprise on her face. "These are fantastic. I had no idea you could draw like this. You've got real talent, Serena. Does your dad know? He'll be so proud."

Serena squirmed under Laura's gaze, but Angelina could tell that she was pleased by Laura's reaction.

"It's nothing special, they're just pictures."

"Nothing special? I could never draw something like this in a million years. You must put them forward for the Valentine's Ball, they'd look fantastic. Please, promise me you'll show them to your dad? You're amazing to be able to draw like that."

As Laura handed back the sketch pad, she gave a loud moan and clutched her stomach.

"What's wrong?" Serena asked in panic.

For a second, Laura struggled to breathe, but then she smiled up at Serena.

"I think this baby has finally decided to make an appearance. I've been having twinges all afternoon, but I thought they'd go away. Guess

I was wrong. Could you call your dad for me?"

"What?"

"It's okay, I think it will be a while yet, but I'd better get to the hospital."

"Yeah, fine. Okay. Fine. Where's my phone?" Serena whirled around in panic.

'I need to calm down,' Angelina told her in a loud confident voice. *'The phone's in my bedroom. I'll call Dad and he'll be here soon.'*

"Stay there. I'll go get the phone."

Serena raced upstairs grabbed her phone. Her voice was so high-pitched that the speech recognition system didn't work, and it took her three attempts to hit the button for her dad's mobile, her hands were shaking so badly. She thundered back down the stairs.

As her father answered, she heard more groans coming from the lounge.

"Dad, it's me," she yelled into the phone.

"Serena? Is everyth…"

Serena interrupted him. "Laura's having the baby. You need to get here. Now!"

"What?"

"The baby, she's having the baby."

"But she was fine this morning."

"She's not now! You need to come home, quick."

"Okay, I'm on my way, but it'll take at least an hour. Do you think she can wait until then?"

Another groan, this time even louder, came from the lounge.

"No, she can't! You need to get here now, Dad."

"I'll be there as soon as I can, but I need you to get her to the hospital. Call an ambulance and I'll meet you there."

"Okay, but don't be long." She cut the connection and dialled 999.

Laura was having another contraction when Serena returned to the lounge. She knelt and held Laura's hand.

"Don't worry, the ambulance is on its way and Dad will meet us at the hospital. Do you need me to get you anything?"

"My overnight bag. It's in the hall cupboard," Laura gasped, as the pain subsided.

Serena got to her feet to fetch the bag, but Laura held on to her hand.

"I'm glad you're here. Thank you."

"That's okay."

Smiling, Serena rushed off to collect the bag. Five minutes later, the ambulance arrived. As Serena opened the door to the paramedics, Angelina exited. She'd done her part tonight and delivering babies wasn't part of her job description.

Angelina waited in the shadows until Laura, supported by the paramedic, shuffled down the driveway. Serena followed behind clutching the overnight bag. When they were all safely inside, the ambulance pulled away and drove off down the road, not even bothering with the siren or flashing lights, much to Angelina's disappointment.

Watching the taillights glow red, as the ambulance slowed to negotiate the corner, she couldn't keep the smile from her face. She was another step closer to making this assignment happen and it felt good. If Dee had thought a level-eleven Fate Switch was beyond her, then she was in for a shock.

Chapter Thirty-one

Serena didn't turn up for registration the next day. Finally, she appeared at lunchtime looking tired.

By hiding in a dark corner of the cloakroom, Angelina heard Serena telling Carrie that, at exactly eighteen minutes past two in the morning, Laura had given birth to a baby boy, Serena's baby brother, well half-brother. They'd called him Lucas, a name Serena had suggested.

It was all very nice, but Angelina didn't have time for 'nice'. She had to get Serena to put her name down for the Valentine's Ball design team as soon as possible. Taking a chance, she jumped into Serena's mind.

'Isn't there something I should be doing? That's it! Showing Mr Stewart the sketch. I promised Laura.' Angelina jogged Serena's memory.

'I'll do it later.' Serena didn't seem quite so keen on the idea today.

'But Laura's bound to ask and she'll give me that disappointed look if I haven't shown him. I'll go now.' Angelina knew that she was sounding desperate, but she needed Serena to act.

Fortunately, Serena squirmed at the thought of disappointing Laura. *'Might as well but I don't want Carrie to know, she'd laugh at me.'*

She looked at her watch and said: "I've got to go and sign in or they'll give me more hassle. I'll see you later."

Serena found Mr Stewart in the art department, preparing the room for his first lesson after lunch. Angelina had always thought that Mr Stewart looked more like an army sergeant than an art teacher, with his cropped, grey hair, trim build and strong Glaswegian accent, but he had a passion for his work and a no-nonsense attitude that made students both respect and like him.

When he spotted Serena at the door, he frowned. "You're too early. Come back when the bell goes."

'I have to show him the sketches,' Angelina urged in Serena's mind.

"I'm not here for class. It's about the design team for the Valentine's Ball."

"That? It's full. Only had six places and had to close it this morning. You've another year yet though, haven't you? I'll make sure you're top of the list for next year."

"You're full? You can't be."

Serena spoke the words as Angelina said them in her mind. This wasn't possible. Serena had to be on the design team, or the assignment was gone.

"Sorry, we have to draw the line somewhere." Mr Stewart turned back to his preparations.

Serena was deflated, Angelina could tell. It had taken a lot for her to even get this far, but Angelina didn't intend to let her go without a fight.

'How dare he? He's not going to tell me what to do.' Angelina tried to rekindle the impudent attitude Serena used to have. *'I'm going to show him.'*

Serena fell effortlessly into her old ways.

"That's why I came to see you." She slammed the open sketchpad on top of the work that Mr Stewart was sorting through. "It's probably too good for this school, anyway." With a glare she turned and stormed out of the room.

"Miss Jackson." The dangerous authority in Mr Stewart's voice stopped Serena in her tracks. "Come here."

Without turning, Serena gave a theatrical sigh and shrugged. "Why should I?"

"Because I want the Valentine's Ball to feature your design."

"What?"

Open-mouthed, Serena turned back to Mr Stewart.

"You heard." Mr Stewart was studying her sketch pad. "You are right. These designs are too good for this school, but I don't see why we shouldn't have them, anyway. Congratulations, you're on the team."

He looked up and with his head on one side stared directly into Serena's eyes. Angelina could tell that it was making her feel uncomfortable, but she didn't seem able to move from his gaze.

"I always knew you were talented. But, with that attitude of yours I thought you'd never apply yourself. Seen so much potential go to waste over the years." He nodded. "I hope you'll prove me wrong. If ever you need to use the art room out of hours let me know."

Angelina could tell that his words mattered to Serena.

"The design team's meeting tomorrow after school in the hall. I'll see you there and don't be late."

"No, sir. Thanks sir."

It was the first time that Angelina had ever heard Serena speak respectfully to one of her teachers. As she clattered down the stairs, Serena was almost giddy with pride.

Having materialised back in the deserted cloakroom, Angelina was also feeling giddy; another part of her plan had fallen perfectly into place.

Earlier that day, she'd taken another risk by jumping into Nathan Bird's mind. Persuading him to join the Valentine's Ball design team had been much easier. It turned out that Nathan had planned to join the team all along, he'd been waiting to see if it clashed with his band's practice nights. As soon as he'd discovered that they would meet on Mondays and Thursdays, which were the same evenings that Taz played hockey, he'd been one of the first to see Mr Stewart and put his name on the list.

It was all working perfectly. Angelina now had Nathan and Serena in the same place at the same time doing something they both loved.

Now I need to get them talking, make them realise that they both share a passion for art and then discover that they've a passion for each other. Okay, so there's still a long way to go. But, at last I'm getting somewhere.

Although she couldn't stop the nagging doubt that things were going a little too well.

Chapter Thirty-two

"You've less than two weeks to go and you're not doing anywhere near enough training to get a decent grade." Dee slammed the training diary on the kitchen table. "According to this, you've only logged the minimum recommended training time."

Thinking back to the hours and hours of Mind Jumps and research she'd performed, Angelina was relieved that Dee couldn't read her mind.

"I thought I was doing enough."

"Enough? To get an A grade you need to Mind Jump, do your influencing and be out within twenty-five minutes. Take longer than forty minutes and you'll fail. That's more likely than a pass at this rate."

Peering over her glasses at Angelina, Dee frowned. "I know I've been busy, but you shouldn't need me to hold your hand on this. It's your future that's at stake."

More than just my future, thanks to you, thought Angelina. Why this sudden interest in me? Is it so that I won't be suspicious when it all goes wrong, because you've been warning me that I need to practice more? Well, guess what, Dee, that's not going to happen.

Acting suitably chastised, Angelina said: "I'll try to do more this week."

Despite her success in getting Serena and Nathan in the same room, things had stalled. The two had barely spoken, let alone started to fall for each other and there were only four more sessions remaining for the art team before the big day. Angelina had to make something happen.

During registration, Angelina overheard Serena telling Carrie that she'd arranged with Mr Stewart to spend her lunchtimes in the art room this week. She wanted to finish the posters that would go on the notice boards around school.

That's interesting. Angelina thought.

At lunchtime, concealed behind a pillar at the entrance to the canteen, she waited patiently for Nathan. He finally appeared with a group of friends from his form.

With a quick check to make sure that no one was looking, Angelina concentrated and jumped into Nathan's mind. The boys were talking about the football match that had taken place the previous Saturday.

"Northpark didn't know what hit them when Matt equalised." Angelina recognised the boy speaking as Paul Flowers from her biology class "And when Nina tapped in that winner with only five minutes to go, their coach nearly had a fit."

"They were favourites to win the cup, this year. They haven't lost a league match all season," said Nathan.

"Well they lost to us in the semi-finals, and that's what counts," said another boy, whom Angelina didn't know.

"I can't believe we've got Stalyborough in the final. They'll be out to slaughter us since we beat them in the league," said Nathan.

"Have you heard when the final is?" asked Paul. "Fourteenth of February! It's the afternoon of the Ball. What a night that'll be if we win."

Nathan turned to Paul. "Fourteenth, are you sure?"

"Yeah, it's up on the notice board. What's up?"

"We're supposed to be putting out all the screens and dressing the hall for the Valentine's Ball that afternoon. What time does it start?"

"Two o'clock kick-off. Won't you be finished by then?" Paul asked.

"I doubt it. I'll have to check with Mr Stewart."

'Oh no.' Angelina interrupted Nathan's thoughts. *'I need to fetch the banners from the art room now.'*

Nathan wasn't concentrating and, thinking it was his own memory, went along with Angelina's thought.

"That reminds me, I've got to pick up some banners. I'll see you outside," said Nathan.

Distracted by the thought of missing the final, Nathan climbed the stairs towards the art department. It was only when he walked through the door to Mr Stewart's room and saw Serena, her head bowed over a Valentine's Ball poster, that he realised he had no idea why he was there.

Serena looked up. "What do you want?"

"I…I…" Nathan had no idea why he was in the art room.

'The banners. I've come for the banners.' Angelina prompted him.

"I've come for the banners," said Nathan, going with the first thought that came into his mind.

"The banners? Why?" Serena's stare fixed him, like a moth pinned to a specimen board.

It was an obvious question, but one that Angelina hadn't prepared for. She'd only thought as far as getting Nathan into the same room as Serena.

"I…"

'They need checking.' It was weak but it would do.

"I wanted to make sure they were still okay." Nathan translated Angelina's thought into something that made more sense.

"Does Mr Stewart know?"

"No," Nathan confessed.

'I think I made a mistake and need to check the banner. The design is so good I didn't want to ruin it.' Angelina gave Nathan an excuse.

"I had a feeling that I'd gone wrong on the lettering and wanted to put it right. The design's too good, it has to be perfect."

Through Nathan's eyes, Angelina caught a flash of pride in Serena's eyes as Nathan spoke. Then her face clouded once again.

"You really like it?" she asked.

This time, Nathan didn't need any prompting. "I think it's amazing. It's so bold and different to anything they've ever done before. I think it'll blow everyone away when they see it. I'm glad Mr Stewart dared to go for it, everyone on the team thinks the same. Don't you?"

"I suppose."

"Do you think Mr Stewart came up with the idea?"

Nathan was so carried away by the conversation that he didn't seem to care who he was talking to, anymore.

"If you must know, it's my design."

"No!" Nathan's mouth literally dropped open.

"Don't you believe me?" The aggressive Serena reappeared but Nathan didn't seem to notice.

"Honestly? You came up with this design?"

"I said so, didn't I?"

"Wow, that is amazing. I thought it must have been Mr Stewart or one of his old students or something. I didn't think anyone our age could have done this. You're really….," Nathan stopped, searching for the right word, "…gifted."

Serena looked taken aback by Nathan's obvious awe and her defensive attitude faltered.

"You think they're that good?"

"Seriously, I'd love to have come up with something like that."

In his enthusiasm he moved forward and sat down at the table next to Serena, examining the poster she was working on.

"This section here." He traced his finger over the artwork bordering the right-hand side of the poster. "It blends into the heart and makes it look like its broken and bleeding, but when you look closer it's nothing of the sort, it's linking the two hearts together. How you get that effect is fantastic."

"You got that? I didn't know if anyone would work it out."

"Most people probably won't. But they'll be able to read into it what they want, which I'm guessing is what you're after."

"Yeah, that's exactly it. You think it works?" Serena tilted her face towards Nathan.

"Definitely." Nathan stopped, remembering who he was talking to and became nervous again.

"Seriously, it's amazing. I'd better check on the banners and leave you to it."

As Nathan inspected the banners, which were laid out along the benches at the back of the room, Angelina added to his thoughts.

'She's a fantastic artist. I'd never have thought Serena Jackson could have designed all this.'

'I shouldn't have said all that to her, though.' Nathan's own thoughts were still incredibly wary of Serena.

'But she seemed okay about everything. Maybe she's not that bad.' Angelina tried to influence his feelings towards her.

'And she knows what she's doing when it comes to art.' Nathan's thoughts warmed a little. *'These banners are fine. Why did I think I'd made a mistake?'*

Angelina remained silent.

As he made for the door, Serena stopped him.

"It's Nathan, isn't it?"

"Yeah." The nerves were back.

"You won't say anything about it being my design, will you?"

Angelina could tell Nathan thought that Serena was threatening him.

"No, no. Don't worry, I won't tell anyone." He was about to rush out of the door but stopped and turned back. "Why? If they were mine, I'd want everyone to know."

The honesty in Serena's face was unmistakable. "If they knew it was mine, the art team would probably refuse to work on it, and no one would give it a chance. They'd hate it because I'd designed it."

"They wouldn't, it's too good."

Serena shrugged. "Thanks, but you know it's true, Nathan."

Seeing Serena so vulnerable had moved Nathan, Angelina could tell. "I guess you might be right. Don't worry, I won't say anything."

He smiled and was delighted when Serena smiled back.

"Thanks," she said.

As Nathan clattered down the stairs, Angelina said in his mind: *'She's quite good looking when she smiles.'*

'Don't even go there.' Nathan dismissed what he presumed were his own thoughts.

'Why not? Good looking, good at art, can even be quite nice on occasions. Worth a try isn't it?'

'But Serena Jackson!'

Leaving that final thought in Nathan's head, Angelina exited.

Before the next Valentine's Ball design team meeting began, Angelina made sure that she was settled in Serena's mind.

'Is Nathan here yet?' Angelina put the question into Serena's head.

Automatically obeying her own thoughts, Serena looked around.

'Can't see him. What do I care anyway?' She dismissed the thought and collected her paint brushes and pallet ready to start work on the screens. Serena was conscious that most people in the art team ignored her. But Angelina knew she wasn't bothered as it meant that she could get on with her work without being disturbed.

For the next five minutes, every time the door opened, Angelina would ask: *'Is that Nathan?'*

Without fail, Serena looked up.

The constant questioning was making Serena feel nervous, even though she couldn't work out why. When Nathan finally did walk into the room and Serena saw him, she couldn't help but give him a huge grin. From her hiding place in Serena's mind, Angelina could sense how surprised Serena was at the warm fuzzy feeling she had on seeing Nathan.

Registering Serena's smile, Nathan tentatively smiled back.

'*I could ask Nathan what he thinks of this.*' Again, the suggestion came from Angelina.

'*No, he wouldn't care.*' Serena argued with what she thought was herself.

'*He knows his stuff. He'll tell the truth.*' Angelina wouldn't let it rest. It took a full two minutes of discussion inside Serena's mind before she finally plucked up the courage to approach Nathan. He was at the sink, mixing powder paint to a deep shade of crimson.

"Hi Nathan." He jumped at the sound of Serena's voice.

"Oh, hi. You okay?"

"Just need some help." Serena looked away. "Will you look at this design I'm working on? See what you think?"

Nathan was obviously taken aback by the invitation but said: "If you want me to."

He followed Serena back to the screen.

"I'm struggling with this section here," she said. "I want it to flow like it did on the poster, but it's not working." She pointed to the bottom left-hand corner of the screen.

When he looked at the display screen, Nathan's reluctance disappeared. He became engrossed in the intricate design and seemed to forget that he was talking to Serena.

"I see what you mean." He stepped back and tilted his head to the side. "Try using longer brush strokes. Be bold; take it right into the corner." He demonstrated the motion with his arm.

"That could work. I should have thought of that."

"It's not always easy when you're so close to the design. Do you want me to help?"

'*Yes!*' Angelina put the idea into Serena's mind so quickly that she didn't give her the chance to disagree.

"You don't mind?"

"No, it'll be fun. Let me fetch my brushes."

Angelina stayed for another ten minutes, listening as the conversation between Serena and Nathan became more friendly and comfortable.

It's working, Angelina thought, the excitement building inside her.

But for some reason, a sense of overwhelming sadness washed over her, as all she could think about was Joe.

Chapter Thirty-three

Valentine's Day had never meant anything to Joe, until today. It was two-and-a-half months since his friendship with Angelina had fallen apart, but he still couldn't get her out of his head.

He'd trained that morning and the swimming pool had been full of couples, or so it had seemed to Joe.

Valentine's Day! What a stupid invention, he thought.

He knew he should finish his homework but, instead, he was lying on his bed thinking about the card and flowers he could have bought Angelina. He could have taken her to the cinema or for a walk in the park or…

He had to stop. Angelina would laugh if she could see how ridiculously romantic he'd become. He smiled at the thought of her telling him to stop being so soft.

This is stupid, he told himself. It's one day of the year and it's no different to any other. Forget about Valentine's Day and forget about Angelina Crossland. She's bad news and isn't even human. I mean, how ridiculous can you get?

Thoughts of the Valentine's Ball floated into his mind. Not that he was going. Not without Angelina. For all he knew, she might be on her way home to a completely different dimension by then, Fate Switch completed, assignment finished.

He looked at his watch: a quarter past twelve. Only an hour and three quarters until Angelina's assignment was due to take place.

This was pointless. He dragged himself up from the bed and switched on the computer. Opening his schoolbook, he tried to concentrate on his ICT homework, but that was the class he shared with Angelina and it just made things worse. Giving up, he decided to treat himself to the new laptop he'd been saving up for. Although he didn't have quite enough money saved to pay the full retail price, he reasoned that if he searched the internet, he would probably find it on sale somewhere.

It didn't take long. After ten minutes he came across a site he'd never used before. It was selling an ex-display version of the laptop he wanted with a twenty-five per cent discount.

"At last, something's going right today," he muttered.

The site seemed secure and independent reviews from satisfied customers seemed genuine. He completed the transaction and was about to print out the confirmation when he stopped.

That can't be right, he thought.

As he checked the details again, a knot formed in his stomach and for a second the walls seemed to close in on him. Shaking he printed out the order confirmation. He looked at his watch again, twenty-five past twelve. Only an hour and a half to go before the Fate Switch.

He had to tell Angelina.

Spring's arrived early, thought Angelina. Leaf buds blunted the branches of bare trees, yellow daffodil heads bobbed and nodded along the grass verge and a freshness hung in the air as Angelina wandered down Hermit Hill Lane. It helped that the sun was out making it feel surprisingly warm for the time of year.

The day added to the nervous excitement that she was feeling. It was midday, two hours to go before the Fate Switch and she couldn't wait. She knew that the design team was meeting at one o'clock to dress the school hall ready for the Valentine's Ball that evening, and she wanted to watch Serena and Nathan for a while before she made the Mind Jump.

Over the last couple of weeks, with Angelina's encouragement, Serena and Nathan had spent more and more time together. Angelina had already suggested to Serena that she might go to the Ball with Nathan but hadn't pushed the idea as it had to be Valentine's Day, just before two o'clock, before Serena asked the question.

Meanwhile, with Nathan Angelina had concentrated on suggesting how it might be nice to have someone like Serena to go to the Ball with. At first, Nathan had ridiculed the thought but with Angelina's persistent suggestions, he'd gradually warmed to the idea.

Before she could concentrate fully on the Fate Switch, she wanted to call in on Rose. Mr Garden's friend, Bob Woods, had died the day before. Apparently, he'd never properly recovered from the heart attack he'd had on Christmas Day. A cloud covered the sun, turning the air chilly as Angelina remembered how upset Rose had sounded when she'd phoned late the previous evening.

Angelina's plans to visit Rose first thing had been spoiled by Dee insisting on going over the assignment that morning.

After what had seemed like hours of form filling and signing endless disclaimers, Dee had finally said: "I'm glad to see that you took my advice and put in some more practice over these past two weeks. You'll have to hope it's enough. If not, well… we'll worry about that if it happens."

"I'll try my best."

"Good. I haven't had a student fail yet. I don't expect to start with you."

You almost sound like you mean that, Angelina had thought. Great acting, Dee, just another few hours to keep it up.

Maintaining her own act, Angelina had said: "I'll try not to let you down, Dee."

"Try to relax, you can't do any more now."

"I thought I'd visit Rose. She's upset about her friend dying."

"Whatever. Make sure you keep an eye on the time. You need to be at the school by half past one. Remember to set your watch: twenty minutes an A-grade; forty minutes you fail."

With that final warning, Dee had packed up the paperwork and left the room.

The delay meant that it was after quarter past twelve when Angelina arrived at Rose Cottage. Despite Dee's advice, Angelina intended to be at school by five to one at the latest.

That gives me twenty minutes with Rose, she thought.

"Why don't you ever answer?" Joe screamed the question into his phone as the automated voice told him that Angelina's phone was unavailable, and did he want to leave a message?

"Angelina, it's Joe. It's half past twelve on Saturday. I need to speak to you now. Give me a call as soon as you get this message."

He knew it was doubtful that she'd pick up the message in time, but he had to speak to her before she got to the school.

Perhaps she was still at home. He could call the landline but what if Dee picked up?

I'll deal with that if it happens, he thought. Fingers trembling, he pressed the speed dial that still held Angelina's home number. As the phone rang out, he paced his bedroom. Seven, eight, nine, ten… he counted the rings in his head. When he reached fifteen, he was about to give up when someone finally picked up the phone.

"Yes, who's that?" The voice sounded annoyed.

It's Dee, thought Joe, closing his eyes in dread.

"Is Angelina there, please?"

"No, she's out. Bye."

"Wait!" Thinking quickly, Joe shouted into the phone.

"What?" Dee sounded even more annoyed.

"Do you know where she is? It's Joe, I need to ask her about some work I have to do for tomorrow."

"Joe? Oh, you're that boy, aren't you? I've not heard her talk about you for a while. Anyway, she's busy, it'll have to wait until later."

"It can't wait. It's for my exams. I need to ask her one quick question so that I can finish some work. It really will be quick, but I'll need the rest of the day to do the work once she tells me the answer. If I don't speak to her now, I could fail my exams. I've tried her mobile and it's off. If you know where she is I might be able to get hold of her. It's important or I wouldn't ask." Joe babbled, knowing that he wasn't making much sense.

He hoped that Dee might help him out just to get him off the phone.

"How ridiculous. You shouldn't leave things until the last minute. Angelina's out all afternoon, so it's your own fault if you fail."

Joe's heart sank, she wasn't going to tell him.

Then Dee spoke again: "Oh, if it's that urgent, you could try her at that woman's house. Iris, I think she's called. Although you've probably missed Angelina by now."

Iris? Joe thought. Who's Iris? Then he smiled with relief; she means Rose. "Thanks, I'll try her there," said Joe, into the phone.

His relief soon turned to despair as he scrolled through his phone's contacts. He didn't have Rose's mobile or home phone number and a quick check on the internet told him the number was unlisted.

There was nothing else for it, he'd have to go to Rose's house. Grabbing his jacket, he flew out of the door.

Having run all the way, Joe's lungs were burning and he was panting hard when he arrived at Rose Cottage. It was twenty to one. He knocked on the door and waited, bending over, hands on his knees, as he tried to catch his breath. There was no answer. Straightening up, Joe hammered with his fist again, as loud and as hard as he could but there was no answer.

In frustration, he tried the handle. To his surprise the door opened, and he almost fell into the hallway.

"Hello," he shouted.

"Rose. Angelina. Is anyone home?"

He took another step down the hall and called again. The house was silent.

I've missed her, he thought. And I'll never get to the school in time.

The school! Perhaps I can get a message to someone at the school, Joe thought. If they're setting up the hall, there might be someone in the office and they could put out a call for her!

Joe knew it was a long shot, but he was running out of options. He pulled out his phone, intending to search for the school's number, but swore when he looked at his phone. No signal.

Holding the phone out in front of him he edged down the hallway, watching for the signal bars to reappear. Nothing. He reached the door to the sitting room and followed his phone inside. Still nothing. Dropping his hand to his side, he swore again and was about to leave when his eyes rested on Mr Garden's computer, in the corner of the room.

I'll borrow that. I know Rose is precious about anyone using the computer, but when I explain how important it is for me to get hold of Angelina, I'm sure she won't mind.

Avoiding the obstacle course of chairs, occasional tables and ornaments, Joe made his way to the computer table. A light was shining from the hard drive.

"It's on, great!" In relief, he said the words aloud.

Settling into the chair, he wiggled the mouse and the sleeping screen lit up asking for a password. The username read 'GARDEN'.

Joe groaned. It could be anything. He turned his head towards the window, desperately seeking inspiration and laughed.

"Of, course, it has to be," he muttered.

Focussing on the keyboard he typed R-O-S-E. Holding his breath, he pressed ENTER. The screen dissolved.

"Yes!"

As the computer's desktop replaced the password screen, Joe froze. A wave of sickness engulfed him as he tried to make sense of what he was seeing.

"I don't understand," he whispered.

On the left-hand side of the screen, Joe found himself staring at an icon he'd only ever seen on one other computer. A thick white letter 'V' revolved inside a dark purple sphere; it was the icon for the Versalnet.

Drawn by a fearful fascination, he double clicked the 'V' icon and the Versalnet came to life, the Umail account automatically loading.

It was as if someone else was controlling the mouse as Joe scrolled through the Umails. He stopped at one he recognised, almost forgetting to breathe as he opened the message. What he read shouldn't have been there and it shouldn't have made sense. But it did, and for the first time, Joe saw everything all too clearly. His throat was dry and his hand unsteady as he printed out the evidence.

Yet, it wasn't the printer whirring away that made him jump; it was the sound of the door opening.

Swinging round he saw Rose standing in the doorway, hands on her hips. She was blocking his only means of escape.

In a high-pitched voice that Joe didn't recognise, she spoke: "What are you doing?"

Chapter Thirty-four

It was a quarter to one. Angelina was already at the school, hiding behind the piles of chairs stacked at the back of the main school hall in preparation for the Valentine's Ball.

When she'd arrived at Rose Cottage, there'd been no sign of Rose. She'd found the door unlocked, but when she'd received no reply to her shouts, Angelina had assumed that Rose was visiting her neighbour again. Pulling the door closed behind her, she'd left for Ingworth High School, intending to try Rose again on her way home.

It was cramped and uncomfortable in her hiding place. A metal leg from one of the chairs was digging into Angelina's side, and a crusty substance that looked suspiciously like dried chewing gum was stuck to the underside of the table near her face. But it gave Angelina a perfect view of the hall.

At one o'clock exactly, Serena and Nathan appeared. They'd obviously come together, Angelina noted. Mr Stewart, carrying a clipboard, followed them into the hall, along with the other members of the design team. The group huddled around Mr Stewart as he gave everyone a task and barked out his instructions.

Nathan and Serena had obviously been put in charge of positioning the display screens that had been decorated over the past few weeks. Still hidden, Angelina watched the two of them, as they fetched, carried, angled and adjusted the screens around the room. She could tell from their body language and laughter that they were enjoying the work, and each other's company.

At exactly one-forty-five Angelina checked her GA issue watch. She was surprised to find that her fingers were shaking as she pressed the buttons to reset the timer, she was more nervous than she'd thought. Today, instead of setting the timer to 60:00, as she did each time she performed a Mind Jump, she set the timer for 20.00. She was determined to get in and out, her Fate Switch completed, within twenty minutes. She wanted that A-grade.

Taking a deep breath, she focussed on Serena, let go and jumped. Feeling the familiar tugging sensation, she relaxed as she plunged into the depths of Serena's sub-conscious. Angelina allowed herself a brief smile as she detected the dusty smell of paints that had recently replaced Serena's smouldering anger, before feeling for the familiar pull that would take her into Serena's conscious mind.

"At this rate, we'll be finished well before the match starts." Nathan was speaking to Serena. "Were you thinking of watching?" he asked.

"I guess. The whole school will probably be going," Serena said.

"We could walk up there together, if you like."

'That's a good idea.' Angelina suggested to Serena.

"Okay," Serena said.

"Great."

'I wonder who he's going to the Ball with?' Angelina posed the question in Serena's mind.

Without really thinking, Serena asked: "Who are you bringing tonight?"

Nathan shrugged. "No one. I'll probably come down with Paul and Taz; she's my sister. She's in year seven now. Are you going with anyone?"

Serena stepped back to check that she'd placed the screen exactly as she wanted it.

"Don't think so, I'll probably meet up with Carrie."

'I could ask him to go with me.' Angelina's thought caught Serena off-guard, and she blushed.

"These are looking good, aren't they?"

To Angelina's frustration, Serena quickly changed the conversation. They spent the next few minutes discussing how the decorations were coming along. Each time Angelina suggested anything to do with Nathan and the Valentine's Ball, Serena experienced a wave of nerves and chose to stay with the safe subject of the hall decorations.

Time was running out. It didn't look as if Nathan had any intention of going to the Ball with Serena either. Angelina was becoming more and more agitated. It had to be getting close to two o'clock by now. She had to ask Nathan to the Ball.

Serena wasn't responding to any of Angelina's ideas. As the conversation moved back to the football, Angelina knew that she was losing control. She had to act quickly if she was going to make this Fate Switch happen.

An idea came to her. If she could show that Nathan was receptive to the idea, maybe that would make Serena more confident about asking him to the Ball. If she jumped between Serena and Nathan, perhaps she could manipulate their conversation. As far as she was aware there was no rule in the exam against entering more than one mind. It had to be worth a try.

Slipping back into Serena's subconscious, Angelina concentrated hard on where she'd seen Nathan standing and jumped out of Serena's mind. Her intention was to land directly in Nathan's mind, but without being able to see exactly where Nathan was, it was a difficult move. If her aim was off, she could end up materialising right in front of Serena and Nathan or even jumping into the mind of someone else. But she'd managed it once before, when she'd had to jump from Matt's mind to Joe's in the swimming pool. The thought gave her confidence.

As she felt herself spiralling down again, she knew she'd arrived in someone's mind. Only when she landed and smelled the familiar scent of paint oil and guitar wood, did she know that she'd hit the target and was in Nathan's mind.

'Why don't I go to the Ball with Serena?' Angelina suggested as soon as she arrived in Nathan's conscious mind.

'I can't do that, Matt'll kill me.' Nathan countered the thought.

That's why he's avoiding the subject. Angelina remembered hearing that Matt and Serena used to be a couple.

'Although it was last year when they were together, and I don't think they're seeing each other now.' Angelina tried a persuasive tone.

'It's not worth the risk.'

'If she asked me though…' Angelina left the thought hanging as she rushed back to Serena's mind, knowing that the seconds were ticking away.

Safely back in Serena's conscious mind, Angelina said: *'I can't believe how much nicer Nathan is than Matt.'*

Serena gave a smile that caught Nathan's attention.

"What's wrong?" he asked.

"Oh, nothing," said Serena.

"It must be something to make you smile like that."

'I was thinking how lucky I was to get rid of Matt.' Angelina placed the thought ready for Serena to repeat.

"I was thinking it's almost six months since I broke up with Matt, and how I'm glad I don't have to go to the Ball with him."

"You two broke up?" Nathan faked surprise.

"Ages ago. Before the summer holidays."

"For good? You won't be getting back together?"

Serena pulled a face. "No way. I can't stand him."

Serena stopped what she was doing and turned to face Nathan, her hands on her hips.

"He was with Chloe Hayes from Year 10 and Pippa Collier from Year 9 at the same time as he was supposed to be going out with me!"

"Right. I didn't know." Nathan looked taken aback by Serena's indignant outburst.

'Nathan would never do something like that. He'd make a great boyfriend.' Angelina tried to stay calm as she planted the thought.

"Are you seeing anyone?" Serena asked.

That's good, but this is going way too slowly, thought Angelina.

"Me? No." said Nathan.

Angelina felt Serena's hopes rise.

"Too busy with this" -he held up the brush- "and school, you know."

Noooo! Angelina wanted to scream as she felt Serena's hopes fall again.

In desperation, she jumped back into Nathan's mind. There was no time for subtleties, Angelina had to be blunt. *'Why did I say that. I should let her know I'd like to see her?'*

'I can't do that.' Nathan was having doubts.

'Why not? What have I got to lose?'

'Everything!' Nathan argued with what he assumed were his own thoughts. *'What if she laughs at me?'*

'What if she doesn't?' Angelina argued back.

Nathan glanced around the hall and Angelina saw the clock on the wall. It was one minute to two. This was her last chance if she was going to get that A grade. Taking control, she said: *'Right, that's it. I don't care what she says, I'm going to tell her how I feel.'*

As she rushed out of Nathan's mind, she could only hope that Nathan followed her instructions. Within seconds she was once again looking at the world through Serena's eyes and caught sight of Nathan glancing sideways at Serena.

Go on, she thought, you can say it.

He opened his mouth and cleared his throat.

That's it, Angelina offered her silent encouragement. You can do it.

"What you said about seeing anyone, well, there is someone I'm interested in..." he broke off.

Say it! Angelina screamed silently.

Serena looked at him curiously. "Who?" Nathan looked away and said quietly: 'You."

'Yes. I like him too! The Ball would make a great first date.' Relieved, Angelina immediately planted the idea in Serena's mind and waited for her to ask the question.

But instead, Serena appeared shocked. "I..."

"Sorry, I shouldn't have said that. Forget it." Nathan started re-adjusting the screen that he'd just positioned perfectly.

'Ask him, ask him, ask him,' repeated Angelina.

"No," said Serena.

No! Angelina couldn't believe what she was hearing.

Serena continued. "I'm glad you said that. How about we go to the Ball together tonight?"

Nathan stopped messing with the screen and looked up, his face splitting into a huge grin that Angelina noticed was incredibly attractive.

"Yeah, that'd be good. Shall I call for you?"

Serena laughed. "Yes, if you want. But we need to get these boards finished first."

As Serena turned, Angelina caught another glimpse of the clock; the second hand was sweeping past the number seven. She'd completed a level-eleven Fate Switch in nineteen minutes and thirty-five seconds. The A-grade was hers.

'Yes,' she shouted aloud, forgetting that she was still in Serena's conscious mind. Luckily, Serena accepted it as her own excitement.

Before she made any more mistakes, Angelina slipped back into

Serena's subconscious. It was then she remembered that she hadn't heard the bell ring to signal that the Fate Switch had taken place.

I can't believe I forgot to listen out for it, thought Angelina, as she prepared to exit Serena's mind for the final time.

Chapter Thirty-five

Swirling up through the sticky blackness, Angelina couldn't help laughing. She'd done it! She'd passed her assignment. She couldn't wait to see the look on Dee's face.

As the movement slowed and she came to a halt, Angelina waited for the bright sunlight to appear, but for some reason, she found herself still enveloped in darkness. For a second, she thought she'd miscalculated her exit and ended up in a closed cupboard or something. But that wasn't right. She must still be in Serena's mind.

Yet, she'd felt the unmistakable release as she'd exited. She couldn't possibly be in Serena's mind, so where was she?

A strangely familiar voice echoed around her.

"You're right, Angelina. You left Serena's body."

Angelina froze, a cold fear seeping into her mind as she struggled to make sense of how someone knew who she was and what she was thinking.

"I have to hand it to you, Angelina. You're better than I gave you credit for. I didn't think you had a hope of getting Serena to ask Nathan to the Ball, never mind getting him to accept. You're good, I'll give you that."

Deprived of her sight, Angelina felt confused and although she thought that she recognised the voice, it was distorted by the echo and she couldn't quite place it.

The voice spoke again: "Pity it wasn't a real Fate Switch. Still, never mind. I'm sure they'll enjoy the Valentine's Ball together."

An icicle of fear sliced through Angelina's heart. What did that mean, not a real Fate Switch? What was going on?

"Worked out where you are yet?" The voice was taunting.

"Who are you?" Angelina's voice shook as she tried to control the panic rising within her.

A high-pitched laugh cackled all around her and it finally dawned on Angelina who the voice belonged to.

"Rose?" she whispered.

The tone became scarily friendly as Rose's familiar voice rang out.

"Well, not exactly, my dear, but I suppose that's how you know me. You could call me Mr Garden, but that wouldn't be quite right either."

"I don't understand."

The deep, growling male voice returned.

"Rose doesn't exist. She's someone I adopted, shall we say? No family. No mind, either. Until I came along, her dutiful great-nephew, she was sitting in a care home like the rest of them, dribbling and waiting to die. Although I don't think she even knew that. I probably did her a favour. She was just a convenient vehicle. Well, not that convenient considering her size."

His laugh chilled Angelina.

"Is Rose all right?"

"Rose? Who knows? Who cares? You've got more important things to worry about than Rose. If you remember, you spent twenty minutes in Serena's mind and now you've spent at least three minutes in my mind. By my calculations we've thirty-seven minutes or so before you're vapour."

It was the calm, calculated tone in which the voice spoke that was most terrifying.

"Why are you doing this?"

"Nothing personal, my dear." He started using Rose's voice again. "Well, not really personal. I have to say, it was a bonus when I discovered that you were the one. You know, dear, your grandfather and all that."

Angelina's confusion grew, what did her grandad have to do with all this?

"I don't understand. Who are you?"

The voice ignored her question. "You know, it's a pity my old friend Dee isn't here to share your demise."

Dee? I might have known Dee was behind all this, thought Angelina. Shocked and bewildered, she was finding it hard to take everything in. All she could think about was how close she'd been to getting away from Earth alive. Or at least, she thought she had. Yet, according to whoever the voice belonged to, she hadn't stood a chance. Anger replaced her fear.

"Why is Dee doing this to me?"

As she asked the question, something jolted Angelina, sending her senses reeling. Totally disoriented, she felt as if she was swimming through the thick blackness, not knowing which way was up. As she struggled to clear her mind, she heard someone calling her name.

"Angelina. Angelina. You need to listen to me."

Dee? It was Dee's voice. Dee was here after all. There was no way Angelina was going to make things easy, and she remained silent.

"Angelina, I can sense where you are." Dee's normally acidic tone was surprisingly patient. "You don't have to speak to me. I know you've been through a lot, but you need to get out of here. There isn't much time. Joe's waiting for you. He'll explain everything."

"Joe? He's in on this?" The shock of Dee mentioning Joe's name caused Angelina to break her silence.

"I'll explain later. Joe's here to help, but you need to move quickly. Relax, focus, and it's like leaving any other mind. I'll stay and sort this out."

"I don't understand."

Dee's voice turned urgent. "Angelina, for once do as I say. He's going to wake up soon. You need to get out of here. Now!"

Not knowing who to trust, Angelina decided that leaving this mind was a better option than staying.

She relaxed and felt the familiar tugging sensation that would pull her up and out of whoever's mind she was in. Seconds later she was standing in a shadowy corner of the school playground.

I'm out, she thought. Exhausted and still bewildered, she stepped into the warm sun.

Hearing a shout, she turned to see Joe running across the play-ground towards her.

As he came closer, Angelina could see the relief on his face. He looked as if he was going to throw his arms around her, but stopped, wiping his blond fringe from his eyes.

"She got you out! Are you okay?" he asked.

"I think so. What's going on, Joe?"

"It's the Fate Switch." He lifted his arm, brandishing the sheaf of papers he was carrying. "The real one hasn't happened yet. It had nothing to do with Serena and Nathan. Come on, we need to go."

Confused, Angelina stayed where she was. "What do you mean? How does Dee know about you?"

"That's my fault. I told her."

"What? I've been trying to protect you from her for the past three months, and you go and do something stupid like that." Angelina looked away in despair, tears forming in her eyes. "You don't know what she'll do to you."

He reached out and touched her arm. "Dee's not the one. It's something to do with Rose and Mr Garden."

"I know that. Whoever's mind I was in back there told me that." Angelina jabbed her hand in the direction of the hall. "But Dee's in on it. He said so."

Joe shook his head. "I don't know what that guy said, but Dee isn't working with him. You should have seen her face when she saw him. She looked like she'd seen a ghost."

"Who is he?"

"I don't know. He was standing in the corridor by the hall. I only saw the back of him before Dee dragged me outside again. All she said was *'if he's done anything to her, I'll never forgive myself'*. Then she told me to wait for you in the courtyard and that she'd sort it out. Dee saved you. And this proves she had nothing to do with it."

He waved the papers again.

Angelina rubbed her forehead, totally bemused.

"How? What are they?"

"It's a printout of the real Fate Switch. It had been intercepted and changed on Rose's computer before it was sent through to Dee."

Angelina held up her hand. "Wait, why were you on Rose's computer?"

"I was trying to get hold of you to let you know about Dee. When I missed you at Rose Cottage, I needed to get the number for the school. My phone had no signal, so I used Rose's internet. That's when I found this."

Angelina shook her head, trying to clear the confusion. "You said you found out about Dee from Rose's computer, so what were you trying to tell me before that?"

"That's the other thing. I'll tell you everything on the way, but we need to go. There's still time for you to do the real Fate Switch if we hurry."

Joe grinned and as he grabbed her hand and pulled her along with him, said: "I know what Dee is up to in her garage."

Chapter Thirty-six

Angelina allowed Joe to lead her by the hand across the courtyard. As he hurried along, he told her about ordering a laptop online.

"I couldn't believe it when I saw the shipping information on the order form." He slowed to watch Angelina's reaction to his news. "The company address was four, Hermit Hill Lane. Your cottage."

He grinned as if he'd said something obvious, but Angelina was still dazed from her earlier experience and this announcement added to the confusion.

"How could it be? We live there."

"Exactly! But it makes sense when you think about all that stuff we saw in the garage. Dee's running an internet business from home. That's why there are so many packages coming and going all the time. That's why she was so busy at Christmas."

"Dee's running a business. Why?"

"She sells goods that would otherwise be scrapped because they were on display or the box is damaged. But it's not just any business, it's a charity. The profits go towards conservation projects around the world. It's all there on the website. Listen to this, they recently spent a quarter of a million pounds creating a wild animal sanctuary in Africa."

Angelina stopped in the middle of the playground, as the implication of Joe's words dawned on her.

"The money! That bank statement I found in Dee's room, it had more than three hundred thousand pounds in it. Is that what the money was for? She wasn't taking a bribe; she was doing charity work?"

"That's what it looks like." Joe had obviously been waiting for Angelina to catch up with his deductions.

Angelina's hand flew to her mouth. "Oh, Joe, I'm so sorry."

Now it was Joe's turn to look confused. "What for?"

"That's why I was so awful to you. I thought Dee was into something terrible and that if she thought you had anything to do with me, your life would be in danger. I was trying to keep you safe."

Joe pulled her into a hug. "I could have helped you."

Angelina returned the hug before pulling away and smiling.

"I knew you'd say that. The only way I could be sure that you'd stay away from me was to make you hate me. All those things I said," she held Joe's gaze, "they weren't true. I just couldn't bear the thought of you being hurt. Look."

She reached under the neck of her jumper and pulled out the angel chain that Joe had bought her for Christmas. "I never said thank you."

Joe's eyes widened in recognition. "You kept it?"

"I haven't taken it off since Christmas morning. I'm so sorry for everything."

"None of that matters now." Joe looked as if he was about to hug her again, but the faint sound of the church clock chiming the half-hour, drifted across the fields and he checked his watch instead.

"It's half past two," he said. "I need to tell you about the real Fate Switch before it's too late."

As they half-ran across the school playing fields, Joe told Angelina about seeing the Versalnet on Rose's computer.

"I nearly had a heart attack when I looked up from the computer and saw Rose standing there." Angelina stopped again, grabbing Joe's arm with her free hand, to make him face her. "How did you get away?"

"She was looking at me strangely and then asked in this weird voice what I was doing. Then I remembered that Rose wouldn't know that I know about the Versalnet, so I played dumb. I said I was looking up the school's phone number to call you and ask you to the Valentine's Ball, but did she know that she probably had a virus on her computer as there was this funny V icon."

"What did she say to that?"

"That's when she started getting even more weird. She got all upset and came rushing towards me. For a minute I thought she was trying to attack me, but she got hold of my arm and tried to drag me away from the computer saying, 'Is it scarlet fever? Bobby had scarlet fever and he nearly died'."

Joe spoke the last couple of sentences in a shrill, high-pitched voice that made Angelina giggle, despite the seriousness of the situation.

"She thought the computer had scarlet fever?" she asked.

"Who knows? Anyway, I went along with it. I said I didn't think it was scarlet fever, but that I'd turn it off just in case. By this time, I was getting worried. She didn't seem herself. Then, when she asked me who I was, I realised she didn't have a clue what was going on. I said I was Joe and that I helped her out with her shopping. She seemed really pleased about that and made me sit down while she went to get me some lemonade."

"You asked for lemonade?"

"No. That's what I mean, she was clueless. I didn't have a signal on my phone so, when she went into the kitchen, I used her phone to call Dee."

He looked apologetically at Angelina. "I know it was a risk, but with her doing all the charity stuff I thought she couldn't be that bad. Besides, by then I didn't know what else to do. For all I knew, whoever was using Rose's computer was going to come back and finish me off, and I had to let someone know that you were in real danger."

"How did Dee take it when she found out that you knew everything?"

"Not brilliantly, but when I told her what I'd found on Rose's computer, she was great. She came straight over."

"Is Rose all right?"

Joe's face turned serious. "I don't think she's been well for a long time. We got a neighbour to look after her. I'm sorry, Angelina. I know she was your friend."

Angelina shook her head, slowly. "I don't think I knew the real Rose. Whoever it was that I did know was only pretending to be my friend."

Joe glanced at his watch. "We need to keep going."

Setting off again, he continued talking. "I found the Umail that you thought was your official Fate Switch on Rose's computer. You know, the one where the priority level had been changed."

Angelina nodded, they were moving so quickly that she was out of breath.

"This Umail was the original, but it wasn't a trainee assignment at all. It was flagged up as a high-priority Fate Switch."

To Angelina's relief, Joe started to slow down.

"Why was it changed?"

"I don't know. All I can imagine, is that someone doesn't want this Fate Switch to happen for some reason."

"Why didn't they just delete it?" Angelina was trying hard to make sense of everything.

"That's the problem, they couldn't. Dee explained it to me. If you don't respond to a high-priority Fate Switch within a set time and in a certain way, it raises an alarm and the FFU investigates immediately."

"I still don't get what that has to do with my assignment," Angelina said.

"Dee worked that out too. The response for assignment Fate Switches is the same as the response for high-priority ones. Dee followed the procedure, thinking that she was sorting out your assignment. That's why it didn't raise an alarm. I'm guessing that whoever's behind this, thought that a trainee wouldn't be able to make such a difficult Fate Switch happen."

"But according to whoever's mind I've been trapped in and what you've told me, that wasn't a real Fate Switch anyway. So why would they care? It doesn't make sense."

Joe nodded. "You're right, it wasn't real. It looks as if they added the bit about Serena and Nathan to keep you busy and well away from the real Fate Switch. It also meant that this man, whoever he is, knew you'd be in Serena's mind at two o'clock. All he had to do was wait for you to exit, and suck you into his mind and trap you, giving him plenty of time to make sure the real Fate Switch didn't happen. That's what Dee thinks happened. She was mad when she found out how she'd been fooled."

"I'll bet," said Angelina.

"But there was no other information on that Umail, remember? We checked. How do you know about the real Fate Switch?"

"It was in the original message I saw on Rose's computer. When I checked the Umail that had been forwarded to Dee, the one with the bit about Serena and Nathan added, I saw that the original Fate Switch hadn't been deleted. It was all there, we just couldn't see it. It was so simple, yet so clever."

"Joe, you're not making any sense."

"Okay, you remember when I looked into the sender history and told you the priority level had been changed?"

Angelina nodded.

"And I said there'd been a font change, as well."

"Vaguely," said Angelina.

"Well that was the clue. The font colour of the real Fate Switch had been changed to white, so because it was written on a white background, we couldn't see anything. It's like the writing disappeared." He shook his head. "Whoever's behind all this has been careful not to raise suspicion. If they'd deleted the original message, it would have shown up in the sender history, a bit like when you track the changes in a word document."

Frowning, Angelina said: "Let me get this right. Because they changed the colour of the words, all that it said was that a font change had occurred, which could have been anything?"

"Exactly," said Joe. "The only risk they had to take was changing the priority level. Even that wasn't really a risk. Dee didn't even know there was a sender history, never mind how to check it! If it hadn't been for us, no one would have found out that the Umail had been changed."

As she took everything in, Angelina found herself standing by a clump of bushes at the edge of the playing fields. Shouts and cheers could be heard coming from the crowd that had gathered to watch the cup final between Ingworth High and Stalyborough High. She looked at her watch, it was twenty to three. The second half of the match was about to start.

"Why are we here?"

"Read this," said Joe.

He passed the papers he was carrying to Angelina. "The real Fate Switch is the football match."

Angelina scanned the message.

To: Dorothy Devin,
From: Notification Department FFU
Sent: 18 October, 10:53

Subject: High Priority Fate Switch

THE FATE SWITCH

Level-eleven Fate Switch, Ingworth, Yorkshire, England, Earth.

Date: Saturday 14 February
Time: By 15.15 (local time)
Location: North playing field, Ingworth High School, Ingworth
Target: Nina Kaur

Action: To score penalty in final five minutes of cup match.

Background available:
Age: 13
Address: 4 Dunlow Crescent, Ingworth
Interests: Football, world events, wildlife.

Desired outcome: Fate Switch to take place.

She looked up at the football match in progress and then at Joe.
"Nina's the target?"

Chapter Thirty-seven

Angelina looked up and saw the mud splattered, red and black clad, Ingworth High players, lining up against the green and white Stalyborough High team.

The school's cup final.

It was all about football!

Joe said: "I heard that a talent scout from the Women's Super League was coming to watch the match. Maybe that's got something to do with it."

Angelina looked at her watch. There was less than half an hour until the Fate Switch was to take place.

"I can't do this."

"Yes, you can. Dee told me to bring you here by quarter to three to give you enough time to get into her mind."

A look of fear on her face, Angelina turned to face Joe.

"No, I really can't do this. It's a level-eleven Fate Switch. I'm a trainee, Joe, I'm not qualified for this."

"But you thought Serena's Fate Switch was level-eleven and you managed to do that."

"That wasn't real, and I had months to prepare. I've got less than thirty minutes to do this. It's not possible. Not by me, anyway. We need to get Dee. She might be able to do it."

She turned and started walking back to the school, but Joe caught her arm. Swinging her round to face him he held her by the shoulders.

"Listen to me. You can do this. You managed to persuade Serena to ask Nathan to the Valentine's Ball. That was impossible, but you did it. I know you can do this. Dee believes in you too; she wouldn't have sent you otherwise."

"You don't understand. A level-eleven Fate Switch needs preparing for. You've got to make lots of little moves before you can make the big move. It can't be done in less than half an hour."

"But you have prepared. How many matches have you watched? It might not be perfect, but it's something."

Joe seemed to have second thoughts. He let go of Angelina and shrugged.

"Maybe you're right. Maybe it's not possible. But you're giving in before you've even started. If you try and fail, then fine, at least you've given it your best shot, but to not even try…"

He looked away, as if trying to work out how to put into words what he was feeling.

"When I missed out on the British squad because I messed up that dive, I was devastated, but I've got another chance in two weeks' time. I might mess up again, but I might dive well and be selected. The only thing I do know is that if I don't even enter the competition I've absolutely no chance of making the national squad."

He squeezed Angelina's hand. "If you have a go at this, you might fail, but if you don't give it a go, you will fail. Come on, what have you got to lose?"

Angelina looked at him. A hundred reasons why she shouldn't even attempt this Fate Switch were running through her head. But knowing how much Joe had risked to get her here, she knew that she couldn't disappoint him.

"It won't work, but let's see what's going on."

Joe grinned. "You'll be fine."

He grabbed hold of Angelina's hand and they ran to join the spectators at the edge of the football field. Angelina saw Nina immediately. She was waiting on the half-way line as the Ingworth players defended an attack from the Stalyborough High team.

Her watch had almost re-charged from her earlier Mind Jumping. Resetting it, she whispered to Joe: "Hide me, I need to get straight in there."

Moving behind Joe, she quickly checked that no one was looking her way and jumped. As Angelina was sucked into Nina's mind, a wave of panic hit, and she wanted to scream and fight her way out.

Then, Joe's face swam into her mind. She couldn't let him down. She wouldn't let him down.

Breathing deeply, she regained control as she landed in Nina's subconscious. A comforting earthy smell of wet grass and mud surrounded her. She smiled, Nina obviously spent all her time playing and thinking about football. In the darkness of Nina's subconscious mind, Angelina composed herself. Thinking of Joe and his faith in her, she relaxed and waited to feel the current that would pull her into Nina's conscious mind.

The first thing that Angelina saw was the grass rushing past at an alarming rate and she almost screamed. Then she saw that Nina had the ball at her feet and kept glancing down to keep control, before raising her head to check on the opposition defence and note where her teammates were. All these thoughts were whizzing through Nina's mind so fast that she was barely acknowledging them. It was almost as if everything she did was automatic, it was so natural.

This game seems even more complicated from in here, thought Angelina, as she tried to keep pace with Nina's thoughts. For a full ten minutes, she watched and listened as the game went backwards and forwards and attack after attack ended up in disappointment. Eventually, she started to tune in to Nina's thoughts and recognised that something was troubling her.

'What's Matt playing at?' Nina's thoughts now came clearly to Angelina.

Through her eyes, she watched as Matt kicked the ball wildly. It flew well wide of the goal.

'I was in a perfect position. He should have passed,' thought Nina.

When the same thing happened again, Nina jogged over to him.

"Matt, watch out for me. I keep getting free."

"So what? You don't think I'd give a little girl the chance to mess things up?"

Matt kept his face pleasant, but the venom in his words made something click in Angelina's head.

She thought back to the evil that had infected Matt's mind and trapped her during her first solo Mind Jump, and suddenly everything fell into place.

That was no accident, she thought. Whoever used Rose to get to me has been using Matt to get to Nina. Well, if that's the plan, then I know exactly how to handle this.

Angelina could tell that Nina was upset by what Matt had said and she fluffed a pass, giving the ball away to the opposition. Matt came past and sniggered.

"Not so good now, are you?"

Nina's confidence dropped further.

'Matt's scared. He knows I'm a better footballer than him,' said Angelina in Nina's mind.

The thought surprised Nina, and her spirit lifted a little. *'Yeah, I think he is,'* she thought.

'I need to show him how good I am. He'll hate that.' Angelina's suggestion.

'But that'll make him angry.' Nina was still unsure of herself.

'Good. Let's put on a real show and see if he can keep up. I'll show him what a little girl can do.'

Angelina continued to bolster Nina's confidence and eventually she could tell that she was beginning to believe in herself again.

The game went on and every time Matt said something to Nina, Angelina immediately laughed.

'Yes! I'm making him really mad. The better I play, the worse he gets.'

It was true. Matt looked as if he was starting to lose his concentration and, as Nina plucked the ball from the feet of a Stalyborough High defender and raced up the pitch towards goal, Matt was nowhere in sight.

Not wanting to distract Nina, Angelina kept quiet as the goal loomed in front of them. Nina was totally focussed as she picked her spot to shoot and put Ingworth High into the lead. But the Stalyborough High goalkeeper had other ideas. With no chance of reaching the ball, the keeper dived in front of Nina, sending her sprawling to the ground.

"Penalty!"

The cry rang out from Ingworth High supporters around the field, as the referee blew his whistle and pointed to the penalty spot.

Angelina felt her heart begin to pound. She'd become so engrossed in the match and keeping Nina's confidence up, that she hadn't kept track of how much time had passed. It was the final five minutes of the game. This was the penalty that Nina had to score. This was the real Fate Switch.

In horror, Angelina watched as Matt collected the ball and calmly stepped up to the penalty spot. Bending over, he placed the ball on the white mark.

271

'I should be taking this, not Matt.' Angelina's urgent comment caused Nina to look towards the touchline.

The coach, Mr Stephens, was gesturing furiously and shouting for Nina to take the penalty.

'Oh, well, Matt's taking it now.' Nina was ready to give in.

'No. He's not doing this to me again. He's going to miss, and we need to score. It's my turn this time. Mr Stephens wants me to do it too.'

'But what can I do?'

'I need to get over there now.' Angelina's comment was so forceful that Nina automatically obeyed.

She approached Matt, who was walking backwards, pacing out his run up as Nina stood in front of him.

"I'm supposed to take this." Nina looked up at Matt, who seemed even taller and more menacing than ever.

"Get out of the way. I take the penalties."

Looking angry, Matt stepped towards Nina.

'No, you're not. I'm taking it. Ask coach,' Angelina said, in Nina's mind.

The young girl stood her ground, looking up at Matt with a fierce determination. "Mr Stephens wants me to take it. Ask him."

Matt loomed over Nina and for a second, Angelina wondered if he might hit her. The referee, who had spotted trouble brewing, marched up.

"What's going on?"

"Nothing, she's going," said Matt.

'Coach wants me to take the penalty,' Angelina reminded Nina.

"I've been told by Mr Stephens to take the penalty," said Nina.

Matt and the referee looked towards the coach.

"Which one?" The referee shouted to Mr Stephens.

Cupping his hands around his mouth, Mr Stephens' reply could be heard by everyone on the field. "I want Nina to take this."

Yes, thought Angelina. But Matt wasn't done yet. As the referee jogged backwards into position, Matt purposely shoved into Nina.

"You're going to miss this, and the entire school will blame you for losing the cup. You'll be the last girl to ever plays in this team, I promise you that." Matt stalked away, swearing at Nina under his breath.

Angelina could tell that the encounter had shaken Nina. Doubts were creeping in as she realised the enormity of what she'd done.

'He's right. What if I miss? I should have let Matt take it.'

'No!' Angelina interrupted. *'I'm the best player on this pitch and Matt knows it. He's trying to freak me out. I need to take my time and concentrate. Look how big that goal is and how small the goalkeeper. I can't miss. I really can't!'*

Hearing the words, Nina relaxed. Angelina could sense a change in her as she stepped up to the penalty spot and worked the ball with her feet until she was satisfied with its positioning.

'I can do this. I can do this. I can do this.' Angelina whispered the chant until Nina took over.

'I can do this. Same as training, pick my spot, focus and hit the ball clean.' Breathing deeply, Nina took six large strides backwards, her eyes never leaving the goal. Nina was in the zone and Angelina stayed silent, knowing that she could do nothing more. It was up to Nina now.

The referee blew his whistle and Angelina held her breath.

For a second everything seemed to stop as Nina concentrated entirely on the ball and goal in front of her. Leaning forward until she lost her balance, she stuttered forward with small pigeon steps that lengthened into a smooth run for the final three strides and as her right foot connected with the ball it shot from the penalty spot towards the right-hand corner of the net. The goalkeeper dived the right way, but had no chance, the ball sailed over his head, hitting the back of the net as the crowd roared in delight.

The Ingworth team, with the exception of Matt surrounded Nina, lifting the young girl into the air in celebration.

Over the screams and cheers, and before she slipped back into Nina's subconscious, Angelina heard a bell ring.

The Fate Switch had happened.

Chapter Thirty-eight

Having materialised behind a clump of bushes at the edge of the playing field and away from the crowd, Angelina, tired but happy, made her way back to where Joe was standing at the edge of the pitch. As soon as he spotted her coming, he gave a shout. He ran up and flung his arms around her, lifting her off her feet and swinging her round, like the footballers had done with Nina.

"I knew you could do it. And we've won the Cup!"

Laughing, Angelina returned the hug. As Joe put her down she noticed he was looking over her shoulder. Following his eyes, she recognised Dee striding towards them, her curly red hair and long purple coat, billowing out behind her.

She's hardly inconspicuous, thought Angelina, as she and Joe ran across the field to meet her.

"She did it," said Joe. "She made the Fate Switch happen."

"Yes, I know. My pager went."

Despite the good news, Dee looked less than happy as she turned to Angelina. She gave a curt nod.

"You did well. I didn't think you'd have a chance, but glad to see I was wrong."

Don't get too carried away with the praise, thought Angelina. At least Joe was still excited about her success.

"She was brilliant, you should have seen her," he said to Dee. "What happens to Nina now?"

"I don't know."

"What? Don't you usually receive an update?" asked Angelina.

"That's the problem. There is no update because there is no record of this Fate Switch. It looks as if it's all been wiped from the records. That's why we have to get to Rose Cottage."

Dee was leading them quickly away from the school and out towards the main road.

"Why Rose Cottage?" asked Angelina.

Dee looked grim. "Because I think that's where Seddon Danvers will be going."

Joe and Angelina were now almost jogging to keep pace with Dee.

"Who's Seddon Danvers?" Joe asked.

"He's the one who almost Vaporised Angelina this afternoon."

Dee came to an abrupt stop at the side of the road, causing Angelina and Joe to almost bump into her.

Swivelling her head from left to right, to check for traffic, Dee continued. "I worked with him at the FFU. So did your grandfather. For the last eight years, I thought he was dead."

Abruptly Dee changed the subject. "We'll have to go by taxi. You'll be too weak to translocate anywhere until tomorrow morning. It takes far more effort than Mind Jumping. I want you to come with us too, Joe."

With that she stuck her fingers in her mouth and whistled to a waiting cab that was parked in the taxi rank across the road. Squashed in the back seat of the taxi between Joe and Dee, Angelina was unable to ask any questions for fear that the taxi driver would overhear. The journey to Rose Cottage passed in silence. As the taxi approached Little Ingworth church, Dee leaned forward.

"You can drop us here," she said to the driver.

Hurrying along the pavement, Dee gave them their instructions.

"I'll go in alone. You two stay outside. Don't come in until I tell you it's safe. Got that? Danvers is dangerous. You can't underestimate him." They were still twenty yards away from the house, but Dee spoke in a low voice.

"How do you know he's here?" Joe asked in a whisper.

"Call it an educated guess."

"I thought you said he was unconscious. What happened?" Joe persisted.

Dee's face hardened as they moved slowly towards the cottage.

"After I knocked him out..."

"You knocked him out?" Angelina interrupted.

Dee looked annoyed at being questioned. "Call me old-fashioned but hitting him over the head with the broom I found leaning against the wall was the quickest way to free you from his mind."

Angelina remembered the jolt that had sent her reeling.

"By the time he came to, I thought I had his mind under control, but he was stronger than I gave him credit for. I couldn't hold him, the..."

For a second, Angelina thought that Dee was about to swear, but the old woman stopped. Instead, she clamped her lips in a tight line and shook her head.

That's why she's in such a foul mood, thought Angelina. She's cross about letting this Seddon Danvers get away. They'd arrived at the gate to Rose Cottage. As they crept down the path, Dee held up her hand.

"Quiet." She turned, glaring at both in turn. "Now stay here. If I'm not out in five minutes, do not come in. Hear me? You get out of here. Run all the way to Hermit Hill Lane if you have to and call the FFU."

Angelina and Joe both nodded, neither daring to question nor argue with Dee. They watched as Dee slowly turned the handle and pushed the door. It was unlocked.

Is that a good sign or a bad one, wondered Angelina, as she watched Dee ease the door open, step over the threshold and disappear into the shadowy darkness of the cottage. Joe grabbed hold of Angelina's hand and pulled her against the wall at the side of the door.

"Less chance of anyone seeing us from inside the cottage," he whispered.

It was almost four o'clock and the sun was now low in the sky. Long fingers of shadows from the trees lining the road reached down the path towards them.

Listening hard, Angelina could hear faint excited barks coming from Sweep, the next-door neighbour's dog, but there was only silence from inside the cottage.

Joe checked his watch.

"Has it been five minutes, yet?" Angelina asked in a whisper.

He shook his head. "Two minutes left."

With every passing second, Angelina became more agitated.

"Thirty seconds left. We need to get ready to go. Something must be wrong."

Joe was counting down the last ten seconds, when the door to the cottage flew open, making them both jump.

Dee's head with its frothy curls poked out. "It's clear. You can come in."

Realising that she'd tensed just about every muscle, Angelina felt her body sag in relief.

"I thought something had happened," she called to Dee as she followed her back into the cottage.

"It takes time to make sure every room is clear," said Dee.

She led them into the lounge and Angelina gasped.

Joe, who was behind her, said: "Woah."

The room was trashed. All the little ornaments, doilies and plants that Rose had had on display were strewn over the floor, furniture was upturned and books ripped open.

"Why did he do all this?" Angelina was close to tears.

"He was looking for something." Dee picked up a fallen table and tilted her head to inspect the floor beneath.

"Judging by this mess, he didn't find it."

"Looking at this mess, I'd say he did find it," said Joe.

He picked his way to the computer, where the monitor had been knocked over. As he righted it, Angelina noticed that at least the screen was unbroken.

"You're wrong," said Dee. "There's too much mess. If he'd found it, he wouldn't have hung around to wreck the place for the sake of it, he'd have been off. No, he's done this out of frustration. Whatever he was looking for might tell us why this afternoon's Fate Switch was so important. It must be a file or document or something and if it's still here we need to find it."

She turned to Joe and waved towards the computer. "I brought you with us to check that thing. See if it still works and find out what you can from it."

Joe nodded. Dee's brusque attitude didn't seem to faze him. It was almost as if Dee had turned into his hero since she'd saved Angelina. He picked up a chair, sat down and switched on the hard drive.

Angelina was still distressed by all the damage when Dee spoke to her. "You can help me go through the rest of the house."

"This is horrible. Can't we clear up and go? Isn't it enough that the

Fate Switch happened? Do we need to know why this Seddon Danvers was trying to stop me?" Angelina asked.

"Scoring a goal in a school football match is hardly important, but Seddon Danvers has obviously gone to a great deal of trouble to stop it from happening and to hide what he was doing. The only thing that makes sense is that it's the starting point for a major chain of events that ends in something terrible. It could take years for it to all come about and there may be other significant Fate Switches that will give Danvers more chances to change the future. That's why we need to know what he's been hiding."

It seemed like a pointless task, but Angelina joined Dee as she sifted through the broken crockery and smashed ornaments. Something was still bothering her.

"Dee?"

"What?" Dee didn't lift her eyes from the papers she was sorting through.

"You said that you and my grandfather knew this Seddon Danvers. Why did you think he was dead?"

Dee sighed, as if she were annoyed at being made to explain things again.

"Seddon Danvers was on the Fate Federation Board at the same time as me and your grandfather. We were all friends for a time."

"What went wrong?" Joe asked. He'd stopped his work on the computer and was listening.

Dee glanced at him.

"What went wrong was Seddon Danvers. There were suspicions that he'd become a traitor and was profiting from selling Future-Vision and other sensitive information to hostile planets so that they'd know their enemy's moves before they made them. Nothing could be proven, but they banned FutureVision just in case. Anyway, the day of the presidential elections, when I was supposed to be elected, Seddon, your grandfather and two other senior GAs were sent on a mission. Only one of them came back, a GA called Blade Magner and he was in a state."

Dee shook her head. "He spent six months unable to say a word. When he finally recovered from the shock, he told us that the mission had been ambushed. The last thing he'd seen before being knocked unconscious was Fern Dean, the other GA being Vaporised.

Apparently when he came around, Seddon and your grandfather had disappeared but there was enough evidence for him to believe they'd all been killed." Dee snorted. "Seems like he was wrong about Seddon."

"What happened then?" asked Angelina.

"Not a lot. I lost the election because I'd sent them on that mission. I returned to Earth and thought I'd heard the last of Seddon Danvers."

"You think that this Seddon Danvers had something to do with Angelina's grandad being killed?" asked Joe.

"Well, seeing he's the one who's alive and trying to get rid of Angelina, I'd say it's a pretty safe bet."

"Why Vaporise me? I didn't even know Serena wasn't the real Fate Switch." Angelina shuddered.

"You'd have found out pretty quickly," said Dee. "Seddon would have known that as soon as I registered your assignment with the FFU, I would discover it was fake. For whatever reason, it looks as if he couldn't risk an investigation. For him, it was much more convenient for you to be Vaporised in a tragic accident."

Dee narrowed her eyes as if she'd worked something else out. She shook her head and gave a humourless laugh before continuing. "He knows the FFU too well. He knew they'd be so busy looking into my health and safety records, trying to blame me for your death, that they wouldn't care about a Fate Switch. Especially one they didn't even know existed."

Angelina looked at Joe. "He'd have killed me, if it hadn't been for you."

"Yes, well." Dee interrupted. "There's no time to worry about that now. If we want to stop him from doing anything else, we need to know what he's up to."

She pointed at Joe. "Keep working on that computer, while we carry on here." With that Dee turned back to the papers that she still held in her hand.

They continued searching in silence. After a few minutes, Joe called out.

"I've got the computer working but he's tried to delete everything." Dee stopped what she was doing and picked her way among the debris to peer over Joe's left shoulder.

"Looks like he's deleted the Versalnet," said Joe.

Angelina joined Dee. Looking over Joe's right shoulder, she could see that the icon for the Versalnet was no longer showing on the computer screen.

"The desktop is a shortcut, but I've had a look and I can't find it anywhere."

"He's got rid of all the evidence?" Dee sounded frustrated.

"He probably thinks he has." Joe had a smile on his face.

"What do you mean?" Dee didn't sound as if she was in the mood for riddles.

Joe looked up at her. "Most people think that when you delete something and then permanently delete it from the computer's recycle bin that it's gone forever. What it actually means is that the computer is free to use that bit of memory again but until it does that information will stay there."

"I have no idea what that means." Dee's voice was dangerously calm.

"If I use the special software programme I have at home, I might be able to bring back everything that this Seddon Danvers thinks he's deleted."

"You can do that?" Dee asked.

Joe hesitated. "In theory, yes. I don't want to make any promises, because the Versalnet wasn't exactly created in this dimension." He shook his head as if he couldn't believe what he was saying. "But I don't see why it should be any different. The operating system is far more sophisticated, yet it still works…"

Dee stopped his technical explanation with a wave of her hand. "Let me know what you find, when you find it. For now, you might as well help us. Angelina you take the front bedroom, Joe you take the back bedroom and I'll carry on here."

Systematically, they searched the bedrooms but found nothing. Eventually, Dee called them downstairs to give the sitting room one final search.

"There's more damage in here than anywhere else, so this is probably where he lost whatever it is he's looking for," reasoned Dee.

The books had all been swept from the shelves. Angelina flicked through the pages of each volume before carefully replacing them. For the second time, Dee sifted through the contents of the bureau drawers while Joe lifted each picture from the wall and checked to see if anything had been inserted or stuck to the back of them.

As Angelina picked up a novel she'd seen Rose reading a few days earlier a piece of paper fell out and fluttered to the floor. Thinking it was a bookmark, she picked it up and was about to replace it when something stopped her. Looking closely, she saw that there were six words written in Rose's or rather Seddon's looping handwriting. It was the word 'Nina' that had caught her eye.

"I've found something." She lifted her head, an excited smile on her face.

At once Dee was at her side.

She plucked the piece of paper from Angelina's hand and read aloud: "Nina, Super League scout conf. What? That's nonsense."

"No, it's not." Joe was reading the paper over Dee's shoulder. "I bet it means that Rose, sorry Seddon Danvers, confirmed that a talent scout from the Women's Super League would be at the school match."

He looked from Angelina to Dee who shrugged.

"They're the people who sign up talented players. That's probably why it was so important for Nina to score that penalty."

"What's the Super League?" asked Dee.

"It's the league that all the top women play in. There's a lot of investment in women's football now. If Nina gets taken on by a top club, she could become a sports star and a world-famous celebrity. Maybe that's why Danvers wanted to stop her." Joe looked at Dee expectantly.

Dee made a noise that was somewhere between a snort and a growl.

"Don't be ridiculous, it's got to be more than that. Significant Fate Switches aren't about football players or people becoming famous. They only happen when something big is at stake and that usually means human lives, which is no laughing matter."

She glared at Joe. "There's more to it. Seddon was trying to stop that penalty from happening. We need to find out what would have happened if Nina had missed the penalty and wasn't taken on, as you say, by this super star league. It must end in something serious, probably a catastrophe of some kind."

Angelina saw Joe's confused expression. "It's how these things often work. An everyday action sets off a string of events that lead to something major happening. Nina's penalty must have been the starting point: because Nina scored the penalty, she impresses the scout; because she impresses the scout, she becomes a professional footballer; because she's a professional footballer…"

She shrugged. "That's the bit we don't know yet. If Seddon had stopped Nina from scoring, her life would have turned out completely different and this disaster, whatever it is, would have been one step closer to happening."

"What do we do now?" he asked.

Dee looked down and poked part of a broken china cup with her toe. "I need to check this out and let the FFU know about Danvers. You two can stay and clear this place up."

Angelina was the first to react. "Can't it wait until tomorrow?"

Frowning, Dee shook her head. "Rose will be in a nursing home by now, but if any of her neighbours pop by or someone from social services turns up and sees the place looking like this, they'll start asking awkward questions. The last thing we want is any more humans poking their noses into this mess."

With that, Dee collected her coat and left, quietly closing the front door behind her.

Chapter Thirty-nine

It was getting dark, so Joe turned on the light and pulled the thick curtains across, hoping that no one would see the light from outside and investigate.

"Where do we start?" Angelina turned in a circle, surveying the mess that had been Rose's sitting room.

"We may as well throw everything away that's broken, that'll probably get rid of most of this stuff. I'll get a binbag from the kitchen," said Joe.

Angelina knelt and started collecting the pieces of debris. Some bits were recognisable, and she managed to match the head of a small, white, porcelain ballerina with its smooth full-skirted body and delicate pointed toes.

"Maybe we could mend some of these things. Is there any glue in there?" Angelina called out to Joe.

He didn't answer. Frowning, Angelina carried the broken ornament into the hallway.

"Joe?"

Pushing open the door to the kitchen she looked around. There was no sign of Joe. Still shaken from the events of the day, Angelina felt the panic once again rise in her chest. Where was he?

"Joe?" Her call was strangled by fear. "Joe, where are you?"

A head popped up from the other side of the kitchen table.

"It's okay, I'm here."

Almost faint with relief, Angelina leaned across the table and could see that Joe was kneeling by the open oven.

"What are you doing?"

Joe pointed to the inside of the oven. "I've had an idea."

"What, sticking your head inside an oven?"

Joe grinned. "Don't be daft."

His face became serious. "I started thinking about why and how this Seddon guy would have lost this important file or whatever it is. After all, no one else has been in here apart from Rose, and Seddon was controlling her for most of the time."

"And?"

"Well, what if he'd got the file ready to take with him after Vaporising you and ruining the Fate Switch? Let's face it, he's not going to stick around here and wait to be caught."

"Surely he'd have known where he'd left it?"

"Exactly!"

"Why bother trashing the place?"

"Because it wasn't where he left it," Joe said.

"That doesn't make sense."

"Think about it. Someone must have moved it. The only person who's been here apart from me is Rose. I didn't move anything, so it must have been Rose."

"But Rose has dementia. Even you said she didn't know who you were or what was going on."

"That's why I'm looking in the oven. My gran started with Alzheimer's a few years ago. It was really sad; she started doing some strange things. Grandad once found the house keys in the butter dish and her gloves in the oven."

Angelina realised what Joe was getting at.

You think Rose found the file and put it somewhere weird?"

"Exactly, and I think the kitchen is the most likely place. It hasn't been trashed by Danvers and we haven't searched it yet. There's nothing in the oven, though, I've checked."

"I'll help. It shouldn't take long." Angelina put down the broken ballerina and started opening cupboards.

The kitchen wasn't big and after ten minutes, Angelina and Joe had exhausted all possible hiding places. They'd even tried looking inside the coffee jar and flour tin, but there was nothing.

"Stupid idea, after all. I was so sure I'd worked it out."

Joe looked dejected.

"It was worth a try," said Angelina. "Let's face it, we don't even know what we're looking for, never mind whether or not it's still here."

"Let's clear up and go home." Excusing himself, Joe nipped to the bathroom while Angelina collected a binbag and returned to the sitting room.

She was adding Rose's smashed telephone to the already bulging bag, when a yell and the sound of feet pounding down the stairs startled her. The sitting room door crashed open and Joe stood there, his eyes wide and a manic grin on his face.

"I've found it!"

Shocked by the commotion, Angelina stared at him.

"I've found it," Joe repeated.

He was waving a memory stick around in his right hand.

"I'll bet you anything that this is what Seddon Danvers was looking for."

"You think he stored the files on that?"

Joe nodded. "Shall we try now?"

Without waiting for an answer, he picked up another fallen chair and dragged it across to the computer so that Angelina could sit next to him.

"Where did you find it?" she asked.

"I had the right idea, but the wrong room." Joe switched on the computer and stared at the screen.

"You mean it was in the bathroom?"

Glancing across at Angelina, he nodded. "In the toothbrush holder. It caught my eye while I was washing my hands and I realised that Rose was just as likely to put something in the bathroom as she was the kitchen. There it was, with the toothbrushes."

He turned back to the screen and uncapped the memory stick.

"Let's hope it's what we think it is."

He carefully eased the memory stick into the port in the computer's hard drive and stared at the screen.

"How long does it take?" asked Angelina.

"It should be instant. Look, here we go."

A window opened on the screen and Joe clicked the link to view the files. Three folder icons appeared.

"We're in. This must be it!" Joe sounded excited. "Right what do you think these are?"

Angelina read the names of the folders: "Log, Manifest - FFU, Xdat. I don't know, start with the first file."

Obediently, Joe double clicked on 'Log' and a long list of files in date order appeared in the open window. As Joe scrolled down to the bottom of the list Angelina saw that the first file was dated almost three years ago, while the last file gave today's date.

"May as well start with the earliest," she said.

Joe moved the cursor until it hovered over the first file and double clicked the left button on the mouse. The document opened.

"It's like a diary," said Joe.

Squinting at the screen, Angelina read the short message.

"Target identified, Rose Cavendish, Bellview Nursing Home, Sheffield." She looked at Joe. "He's been planning this for years. Rose Cavendish must be the woman we know as Rose Garden."

Joe nodded and clicked on the next file down. It was dated three weeks after the first. The words on the screen read: 'Target extracted from nursing home. No issues.'

"He stole her from a nursing home. How could he get away with that?" Joe asked.

"Seddon said something to me about Rose being in a home and having no mind or family. What was it he said?" Angelina looked away from the screen, frowning in concentration. "That was it. He said she had no family until he came along, her dutiful great nephew. I bet he pretended to be a relative and abducted her."

Joe nodded. "That would make sense, but you'd have thought they'd have checked up on him."

"Even if they did, he'd probably have had forged papers or something. Try that one." Angelina pointed to a file further down the page, the title read 'Location confirmation'.

"Location verified as Ingworth High School, UK," read Angelina. "You know that's almost two-and-a-half years before it was due to happen. That's early to find out about the location. Usually, the FFU sends that kind of information out only a few months before the Fate Switch is due to happen."

"Didn't Dee say he'd been suspected of stealing some FFU secrets? Maybe these were the secrets he stole."

They spent another ten minutes opening and closing files, reading snippets that told the story of Seddon Danvers establishing a life in Little Ingworth disguised as Rose Garden.

As Joe scrolled down the list of files a title caught Angelina's eye. "Stop there."

Joe lifted his finger from the mouse.

"No, back a bit. Yes, that one, there."

She pointed to an entry towards the bottom of the screen, it read 'Operative identified.' It was dated the Sunday that Angelina had first arrived in Little Ingworth and met Rose on the train.

Joe dutifully opened the document.

"Contact made with operative. Bonus – Morton's granddaughter!!! Easy to manipulate. Figment worked well. Dialogue established for future meetings," he read. "What does that all mean?"

Angelina felt the walls close in as her arrival on the train replayed over and over in her head.

"It was all a set up." She groaned and put her head in her hands.

Joe whipped his gaze towards her, concern clouding his features. "Are you okay?"

Staring down at the table, she said: "I knew I'd checked that train before I started the Physicalisation process."

She raised her head, realising Joe didn't know what she was talking about. "That's what we call it when we first materialise on a new planet. It's the same process as when we return from a Mind Jump, but it takes much longer as you've got to kind of build your body in a new dimension. That's why we must do all these checks to make sure that none of the planet's inhabitants see it happening. I thought I'd checked properly but there was a conductor on the train who saw everything and Rose was in the carriage too."

"What does it mean by a figment?" Joe asked.

Angelina gave an angry sigh. "I'll bet the conductor was the figment. It's a trick. Something that looks real but isn't. It can be anything, a place, a person, a thing that's made to look life-like by this special projector called a Figment Reality Augmentation Capsule. They were banned by the FFU when they first came out but if you know the right people, or rather the wrong people, you can still get hold of one. Seddon would have had no problem with all his shady contacts."

"The conductor you saw, he wasn't real?"

Angelina shook her head. "Doesn't look like it. I couldn't work out why Dee didn't find out about Rose and the conductor from my Arrival Report. But, as Seddon Danvers had taken over Rose's body, she wouldn't be classed as human and if the conductor wasn't real, there'd be nothing to report. It explains everything. And it gave Rose, or rather Seddon, an excuse to talk to me."

Joe looked thoughtful. "I've been wondering why this Seddon Danvers picked Rose, but when you think about it, she was perfect. Let's face it, who wouldn't trust a harmless, little old lady? He had it all worked out."

"But why? There's nothing here to tell us why Danvers went to all this trouble."

"Let's try one of the other folders."

Joe opened the folder labelled 'Xdat', but all the files were referenced by a letter and number code and when he double clicked on the first file it wouldn't open. "He's removed the programme to open these files," said Joe. "I won't be able to restore it now."

Angelina didn't hold out much hope of finding anything else, but Joe was already clicking on the final folder and contents of 'Manifest-FFU' appeared on the screen.

"Most are word processing documents, I can open those. There's another folder, 'FV', whatever that is."

The document file names didn't mean anything to Joe, but Angelina leant forward, immediately recognising what she was looking at. She pointed at the subject title.

"You see the way these are labelled, all starting with FFUEncrypt? They're confidential FFU files. I've only ever seen examples in text-books before. This must be what Seddon Danvers stole and why he knew so much."

Joe clicked on the first file.

"It looks like minutes from a meeting," he said. "My dad brings things like this home from work. It's a record of what was said and agreed at committee meetings."

They scanned the words but there didn't seem to be anything about Nina. Joe closed the file and opened the next to find more minutes from another meeting.

"These are from years ago," said Angelina looking at the date.

Joe continued opening the documents and scanning the contents. Eventually, he leaned back in his chair. Yawning, he stretched his arms above his head, clasping his hands together as if he were about to enter the water during a dive.

"This is background stuff. It'll take us ages to go through it all," he said, letting his arms drop back to the table. "What I don't get is why has Seddon Danvers has gone to so much trouble to mess up Nina's football career?"

"I know what you mean." Angelina reached across and took control of the mouse. "Dee's right. There must be more to it. Let's see what's in here, then we'll leave it."

She clicked on the folder labelled 'FV' to reveal two files.

Joe sat up. "They're video files."

Angelina clicked on the file labelled 'Positive Outcome'.

"That's what happened today," said Joe, as a film of Nina scoring a penalty filled the screen.

The image flicked to a news report of a young woman running out on a football field, the stadium filled with people.

"That's Nina. She's older. She looks at least twenty."

"Shh," said Angelina, as the voice of a commentator came through the speakers.

"And give a huge welcome to Nina Kaur, making her England debut."

"What is this?" Joe glanced at Angelina.

"FutureVision," she said. "It shows Nina's fate now she's scored that penalty and caused the Fate Switch to happen. Watch."

The screen flickered again. Another news report. This time Nina was standing at a podium perched on an outdoor platform. The camera swept round to show an enormous crowd. Hundreds and thousands of people chanting Nina's name.

"That looks like the White House in America. Does that mean, in the future Nina meets the President of the United States?" Joe couldn't hide the awe in his voice.

"When a Fate Switch goes the right way, you get a positive outcome. So, yes, that's Nina's future if things stay the same," said Angelina. "But there might be other Significant Fate Switches in the future. It could still change."

The film jumped again, showing what looked to be a nature programme. The camera swooped over vast landscapes of trees, mangrove swamps and oceans. Then a clip of Nina as a mature woman appeared. She was applauding a group of teenagers holding up a sign saying ZERO EMISSIONS.

"Look, Nina gets involved with climate change in some way." Joe frowned. "Stopping her from becoming a footballer wouldn't change that, and why does she meet the US President?"

"Maybe this will tell us," said Angelina, clicking on the second file labelled 'Negative Outcome'.

The film showed Nina in a black gown with a purple sash, a black, tasselled mortar board on her head and a smile on her face. She was obviously graduating from university.

"She seems happy. Why is that negative?" Joe asked.

The film jumped forward. Nina in her mid-twenties, hands cuffed behind her back being escorted by two police officers. In the background a small group of protesters were scuffling with more police. The camera zoomed in on a discarded homemade placard bearing the slogan 'There is no planet B'.

The screen went black.

Joe frowned and clicked an icon on the screen that brought up the background data.

"That's strange," he said. The file looks to be okay. It's even showing the date, it's fifty years from now. I don't understand why there's no picture."

"That is the picture," whispered Angelina. "It's showing the future."

"But there's nothing there." Joe fiddled with the brightness control.

"Exactly." Angelina's voice was hollow. "There's nothing to see. If this had been the outcome, there is no future for human life."

Angelina glanced at Joe, now pale and staring at the screen with new understanding. He fast-forwarded to the end of the clip but there was nothing but blackness.

"It's the Fate Switch, Joe. It's not about Nina, but about what she does. By becoming a famous footballer, it gives her a voice on the world stage. World leaders listen to her and obviously act. Football puts her in a world where she can reach millions more people. Where she has influence."

Joe ran his hand through his hair. "That's what Seddon wanted to stop." He turned to Angelina. "I'm glad you helped Nina score that penalty."

"Me too." Angelina closed the file. "Although, this might not be the end. There could be half a dozen Significant Fate Switches in the future that could knock Nina off track. I'm guessing that's why Seddon

Danvers needs this file. I bet those files we can't open identify the next Significant Fate Switch and the next chance he'll have to stop Nina."

"You mean this could still happen."

"Possibly. It's like one enormous game of chess. You've got to plan your moves years in advance to get the result you want."

Joe turned his attention back to the computer. "I'll take a copy of what's on the memory stick, but is there anything else on here we need to know about?"

"Not now." Angelina stood. "Come on, we need to get this back to Dee. She'll know what to do. I'll get another binbag. I've almost filled this one."

When she returned from the kitchen, the computer had been switched off and Joe was standing in the middle of the room.

"It shouldn't take long between us," she said.

Kneeling, she started shovelling handfuls of broken crockery into the bag. After a few seconds she looked up, realising that Joe hadn't moved.

"Aren't you going to help?" she asked.

A strange smile spread slowly across Joe's face and as she looked into his cold dead eyes, Angelina felt her heart freeze.

Joe's mouth opened, but the voice that came from his body didn't belong to him.

"Good to see you again, Angelina," said Seddon Danvers.

Chapter Forty

Shock sent Angelina scrabbling backwards on her hands and heels until her back hit the wall. Pressing hard against it, she edged upwards into a standing position, sliding her palms over the rough wallpaper, trying to get as far away as she could from the chilling image in front of her. Yet, for some reason, she couldn't tear her eyes away from Joe's dead stare.

Her fear seemed to amuse Seddon Danvers, as the smile on Joe's face grew wider.

"Thought I'd better say thank you for finding my files."

Still frozen by the monstrous sight of Seddon's deep growl coming from Joe's mouth, Angelina couldn't reply.

"Although I have to say, having you interrupt my search was annoying. It was terribly inconvenient having to go off and hide when I saw the three of you marching down the path."

He stepped towards her, Joe's features curled into an unfamiliar snarl. Angelina flinched pressing her back harder against the wall.

Seddon laughed at her terror.

"I have to say, Sweep came in useful. I knew that even Dee wouldn't think to look in a dog's mind. Although I thought his barking might give me away at one point."

He frowned as if to emphasise his concern but then his expression immediately brightened.

"It all turned out fine in the end, though. I'd never have thought to look in the toothbrush mug. Bright lad, that boyfriend of yours. I could tell that the first time I entered his mind."

"What?" Angelina finally managed to croak the word out from between her dry lips.

"Don't worry. It was only a quick visit last time. Long enough to ruin that competition we went to watch but just a bit of fun, really."

Fear had slowed Angelina's thoughts and it was a moment before she understood what he was talking about. Then she remembered the diving competition she'd gone to with Rose and how Joe had insisted that his mind had gone blank when he'd landed on the end of the board. He'd been right. It had, thanks to Seddon Danvers messing with his head and all for a 'bit of fun'.

Anger that this evil being had interfered with Joe's dreams, rekindled Angelina's fighting spirit and she pushed away from the wall.

"You're pathetic. Joe had nothing to do with this. You ruined his chances of getting picked for the national squad. What was the point?"

"Point? Oh, there wasn't a point. I thought it might distract you both for a while. Stop you from thinking about the Fate Switch. And I quite enjoyed seeing him lose."

He was taunting her now. Joe's head was tilted to one side, his eyes looking down, casually checking his fingernails. The mannerism was so alien to the Joe she knew, that Angelina could no longer think of this body in front of her as anyone but Seddon Danvers.

She stepped towards him, her voice trembling with fury as she spoke. "You've got less than an hour before you have to be out of that mind. When you materialise, I'm going to make sure you pay for everything you've done."

"Ah well, you see that's where you're wrong."

The assured, conversational tone sent another shiver of fear through Angelina.

"What do you mean?"

The dead eyes stared straight at her.

"At the moment, your beloved Joe is unconscious but in less than one hour, the rather aggressive infection I've planted will have destroyed his mind completely. Without me in here, he'll be a living corpse. He'll be even worse than Rose. At least she could still walk and talk, even if she didn't know who she was."

Angelina felt her knees start to give way and she leaned back against the wall.

Seddon continued, all trace of humour now gone from his voice: "You know as well as I do that that's better for me. The weaker the mind, the longer we can stay without risk of Vaporisation. With Rose I had almost twenty-three hours a day. I only had to become Mr Garden for an hour a day, but with Joe completely brain-dead, I can occupy his body for as long as I want. With no mind to conflict with mine, there's no risk whatsoever. Providing I use Joe's voice, no one need ever know. He'll be the perfect cover and I'll get to stay close to Nina and wait for my next chance to change her life forever."

"You can't do that." Terror had choked Angelina's voice and her words came out as a whisper.

Seddon's expression darkened. "Oh, but I can. As it was Joe who messed everything up for me, it's the least he can do." The dead eyes sparked with anger. "You've no idea how much this contract is worth to me."

Desperately Angelina searched for a way out.

"It won't work. We're already late, Dee will come looking for us soon."

It was a feeble threat and Angelina knew it. Unfortunately, so did Seddon Danvers and, smiling, he shook his head.

"I watched Dee leave and she's not the type to check up on anyone. She gives you an order and expects you to follow it. Always has done. Dee won't be coming back here today."

"She'll know what you've done when I tell her. She'll have the entire FFU after you and I'll know where you are."

Seddon looked amused. "How do you plan to tell her? You're still not capable of translocating and the doors to the cottage are locked."

He pulled Rose's keys and chain from the back pocket of Joe's jeans and let them dangle on the end of his finger.

"You can't keep me here forever."

"I won't need to." He pocketed the key. "I know I can't touch you now, not with Joe still alive. If I try to harm you, it will be Joe's body that gets hurts. But once he's brain-dead and I take over, this body will no longer be occupied by a human mind and your Transference mechanism won't be able to protect you."

Seddon made a show of looking at Joe's watch.

"I'd say you've got about fifty-six minutes left to live Angelina, which is about two minutes longer than your boyfriend. Any last requests?"

Something inside Angelina snapped and instinct took over. Without being aware of what she was doing, she lunged forward with a roar that caught Seddon Danvers by surprise. She saw him step back, the dead eyes widening in shock. Then a split second later, her body dissolved into millions of atoms as she was sucked into Joe's mind.

Chapter Forty-one

The first thing that hit her was the smell. The infection had wiped out the comforting banana smoothie scent that had previously occupied Joe's mind and now the blackness was thick with a sickening stench that almost made Angelina gag. Seddon wasn't bluffing; the infection was strong.

Angelina forced herself not to think about what was going on, or what she was about to do. She knew she had to be fast and get to where she was going before Seddon worked out what she was up to.

Relaxing her mind even further, she entered the twilight zone that exists between sleep and wakefulness, as she had when she'd been trapped in Matt's head. But this time she was sinking through the layers of Joe's mind. The deeper she fell, the more acute her senses became until she was so in tune with Joe's mind that a sense of vision returned. As a cavernous space widened around her, she knew that she'd arrived in Joe's deep subconscious.

With no time to waste, she ignored the whispers and the fluttering ideas and forgotten thoughts that flew all around her. She didn't even turn towards the banks of knowledge stacked neatly along one of the shifting walls. Neither did she look towards the shadowy corner where she could sense evil. That was where the infection had taken root, multiplying by the second and waiting until it was strong enough to destroy Joe's mind.

Thankfully, there was no scent in the deep subconscious, but knowing the infection was there was enough to turn her stomach. She had no desire to see how the person she loved was being polluted by the vile disease. Instead, she focused only on the glowing orb, hanging motionless and constant in the centre of this ethereal space.

Although she knew that it was a trick of her mind, it was as if Angelina could see her own body as she moved towards the orb: towards the very heart of Joe's spirit. Her arms reached out and gently she wrapped her hands around the sphere, pulling it away from the life-force that held it in place and kept Joe alive.

While it looked to Angelina as if her hands were holding Joe's life, she knew that it was the power of her mind that was now keeping the orb suspended.

It was the most dangerous and reckless thing that she had ever done, but she was out of options and couldn't think about that now. One slip of concentration and without any force to maintain its form, the glowing sphere would disintegrate, and Joe's life would be lost forever.

Keeping perfectly still, she waited for Seddon Danvers to arrive.

It didn't take long.

The negative energy radiating from him, travelled like shockwaves through Joe's deep subconscious, bouncing off the walls of Joe's mind and echoing all around. The whispers fell silent and the fluttering thoughts fled, hiding in the shadows of the shifting walls.

Angelina stood firm, maintaining her focus on the orb, even as she sensed Seddon Danvers moving towards her. Then she felt him stop and gasp. He'd finally seen what she was holding.

"You silly little fool. What do you think you're doing?"

His voice was low, the words coming out in a hiss and for the first time since meeting him, Angelina detected a note of uncertainty.

Without looking up, Angelina said: "Exactly what you think I'm doing. When I let this go, Joe dies, and because we're in his mind, we do too."

"You wouldn't kill a human, especially not this one." But there was doubt in his voice.

Angelina felt him take a step towards her, but she stayed calm and focussed, knowing he wouldn't dare to come too close.

"Why not? You're going to kill me anyway, and Joe will be as good as dead. In fact, death will be better than the life you've got planned for him."

Striving to keep her voice strong, she continued: "What have I got to lose? At least this way I can stop you from doing any more harm."

The cavern fell silent. Seconds ticked by as Angelina used every ounce of strength she had to focus on keeping Joe alive.

Eventually Seddon spoke again, his tone calm and soothing: "Okay, Angelina, you win. I'll leave his mind. Put the orb back."

"You're forgetting something Seddon. You can't leave, Joe's mind is infected."

"He's unconscious, the infection can't keep me locked in." Seddon's voice sounded more assured.

"I know, but if you try to leave, I'll let the orb go. You know you'll never make it out of his mind in time."

"What do you want?"

"Get rid of the infection now. I know you have the antidote with you. You'll need to get rid of the infection once Joe is brain-dead, otherwise it will infect your mind as well. I know you're not that stupid."

Silence returned but this time Angelina wasn't prepared to wait. She was growing tired and her concentration was starting to falter.

"Do it now, or I let go," she shouted.

"Take it easy…"

"I'll count to three. One…"

"Stop!" Seddon called out. "I'll do it. Just put the orb back."

"No way. Do it now or I drop it. Two…"

"All right, I'm doing exactly as you ask."

She felt him move away from her and towards the shadowy corner of Joe's mind. Although she couldn't see exactly what he did, she sensed a lightness in the cavern. It was as if the infection had acted like a magnet pulling everything towards it, making the atmosphere heavy and dense.

"It's done. You've got what you wanted, the infection has gone," said Seddon.

Angelina knew he was telling the truth. If it was possible, the cavern had become even more vivid: the feelings even more acute. Even though Seddon Danvers was still there, the whispers had returned and, with a flurry, thoughts and ideas flew from their hiding places.

"You can put it back now," he said.

"No." Exhaustion was starting to set in, but Angelina held her nerve.

"The infection's gone. Now put the orb back." Seddon was starting to sound desperate.

She knew that if she obeyed Seddon now, he'd find some way to destroy her, she had to hold out a little longer.

"I want you out of Joe's mind."

"What?"

"You heard. Go. Now. I'll know when you're on the outside."

"You stupid…" He stopped. "Make sure you keep hold of that thing."

Another blast of shockwaves hit Angelina as she felt his presence fade from Joe's subconscious, causing the orb to tremble and for a terrifying moment, she feared that it would fall. Concentrating hard she regained control and seconds later sensed that Seddon had left Joe's body.

The relief was almost overwhelming but she couldn't relax yet. One slip now and both she and Joe would die, while Seddon Danvers would be free to find another victim. She had to stay focused for a few more seconds.

Her concentration was on the verge of breaking. Her arms looked as though they were trembling, and her breath was coming in short, sharp gasps as she edged the orb back towards the column of force that would keep Joe's life safely suspended.

As she tried to balance the orb within the forcefield, Angelina almost lost her grip. It had been much easier to remove the orb than it was to return it, the force was strong and kept throwing the orb off line. Three times she allowed her concentration to ease, her hands inching slowly away, but then the orb would shoot sideways, forcing her to intensify her concentration to prevent it from falling and disintegrating.

The effort was exhausting and the longer it went on, the more her arms trembled. It was no good, she couldn't do it. Seddon Danvers would win after all. Her concentration was breaking, the negative thoughts weakening her hold on the orb. The trembling in her hands increased, until she could barely keep hold of the sphere.

"Breathe," she whispered. "Close your eyes and breathe slowly."

With one last effort, she slowed her mind until the trembling stopped. This time, she kept her eyes closed, feeling for the column of life-force and letting her concentration become one with the energy flowing around the orb.

She gasped as it began to lift from her hands and was gone. She was no longer in control. Opening her eyes, she could see that the orb was once again fixed in place, hanging motionless in Joe's subconscious.

She'd done it.

Despite the exhaustion, she felt elated. She was about to turn away when she noticed something that set her heart racing with fear.

The glow within the orb appeared dim. What if the infection had already started working and Joe was dying anyway?

Wasting no more time, Angelina raced across to a block of Joe's emotions to what looked to her eyes like the button you'd find on a doorbell. She slammed her hand against the button and then was gone, moving up through the marshmallow consistency of the layers of Joe's mind and into his subconscious.

She sniffed but the stench of infection was gone and had been replaced by a sharp antiseptic tang.

The antidote, thought Angelina as she swiftly exited Joe's mind.

Chapter Forty-two

Angelina found herself back in the sitting room at Rose Cottage. The first thing she saw was Joe's body lying on the carpet, one leg curled awkwardly underneath him.

With a cry, she fell to the floor next to him and placed her cheek against his face. She could feel a faint movement of warm air. He was still breathing. Just.

She was so exhausted that she could barely move, but somehow she managed to heave Joe's head on to her lap and she sat stroking his forehead.

"Don't worry, I'm going to get you help," she said, her voice barely a whisper.

"Touching. Very touching."

Startled, Angelina jerked her head towards the voice. She'd been so concerned about Joe that she hadn't noticed Seddon Danvers sitting on the sofa waiting for her.

It was the first time that she'd seen him in human form, and the sight of him was shocking. It wasn't his appearance that bothered her. He was a small, pudgy man, with a receding hairline and non-existent chin, his shoulders seemed to slope down from his neck making everything about him look weak. It was a look he'd chosen on purpose, one that was nondescript and forgettable, and Angelina knew that it had worked.

She'd seen him before. Many times. She'd just never taken that much notice of him, even though he'd always seemed vaguely familiar. He was the assistant caretaker at school. And knowing what she knew now, it finally dawned on her where she'd first seen him.

He stood and stretched lazily, fixing her with a stare that held a chilling intensity.

"About time," he said. "I thought you must have been having a party in there without me."

The confidence was back, Seddon Danvers knew that he was in control again.

Angelina didn't speak.

"What? Don't tell me you're surprised to see me. You didn't think I'd just up and leave did you?"

Ignoring his question, Angelina narrowed her eyes.

"I've seen you before." she said. "At school, you're the caretaker. And the day I arrived. I saw a man sitting next to Rose on the bench at the station. That was you, wasn't it?"

Seddon shrugged. "Possibly. I enjoyed a break from the old woman's mind whenever I could. Anyway, enough talking. I might not be able to use this useless body anymore," he stood up and kicked Joe's foot. "But I'm going to make sure that neither of you leave here."

A wooden leg from one of the broken chairs was resting at the side of the sofa, where Seddon had been sitting. He picked it up and Angelina looked at it in horror.

"Don't. You can get away without being caught. There's no need to do anything else to us."

"Oh, but there is. You both know too much."

"Joe doesn't. He's nothing to do with this. Leave him alone." Angelina's plea was frantic, but Seddon ignored her.

"I can't do that. If he ever comes round, he'll talk. You've both seen the files, but you're the only ones who know what's on them. I can't leave you alive."

Seddon raised the chair leg above his head ready to strike and as he advanced towards her, Angelina cowered away, waiting for the blow to land while doing her best to protect Joe with her body. The blow never came. Angelina risked a glance in Seddon's direction.

The arm holding the chair leg had dropped to his side and he was listening intently.

"You!" He spat the word at Angelina. "It was you, wasn't it? You set off an AutoESC in his mind, didn't you?"

Angelina almost smiled with relief. She'd known that Seddon would probably be waiting for her as soon as she'd left Joe's mind, so she'd pressed the manual override for his Automatic Emergency Saviour Call, Joe's internal panic button. It was the same alert that had taken Angelina to the roadside to save the mother and her baby. Only she hadn't been sure that the alert would arrive in time. There was always a delay while it was routed through the system.

Seddon was still raging at Angelina. "Did you think I wouldn't know? Did you think Dee and every other GA within range would turn up and catch me? Is that what you were planning? Well I'm still a GA, or had you forgotten that I get the call too? Your stupid little trick isn't going to work."

No, thought Angelina, you're wrong. It is working.

Her only hope had been that Seddon would receive the alert. No one was coming to save her. Dee didn't even acknowledge AutoESCs anymore and since the new rules came in, the call was sent no further than half a mile.

Her plan rested on Seddon Danvers not knowing about the changes, and him assuming that the alert would be sent to all GAs in the country.

"They'll get you. You've no chance of getting away." She forced herself to stare into his chilling eyes.

Seddon leaned over Angelina so close that it was almost as if she could feel the anger radiating from his eyes. She flinched and turned away, wondering if he'd decide to take a chance and stay around to kill them both after all. She felt his hot clammy breath on her cheek as he hissed a final warning.

"I know exactly how long it takes to respond to one of these and I'll be far away from this world before they get anywhere close. I tell you, Angelina Lachesis, I won't forget about you, or your boyfriend."

He gave Joe one last kick.

Then was gone.

The sudden silence startled Angelina.

She listened, waiting for his voice to return but the silence remained.

He was really gone.

The relief was fleeting. Joe was still unconscious, his breathing shallow.

"Joe? Joe? Can you hear me?"

Gently, she shook his shoulders. No response.

Placing a cushion under his head, she ran to the kitchen to fetch a cloth. Kneeling beside him, Angelina squeezed a few drops of ice-cold water onto his forehead, before dabbing them up again with the cloth. All the time, she was telling him everything would be all right, though her words didn't ring true.

He had to wake up. He had to.

Twice she returned to the kitchen for more water, and she felt like she'd been there forever, trying to wake Joe up, yet only ten minutes had passed. Exhausted, she knelt back on her heels staring into Joe's motionless face. She had to get help. Dee would know what to do.

"Oh, Joe. I'm so sorry, I should never have got you involved."

Struggling to her feet, Angelina stared helplessly around the broken room. Rose's phone was smashed beyond repair and she had no idea where her own mobile was. Then she remembered. Joe had had his phone with him, but where was it now? The computer, she'd seen it near the computer.

As she turned to look for it, she heard a moan, or thought she did. "Joe?"

She dropped back to her knees and gently shook him.

"Can you hear me?"

Ever so slightly Joe's lips parted, and another moan escaped from them. It was so feeble that Angelina wasn't sure if she'd imagined it. She leaned forward.

"Joe, it's me. Joe, can you answer me."

His eyelids flickered and slowly opened. Angelina gasped and covered her mouth with her hand as the tears started streaming down her face.

There was no life behind the eyes, they still held the dead stare that she'd seen when Seddon Danvers had possessed his mind. She thought back to the way the light had dimmed in the orb before she'd left. The infection must have done too much damage. Even worse, perhaps she'd harmed him by moving the orb in the first place.

The thought that she might have been the one to kill him sliced through her heart and more tears swamped her vision.

"Angelina?"

Had she really heard the whisper? She swiped at the tears, trying to clear her vision so that she could see Joe's face properly.

"Angelina?"

The whisper came again, this time slightly stronger and she saw his lips move.

"Joe?"

This time, when she risked a look into his eyes, it was relief that coursed through her. There was no mistake, Joe's eyes returned her gaze.

He was back.

Chapter Forty-three

"How are you feeling?"

It was Sunday afternoon and Angelina had arrived at Joe's house. Under strict instructions from his mother to rest, Joe was sprawled on the sofa, his head and shoulders propped up by two plump pillows. Angelina was sitting in the chair next to him, nursing a mug of hot chocolate, her legs curled underneath her.

"Apart from a chronic headache, I'm fine."

Angelina looked apologetic. "Sorry, Dee says that's my fault. One of the side effects from messing about with your life, but she said to tell you that it should settle down within twenty-four hours."

"Don't worry. From what you've told me, a headache for a day is nothing compared to what Seddon Danvers had planned."

"True. By the way, what did your mum say last night?"

After making sure that Joe had suffered no long-term damage to his mind, Dee had insisted on taking Joe home in person. When she'd opened the door, his mother had naturally been upset at the sight of her son looking so ill.

"She believed our story about me falling off a wall and knocking myself out. Let's face it, she's hardly going to suspect the truth, is she?"

Angelina grinned. "Never in a million years."

"She's worried though. She insisted on taking me to the hospital, which was so busy, we were there until almost midnight. Not that they could find anything wrong. The doctors told me to rest up for a day or two, and Mum's making sure I do. She won't even let the twins come in. She's frightened they'll start jumping all over me."

He banged his forearm on the sofa's cushion.

"This is as far as she'll let me go today. Although to be honest, there's no way I could have gone training with this headache."

"Have you remembered anything else, yet?"

He shook his head. "Ow." He held his head. "Sorry, I keep forgetting it hurts when I move quickly."

He closed his eyes for a couple of seconds as he waited for the pain to subside.

"Everything's blank from when you left the room. I don't remember seeing Seddon Danvers or feeling anything until you woke me up."

"You've probably lost those memories forever because of the infection. It's a good job we stopped it early, though. Apparently that strain grows exponentially, Dee told me that means it doubles in size every few minutes. It takes a while to become established but once it does, it can wipe out your entire mind within half an hour. Dee thinks we probably had about five more minutes before it started to do serious damage."

Joe looked sombre, as if he understood how close he'd come to never waking up.

Angelina reached across and gave his hand a quick squeeze.

"It's okay. Danvers has gone and he won't be back on Earth in a hurry."

"It's not me I'm worried about. It's what he'll try next. He took the memory stick, and you said he'll mess with Nina's career the next chance he gets."

"Seddon won't get any more chances, not now that the FFU knows about him and, thanks to you, we have a copy of the information Seddon stole. Even though they haven't caught him yet, it can't be long before they do."

Angelina relayed the news that Dee had given her earlier that morning. The FFU had tracked Seddon's exit from Earth but then the trail went cold and they lost him.

"Dee thinks he's gone back to wherever he's been hiding all these years. If he's any sense, he'll stay there."

Joe still didn't seem happy. "What about you? Won't you get struck off or something, because of me?"

Angelina couldn't keep the smile from her face.

"That's what I wanted to tell you. Dee's keeping your involvement out of the official report. She said if I don't say anything about her business and charity work, she won't say anything about you and me. As far as the FFU's concerned, you were as much a victim as Rose was. And" -Angelina dropped her eyes to her lap before returning her gaze to Joe's face, anticipating his reaction- "if you're up for it, Dee wants you to help her go through Seddon Danvers' computer. Kind of working with her, but without anyone knowing. If that's okay with you?"

"You're kidding?" Joe's face lit up. "Wow, that'll be fantastic. Dee's okay with that?"

Angelina giggled. "She suggested it. I think she's got a soft spot for you, not that she'd ever let on."

"Everything's worked out. I get to work on a computer programme from another dimension, and you made the Fate Switch happen and passed your assignment."

"Well, not quite. You see, I haven't officially passed my assignment. I shouldn't have had anything to do with Nina's Fate Switch. That was meant for Dee. Serena and Nathan getting together didn't cause a Fate Switch so I didn't complete my assignment."

Joe looked confused. "I don't understand. You changed the future by getting those two together, surely that was some kind of Fate Switch."

"Believe it or not, that didn't change the future. Serena and Nathan were already destined to become boyfriend and girlfriend. It would have taken a few more years without my interference, but that's not the same as changing the future and activating a Fate Switch," Angelina explained.

"I would never have put those two together in a million years, let alone a few years. But if Serena wasn't the real Fate Switch, which one should you have done?"

"Do you remember Dee telling you how you have to respond to high-level Fate Switches and trainee assignment Fate Switches in the same way?"

"What's that got to do with..." Joe stopped as he worked out what Angelina was trying to explain.

"I get it. Danvers switched the two emails. Don't tell me, Dee did your assignment Fate Switch thinking it was a high-level Fate Switch."

Angelina nodded. "Exactly. It was one that she performed on Friday evening. You know Carrie, Serena's best friend? Dee had to persuade Carrie to walk home from school instead of taking the bus. It meant that she saw an advert for street dancing lessons and next week signs up for the class. It gives Carrie a purpose now that Serena has her interest in art, and Nathan."

"That's hardly a big deal. Didn't Dee think something was wrong?"

Angelina shrugged. "Nina scoring a penalty isn't a big deal but it's the future consequences it affects. Dee was a bit suspicious when the follow-up report said that it was an assignment and not a Significant Fate Switch. She said it wasn't the first time that the FFU has messed up with priority levels, and she was going to complain about it at the AGAIM, that's the Annual Guardian Angel Interplanetary Meeting. It's in December, so she was going to wait until then."

"What does that mean for you?" Joe lifted up from his pillows and leaned towards her, his voice hopeful when he spoke. "Do you have to stay on Earth and do another assignment?"

Guilt wrapped around her heart and squeezed, as Angelina knew that she was about to hurt him again.

"Dee's confident that they'll accept Nina's Fate Switch as my assignment, especially with it being such a high level."

"Is there a chance they won't, and you'll get to stay?"

The eagerness in his eyes, only made her feel worse as she slowly shook her head.

"I'm not supposed to know, but the FFU is giving me an award. The Amethyst Interplanetary Defender Award, for bravery beyond the call of duty. It's never been given to a trainee GA before. If they're willing to do that, they won't be able to fail me for a technicality."

Joe sank back against his pillows. "That's amazing. I didn't mean that I wanted you to fail. After everything you did, you deserve it. I'm proud of you."

Despite the words, Joe's disappointment was raw. "When do you go?"

"I've a few days left, while Dee sorts the paperwork out."

Joe nodded. "This time next week you'll be gone?"

Angelina held her breath, willing herself not to cry.

"We can keep in touch. Dee says you can Umail me whenever you want."

"Yeah." He gave a snort of bitter laughter and looked away. "That will be fun. Me here on Earth while you're flying halfway around the

Milky Way."

"Please don't." Angelina lost the fight with her emotions and tears choked her voice. "You know I've no choice. I have to go."

She pressed her palms against her eyes, trying to stem the tears. Suddenly Joe was kneeling in front of her, pulling her hands away from her face.

"I'm sorry." He whispered. "I've only just got you back and now you're going again. I'm going to miss you so much."

He put his arms around her and pulled her close as she sobbed. He held her tight, and she could feel his cheek resting against the top of her head. Eventually, he pulled away and held her at arm's length.

He smiled and gently wiped a tear from her cheek. "I guess we'll have to break the record for long distance relationships."

"It won't be long. Dee's already agreed to let me come back for the holidays. I'll be fully qualified soon and can say where I want to be stationed. Dee will support me if I apply to work with her."

"I know. Hey, I'll be the only person who can honestly say that his girlfriend is out of this world."

Angelina gave a half-laugh, then saw that Joe had grown serious again. He was looking at her with a strange intensity that seemed to stop time. He pulled her gently towards him.

"Is it against the rules to kiss an angel?"

Barely breathing, Angelina smiled. "Probably. But seeing as we've broken almost every other rule, I don't think one more will matter."

Epilogue

Two weeks later.

Shouts, screams and whistles bounced off the walls, echoing and crashing into one another, until all that could be heard was a deafening buzz of noise.

"Are all swimming pools this noisy? And hot?"

Edging her way between the row of seats on the spectator balcony, Dee shrugged off her purple coat and folded it over her arm, frowning at Angelina as if it were all her fault.

"It will be quieter when they close the main pool for the competition."

Angelina slid into the seat next to Dee. Leaning forward to peer over the balcony, she watched the divers, coaches and white-suited officials milling around the diving pit. She noticed that the highchairs and tables were in place for the judges and officials, and the electronic scoring system was switched on.

Finally, her eyes rested on a familiar figure. Joe had his back to the balcony and was still in his T-shirt and shorts, warming up. She watched as he used his left hand to pull his right arm across his chest loosening the muscles in his shoulder, holding the stretch before changing arms and repeating the move in the opposite direction.

He was obviously discussing the competition with his coach. Nick was demonstrating what looked to be the take-off, animatedly gesturing with his hands towards hip and arm positions, while Joe nodded in understanding.

Nick was facing the spectator gallery and must have spotted

Angelina as he said something to Joe and nodded towards the balcony. As Joe turned around, his curious expression widened into utter delight as he caught sight of Angelina. He waved and Angelina felt a smile, so wide that it made her cheeks ache, spread across her face.

For a second, the background noise faded into silence as she realised how much she'd missed him. Knowing that Joe needed to concentrate on the competition however, she mouthed 'good luck', smiled and waved. Joe waved an acknowledgement and turned back to Nick.

Sinking back into her seat, Angelina turned to Dee. "Thanks for arranging for me to come back for this. You don't know how much it means to me. And to Joe."

In her usual brusque manner, Dee dismissed Angelina's sentimental outpouring. "We had to do your review at some point. This weekend was as good as any."

Angelina knew that what Dee had said wasn't strictly true. Reviews were usually a paper exercise, with no need to return to the assignment location, yet Dee had requested a personal debrief, using the excuse that Angelina's experience had been far from routine and that she must be allowed to return to Earth.

The real reason, Angelina knew, was so that she and Joe could see each other again – not that Dee would ever admit it. She suspected that it was also the reason why Dee had applied for Angelina to return to Little Ingworth for work experience during the holidays.

"Thanks anyway."

Without thinking, Angelina gave her mentor a quick hug that caught Dee by surprise.

"How long do we have to wait?" Dee asked, changing the subject.

"Not long." Angelina checked her watch. "Look they're clearing the public from the swimming pool now."

The balcony was filling up with spectators and Angelina nodded a greeting to Nick's mum, dad and grandma as they settled into their seats two rows behind where Angelina and Dee were sitting. As Angelina turned to her left, she gasped as she saw who was walking towards her.

Glancing quickly at Joe, she could tell that he hadn't noticed them. She turned back, smiling as Joe's mum and dad sidled between the row of seats towards her.

"Hello, Angelina. Are these seats free?" Joe's mum asked.

"Yes, of course. I didn't know you were coming."

His mum smiled. "I didn't tell Joe in case I couldn't get a sitter for the twins. I hope it will be a nice surprise for him. David" -she turned to her husband- "this is Angelina, Joe's friend and her aunt, Dee."

Susan Brennan leaned forward so that she could speak directly to Dee.

"I want to thank you again for looking after Joe the other week. I dread to think what could have happened if you hadn't been there."

Dee nodded. "Not a problem. He's a good lad is Joe."

Angelina had barely taken her eyes from Joe and she saw him look towards the balcony as he stripped off his shorts. He was pulling his T-shirt from his head when she saw him stop as he caught sight of his parents.

Susan, who had been chatting with Nick's family, turned back towards the pool and saw him looking.

"There he is." She leaned forward and waved.

Joe's mouth sagged open in disbelief as he raised his hand in response to the greeting. At that moment, the personal address system crackled into life and the booming voice of the referee ordered the diving boards to be cleared.

The competition was about to start.

Whether it was knowing his parents were supporting him or that he'd had more chance to prepare Angelina didn't know, but Joe dived even better than when she'd last seen him compete. By the final round of dives Joe was leading the competition, fifteen points ahead of Seth Palmer. His last dive of the competition was a forward three-and-a-half somersaults piked. The same dive that Seddon Danvers had ruined.

Angelina didn't think that she'd ever felt so nervous. Her heart was beating fast and she was almost shaking as she watched Joe climb the stairs and step on the board.

Hardly daring to watch, she whispered to Dee: "If he does the dive first time, he can't lose."

As Joe took his first step along the board, Angelina held her breath. Raising his arms and left knee in the hurdle step, he jumped on to the end of the springboard.

"Please don't stop, please don't stop," Angelina muttered under her breath.

He didn't. Unlike the last time she'd seen him, Joe soared into the air, spinning so fast that he had plenty of time to make the three and a half somersaults before lining up for his entry into the water.

With a scream of delight, Angelina jumped out of her seat, clapping and cheering.

Joe's grinning face broke the water as the judges scores were being read by the announcer.

"Seven, seven, six and half, seven, seven and a half..."

Angelina cheered again. "He's done it."

Excitedly, she hugged Joe's mum, who, like nearly everyone else on the viewing balcony, was giving Joe a standing ovation. As Angelina broke the embrace, she saw the look of pride on David Brennan's face.

After the medals had been presented, Angelina and Dee retired to the café to wait for Joe.

After congratulating their son, Susan and David Brennan had left to collect the twins from the babysitter.

Angelina was sipping on a mug of hot chocolate and Dee was on her second cup of camomile tea (which Angelina still thought smelled of old socks) when Joe finally appeared.

With a squeal, Angelina jumped up and threw herself into his arms. "You were fantastic."

Laughing Joe returned the hug.

"Well done, Joe," said Dee. She pushed a banana smoothie across the table towards him. "I understand that's your favourite."

"Thanks, I'm ready for this." He joined them at the table.

"So?" Angelina was so excited she could barely sit still. "Have you made the national squad?"

Joe frowned.

"Well," he said.

Hearing Joe's serious tone, Angelina's face dropped. "What's wrong? They must pick you. You were amazing."

Joe couldn't keep his face straight any longer, and it broke into a huge grin.

"Course they did. I'm in!"

With another squeal, Angelina threw her arms around Joe again, almost knocking over his glass.

"Careful!" but he was laughing. "Hey, can you believe, Mum and Dad came to watch, as well? Even Dad enjoyed it. He apologised for not being more supportive. Said he didn't want me to take it seriously in case I didn't make it. Apparently, he missed out on the chance to play county rugby and never got over it. He's promised to come to all my competitions, even if Mum can't because of the twins."

He's told Joe the truth at last, thought Angelina, remembering the thoughts she'd heard in David Brennan's mind.

"That's brilliant news," she said.

"Wait a minute." Joe peered suspiciously at Angelina. "You didn't have anything to do with my dad coming today, did you? You didn't do any Influencing or anything?"

"Me? No. I never gave it a thought. Besides, I only got back this morning."

Angelina's surprise was genuine, and Joe must have believed her as his face widened with pleasure.

"Then he came because he really wanted to."

"Joe!"

They all turned to where the call had come from. It was Nick, he was standing at another table talking to a man in a tracksuit emblazoned with the Great British emblem.

Nick beckoned to Joe.

"That's the head coach, Nick's talking to. I'd better go." He slid out of his seat. "You'll stay and wait for me, won't you?"

"Of course," said Angelina.

"Joe." Nick called again.

Giving Angelina a quick kiss, Joe rushed off to join Nick. As she watched him go, a sudden thought struck her. She turned to Dee, who had been uncharacteristically quiet, during the exchange.

"Dee." Angelina drew out the word into two syllables. "This thing about Joe's dad turning up for the competition. It wouldn't have anything to do with you, would it?"

Dee dropped her eyes to her cup of tea, before answering.

"You've still a lot to learn, my girl." Dee raised her eyes to meet Angelina's gaze. "One of the most important things to understand is that when it comes to humans you can't always leave everything to fate."

Coming soon...

From Jeanette Dyson

THREAD OF DESTINY

The second book in the Fate Switch trilogy